BESTSELLING AUSTRALIAN AUTHOR

BARBARA HANNAY

Outback Skies

MILLS & BOON

OUTBACK SKIES © 2022 by Harlequin Books S.A.

OUTBACK WITH THE BOSS
© 2000 by Barbara Hannay
Australian Copyright 2000
New Zealand Copyright 2000

First Published 2000
Fifth Australian Paperback Edition 2022
ISBN 978 1 867 25564 2

OUTBACK BABY
© 2000 by Barbara Hannay
Australian Copyright 2000
New Zealand Copyright 2000

First Published 2000
Fourth Australian Paperback Edition 2022
ISBN 978 1 867 25564 2

A BRIDE AT BIRRALEE
© 2002 by Barbara Hannay
Australian Copyright 2002
New Zealand Copyright 2002

First Published 2002
Fifth Australian Paperback Edition 2022
ISBN 978 1 867 25564 2

This is a work of fiction. Names, characters, places, and incidents are either the
product of the author's imagination or are used fictitiously, and any resemblance
to actual persons, living or dead, business establishments, events, or locales is
entirely coincidental.

Published by
Mills & Boon
An imprint of Harlequin Enterprises (Australia) Pty Limited
(ABN 47 001 180 918), a subsidiary of HarperCollins
Publishers Australia Pty Limited (ABN 36 009 913 517)
Level 13, 201 Elizabeth Street
SYDNEY NSW 2000
AUSTRALIA

MIX
Paper from
responsible sources
FSC
www.fsc.org   FSC® C001695

® and ™ (apart from those relating to FSC ®) are trademarks of Harlequin
Enterprises (Australia) Pty Limited or its corporate affiliates. Trademarks
indicated with ® are registered in Australia, New Zealand and in other countries.
Contact admin_legal@Harlequin.ca for details.

Printed and bound in Australia by McPherson's Printing Group

CONTENTS

OUTBACK WITH THE BOSS   5

OUTBACK BABY   163

A BRIDE AT BIRRALEE   313

Barbara Hannay was born in Sydney, Australia, educated in Brisbane and spent most of her adult life living in tropical north Queensland, where she and her husband have raised four children. While she has enjoyed many happy times camping and canoeing in the bush, she also delights in an urban lifestyle—chamber music, contemporary dance, movies and dining out. An English teacher, she has always loved writing, and now, by having her stories published, she is living her most cherished fantasy.

Outback With
The Boss

CHAPTER ONE

GRACE ROBBINS REACHED into her carryall and reluctantly drew out her black lace lingerie. Nervously, her fingers traced the delicate ribbon trim while she wondered how on earth she could go ahead with Maria's outrageous suggestion. Until now, she'd only ever worn these revealing garments under her faithful 'little black dress'. She'd *never* considered displaying her low-cut underwired bra and high-cut wispy knickers on their own.

'The problem is you're a natural prude,' Grace told her reflection in the mirror. She didn't enjoy parading in front of a man. Wearing a bikini on the beach was bad enough.

She sighed. Perhaps the solution was to take this one step at a time. She'd already let herself into her boyfriend's flat. If she put the underwear on beneath her other clothes for now, she could decide whether to go ahead with the rest of her friend's crazy plan later.

Halfway through this process, Grace paused and studied her image in the full-length mirror. The dramatic effect of her body, framed by a doorway and encased in nothing but skimpy, sensuous black lace, was surprising. Maria was probably right. It would take Henry by surprise too.

But how on earth could she carry this off? And if she did, what could she possibly say to justify such madness?

She sent the mirror a grimacing grin and tried striking a sexy pose, announcing to the empty room, 'Ta-da! National Underwear Display Day!'

No, she thought with a shudder. She looked and sounded ridiculous.

She tried another, more demure pose. 'I'll show you mine, if you show me yours?' *Definitely not.*

Oh, heavens, thought Grace, why am I even bothering? This just isn't me. Bringing her hands to her face in mock horror, she tried one more time. 'Henry, the little black dress thieves have struck and left me with nothing to wear!'

Groaning, she decided it was absolutely no use. Playing *femme fatale* was definitely not her scene. She couldn't ever make this work.

Grace glanced at the clock on the dressing table and decided there was no need to panic just yet. She still had at least an hour before Henry would return. She had to think this through calmly and rationally.

She grimaced. *Calmly and rationally?* She hadn't been able to place one logical thought next to another for days. Her fists clenched. *It was all Mitch Wentworth's fault!* The new boss had forced her into this pickle!

For the past fortnight, just thinking about Mitch Wentworth's arrival to take over the company had seemed to banish every composed and sane idea from Grace's usually clear-thinking head. And it was her fuming and fretting about this man that had launched Maria's lame-brained idea in the first place.

The whole wild plan had started at lunchtime when Maria had rested her plump elbows on the cafeteria table, and leaned towards Grace with her best lecturing expression. 'For goodness' sake,' she'd sighed. 'Stop stewing about Mitch Wentworth and concentrate on the bonuses. *Our new boss is a stud!* He's flying in to take over Tropicana Films any day now, and as you're his assistant you get to work side by side with him. Did you see his photo on the cover of *Movie Mag*?'

Out of her voluminous handbag, Maria had dragged a glossy magazine and tossed it onto the red laminated tabletop.

'Of course I've seen it,' Grace had retorted, her nose crinkling in disgust. 'I took one look at his self-satisfied smirk and the bimbos hanging off each arm and wanted to hand in my resignation, pronto.'

'Self-satisfied smirk?' Maria's dark eyes twinkled with tolerant disbelief. 'Come on, that's a really cute smile in anyone's books. Mitch is the ultimate in T. D. and H.'

'Pardon?'

'Tall, dark and hard to get.'

Grace's lips had pursed into a tight circle as she'd pushed the magazine aside. 'I'm sure, in *his* case, it'll be tall, dark and hard to please. Working for him will be awful.'

Maria threw her arms in the air. 'Half the women in the movie industry would be lining up for your job just to breathe the same air as Mitch Wentworth.'

'That's enough!' Grace moaned. 'All I hear about from Henry is how lucky I am to be working for the great Mitch Wentworth.'

'Henry?' Maria clicked her fingers in triumph. 'Now I get it! It's not Wentworth who's your problem. It's the boyfriend, Henry. I should have guessed.'

Grace rolled her eyes. 'I made the mistake of outlining the plot of Wentworth's next movie *New Tomorrow* and now Henry spends every night designing fancy computer graphics he's absolutely convinced Wentworth will want to use.'

'So he doesn't have any time for you?'

'Exactly,' Grace snapped.

She'd met Henry soon after arriving in Townsville from Sydney and it had been good to have someone to show her around. But over the past fortnight, as his obsession with impressing her new boss had gained momentum, her enthusiasm for him had diminished rather rapidly.

Grace's track record with men made her extra wary. She was still plagued by memories of Roger the Rat, a super-suave mover and shaker, who'd broken her heart. After that shattering experience, it hadn't taken long to convince her that the business world was a breeding ground for men who were superficially quite gorgeous, but so full of their own egos, they trampled all over women and usually left them feeling used and abused.

That was why she'd dated Henry. He wasn't handsome, but he had other virtues Grace preferred these days. He was scholarly and serious and, most importantly, safe.

She'd shrugged. 'I—I don't think it's that Henry's not interested. It's just that he gets kind of…distracted.'

A disgusted grunt had prefaced Maria's response. 'Distracted? What can divert a real man from your long legs and green eyes, not to mention the bits in between?'

Grace let out a short, self-conscious laugh. 'Computers are very fascinating toys.'

With a groan, Maria threw her head back and had stared at the cafeteria's ceiling. Then she had slowly lowered her gaze. 'You two are getting physical, aren't you?'

Feeling distinctly uneasy, Grace ran nervous fingers through her thick tawny hair, flicking it away from her collar. 'We will— I'm sure. I feel quite—er—fond of Henry. It's—it's all a matter of—timing.'

'Timing?' Maria almost shrieked. She shook her head in dismay. 'My dear girl, the answer's clear-cut. You forget about Henry and set your sights higher.'

'Higher? How much higher? What do you mean?'

'Mitch Wentworth, of course. You could snaffle the new boss. You've certainly got everything it takes.' Maria had looked down at her own chubby figure and groaned. 'If only I didn't love chocolate.'

Grace jumped to her feet. 'The new boss? For crying out loud, Maria, where's your loyalty? Think what he's done to our old boss, George Hervey. The poor old fellow's been tossed on the scrap heap by this take-over. Wentworth just blasted his way into Tropicana Films and we're expected to whip straight into "Yes, sir. No, sir".'

She sat down again and reached for her friend's hand. 'Thanks for the sympathetic ear, but you're way off beam. I can't stand the idea of even working for the man, let alone…' Her mind had darted frantically away from the mere thought of making a play for her boss. She slumped back into her chair. 'I'll definitely stick with Henry.'

'You're sure?'

Suddenly Grace had been very sure.

Having a boyfriend like Henry was sensible and safe—like wearing a seat belt in a car. But giving a bully-boy showman like Mitch Wentworth so much as a second glance was as wise as skinny-dipping with sharks. 'I've just got to find some way to get Henry away from his computer and interested in me again.'

Maria's face was split by a sudden grin. 'Don't worry, my dear. I can feel a bright idea coming on. We'll put an end to this nonsense of Henry's. Tonight's the night. Before our Mr. Wentworth gets here to totally distract your boyfriend, we'll *undistract* him. We'll *make* Henry notice you!'

'Oh, I don't know if that's necessary.' Maria had started to get just a touch too pushy. How had one little gripe about Mitch Wentworth escalated to the point where her friend had been about to launch a rescue mission on her love life?

'I appreciate your good intentions,' she'd hedged, disliking the hard edge in her tone, but too tense to do anything about it. 'But I'm not quite dateless and desperate. And I really think this is just between Henry and me.'

Grace's glance fell to Mitch Wentworth's grinning face on the cover of *Movie Mag* and an image of him standing in her office had floated dangerously into her thoughts. Once her new boss arrived, that cheeky smile, those naughty-boy eyes and those highly indecent muscles would be mere inches away from her.

Maria eyed her shrewdly and Grace had the terrible feeling that the other woman knew exactly what was bugging her! How on earth could she carry on with her work each day while a man like Mitch Wentworth flaunted his lethal, sexy weapons around her office?

He hadn't even arrived yet and already her thoughts had been trailing in his direction like ants to a picnic basket.

That shocking realisation had prompted Grace into action. 'Okay, you win,' she'd told Maria. 'I'll give Henry one last chance. What's your brilliant idea?'

But listening to Maria's action plan had been the easy part.

Now, as Grace stood eyeing her reflection in Henry's mirror, the sight of her wide, anxious eyes and her nervous, fiddling fingers reminded her that she wasn't really up to the task ahead.

She could deal with the twinge of guilt she felt about leaving work early and letting herself into Henry's flat. The missed time could be made up on another day.

But she couldn't face the final step.

This mission was impossible. There was no way she could pose at Henry's front door and carry out the rest of the plan.

The sense of elation Mitch Wentworth had hoped for when he'd arrived in Townsville was somehow evading him. It must be jet lag, he told himself as he ran a weary hand over his eyes. A flight from San Francisco with only a few hours' stopover in his home town, Sydney, before heading north to Townsville would knock the stuffing out of most travellers. And it was probably a mistake to take a peek at his brand-new baby—the Tropicana Films studios—unannounced and so late in the day.

At this stage, there was only an advance team working on the project, so he'd expected half the offices to be empty. And it *was* six-thirty in the evening, so it was not surprising that all his employees had gone home.

Even the formidable Ms Robbins.

Her name was on the door of the office in front of him. Grace Robbins. After all George Hervey had told him about this woman's efficiency, dedication to the company and amazingly wide range of skills, he thought that perhaps—just *perhaps*—she might have stayed behind to meet him. In fact, once he'd faxed her his flight times, he'd almost expected her to greet him at the airport.

As he'd made his way through the Townsville terminal, he had kept a weather eye out for a middle-aged woman, conservatively dressed, brandishing perhaps a clipboard or some other weapon of efficiency. That was how he pictured Grace Robbins after listening to George's twenty-minute eulogy of her.

Clearly George's praise had been way too enthusiastic and his claims too exaggerated. It was a regrettable oversight, Mitch decided as he moved into her office. He was going out on a financial limb with *New Tomorrow*. With almost all his own money invested in it, this movie had to be a resounding hit and he needed the best possible staff to support him. He expected Ms Robbins to be a key player in the project.

Shrugging aside his annoyance, Mitch tried to be reasonable. Perhaps he shouldn't judge the woman just because she wasn't still here when he crept into town virtually unannounced. He'd only sent the fax just before he left Sydney and she might have had an appointment—any number of reasons for rushing home.

His eyes scanned the office. He couldn't judge much at this stage. Her computer was shut down of course. There was a pile of faxes on her desk, but he had no intention of snooping. At least she wasn't someone who littered her desk with personal knick-knacks or family photographs. Mitch approved of that. He liked a staff who kept their business and personal lives completely separate.

His glance caught the latest copy of *Movie Mag* lying at the edge of her desk.

Frowning, Mitch picked it up. The frown deepened and his eyes narrowed. Someone had taken a thick black marker pen and added graffiti to the cover. His picture sported an Adolf Hitler-style moustache and enormous black-rimmed spectacles. Several of his teeth had been blackened, leaving him with a ludicrous, gap-toothed smile.

Mitch's shoulders rose, then slumped as he drew in a long breath before expelling it slowly in a hiss through his teeth. With slow, deliberate movements, he folded the offending magazine and placed it thoughtfully in his coat pocket.

And as he prowled back through the empty building he felt more jet-lagged than ever.

When he reached the thick glass doors at the entrance to the studio, a tall, dark shape outside caught his attention. An agitated young man was gesticulating wildly—pointing to himself and then to Mitch. For a moment, Mitch experienced a surge of hope. Had one eager employee returned to greet him? But just as quickly he dismissed the fanciful notion. Anyone working for the company would be able to let himself in.

Mitch opened the door and the fellow launched forward, his hand outstretched.

'Mr Wentworth?'

Mitch nodded as the man stepped through the doorway and he shook the proffered hand. 'How do you do?'

'Henry Aspinall. And I'm very well, sir. I must say this is indeed a great honour. Oh, boy, it's such a stroke of luck meeting you here, Mr Wentworth, sir. I've been trying to ring Grace all afternoon to check your arrival time and...'

Mitch interrupted the enthusiastic outburst. 'Grace? Grace Robbins? You know her?'

'Sure.' Henry nodded. 'When I couldn't reach her at her flat, I thought she must still be here.'

'No, there's no one here—not even Ms Robbins,' Mitch confirmed.

'Oh, well, not to worry.' Henry grinned. 'It was really you I wanted to meet. You've received my e-mail messages?'

Mitch rubbed his brow, cursing the tiredness that fogged his memory. 'Aspinall, Aspinall...' He needed to recall whether this was someone really important he should remember, or just a nuisance fan.

Henry took advantage of the hesitation. 'Grace told me about New Tomorrow and I've designed some computer graphics to blend in beautifully with the North Queensland outback...'

Mitch held up his hand to halt the flow of Henry's enthusiasm. 'Of course. You swamped my Los Angeles office with messages. You've done some graphics for the battle scenes.'

Henry looked jubilant. 'That's it, sir! What do you think? Would you like to see them?'

Mitch shot Henry an appraising glance. 'Do you mind if we start walking? I'd kinda like to get to my hotel.'

'Yes, sir. No problem. Where are you staying? The Sheraton? I'd be honoured to give you a lift.'

Mitch shrugged. Why not go with the fellow? It would save hunting up another taxi. While under other circumstances he might have found Henry Aspinall's zeal annoying, like the unwanted attentions of an over-enthusiastic puppy, this evening it appealed to his dented ego. At least someone was keen to see him and seemed eager for his film's success. He grunted his acceptance of the offer.

As they stepped onto the street, Henry skipped along the pavement with excitement. 'My flat's on the way. I've got everything set up. We could call in and I could quickly show you—'

Mitch held up his hand and nodded. 'Sure thing,' he agreed as Henry opened the passenger door of a battered and rusty sedan. 'Take me to your disk.'

To his relief, they pulled up in front of a set of low maisonettes within five minutes. The car door squeaked on its hinges as Mitch prepared to follow Henry into his flat. After sitting for even such a short time, his weariness had returned with a vengeance. He would make this call as brief as possible. All he wanted now was to crawl into crisp, clean hotel sheets and sleep for three days.

'That's funny,' commented Henry as they crossed the short strip of weedy front lawn. 'I don't remember leaving any lights on.' He shrugged a puzzled smile Mitch's way before sorting through his keys for the one he needed.

But his key never reached the lock.

As their footsteps echoed on the concrete paving of the narrow entryway, the front door flew open.

'Surprise!'

A blaze of light flooded the doorway, illuminating a beautiful creature wearing next to nothing. Her eyes were fixed on Henry.

'It's Tuesday! National Girlfriend Exposure Day!'

Standing back in the shadows, Mitch was vaguely aware of strangling noises coming from Henry, but he was too stunned to move or speak.

A goddess, tall and tawny-headed, posed before them, dressed in the briefest of black lacy undergarments. She was absolutely breathtaking. Her creamy skin was satin-smooth and her womanly curves perfectly shaped—delicate slenderness and lush fullness balanced in proportions designed to impel a man to reach out for them.

He blinked, but shot his eyes wide open again in case he missed something.

And what he noticed was the 'something' in her eyes that didn't quite mesh with this vision of alluring temptress. Was it fear, embarrassment? The shy tilt of her head and the downward curve of her shoulders made him think of a little girl pushed into the stage's limelight by an overly ambitious parent. This woman had the body of a sultry seductress and the mien of a vulnerable child.

'What on earth are you doing?' Henry yelled.

His voice sent her slumping against the door frame like a puppet whose strings had been cut. But, almost instantly, her eyes flew to Mitch and she suddenly jerked again to terrified life.

'Oh, my gosh,' she moaned, and stared at Mitch in absolute horror. She clasped her hands to her chest. 'Oh, no! *Oh, no!*' she cried.

Her arm shot out and the door slammed in their faces.

CHAPTER TWO

'GRACE! WHAT *HAS* got into you?'

Grace turned, shaking with terror, her eyes wide and her hand covering her mouth, as she watched Henry stride across his living room towards her. His crimson face was twisted with anger.

'Do you realise what you've just done?' he shouted. 'Do you know who—?' Henry stopped shouting abruptly, as if he realised he was making this fiasco much worse. His voice dropped to a panicky whisper. 'That's Mitch Wentworth at the door!'

'I know, I know,' Grace moaned. Her eyes hunted around the small room, searching frantically for any item of clothing she could grab. Where was a gaping black hole when she needed to leap into it?

'How could you do this to me, Grace? What's he going to think?'

As if the answer to his own question suddenly popped into his head, Henry swore, spun on his heel and darted back to his front door.

Grace made a speedy escape to the bedroom.

'He's gone!' she heard Henry roar. 'Wentworth's left already!'

She sank with relief onto the bed. Thank heavens for that. With shaking hands, she pulled a T-shirt over her head.

Henry burst into the room. 'You've ruined me! You do realise that, don't you? I'll never get Wentworth to look at my graphics now.' Flinging his hands into the air, he glared at her. 'I had Mitch

Wentworth here, Grace. Here in my own home. He was going to look at all my designs tonight! Tonight! You stupid woman! You've spoilt everything.'

Grace shuddered. 'I'm sorry, Henry,' she replied dully. 'How was I to know you'd bring him home? I didn't even know the man was in Townsville.' With nervous, wrenching movements, she pulled on her jeans. All she could think of was how badly she wanted to get away.

And never come back!

Henry was carrying on like a spoilt little boy who'd dropped his ice-cream cone in the dirt.

'I'm sure you'll be able to show your ideas to him some other time,' she muttered. Why had she ever wasted one moment trying to arouse Henry's interest in her? He couldn't have been less appreciative of her efforts if she'd trashed his entire flat.

She shoved her feet into trainers. 'I'm sorry my silly plan was such a flop,' she told him as he slumped and sulked on the far side of the bed. Her shoulders rose in a dismissive shrug. 'It—it seemed like a good idea at the time...'

But not any more! A wave of shame drenched her with fresh horror. Never had she been more aware of being in the wrong place at the wrong time.

Henry shook his head and growled. 'I thought you were supposed to be smart, but that was about the dumbest thing I've ever seen.'

One thing was for sure, Grace promised herself silently: Henry wouldn't see anything like that ever again. Jumping up, she grabbed her carryall and offered him a mumbled, 'I won't hang around,' before blinking back embarrassed tears, hurrying past him and out of the room.

But as she left his flat Grace winced at the thought of a much more pressing concern than Henry's fit of the sulks. Her big, bigger, *biggest* problem was so horrendous she wished she could take off on the next space shuttle! She'd gladly spend six months on a space station in the far reaches of the universe.

There was no way on earth she could face her new boss in the morning.

* * *

Please, please, *please* don't let him recognise me.

When Mitch Wentworth stepped into her office next morning, Grace huddled over her computer and prayed as she had never prayed before.

She was prepared to repent in sackcloth and ashes. She would make a big donation to charity. She could do both. Anything. Just as long as her boss didn't connect her with that humiliating moment in Henry's doorway.

This morning, she'd taken great pains to look as different from the previous night's pouting sexpot as she possibly could. But was it enough? Suddenly, with Mitch Wentworth's expensive, hand-stitched shoes firmly planted in the middle of her office, Grace doubted the ability of hair gel and a primly fashioned bun to effectively change her appearance. And how helpful were the heavily framed glasses she'd borrowed from her neighbour? Her only reassurance was that last night Mitch had glimpsed her very briefly. And surely the shapeless, dull brown dress disguised her body?

What had actually been said at Henry's front door was all an embarrassing blur, but with a hefty dollop of luck Mitch Wentworth would have no idea she was remotely connected to Henry Aspinall—or the trollop who'd greeted him last night.

Nevertheless, as he moved towards her, her shoulders lifted and squared as if she was braced to take a blow.

'Good morning. I presume I have the pleasure of meeting Ms Robbins?' His dark eyes assessed her carefully, but they showed no sign of recognition.

Yes! Relief flowed and swirled through Grace, but she still couldn't dredge up a smile as she replied, 'Good morning, Mr Wentworth.' She stood and held out her hand to greet him formally, and the room buzzed with her tension. His handshake was predictably strong and firm.

My, he was tall! And broad-shouldered. She'd been prepared for the well-defined bone structure, the thick dark hair and the eyes designed purely for seduction, and last night she'd realised he was a big man. But now, in her small office, he took up far too much space. There was no escaping his spectacular style of masculinity: the kind of looks she'd learned to mistrust instinctively.

'You come highly recommended. George Hervey gave a glowing report.'

She smiled faintly.

Mitch did not smile back. 'But, of course, that's all over now. With me, you will have to prove yourself.'

Prove myself?

Despite her nervousness, a surge of defiance heated Grace's cheeks. *Here we go! The bloodthirsty pirate takes the helm!* Her chin lifted automatically, but, just in time, she remembered to mask her stormy reaction by lowering her gaze. Her green eyes had a bad habit of attracting unwanted attention when her dander was up. And already she could feel her hackles rising.

Mitch spoke again, his deep Australian drawl blending with the American twang he'd acquired after many years in the United States. 'I expect one hundred per cent commitment and loyalty.'

'Of course, Mr Wentworth.'

He drew in a sharp breath and Grace suspected that her softly spoken subservience irked him. Nevertheless, he continued without missing another beat. 'You're a vital key to the success of this *New Tomorrow* project. But...' his voice dropped and he paused for dramatic effect '... I *am* that project. You're working for me now, Grace Robbins. When you think of *New Tomorrow,* you think of me.'

He was as full of himself as she'd expected! However, she couldn't ignore the fact that his brainchild was very exciting—a project she itched to become more involved with.

'Your film has a brilliant premise,' she replied, and would have continued, but, with an ominous flourish, Mitch reached into his pocket and withdrew something that looked like a magazine.

He threw it onto the table.

Her boss grinned up at her, *his face disguised by a bristly moustache.*

Rimless spectacles.

And blackened teeth!

Grace's stomach felt as if it had been pumped full of concrete.

Slashed onto the page with thick, black, angry strokes, her graffiti was clear evidence of the tantrum she'd thrown in this very office after her lunchtime discussion with Maria.

How on earth had he found it?

She flinched.

And suppressed a whimper.

Gulped down the urge to scream. Why couldn't real life be like making a movie? If only a director could jump into her office and yell, 'Cut! I don't like the way this scene's falling. Let's start again and *this* time we'll leave out the magazine...'

But no.

No one was going to rescue her from her own reckless actions. For several seconds Grace hoped she might faint.

No such luck.

Her legs trembled, but didn't give way. No comforting blackness descended. And Mitch Wentworth remained standing squarely in front of her, pinning her to the spot with his cold, unflinching stare.

'It seems you have a problem,' he challenged.

She swayed slightly and grasped the back of her chair.

'Obviously, you've got a problem with me,' Mitch repeated in a cold, flat voice.

Where had she heard that the best defence was to attack? With a shaking, accusing finger, she pointed at him. 'You—you've been spying on me!'

He stared at her in simmering silence. Then, to her surprise, he shook his head and walked away. For several seconds, Mitch stood with his back to her, but Grace could sense his anger in the rise and fall of his shoulders. He turned swiftly to face her again. 'I don't spy, Ms Robbins! I called here yesterday evening to check out the office. *My* office. And it didn't take the help of a special service investigator to uncover what you left lying so blatantly on your desk. Right here!'

Grace looked away. He was about to sack her. She knew it. And if she stretched her imagination to take in his point of view she probably couldn't blame him.

But she loved this job. Over the past four years, it had become the single most important thing in her life! Somehow, she dragged her eyes upwards again to find Mitch studying her. His hands were now shoved deep into his trouser pockets. If he was going to fire her, she wished he would get it over quickly.

'Do you want to see this project through?'

'Huh? I—I mean I beg your pardon?'

'*New Tomorrow*. You want to stay on the team?'

'Yes, I do. Very much. I'm actually very committed to *New Tomorrow*. I—'

'You want to work with me?'

For a fraction of a second she hesitated, but it was long enough to elicit another of his quick frowns.

'Yes. Yes, I do.'

Mitch picked up the offending magazine and tossed it into her waste-paper basket. Then he began to pace the small square of carpet in the middle of her office. 'Okay. We'll forget about this, Grace.'

Grace? He'd dropped the Ms Robbins?

'I don't have any problems at this stage,' he continued. 'If you have problems you should get them off your chest.' He shot a questioning glance her way.

She shook her head.

'You're quite sure?' he persisted.

Of course she had objections about Mitch Wentworth. She had a list as long as both his arms. But what could she do with them?

Especially now, when he'd skilfully backed her into a corner?

How could an employee criticise her boss for the way he'd bulldozed his way into taking over George Hervey's little film company? As for her other problems—there was no way she could lambaste a man for his killer good looks.

She really had no choice but to offer an olive branch. 'I have no complaints,' she told him. 'And—and I apologise. You were never meant to see the silly doodling on that magazine. I admit... I've been...rather thoughtless.'

He half turned and eyed her speculatively, his hands resting on his hips, pushing his suit coat aside. He was still too damned good-looking to be let loose in small spaces.

'But,' she finished defiantly, 'can you spare me another speech?'

He chuckled and, for the briefest of moments, his eyes danced before his frown slid quickly back into place. 'No, Grace, I'm afraid you'll have to bear with me for a little longer. You see, from now on, people will have to get used to following my orders. And the *New Tomorrow* project must dominate everybody's thinking. It's my single focus and it's got to be the focus for everyone else on the team. For anyone who's not on that wavelength, there's going to be a lot of pain and suffering. And if heads have to roll...' his own head cocked to one side and he glared at her '...then so be it.'

'I understand,' Grace responded, a little flush mounting on her cheeks. How dared he suggest she wasn't focused? She'd always taken great pride in her professional commitment. 'I'm quite well aware that I'm playing with the big boys now.'

Perhaps she had gone too far. Grace squirmed uneasily as Mitch's jaw clenched and his frown lingered while he studied her face. 'The big boys...' he repeated softly. His dark eyes linked for an uncomfortably long moment with hers. They moved to her mouth.

And Grace felt as if she'd stepped into quicksand.

How did he do it?

His hands were now lodged firmly in both trouser pockets and he was standing a good metre and a half away and yet, the way his eyes touched her—she felt as if his mouth was caressing hers—*intimately.*

This was ridiculous!

She tightened the lips he seemed to be studying so intently. And, her mind racing, she began to talk—anything to cover her turmoil. 'I—I think you'll find that I've been networking successfully on the location options, Mr Wentworth. I've already contacted the property owners in the Tablelands and Gulf regions. I've been inundated with offers of accommodation from tourist operators in the north. I have contour maps from the army, information on the roads... The internet is invaluable...'

Mitch held up his hand. 'Hold it. Okay, I'm impressed, but I don't need an itemised account just yet. I'm sure it's all in your report.'

Her eyes blazed. 'How can I help babbling? You make me nervous when you…when you keep *staring* at me…like that.' A swift flood of heat rushed into her cheeks.

Mitch took a step closer and, for a breath-robbing moment, Grace thought he was going to touch her. 'You don't like men looking at you?' he asked lazily.

'Of course I don't,' she snapped while her heart thundered.

His eyes left her then, and he turned to the opposite wall, but an annoying little smile tugged at the corner of his mouth.

'No woman does!' she said indignantly. *What was so darned amusing?*

'Ogling women is certainly inappropriate in the workplace,' Mitch agreed, while he appeared to examine with fascination a 'Save the Rainforest' poster on her wall. 'I apologise if I seemed to be staring. You have an intriguing…face.'

Grace gulped, uncertain how to react.

He moved to the door then stopped. With his thumb, Mitch traced the straight timber edge of the door frame.

Grace's heartbeats continued to trouble her. He hesitated as if he still wanted to tick her off about something and she wished he'd get it over and done with.

A dreadful thought struck and her hands clenched so tightly her fingernails dug into her palms. *Surely he wasn't about to announce that he'd recognised her after all? He knew she was the hussy in the wispy triangles of black lace?*

Not now?

But when his eyes swung back to hers, although they glinted with secret amusement, he merely nodded his head and said with studied politeness, 'Nice to meet you, Grace. I'll look forward to reading your report.'

He turned and left and Grace's knees buckled. She sank onto a chair.

Groaning, she tried to reassure herself that Mitch couldn't have known about last night in Henry's flat. She was panicking about nothing. If he'd recognised her, he would have brought it out in the open—the way he had with the magazine.

Yikes! The magazine! With a moan of despair, she buried her face in her hands. *The magazine! The underwear!* How could she cope?

Staring through her fingers at her keyboard, Grace knew the full meaning of regret. But, she decided after a few minutes of blistering remorse, what she regretted most was that the human brain wasn't more like a computer. If only there was a safe way to wipe a man's memory…and get away with it.

CHAPTER THREE

MITCH CLOSED GRACE'S preliminary report on location options for *New Tomorrow* and placed it carefully on his desk. Leaning back in his chair, he glanced at his watch and stretched his arms above him. He was surprised that it was already seven p.m. No wonder his stomach was growling with hunger. In the past three days since he'd arrived in town, there'd been so much work to get through that he'd stayed back in the office each night, then grabbed a snack from the sandwich bar next door rather than eating properly in the hotel's restaurant.

He allowed his arms to drop again and inter-linked his hands behind his neck. It was his favourite position for thinking.

And he needed to think about Grace Robbins.

This report she'd submitted was impressive. The clear, concise writing, the maps and illustrations, the impeccable layout and thorough attention to detail showed beyond doubt that Grace was absolutely professional. She was one smooth operator.

In the two months since she'd moved from the Sydney office to be part of the advance team working out of Townsville, Grace had assimilated an amazing amount of information about the northern region and all of it was highly relevant to their project. While reading her report, Mitch had become excited by all the potential location sites she'd outlined.

What had really surprised him was her uncanny grasp of what

he was trying to achieve with this movie. He'd only sent a fairly sketchy proposal; she hadn't even read a full script. But it was as if he and Grace had already shared several in-depth conversations about his hopes and expectations for *New Tomorrow*.

An assistant who could methodically work her way through extraneous details to find exactly what was relevant was a great asset. But one who could also share his artistic vision was a rare find. When her efficiency and presentation skills were also considered, Mitch knew George Hervey had been right. Grace was of inestimable value to the company.

It was a pity these qualities didn't come with a pleasant, sunny personality. There was only one way to describe Grace—well-balanced—with a huge chip on both shoulders!

Throughout the three days he'd spent in the office, her face had remained a polite, but frowning, almost unfriendly mask. And, while it didn't particularly bother him, Mitch was beginning to think he'd dreamed up that vision of an alluring, provocative beauty framed by the doorway of Henry Aspinall's flat.

The way she scurried around the office with her head down, dressed in sombre browns and greys, she looked like a drab brown mouse. It was hard to believe she'd ever made a sexy come-on in her life.

Perhaps he should have said something to clear the air. But he hadn't wanted any blurring of business and private matters between himself and the woman with whom he had to work so closely.

He flipped open the plastic cover of the report and turned again to Grace's recommendations. Pen in hand, he read through them once more, circling certain points and making notes in the margins. She had certainly presented some thought-provoking options.

Grace was in the mood for cooking something special. It was an inspiration that didn't hit her often, so she tended to make the most of it, preparing large quantities that would last her for many meals. Occasionally she felt expansive and threw a dinner party, but tonight she was making her favourite curry and she wasn't planning on sharing it with anyone.

On the way home from work, she stopped off at the local supermarket and bought all the necessary ingredients. And after a long, warm soak in scented bath oils, she padded into her kitchen, drew the red gingham curtains closed and slipped her favourite Spanish guitar CD into the player.

In the four years she'd worked for Tropicana Films, she'd always made a deliberate effort to separate her work and her leisure. At the end of the working day, she relished time for herself to clear her thoughts. Now it was especially important to forget about her new boss and the persistent, niggling worry that he might have recognised her as the figure flaunting herself in Henry's doorway.

What if Henry had said something to Mitch?

Shaking her head furiously, she tried to push aside such invasive thoughts and turned up the volume on the CD player. The fluid sounds rippled around her and she began to feel better than she had in days.

Three days.

She hummed softly under her breath as she diced lamb, and chopped onions and garlic. And within twenty minutes the small kitchen was redolent with the rich fragrance of lamb simmering in curry leaves, fresh coriander, crushed cummin and chilli.

Totally absorbed in her task, she was stirring in the final ingredient, coconut milk, when a knock on her door startled her. Quickly, she lowered the heat and snatched up a towel to wipe her hands as she headed for the door.

The last person she expected to find on her doorstep was Mitch Wentworth. Grace's heart plummeted.

'Wow, something smells wonderful.' He sniffed the air appreciatively.

'Er, hello, Mr Wentworth,' she murmured, only just resisting the temptation to slam the door in his face. At least she was fully clothed this time. Not that her favourite old tracksuit was exactly suitable attire for greeting the boss. Especially when he was still in the elegantly tailored business suit he wore to the office. Her hand strayed to her hair which, aided by the soak in the bath and the warmth of the kitchen, had loosened and begun to fall in wispy strands around her face. She rubbed one bare foot against the other. 'What can I do for you?'

'Do I smell roghan josh curry?' Mitch asked.

Her eyes widened. 'Madras, actually,' she answered warily. Surely he wasn't looking for a meal?

'Ah, yes. I should have noticed.' Mitch smiled and Grace took a step back. She needed to put some distance between herself and that smile. 'There is faint aroma of coconut,' he agreed. 'Roghan josh has yoghurt, doesn't it?'

'You—you like curries?' Why did she ask? Every man she'd ever met liked curries. But rarely were they so familiar with the details of the ingredients. 'This one needs to simmer for a good while yet,' she hastened to add, in case he had any bright ideas about inviting himself for dinner.

'There's no need to look so nervous, Grace. I won't be invading your privacy for very long,' Mitch reassured her as if he'd been reading her mind. 'And I'm sure Henry Aspinall would have something to say if I ate his share of dinner.'

'Hen—Henry?' Grace stammered. *What exactly did he know about Henry?*

'He's been chasing me to look at his graphic designs and when I first met him he mentioned you and he were...good friends.'

'Oh.' Grace gulped. Nervously, she waited to see if Mitch was going to expand on this information. When he didn't, she added, 'So why have you come here?'

'Do you mind if I come in for just a moment? There are a few things I need to discuss with you and I'd like to clear them up tonight.'

Mitch expected her hesitation, but he also knew Grace would invite him in. She had seen that he was holding the folder with her report and curiosity sparked from her green eyes. Valiantly ignoring his hunger pangs, he followed her into the small sitting room, rich with the fragrant, spicy smells that drifted from her kitchen.

He couldn't help noticing that it was a lovely room—not extravagantly decorated, but comfortable and welcoming. And the raw, emotive passion of the guitar music in the background was a surprise. Another layer to the Grace Robbins enigma.

Mitch's gaze roved slowly around the cosy setting. The lighting was low, creating a soothing mood. And the warm, natural earth colours of the terracotta tiled floor and the two large Aboriginal paintings dominating the main wall gave a sense of mellowness. In the opposite corner, beneath a black and white movie poster of Bogey and Bacall, a fat earthenware pot held a sheaf of dried grasses. Beside it sat an overly plump floor cushion covered with a stone-and claret-coloured design.

He'd rarely settled in one spot long enough to establish his own home, but when he did make purchases these same earthy tones, sunburnt ochres and browns were the colours that always attracted him.

The chocolate brown sofa was deep and soft and Mitch sank into it gratefully. Grace sat opposite him on a woven cane chair and clutched at a sienna and black striped cushion as if her life depended on it. Nevertheless, he didn't miss the way she curled into the deep chair with catlike elegance.

'You decorated this place yourself?' he asked.

'Yes. I thought the *New Tomorrow* project would take long enough to warrant moving all my gear from Sydney.'

Mitch nodded. 'It's very attractive. I'm looking forward to finding a home base for myself.' His glance drifted to the fish tank on a stand behind her chair. Two goldfish and a black fish. 'I have a sister-in-law who is a feng shui expert. She claims that aquariums are very helpful for creating...' he paused, searching for the right word, but gave up with a smiling shrug '...a happy environment.'

Grace's mouth twitched as she gestured to the fish. 'I've read that. These guys are the Marx Brothers.'

'Let me guess. The black one is Groucho.'

'Of course.' She laughed. Then she looked startled as if she hadn't meant to let down her guard. 'Um—what did you want to speak about?'

She was edgy—probably in a hurry to get rid of him before Aspinall turned up. Mitch suppressed a sigh as he pictured the other man wolfing down her delicious meal. He avoided thinking of any other delights in store for Henry Aspinall by flipping her report onto his knee and tapping his finger against the cover.

'This is good, Grace. Very good. I have to say I'm very impressed by how quickly you've made yourself familiar with the North Queensland territory.'

Her eyes lit up with pleasure. Mitch found their sudden sparkle arresting.

'It's very interesting country,' Grace replied, unconsciously crossing one long, towelling-clad leg over the other. 'As I said in my report, I think there are many location options on our back doorstep.'

Mitch had never noticed before just how sexy faded blue terry towelling could be. He dragged his gaze away. Her body shouldn't, couldn't be a factor here. Praising her business skills was the way to win over Grace Robbins. 'Your report is very persuasive. That's why I'm here tonight. I'd like to start investigating some of these outback locations straight away.'

'Immediately?'

'Tomorrow morning.'

She nodded thoughtfully and Mitch could sense her thoughts whirling behind those wide green eyes as she calculated what needed to be done. 'You'd definitely check out Undara?' she queried.

He referred to his scribbled notes. 'The ancient lava tubes? Yes. They sound fantastic for the underground scenes. And I want to look at some of the old deserted mining towns, too.'

'Like Ravenswood or the Mount Surprise district?'

'They're the ones.' Mitch nodded.

'You'd hire a four-wheel drive?'

Mitch could tell that she was catching onto his enthusiasm. The cushion she'd been clutching earlier slipped unheeded to the floor.

'I think that would be best. Then I could mosey on and explore more of the outback. I want to take a good look at the Gulf country. There's so much great wilderness terrain out there.'

'And with its own peculiar kind of beauty,' Grace supplied. She leaned forward, an excited pink tinting her cheeks. 'I'm sure you'll find just what you're looking for in the Gulf.'

For the briefest moment, Mitch had the eerie feeling that there was something deeply prophetic about her words—as if he would actually find something much more meaningful than a location for his film. He blinked and shook his head. Grace might be clever, but she could not see into the future. Working overtime on top of jet lag could produce the weirdest sensations.

He smiled at her. 'You understand what I'm looking for, don't you?'

'I—I think so.' Perhaps he was staring too intently. Her cheeks grew pinker and she looked away for a moment.

'This industry is a dog-eat-dog world. And filming at a great location will give my movie the kind of competitive edge I need.'

She seemed to recover, giving a little shake, and as she spoke she met him once more with a level gaze. 'As I understand it, you're hoping to create a kind post-World War III scenario—a world where the people who are left will start all over again. The old world is lost or contaminated except for this small section of land and it is pure and unpolluted. So you want something iso-lated—pristine, untouched.'

Mitch jumped to his feet. 'That's exactly what I'm looking for. It's great that you understand. And that's why you'll be coming with me.'

The look of horror that swept across her features shocked him. He hadn't expected opposition from someone so deeply involved with the film.

'You'll help me check out the locations, of course.'

'Oh, no. I can't. I—I can't possibly,' she stammered.

'Why not?' He'd set his mind on having her with him. Her knowledge, the research she'd already undertaken, was invaluable.

'I have so much to do.' Her hands were twisting nervously in her lap. She looked so frightened, Mitch wanted to grab her by the shoulders and shake some sense into her. What kind of a man did she think he was?

'I'm the boss, Grace. I know exactly what you have to do. And I know you can spare the time for this trip.'

What had he done wrong to upset her so badly? How could she be so keen one minute and then suddenly back off as if he'd turned into a ghoulish monster? Mitch paced the length of her fashionable hand-woven rug. Caught up with the positive tone of her report, he had come tonight with the expectation that Grace would see it as her professional duty to accompany him—no matter what her personal hang-ups were. And now he was prepared to be as stubborn as was necessary.

He wasn't leaving until she said *yes*.

CHAPTER FOUR

'GRACE, I'M OFFERING you a chance to get out of the office—to
get away in the outback and to really explore this project with me.
How could you refuse?'

'By saying no!' she snapped, and leapt to her feet. She was incensed by Mitch's arrogant assumption that she'd give her eye-teeth
to slip away with him. 'I realise that's probably a new experience
for you, Mr Wentworth.'

He shot her a startled glance, before throwing his head back
and releasing a quiet chuckle. 'Of course I've had my share of re-
jections, Ms Robbins.'

Mitch eyed her shrewdly while he paced her floor and Grace
felt like a witness in the dock about to be cross-examined. There
was a long, awkward silence before he spoke again. 'Would we be
talking about relationships here? The man-woman kind? Or are
we talking about business and the world at large?'

She didn't answer, but when he retaliated by crossing the short
strip of matting towards her Grace held her breath, desperately
willing her heart to stay calm and wishing that she could think of
a smart retort that would stop him in his tracks. In spite of all the
warnings her mind issued, her body started overreacting whenever
this man got close. He must know the effect he had on women. He
should be considerate and keep his distance.

'Which Grace Robbins is rejecting my request?' Mitch drawled softly, while he shook her report in her face. 'The Grace who wrote this report wouldn't hesitate to help check out these locations.'

Suddenly she was very unsure of her ground.

'Is there something deeper going down here?' Mitch frowned and rubbed his chin thoughtfully. 'Perhaps I was wrong to throw that magazine with your artwork in the bin and assume we could start afresh? Do you dislike me so much that you can't bear to make this journey in my company?'

She shook her head, trying to convince herself that her protests were well-founded, but for the life of her Grace couldn't articulate her objections. Surely she had good, solid, professional reasons to offer him beyond the pitiful fact that he was so sexy that her clear thinking, precise mind turned to candy floss when he was around? And now he expected her to go away with him!

Just the two of them!

Until now she had always been prepared to cooperate whole-heartedly with her employer. But her previous boss, George Hervey, had been a thoughtful and considerate, elderly gentleman. Working for him, she had always felt safe and sure of her role.

Now, trying to come up with a plausible explanation for her refusal, she couldn't get her head past Mitch's suggestion that her objections were more to do with how she felt about him than how she felt about her work.

Mitch was still spearing her with his dark gaze. 'Would it make a difference if I promised Henry Aspinall not to lay a finger on you for the duration of the journey?' he asked.

'Henry?' Her cheeks flamed. Why did he keep mentioning Henry? 'Henry has nothing to do with this. He's mistaken if he thinks we're still...friends.'

'Indeed?' He considered her response for another uncomfortably long moment. 'You look terrified. What is there to be afraid of?'

Mitch stepped forward and, with an assurance she was sure came from years of experience, reached out his hand to rest it lightly at the nape of her neck. Her skin grew hot beneath his touch and she fully intended to pull away. But, with the same ease that a bright flower attracts a giddy butterfly, he slowly drew her towards him and her good intentions melted. Her lips hovered just below his. 'Is this what you're frightened of, Grace?'

Her heart fluttered frantically.

There was no doubt he intended to kiss her.

And Grace also sensed at that moment, that if she cried out, or tried to beat Mitch Wentworth off with her fists, he would certainly let her go. She might have asked him to stop if she hadn't been having such difficulty with her breathing, but instead she allowed him to close that last short gap.

As Mitch's warm mouth settled over hers, a tiny sob escaped her and she felt him pull away slightly.

But she was already under his spell.

Her eyes were already closed and her face was tilted at a shamefully helpful angle. And, after that one brief touch of his lips, she was mentally begging him to taste her, to explore her mouth with his own. And when he did Grace sank against him as if she needed his strength.

There was nothing arrogant or pigheaded about the way Mitch's hands tenderly cradled her face, or the way his mouth lazily investigated hers. It was a journey of discovery beyond her wildest dreams. Wherever he touched her, her skin seemed to flare with delicious sensitivity. The way his mouth moved, slowly and seductively against hers, felt so-o-o good. Utterly spellbound, Grace's lips opened, pleading for more. Mitch's kiss deepened and, as if they had a mind of their own, her arms rose shyly to link themselves around his neck.

There was nothing threatening about being in his embrace. Never before had she felt so womanly, so desirable, so eager for a man to explore *more* than her lips. When Mitch finally broke away, it took all her strength of will not to moan in soft protest.

He looked down at her, his gaze smoky with emotion. 'Another question answered,' he murmured softly.

And the spell was broken.

Shocked, Grace staggered backwards, her hand at her mouth as if she couldn't quite believe she'd allowed such a thing to happen.

'What do you think you're doing? You can't just get your way by trying to seduce me,' she cried, her voice shrill with self-recrimination.

'Of course not,' Mitch responded quickly. 'I wasn't using a kiss as a persuasive device. It was just—how shall I put it? An experiment. I needed to discover something.'

Incensed, Grace grabbed a sofa cushion and hurled it at him. 'How dare you? How *could* you experiment with me?'

Mitch caught the cushion neatly and stood holding it in both hands. Hands which only minutes earlier had been caressing her. 'I don't know, Grace,' he replied, a tiny smile playing at the corners of his mouth. 'Can you explain how we seem to be such a great team when it comes to kissing?'

Of course she couldn't! It was the stupidest thing she'd ever done. Well, almost, she corrected as her memory replayed two other occasions this week when she'd made a first-class fool of herself in front of this man.

'Don't think a little kiss will make me want to go off travelling in the outback alone with you,' she hissed.

'What if I promise never to kiss you again?'

'Oh?' Grace gasped. *Never?* She hoped her reply held no echo of the ridiculous wave of regret that flooded right through her.

'Boy scout's honour,' Mitch replied, tossing her a grin and a two fingered salute. Then he shot her a cheeky sideways glance and added, 'Of course, I'd be prepared to build in an escape clause.'

'Escape?' she echoed faintly.

'I'll only kiss you if you want me to. The next time I take you in my arms will be when you ask me to, Ms Robbins.'

That brought her to her senses. 'In your dreams, Wentworth.'

'I'm afraid I can't promise what might happen in them.'

Grace glared at him as she folded her arms across her chest and took several deep, fortifying breaths. The impact of that kiss was still reverberating through her body. Her heartbeats weren't just racing, they were stampeding. Anybody would think she'd never been kissed before. She suppressed the recognition that she had never been kissed like *that* before. Roger the Rat had been nowhere near as good.

To think she'd joked the other day about playing with the big boys. Clearly, Mitch's kisses were in a league of their own.

His businesslike tone cut through her wayward thoughts. 'I really do need you to make this trip with me. You understand exactly what I want. You've already done all the groundwork. No one else will be nearly as useful. Give me some credit. I swear I'm not a boss who preys on his female staff. I want us to work together as a great business team.'

Forget about the kiss, she chided. *He means it. It's not going to happen again. Concentrate on the job.* 'How many days would we be away?' she asked softly.

Mitch beamed at her. 'I knew you wouldn't let me down.' He glanced again at the notes he'd made on the end of her report. 'Five days should just about do the trick.'

She nodded weakly.

His answering nod of acceptance, as if he knew all along that she would capitulate, annoyed Grace, but she forced her mind to stay focused on practical business details. 'Do we need to make any bookings?'

'I'll book for tomorrow night at Undara,' he replied. 'After that I'd like to be as flexible as possible. We'll take my mobile phone and book ahead as we go.' Mitch's eyebrows rose and he jerked his head in the direction of her kitchen. 'That curry of yours should be just about ready by now, shouldn't it?'

'Don't push your luck, Mr Wentworth,' Grace warned, pointing to her door. 'If I have to spend the next five days with my boss, I need a little solitude tonight.' More than anything else, she needed to think about how on earth she'd ever allowed that kiss to happen.

Her very worst fears about Mitch had already proved well-founded. He was the kind of man who could charm a nun away from her prayers. And now she was going to be travelling alone with him! Grace believed he'd keep his promise about not kissing her again, but she needed to develop strategies to ensure her body didn't come up with any silly ideas of its own.

Mitch didn't try to hide his disappointment that he wouldn't taste her curry, but to her relief he had just enough manners not to push the matter. 'I'll have the vehicle ready for nine o'clock in the morning,' he said as he went through her doorway. 'I'll pick you up from here.'

Punctuality was not her boss's strongest feature, Grace decided next morning when he eventually pulled up outside her flat a good thirty minutes late. He was driving a large, solid-looking off-road vehicle with a tray back.

She had expected something more flashy and sporty—perhaps a shiny black and gold, city-style, four-wheel drive. This was a regular bush vehicle.

When Mitch swung the driver's door open and jumped down, flashing her a boyish grin, she was surprised by the way her own spirits lifted. She was hardly feeling her best after a long night tossing restlessly in her bed, worrying about spending five days rattling around the North Queensland outback side by side with her employer.

But this morning, dressed in jeans and an army-green bush shirt, he was looking so genuinely excited, like a boy allowed off on his very first Huckleberry Finn adventure, that her fears subsided somewhat. His enthusiasm, as he patted the truck's sturdy bonnet, was almost infectious. Not that she was prepared to let him see a chink in her armour. She nodded an unsmiling greeting.

Mitch wasn't to be put off. 'I've made sure I got a vehicle fitted out with absolutely everything we could possibly need. Spare water tanks, special tow ropes and winches in case we get bogged. Tarps and cooking gear if we decide to rough it. That's why I'm a bit late—making sure we had all those extras.'

'Did you get G.P.S.?'

'A global positioning system?' Mitch frowned, looking slightly put out. 'What do you know about that sort of thing?'

'Oh...' she shrugged '... I've read about it. It seems like a brilliant system for making sure you don't get lost. The army use it a lot.'

'I doubt we'll need gear that sophisticated to help us navigate. We've got maps and a mobile phone and a good sturdy vehicle—and neither of us is a fool. We're not going to get lost.'

'I guess not,' she agreed, but she pulled a face that allowed just a hint of doubt to linger in the air as she lifted her carefully packed kit bag and heaved it onto one shoulder.

'Here, let me take that,' he offered.

Finding it rather a strain to remain ungracious in the face of his helpfulness, Grace allowed him to take her pack. As she did so, he dipped his face close to hers and his dark eyes danced as they studied her. 'Aha! I think I detect a faint smile,' he teased.

'A slip of the lip,' muttered Grace.

Mitch sighed as he hefted her bag into the back of the truck. 'So that's the way it's going to be, is it, Ms Robbins?' His glance slid to her jeans. 'Five days of venom in denim.'

His words found their mark and Grace's cheeks burned. Perhaps she was behaving unprofessionally—more like an immature kid.

'Sorry,' she said, shooting him a fair attempt at a smile. 'I'm a bit tired.'

'Then you should just sit back and relax and let me take care of the driving. Did you want to bring any of your favourite CDs to help while away the miles?'

She stared back at him, surprised. 'That's a great idea! I won't be long.' About to dash into her flat, she paused. 'Do you have any preferences?'

Mitch leant his long frame against the truck's door and sent her a slow, conspiratorial smile. 'I think there's a very good chance we have similar tastes, Grace. I'm prepared to go along with whatever you choose.'

As she collected a pile of CDs, she sensed her mouth softening into the beginnings of a genuine smile.

Grace wasn't sure who was more surprised, she or Mitch, when they covered the six-hour journey up the narrow road to Undara without any sparring or tense silences. They only saw a few vehicles during the journey. They listened to her music, chatted about *New Tomorrow,* about people they knew in the film industry, or sat in comfortable silence as the countryside flashed past them in streaks of brown and grey-green against a bright blue sky. There were even moments when she actually laughed out loud at stories he told about colourful Hollywood personalities.

But whenever she started to relax Grace quickly reminded herself to be wary of her boss. He could pour on the charm when it suited him, but she knew from bitter experience that she must never lower her resistance.

From time to time Mitch stopped the truck to look at a point of interest. A flock of emus caught his attention, and he slowed to take a closer look.

'I'll bring them in near us,' he told her.

Grace eyed him dubiously. 'So what exactly are you going to do? Warble their mating call?'

He darted a withering glance in her direction. 'Just watch this, city girl.' Winding down his window, he held out his wide-brimmed hat and waved it at the emus. The birds stopped abruptly, staring at the movement. As Mitch continued waving, one of the scraggy, long-legged birds slowly stepped forward, a beady eye fixed on the hat. Then the others followed cautiously, until several dark-feathered adults and three stripy chicks were all gathered at the edge of the highway, staring fiercely at Mitch and his hat.

'That's a cool trick,' breathed Grace. 'Where'd you learn it?'

'Oh, I knocked about in the bush quite a bit when I was younger. I'm not a complete city slicker. Look!' He pointed as one of the adults herded up the chicks. 'You don't often see the mother emu with her babies.'

Grace cleared her throat. 'Actually, city boy, it's the male emu that incubates the eggs and looks after the chicks.'

'Poor bloke,' Mitch muttered under his breath as he accelerated back onto the highway. He shot Grace a baleful glance. 'And where did you learn that?'

'Oh, I read a lot...' she answered airily.

They travelled on, companionably silent, as the bush flashed past them—the rough black trunks of ironbarks, the silvery smooth limbs of woollybutts and the deeper red of bloodwoods.

Later in the day, more animals emerged. A butcher-bird startled Grace when it took off suddenly from the side of the road with a long, thin snake in its beak. In the shadowy verges, kangaroos and wallabies slowly edged out for an afternoon graze. It was late in the day by the time they rattled down the final stretch of dirt road to reach Undara.

'You've organised our accommodation, haven't you?' she asked warily.

'Sure have,' Mitch assured her. 'We're also booked in for a meal tonight and our underground tour in the morning. I'll just head into the office there and pick up our keys.'

Grace watched as he bounded up the three steps and crossed the timber veranda to the reception area. Somehow, despite his city lifestyle, Grace had to admit that Mitch had avoided the urban cowboy image. He really looked as at home in faded blue jeans and scuffed riding boots in the bush as he did in his expensive Italian suits and hand-stitched, shining shoes in the city.

She had the uncomfortable feeling that Mitch was the kind of guy who would look good in any setting—in any clothes. Or without clothes, came the errant thought. She dismissed it quickly.

As he headed back to the truck, he was frowning. He flipped open the door and swung his long frame into the driver's seat. 'Minor hitch,' he mumbled.

Grace's heart jumped a beat or two. 'How's that?' she whispered.

'I don't know how it happened, but there's been a misunderstanding about our accommodation.'

'A misunderstanding? Didn't you know the accommodation here is converted railway carriages?'

'Yeah. That's not the problem.' His dark eyes rested on her and his mouth twisted into a lopsided grin. 'Actually, there's no problem really. At least, there won't be if you don't throw a tantrum.'

Alarm sent tiny shivers darting through Grace's innards. 'Tantrum?' she squeaked and then she struggled to gain more composure. 'I haven't thrown a tantrum since I was two years old. For heaven's sake, what are you rambling on about?'

He twisted the key in the ignition and, as the engine chugged back to life, he told her. 'A couple of busloads of tourists have filled the place up and there's only one spot left for us. Honestly, I don't know how they got the idea we were a couple.'

Grace shot him a suspicious glare. 'You—you mean we have to share a...'

'A room,' Mitch supplied.

'Twin share?'

''Fraid not. Double.'

'We can't!' Grace yelled back. She ran nervous hands through her hair. The comfortable safety shield she'd been building all day had suddenly developed huge gaping cracks. 'This is ridiculous!' she shouted.

'We're not in the city now, Grace. In the bush you take what's offered.' Mitch nudged the truck towards the distant row of brown-painted railway carriages lined up in the shade of gum trees. 'In case you didn't know, beds are for sleeping, not just for sex. We can build a little barricade with pillows.'

Grace clamped her teeth closed as a screech of frustration threatened.

Mitch shot her a sideways glance. 'I didn't think you'd take this news too calmly. Look, it's a long drive back to anywhere else and we'd only have to come back out here again in the morning,' he commented. 'You get all kinds of hazards in remote areas, but I'm game if you are.'

'Of course you are!' she cried.

Mitch stopped in their allotted parking bay, outlined by rough bush timber, cut off the engine and turned to her. 'What's that supposed to mean?'

'It's no skin off your nose to spend one more night in bed with a woman you hardly know. It—it's your—*hobby*!' She flung her hands upwards to emphasise her words.

Mitch grabbed the hand nearest him and held it in a vice-like grip. 'If we're talking about hobbies, Ms Robbins, perhaps I should remind you that I've been an eyewitness to an interesting hobby of yours. It's not every girl who has a penchant for greeting men at the front door in her underwear.'

Oh, no! Grace's mouth hung open as she stared at Mitch in speechless horror. *All this time he'd known!*

For several long seconds, Mitch eyed her sternly and his grip on her hand tightened. 'So now you can stop behaving like a puritan and be adult about this. I've already seen what you have on offer. And, for Pete's sake, I've already promised I won't touch you.' He dropped her hand and swung his door open. 'If you'd like to be first in the shower, it's at the end of the carriage and you'd better get moving.'

With stiff, robotic movements, Grace climbed out of the truck, while her mind recoiled from the onslaught of Mitch's speech. She wasn't sure what had offended her more—his revelations about the embarrassing episode in Henry's flat, the claim that she was behaving like a silly little girl, or the implication that he wasn't remotely interested in her as a woman.

Get a grip, girl! she chided herself as she followed him into the carriage. *One minute you're terrified this man might touch you, the next you're upset because he promises not to.*

She'd been making Mount Everest out of a molehill. The very fact that he hadn't mentioned the incident at Henry's flat until now proved that her boss was no more interested in her personal life than she was in his.

It was important to remember that, just because she couldn't help thinking about his kiss and the delightful way he'd touched and held her as if she were a very special prize, there was no chance Mitch Wentworth actually considered her as anything other than his efficient employee. And that was, after all, what she wanted.

Maybe his kiss had scored right off the Richter scale, but she would have to put it out of her mind. He had probably forgotten about it before he'd left her flat. He'd been more interested in her curry than her kiss.

Nevertheless, the relaxed camaraderie they'd enjoyed during the day was rather more strained at dinner. The threat of the night ahead loomed over Grace and as she sat opposite Mitch, she felt ridiculously nervous.

Undara Lodge's dining area was a wide timber deck protected from the elements by huge canvas awnings, and all around them relaxed and happy tourists laughed and chatted in a mixture of languages. Their mood contrasted sharply with Grace's. These were people on holiday, keen for adventure in the Australian out- back and having a good time.

She toyed with her chicken marinated in wine, wattle seeds and mountain pepper and Mitch tucked into Georgetown sausages while he outlined the key factors they needed to focus on when they toured the lava tubes in the morning. But Grace knew he was laughing at her embarrassment and inner turmoil.

On the surface he appeared cool and businesslike as he flipped a small notebook out of his shirt pocket and made notes of pertinent questions they needed to ask if they wanted to use this site as a film location. But she could tell that he was laughing inside. The playful spark in his eyes betrayed him.

'I presume that amongst all this reading you do, you've boned up on the geological formation of these tubes?' he asked.

Grace patted her lips with her serviette and replied with as much dignity as she could muster. 'As a matter of fact, yes, I have.'

'Can you give it to me in language a simple movie man can understand?'

She took a sip from her wineglass and favoured him with what she hoped was a look icy enough to freeze the smile right off his face. 'A hundred and ninety thousand years ago, volcanoes erupted in this area and huge rivers of lava spilled everywhere, mainly following the old water courses. As they flowed, the lava on the outside cooled at a faster rate and it began to harden, but the very hot lava at the core kept flowing, pushing a hollow tunnel inside. The tubes here are the best preserved and most impressive in the world.'

'Thank you, Grace.' A small muscle near the corner of his mouth twitched as he poured some more wine into their glasses.

Grace stared at her plate in silent rage. She was more sure than ever that, while Mitch appeared to be polite and detached, he was playing with her, in much the same way a cat toyed with a mouse.

How on earth had she got to this point? She hadn't wanted to share office space with this arrogant man who'd blasted his way into the company, and now she was sharing—*his bed!*

By the time Mitch had finished his first course, she was a dithering mess. 'I'm not very hungry,' she said as she placed her knife and fork very carefully to one side of the half-eaten meal on her plate. 'I won't worry about dessert or coffee. But please, you stay and have as much as you like.'

Mitch stood politely as she left the table. 'Make sure you're tucked in tight and sound asleep before I get back,' he said softly, while his eyes danced with undisguised amusement.

Grace's shoulders stiffened. 'You're being utterly detestable,' she sneered over her shoulder as she sailed off the deck.

Storming down the short bush path to their carriage, she charged inside and banged the door. She leaned against it, shaking. He was hateful! How could poor George Hervey possibly enjoy his enforced retirement when he knew this bully boy was wrecking their happy little company? He might have money and ideas, but Mitch Wentworth's people skills left a lot to be desired!

Still raging, she changed into her pyjamas. Thank goodness she had a sensible cotton pair with a high neck, long sleeves and long legs. It was a pity they were hot pink and dotted with little white hearts, but at least they left no part of her exposed. She tucked the top into the trousers and drew the drawstring tightly into her waist before securing it with a double knot.

Then she removed her make-up and cleaned her teeth. About to leave the bathroom, Grace paused, and, avoiding the message her reflection revealed about how distraught and anxious she looked, she inspected her teeth in the mirror, and cleaned them again. And she dabbed some perfume behind her ears. Then she stared at her reflection, horrified. Why on earth did she want to smell nice?

Shaking with confusion, she carefully drew back the bedspread and climbed between the sheets. Then, rolling onto her side, she turned out the bedside lamp. In the dark, she lay ramrod-stiff with the sheet tucked high beneath her chin and waited for the sound of Mitch's returning footsteps...

But, no matter how hard she tried, Grace couldn't stop her wretched mind from imagining the night ahead. What was it going to be like, lying side by side with Mitch? Would he stick to his half of the bed? Would he roll onto his back and fling one arm out so that he touched her? And what would she do then? Might they wake in the morning to find themselves wrapped in each other's arms?

As she lay in the dark room, listening to the creak of the overhead fan, her tortuous imagination played out dozens of possible and impossible scenarios until she wanted to scream with the stress of it all. How could this same brain that served her so methodically and well when it came to assimilating information and absorbing facts turn itself inside out when she contemplated Mitch Wentworth?

Everything about him—his good looks, his powerful presence, his annoying self-confidence—placed her on the alert. Mitch was so much like Roger. Such men ate young women for breakfast before heading off to build their empires.

Were there no decent men in this world? Roger had broken her heart. Henry had enraged her. And Mitch?

Mitch doesn't factor in this equation, she reminded herself. *He's a boss, not a boyfriend.*

But any tensions Grace experienced when she first went to bed were magnified a hundred times over during the next hour or so. Rather than hearing footsteps returning to the cabins, the only sounds that drifted on the still night air were laughter and happy voices coming from the diners on the deck. Out in the bush, everything else was so very quiet that these sounds seemed even louder than normal. And, as the weary night wore on, the cheery voices grew merrier—probably as people drank more, she guessed. She could tell by the sudden guffaws of laughter that jokes were being shared and glasses were being clinked together in endless toasts.

Mitch had no doubt forgotten all about her and was joining in the fun. And, of course, the harder she tried to get to sleep, the wider awake she became!

When she heard the strains of 'Waltzing Matilda' sung in a mixture of German, Danish and English accents, Grace snatched up a second pillow and tried to block out the gaiety. She hoped every single one of those people had a huge hangover in the morning.

Eventually, after an interminable wait, the voices separated and she heard people moving to their carriages. At long last her own door was pushed open. Grace lay rigid with tension as she listened to Mitch stumbling around in the dark. She heard one thump then another as his boots hit the floor—the scrape of his zip and the slide of denim as he stripped off his jeans. Any minute now, she would feel the mattress give as he lowered his long frame onto it...

CHAPTER FIVE

GRACE HELD HER BREATH.

There was a little more quiet scuffling and bumping, and then silence.

And more silence.

Alert as a time bomb about to explode, she lay in the bed desperately trying to make sense of this lack of sound. Where on earth had Mitch gone now? A sickening thought struck her. Had he crept out to visit someone else's bed? Not knowing was more than she could bear. She snapped on the bedside light.

'What's going on?' From the floor on the far side of the room, Mitch sat up, blinking.

She could only see him from the waist up, and as far as she could tell he wasn't wearing anything. He was looking tousled and tired, and in the soft lamplight she found herself staring at the tumble of hair in his eyes, the late-night shadow on his jaw, the breadth of his shoulders. The visible half of his body was as sleek and beautifully muscled as a sculpture by Michelangelo.

'I—I didn't know where you were,' she stammered. 'What are you doing on the floor?'

'Trying to sleep,' he muttered.

'But—but why down there?'

He rubbed his eyes sleepily, then blinked again before staring back at her. She sank against the pillows as the slow-burning pressure of his gaze set her heart scampering into a crazy, dancing rhythm. This was how he'd looked at her last night—just before he'd kissed her.

Then he grinned through the gloom. 'It's okay, Grace. I spoke to the management and explained about our...our little problem. They were great. They lent me a swag, so I'm fine. I'll kip down here tonight.'

As he settled back onto the floor, Grace flicked off the light and hot anger seethed through her entire body. It was so ridiculous! Mitch was handling this awkward situation like a gentleman and she should be grateful. Of course she was grateful!

Why wasn't she grateful?

She flung herself restlessly across the bed, trying to find a comfortable position, and his disembodied voice reached her through the darkness.

'It was a pity you were so tired; you missed a great party.'

Somehow she managed to turn a scream of fury into a mumbled, 'G'night.'

One last time, his voice, deep and rich as chocolate liqueur, came through the night. 'Pink looks okay on you, but not as sexy as black lace.'

After that Grace spent a long, empty night tossing and turning while she listened to Mitch's regular, relaxed breathing.

The Undara lava tubes blew Mitch away. He had expected the underground formations to be interesting, and he'd hoped they would be grand, but he'd never expected them to be quite so spectacular.

'Blow me if this isn't just too good to be true,' he whispered to Grace as they followed the trail of tourists along the wooden walkway in the first enormous lava tunnel. High above them, like the richly decorated ceiling of a towering cathedral, arched glorious patterns. The intricate red, pink, ochre and cream designs, which, their guide explained, had formed when iron and calcium leached through the basalt, would look superb through a camera lens. 'Couldn't be better for what we want!' he enthused. 'The scenes dealing with underground survivors are so vital to the movie. This is magnificent!' He patted Grace's shoulder. 'And *you're* magnificent.'

She jumped at his touch and turned startled green eyes his way. 'I beg your pardon?'

'You showed a masterstroke of pure genius when you suggested checking out these tubes.'

Grace blinked at his praise. 'I realised they must be pretty sensational when I read that you could fit two trains on railway tracks in here and there'd still be room for another level on top of that.'

'We could never create anything quite so awe-inspiring with computer graphics, or by trying to build a set in a studio.' Mitch realised his hand was still resting on her shoulder. She was wearing some kind of halter-neck cotton top and her shoulder was bare. Beneath his fingers, Grace's skin was silky and soft and he was surprised by his urge to give her shoulder an enthusiastic squeeze.

Not a wise move, Wentworth, he reflected with a laconic shrug. Best to change his line of thinking before he did something he regretted.

But, as they continued into a narrower section of the stone tunnel, the surroundings became less absorbing and Mitch became much more conscious of Grace's perfume filling the enclosed space. The scent she wore was very fresh and flowery, without being too sweet. And every so often, he caught traces of the fragrance of her hair. There was nothing artificial about its smell, and it reminded him of a fresh autumn morning, gentle sunlight and clean, tangy lemons.

'What are you doing?' Grace's sharp words in his ear cut into his wandering thoughts. What *was* he doing? How had his arm crept back around her shoulders? He dropped it abruptly.

'Got carried away with the excitement of all this natural splendour,' he responded, in what he hoped was a deceptively casual reply. He diverted his attention to the primeval rock formations around them, rather than the neat curve and slope of her shoulders and the straight, perfect symmetry of her collarbones—natural splendours, way out of his territory. 'Don't the psychologists tell us the cave represents the womb?' he elaborated. 'It must be why I'm feeling kind of...primitive.'

Grace opened her mouth as if to comment, but must have thought better of it.

'What about you?' he joked. 'Any primitive urges?'

'I—I feel perfectly normal,' she said, defying her words by nervously wiping her hands on her linen shorts.

Mitch considered the way she walked a little faster, putting more distance between them. This puzzling woman was getting under his skin. There was so much that he liked about her and yet, around him, she was permanently uptight—always on tenterhooks, as if she suspected he would pounce on her and have his wicked way with her at any moment.

Anyone would think she'd lived her life locked away in a tower.

But that couldn't be the case. He'd seen her looking more sexy and alluring in fetching black lingerie than any siren of the silver screen. And the other night, when he'd kissed her—why, her enjoyment had been breathtakingly unrestrained. He'd been absolutely stunned by the eagerness of her sweet, receptive mouth and the yearning he'd sensed in her soft, submissive body—as if she'd come to life in his arms.

It was a fanciful notion, but, for a moment, she'd made him feel like the prince who kissed Sleeping Beauty, waking her from one hundred years' sleep.

How he'd walked out of that flat without throwing her onto the sofa and taking her there and then was nothing short of miraculous. Perhaps Grace had every right to be nervous of him.

It was mid-afternoon before they finished their interviews with the management at Undara. They were delighted to discover that obtaining the official permits for filming would not be a problem, as long as Tropicana contracted to meet certain environmental considerations.

Once they left, Mitch was determined to head further northwest, to explore what he called the real Gulf country. 'I'm not sure of exactly what I want, but I'm looking for something stark. I'll know it when I see it,' he told Grace.

And she had to be content with that.

In a way she was rather grateful to be able to sit back and let the miles drift by as Mitch drove through the late afternoon. They didn't bother much with conversation. She'd spent the last two nights tossing sleeplessly and now she was weary. And, with Gershwin's 'Rhapsody in Blue' playing softly while the truck sped along the straight, monotonous stretch of road towards Georgetown, she felt herself nodding off.

Luckily, Mitch seemed caught up in his own thoughts as he stared ahead at the single-lane bitumen road. It looked like a thin, red-stained ribbon stretching across the wide savannah. She made a pillow by folding her leather jacket and propping it up against the window. Curling up her legs as best she could, she rested her head against it. Before too long, she drifted off to sleep...

Her forehead banging hard against the window woke her.

It was dark. Grace struggled into consciousness, surprised to discover that their truck was swaying, banging and thumping its way through the dark across very rough and rocky terrain. Feeling stiff and a little groggy from sleep, she struggled to sit straight. Her neck was cricked and sore from the way she'd slept.

'Where are we? Where's the road?' she mumbled as she tried to make sense of the brief glimpses of wild landscape shown up by the jumping headlights.

'Good evening,' Mitch grinned. 'You're awake.'

She was about to ask the time, but the clock on the dashboard in front of her told her that it was almost eight o'clock. 'Good heavens. I've been asleep for nearly three hours!' she exclaimed as she shoved her arms into the sleeves of her leather jacket. The temperature had dropped quite dramatically.

'You've been snoring your head off.'

Her response was pure outrage. 'I don't snore!'

'Whoever told you that?' he drawled.

'Why...' Grace gritted her teeth. She'd been awake for no more than thirty seconds and already her boss was taunting her. What business was it of his who knew about her sleeping habits? In reality, the number was exceedingly small. But there was no need to share that kind of personal history with a world-class playboy like Mitch Wentworth. 'No one has ever complained about my snoring,' she answered honestly.

Even in the dark interior of the truck's cabin, she could see his eyebrows rise. And his sideways glance was loaded with inference.

With a disdainful sweep of her eyelashes, Grace refused to meet his teasing gaze and turned instead to peer through the window beside her. 'You haven't answered my question,' she said, eyeing the rugged terrain. 'Where are we? What happened to the road?'

'The road's right where it's always been. We're just not following it at the moment.'

This deserved an explanation. Warily, she faced him again. 'But why, for heaven's sake? Have we been through Georgetown?'

Mitch swung the steering wheel sharply to swerve past the rocky outcrop that suddenly loomed in their path. Grace braced herself as, despite her seat belt, she was thrown against the door.

'Sorry about that,' he muttered, once they were safely on the other side. 'To answer your question, we passed through Georgetown over an hour ago. But then I came across a signpost to an old mining site and thought it might be worth taking a look.'

'So you just left the road and took off blindly into the scrub in the middle of the night?'

In the glare of the headlights, she saw the line of Mitch's face stiffen. 'It was still light then and there were clear tracks. And the kind of location I'm looking for is hardly likely to be sitting right next to the highway. I need to be prepared to take a few risks.'

'And has it been worth the detour?'

He shrugged. 'Not really.'

Pounding through the dark along an unknown track in one of the remotest parts of Australia seemed a touch reckless. Grace couldn't resist another question. 'Do you know where we are now? It's so dark you'd be lucky to see a kangaroo hopping straight in front of you, let alone the way back to the main road. I don't fancy spending the night out here.'

'Of course I know where we are. I've turned back. We'll hit the bitumen again any tick of the clock and you'll be in Croydon in time for a late dinner.'

Grace shivered inside her jacket. She wasn't especially cold, but the grim, deserted landscape and the inky black world beyond the headlights' beam looked menacing. 'This track doesn't look like it's had much use. I'm sorry to keep harping on this. But *how* do you know we're going in the right direction?'

Drawing in a deep, exasperated breath, Mitch glared at her. 'For crying out loud, woman, are you going to question my every move? I was following a good track, but it petered out. Okay? But there are enough signs here for me to follow. We'll be all right. Give me another half-hour, and if we haven't come across the road by then we can rethink our position.'

She clamped her lips tightly shut. In this situation, there was no sense in upsetting Mitch any further, so she sat straight and silent, clutching the safety rail, with her eyes peeled for the first hint of danger ahead. The way was very rough and, to her mind, Mitch was driving too fast. Anthills and boulders seemed to loom suddenly out of the dark and he was forever having to swerve to avoid some kind of hazard. She hoped he wasn't being overly confident just because he had an off-road four-wheel-drive vehicle.

Suddenly the headlights picked up a flash of something ahead. Shadowy black shapes streaked across their path. 'Look out!' she cried, and Mitch slammed on the brakes.

'A mob of wild pigs,' he growled.

The shaggy beasts, some huge and with gruesome tusks, were frightened by the truck's lights and scampered away, squealing and screeching into the murky black world beyond the headlights. Shaken, Grace glanced at Mitch and he flashed her a quick grin. 'How are you holding out there, Ms Robbins? Exciting, isn't it?'

'I think I could do without this kind of excitement,' she replied.

He reached over and tweaked her hair. 'We're not in any danger, Grace,' he said, his voice suddenly gentle. 'We've a sturdy vehicle, plenty of fuel, water and warm clothes. If we have to face the worst and we can't get back onto the road tonight, we can always pull up. You can sleep in here inside the cabin and I'll curl up in the back of the truck.' He leaned over and looked as if he was going to drop a warm kiss on her cheek, but at the last minute changed his mind and straightened again. 'Cheer up. Throw in another CD and let's have some music.'

The truck lurched forward as he accelerated once more and Grace, because she could think of no better suggestion, slipped a CD into the player. In the pitch-dark, she had no idea what she'd selected, but within moments Simon and Garfunkel's soothing voices began to sing the familiar harmonies from the sixties.

And before too long she felt a little better. Mitch was right, she grudgingly admitted. This was a kind of adventure. And if they really had to they could camp out for one night. After last night, she knew she wouldn't have to fight him off. There was no one around and they'd be perfectly safe. It wasn't the wet season, so they weren't in danger of getting bogged or flooded.

She zipped up her jacket, shoved her hands into the pockets of her shorts and wished she were wearing jeans. If she did have to spend the night out here, she would have to change into something warmer.

As their vehicle forged its way through the dark bush, her spirits gradually lifted, and by the time Simon and Garfunkel were singing one of her favourite songs, Grace was relaxed enough to hum along with them. Even if Mitch was a touch devil-may-care, he was a competent driver, she decided. His strong hands held the steering wheel confidently and he changed gears with the ease of a racing car professional.

Even now, as he slipped into a lower gear while they careered around another unexpected mound of boulders, he was completely in control.

Almost!

They both saw it at the same moment.

Before them in the headlights' glare, a gaping, deeply eroded washout cut through the track.

Mitch swore.

There was no chance for him to stop; the channel was far too close and sudden braking would send the vehicle skidding straight down into the deep ditch.

He gunned the motor, knowing his only hope was to jump the truck over the gap. Teeth gritted, he depressed the accelerator and willed the vehicle forward. His heart lurched as the front wheels left solid ground.

He thought they'd made it. But the rear of the truck dipped abruptly, then smashed down into the gully. With a savage jolt, the vehicle crashed to a sickening, sudden halt and ghastly sounds of crumpling metal filled his ears. Mitch's body pitched forward, then the sudden rush and hiss of an inflating airbag burst in his face.

He swore and turned to Grace, who was similarly battling with a safety airbag. 'You okay?' he gasped.

'I think so.'

He heard the clunk and squeak of her door opening and the thud of her feet hitting the ground as she jumped down. Over her shoulder, she called, 'I'll try to see what's happened.'

Mitch grimaced and he punched the airbag in helpless rage. He knew what had happened. A right royal stuff-up! How would he ever urge this vehicle out of such a steep ditch? The motor had stalled, so he reached for the ignition key and flicked it on.

'Hold it!' Grace's sharp cry came from somewhere in the grim darkness outside. 'Wait, Mitch! I think there's a rear wheel torn from its axle. And—and I can smell petrol.'

Frustration had him roaring back at her. 'Stand back! I've got to give it at least one go.'

'No, Mitch, no!'

Ignoring her cries, Mitch turned the ignition key again. He heard the motor try to grind into action. Then everything happened very quickly.

Sparks flashed from somewhere in front of him, followed by the smell of smoke and a muffled explosion.

From a long way off, he heard Grace screaming, 'Mitch! Get out!'

He didn't need a second invitation. Unbuckling his seat belt with frantic fingers, he shoved his door open and dived sideways. With a horrible flaring blast, the truck burst into ugly flames. Mitch rolled across the rocky ground and cleared the conflagration just in time.

Stunned, he lay still on the dirt track for the few short moments it took his mind to catch up with his body. 'Grace?' Where was she? Refusing to notice the cuts and grazes he'd scored, Mitch hauled himself to his feet. All he could see were flames—orange, scarlet and blood-red, disappearing into a cloud of evil-smelling black smoke.

'Grace!' he called again.

And then came the faint reply. 'I'm all right. I'm back here.'

Relieved, he switched his attention to the inferno beside him, and he decided in a flash that there was no way he could just let their only source of transport and shelter burn up!

Desperately, he scraped at the dirt and tossed it towards the flames. Again and again he tried. But eventually, with a sinking stomach, Mitch had to accept the truth. Even if he had a shovel and a whole mountain of sand, he could not put out that fire.

'Mitch!' Grace called, and he staggered towards the sound of her voice, almost stumbling over her where she sat, huddled beside a boulder.

Feeling dizzy and miserable and several versions of an idiot, he knelt quickly at her side. 'Are you all right?'

'Yes,' she replied in a small voice. 'What about you?'

'I'm okay. Just furious with myself.'

'Furious' wasn't a strong enough word for his sense of rage. He'd just hurtled them headlong into the worst kind of danger. And when Grace had mentioned a petrol smell he should have known that meant the fuel tank was ruptured. Now they were stranded without food, water, warmth or any means of communication.

In the middle of nowhere.

Although he'd put on a brave face for Grace, he had absolutely no idea where they were. His head sank into his hands and he groaned aloud.

Her hand patted his shoulder. 'I managed to grab my day pack out of the back of the truck.' Grace held the canvas bag out for him to see.

'Top stuff, Grace.' He sighed. 'You're the only one around here with any brains.' With another groan, Mitch smashed a balled fist against his palm as he looked back at the orange flames engulfing the truck. 'Damn it to hell!'

And once again he felt Grace's cool hand on his wrist. 'It's happened, Mitch,' she said softly. 'There's nothing more we can do. We just have to stay clear-headed now and think this through.'

Mitch closed his eyes and clenched his teeth. This whole mess was his fault. He was surprised that Grace was taking everything so calmly. Now they didn't even have any shelter. *What kind of a boss did that make him?* 'I'm sorry,' he muttered.

She didn't respond. There was another explosion, followed by another flash and a burst of flames from the truck. 'Let's move further away,' Mitch said, and reached down to help Grace to her feet.

They found a couple of flat rocks to sit on and Grace settled her small canvas pack beside her, undid the buckles and began to rummage around inside. 'I'm just checking out all our worldly goods,' she said. After a moment, she turned to him. 'It's not so bad. We have a litre of water, which is pretty important. Two muesli bars, two apples. And…and a map and matches! Thank heavens for that!'

'I didn't even think to grab the mobile phone,' confessed Mitch. He threw his arm around her shoulders. 'I told you this morning, you're magnificent.'

'There's not much else,' Grace replied, apparently ignoring his praise. She was digging down deep and, to his surprise, he heard her giggle. 'Now this is really useful. I've got a spare pair of knickers.'

'You don't say?' In spite of everything that had happened and the mountain of guilt he shouldered, he sensed a totally inappropriate physical response. Mitch forced his voice to sound casual. 'What colour are they?'

And, for some ridiculous reason, Grace laughed. Mitch's shoulders relaxed and his own chortle joined hers. This girl might be uptight and prickly in the office, but when it came to the real crunch she had guts.

After their chuckles subsided, they sat together in the dark with the flickering flames of the wrecked truck lighting up the bush around them. The air was still tainted by the acrid smell of burning rubber.

Mitch's sigh hissed like air escaping from a punctured tyre. 'I guess we'll have to try to make the best of this,' he said at last. 'At least we can save your matches for now, seeing as we've got this flaming truck barbecue to ignite our timber. I'll see if I can find some wood for a fire. It's going to get quite cool tonight, I imagine. But we may as well stay here till morning and then take stock of our surroundings.'

He built their fire some distance from the burning truck, in the shelter of a small rocky outcrop. When he'd finished, Grace came and sat beside him and they shared one of her muesli bars and had a few sips of water each and stared at the flames. All around them the bush was deathly quiet, so that the only sound they could hear was the snap and crackle of wood burning or, in the distance, the occasional faint howling of dingoes.

'No one knows where we are?' asked Grace.

''Fraid not.'

For the first time, she was frightened. 'When I was asleep, you didn't phone ahead to Croydon?'

'I tried, but the phone wouldn't work. Must be out of the network.'

'So there's no one at all who knows which way we headed after we left Undara?'

'I'm afraid not.' Mitch sighed, and they continued staring at the fire in silence for several minutes before he spoke again. 'Thanks for being such a champion about this. You have every right to lecture me.'

Grace gazed deep into the flames and her lips curled into a self-deprecating smile. It was weird how she could stay so calm in the face of this present danger and yet, at other times, she'd been reduced to a quivering mess by the mere hint of Mitch's awareness of her as a...woman.

'Neither of us is going to drop straight off to sleep,' Mitch added, and Grace found his deep voice a strangely comforting sound filling the silence. 'I guess there's not much for us to do except get to know each other a little better.'

'How do you mean?'

She saw Mitch's grin in the reddish flicker from the fire. 'Calm down, Grace. I'm simply asking you to tell me a bit more about yourself. Tell me about your family.'

Grace drew in a deep breath as she sat with her knees drawn up and her chin resting on them. She switched her gaze from the glowing timbers to the starry sky above, unsure to what extent she wanted to bare her soul to this boss she found so disconcerting. 'Just because we're stranded in the middle of the wilderness, that doesn't mean we have to become bosom buddies.'

Mitch's eyes betrayed his amusement. 'You are exceptionally safe Ms Robbins. We've a long way to go before we reach that point.'

Grace sniffed. 'If you must know,' she replied in a prim, tight little voice, 'I was born on a distant planet and came to earth in a space pod when I was just five centuries old. Two kind earthlings adopted me.' Her glance flicked to Mitch to gauge his reaction.

'That explains a great deal,' he said with a deadpan expression.

'I'm glad to hear it.'

'Now I understand why you're such an intriguing puzzle. I can see that you're superwoman and yet you're afraid of earthmen.' He lay back, linked his hands behind his neck and grinned. 'And you also don't want to talk about your private life.'

'Oh, for heaven's sake,' Grace cried, shaking her head in exasperation. 'Do you have to psychoanalyse me all the time? Okay here come the fascinating details.' She folded her arms across her chest and spoke slowly, her expression flat, as if giving evidence to the police. 'I'm an only child. My parents were fairly old when I was born. I had a very…quiet childhood.' She could have said repressed or boring, but now, in the middle of nowhere with this infuriating man, the safety of home, no matter how dreary, seemed more appealing.

'You were a good student?'

'Oh, yes. I was very studious. Winning prizes on speech night was the best way to please my parents.'

Mitch poked at the fire with a long stick. 'So how did your parents feel when you took a job in the film industry?'

For some reason his question pleased Grace. It made her feel as if he had really listened and was genuinely interested and thinking about what her home life had been like. 'They were devastated at first,' she admitted. 'Especially Dad. He had such high hopes that I would become a doctor or a lawyer or something equally prestigious. But when I was young we never went to the cinema and so—I don't know—maybe I overreacted after all that stifling—but when I first started getting out to the occasional movie as a teen-ager I was absolutely entranced—totally wrapped. I knew I had to end up involved with them somehow. Mum and Dad eventually got over their disappointment after they saw my name in the credits at the end of the first feature film I worked on.'

'What about the men in your life?'

She sat bolt upright. 'What about them?'

Mitch shrugged. 'Idle curiosity. I know you like to give the impression that you're not interested, but...'

She drew in a breath sharply. Perhaps it would be best if she set him straight right from the start. 'I'm very choosy about men,' she told him quickly, well aware that she sounded nervous.

'Now, why doesn't that surprise me?'

Briefly, she considered mentioning Roger the Rat, but just as quickly she rejected the idea. 'And it works the other way, too. I have limited appeal.' She said this, not daring to look at him as she made her admission. 'I'm too serious and quiet. Men don't find those qualities particularly appealing.'

Mitch was staring at her. His eyes were wide and considering and a faint, sad smile played at the corners of his mouth. 'Not even Henry Aspinall?'

'Especially Henry Aspinall,' Grace responded with a scowl. She leaned forward abruptly. 'That's enough about me. How about you?'

Slowly, he scratched in the dust with a twig. For a long moment he seemed wrapped in his own thoughts, then his head jerked up. 'What was that? My family? My father died when I was ten and my mother had a real struggle to raise my three brothers and me.'

He threw the broken twig into the flames and Grace watched it curl into a blackened crisp. 'My mum wasn't much like your parents, by the sound of it. She wasn't all that interested in academic prizes, but she used to come and watch me play footie...'

'You ended up playing rugby for Queensland, didn't you?'

He looked surprised. 'How on earth do you know that?'

'Oh, I've told you before, I read a lot and I have a good memory.'

Mitch grinned. 'Anyhow, what really pleased my mother was when we boys got part-time jobs that helped to make the dollars go round. For years, I had a paper round and a lawn-mowing service. Later I earned money fixing my mates' computers.' He frowned at Grace. 'Now why are you looking at me like that?'

'Sorry,' she mumbled, ducking her head. Her surprise must have been showing more than she realised. For some reason she'd imagined Mitch sailing through a comfortable, pampered boyhood, with doting parents to launch him into his brilliant future. 'I'm just coming to terms with the humble beginnings of the famous Mitch Wentworth.'

She watched as he shrugged and smiled. 'If we're doing this fair and square,' she said, waiting for his expression to grow serious again, 'I suppose I should ask you about the women in your life.'

'But you don't need to ask, do you?' The grin lingered.

'I don't?'

'You've already done your research and you know everything there is to know about me. You seem to know, for example, all about my hobbies with women. My habit of going to bed with women I hardly know...'

'I've read what the magazines report. And where there's smoke there's usually...' Grace's cheeks burned as brightly as the flames she stared at, and she lost the necessary confidence to finish her reply. Her boss's private life wasn't really any of her business.

To her relief, Mitch seemed just as keen to let the matter drop. He threw back his dark head and stared up at the sky. 'Just take a look at that. Stars stretching for ever. I've never seen so many.'

Grace followed his gaze. From one distant horizon to the other the great sky curved above them in a huge dome—absolutely crowded with millions of tiny, softly twinkling, silvery stars.

He reached over and gave her a gentle punch. 'And to think some hotels boast about five-star accommodation, Grace. We're beating them hands down tonight.'

She couldn't help smiling back.

His face grew serious again. 'It's a humbling concept—the vastness of our universe. Have you come to any conclusions about it?'

'It's big?'

Mitch threw back his head and laughed loudly.

'Before you rupture something,' she went on defensively, 'did you know that there are more stars and planets in the universe than there are grains of sand on the beaches of the earth?'

'No.' He laughed. 'I'm afraid that detail had escaped me.'

'I guess you expected something deep and meaningful from me, seeing I claim to be thoughtful and serious,' she amended when his mirth eventually subsided. 'But what I really meant was that the universe is *so* big, that I haven't found any man-made explanation of it all that satisfies me.'

Watching the flames once more, he nodded.

'Actually, we should be able to use the stars to help us work out directions.'

'You think so? I always understood the sun was more reliable. Isn't there some trick you're supposed to be able to do with your watch and the sun?'

Impulsively, Grace leaned over and grasped Mitch's left wrist. An unexpected flash of heat shot through her when she touched him, but she tried to ignore it as she looked at his watch and laughed. 'I doubt a digital watch would be much use. No hands to line up with the compass points.'

'I suppose not,' Mitch agreed. 'I guess the bits and pieces of bushcraft I picked up in my youth are a bit outdated now. So what wonderful little gem of information do you have about direction-finding?'

She stared at the silver speckled sky, searching her memory for exactly what it was she had read. 'I'm sure I've seen somewhere that you can use the Southern Cross. It's somehow connected to the Cross's two pointer stars.'

'What direction does it indicate?'

'Why, south, of course.'

'I would hazard a guess that it was something to do with the line from the long arm bisecting a line drawn through the pointers,' Mitch suggested.

'Yes!' exclaimed Grace. 'I remember now. That's it! That gives you a southerly direction.'

'So, if we follow that point down, we should remember that really tall ironbark over there—the one standing out against the sky—should be more or less south.' Mitch reached out and shook

Grace's hand. 'Well done, team.' He held her hand for a moment and stared at her as if he wanted to say more.

Grace's heart jumped. A man lost in the wilderness had no right to look so breathtaking. Somehow, when he was tousled and unshaven, he looked more dangerously attractive than ever.

To her relief, he eased himself backwards so that he lay once more with his hands behind his head, looking up at the huge sky. 'I've just remembered a game we used to play when we were kids. Have a crack at this, Grace. If you were a piece of furniture, what would you be?'

'What *furniture* would I be?' she asked, wondering if he'd banged his head during the smash and was suffering from delayed concussion.

'Yeah,' he urged. 'I know it sounds strange, but it's an interesting exercise. You'll get the hang of it. So, what would you be? A rocking chair, a garden seat?'

'Oh, what the heck?' Grace laughed. 'I'm definitely a mahogany roll-top desk.'

Mitch looked at her and grinned. 'So you are—elegant and immensely practical. And what kind of fruit are you?'

Grace rolled her eyes.

'Fruit? Mitch, I don't know. You must have been an imaginative bunch of kids.'

'I guess we were.'

'I'm probably a…a mango. No, I'm not.' She laughed. 'I'm a slice of perfectly ripe, chilled pawpaw.' Grace shifted onto her side and looked at Mitch as he lay with his handsome profile etched in starlight. The wild, menacing wilderness that surrounded them seemed to diminish and she couldn't help her light-hearted, spontaneous comment. 'And you are a…black sapote.'

'I'm a what?' he asked, turning towards her, his eyes wide with curiosity.

'A black sapote. It's a tropical fruit and it tastes sinfully delicious, like rich chocolate mousse.'

'Am I, now?' mused Mitch. 'I like the sound of that.'

And suddenly Grace was embarrassed, as if she'd let her feelings run away with her. 'But as far as furniture is concerned,' she hurried on, hoping to cover over any unwarranted enthusiasm, 'you'd have to be a...'

'Director's chair?' Mitch asked.

'No. That's far too obvious. No, you're a telephone table.'

He shot her a look of surprise. 'How on earth did you come up with that?'

'Well, you're the boss. You can just stand in hallways and yell and everyone comes running to you.'

Mitch chuckled. 'I can see you're warming to this. Now let me see, if you were a musical instrument, I'd say you'd be a saxophone—playing soft blues or jazz at midnight—sexy, moody and unpredictable.'

Sexy? Grace was glad it was dark so he couldn't see the fierce blush that followed his description.

They were back on dangerous ground and an uncomfortable wave of unsettling yearning flooded through her. This would never do. 'There's no doubt what musical instrument you'd be,' she retorted, her tone more waspish than she'd intended.

'Oh?'

'You'd be a trumpet in a brass band.'

Mitch sighed loudly. 'Now why do I think this sounds like a direct hit at my ego? Do you imagine I'd want to blow my own trumpet as often as I liked?'

'If the cap fits...'

He frowned and levered himself up into a sitting position. 'The party's getting rough. I'm afraid your true feelings are coming out, Ms Robbins.'

Grace was suddenly regretful that she'd been quite so sharp-tongued. Mitch had really been very pleasant company. Overwhelmingly charming company. 'Actually, I was thinking more of what a bright, triumphant sound a trumpet makes,' she suggested, in an effort to make amends.

'Liar,' growled Mitch, but in the firelight his eyes twinkled with good humour. He stood and picked up a log, which he carefully positioned on the fire. 'We can't hope for comfort and we don't know what's ahead of us tomorrow, so how about we try for some rest?'

She nodded, realising how clever he'd been to keep her talking, even laughing. She'd almost forgotten just how serious their situation was.

'You're allowed to snuggle into my back if you get cold,' Mitch said as he settled his long frame down on the ground once more.

'I'll be all right,' Grace murmured. She lay stiffly near the fire and the sharp stones of the surrounding gravel dug into her legs. But as she stared at that big, warm, comforting back she wished desperately that she had more courage. There had never been a back she wanted to snuggle up to more.

CHAPTER SIX

IT WAS A terrible night.

Grace found trying to keep warm almost impossible. The side of her body away from the fire became bitterly cold, but if she wriggled any closer the heat was unbearably scorching. So she tossed and turned on the hard, unforgiving dirt and felt like a sausage being grilled on a barbecue. And she lay awake for hours, staring at the blinking, distant stars, feeling hungry, thirsty and utterly miserable.

But she wasn't frightened.

She felt strangely confident that they couldn't really be lost. When the sun came up, she and Mitch would get a better look at their surroundings and, with the aid of her map, they'd discover how to get back onto the road. Then it would just be a matter of waiting for someone to drive past. She lay on the hard earth and tried to comfort herself by picturing their rescue.

Mitch slept like the proverbial log. And that didn't help her to cope any better with the long, dark, lonely hours.

When eventually the distant horizon showed the faintest, thin line of pale light, Grace almost wept for joy. Never had she been more relieved to see a new day. And it arrived quite spectacularly, as only an outback sunrise could. Rosy-pink fingers, growing warmer and more deeply hued every minute, spread outward across the huge sky from a brilliant red-gold fingertip of sun. Slowly the burning ball crept higher. No wonder ancient people worshipped the sun, she thought as she watched the enormous glowing circle pulse its triumphant light across the plains.

They breakfasted on a shared apple and a few sips of water. 'I guess this is not very hygienic,' Grace said as she handed Mitch the half-eaten apple and watched his mouth close over it.

The crisp white flesh that had just been in her mouth was now disappearing into his. It was so incredibly intimate—like sharing a toothbrush—the kind of familiar exchange lovers enjoyed.

'You didn't mention any worries about an exchange of germs when I kissed you the other night,' he tossed back at her.

That shut her up and she fumed as he hungrily polished off the fruit—core, seeds, the lot. While he munched, she studied their surroundings.

'Hardly any landmarks worth noting,' Mitch observed gloomily.

Grace had to agree. The Gulf country, which stretched all around them, was almost featureless—flat country with no hills or mountain ranges and covered with sparse scrub and hundreds of red termite mounds.

'We at least have some ideas about direction,' she offered. 'There's our southerly ironbark tree that we noted last night, and I took careful notice of where the sun came up. It was over here. So that's more or less east. North must be this way.' She pointed slightly to their left.

'That's what I was afraid of,' muttered Mitch, and he kicked at a loose stone with his boot and sent it skimming across the hard-baked red earth.

'Afraid?' she echoed. 'Why's that?'

His mouth pulled into a grimly drooping curve as he turned and pointed back towards the burnt-out shell of their truck. 'Look at the way we were heading last night.'

Grace squinted. Beyond the truck, she could make out the faint line of the track weaving its way past termite mounds and scraggy pandanus. Then she looked again towards the point they had determined as south. 'Oh, my goodness, you were driving towards the north,' she said softly. 'Perhaps north-east.'

'When I should have been heading south. South-west, if we were hoping to get to Croydon.' Mitch swore colourfully. 'I can't believe it. How did I end up driving in completely the wrong damn direction?'

Grace bit her lip. Mitch looked so angry with himself and so ashamed, she experienced a flicker of sympathy for her boss. 'Should we look at the map and try to work out where we are?' she asked hesitantly.

He stared at her and his eyes suddenly brightened with their familiar, teasing glint. 'A top-drawer suggestion, Ms Robbins. If you'd be so kind...' With a flourishing gesture, he held out his hand for Grace's map.

She unfolded it and spread it on the ground, so they could both see it. As they crouched in the dirt, Mitch's hand rested lightly on Grace's shoulder so that his fingers, his warm skin, touched hers. She shivered. Didn't he realise what a casual touch like that could do to a girl?

'Here's Georgetown,' she said, trying to ignore the skitters of reaction caused by his proximity. He had hunkered down so close to her that his thigh pressed against her as well. 'Where do you think you left the road?' she asked, a trifle breathlessly.

'About here,' Mitch replied, indicating the spot on the map with his free hand. 'I started heading north, but then I was sure I had turned back to the south.'

'You must have veered off in a bit of an arc and then, without noticing, slowly swung around to the north again,' Grace volunteered.

Mitch rubbed his thumb over his stubble lined chin and fixed her with his dark eyes. Grace drew in a sharp breath. Fringed by black lashes, his eyes held hers, so that, for a moment, she forgot what they were discussing. Forgot totally that their lives could be in great danger. She was dimly aware that she should have been absolutely panic-stricken! But something much more important was happening. She was drowning in the depths of those beautiful, dark, sensuous eyes.

And, as he squatted in the dirt, he was staring at her as if he'd never seen her before. With a sinking heart, she realised that she probably looked quite terrible. Exhausted and dirty, with no hairbrush, no chance to wash her face—no woman would want a man like Mitch Wentworth to see her in such a state! Self-consciously, she ran her fingers through her hair.

'The wild, untamed look definitely suits you, Grace,' he said softly. 'When we get you back to the office, we'll have to do something about your image.'

With a sickening jolt, Grace came to her senses. 'Will we?' she asked coldly, and she ground her teeth. For a reckless moment there, she had almost allowed herself to think of Mitch as someone other than her boss—as an attractive man. A man she could grow fond of.

What a stupid, stupid mistake. Not only was Mitch Wentworth her boss, he was the Dark Invader. He'd trampled all over poor George Hervey, to forge his way into the company. He was another user, like Roger the Rat.

She wriggled her shoulder away from his touch and stared hard at the map. 'Our chances of ever getting back to the office depend on some pretty careful planning now,' she snapped. 'How long do you think you were driving in the wrong direction?'

'About two hours,' Mitch admitted with a grimace.

'So, taking the rough track into consideration, we're probably about a hundred and fifty kilometres up this way,' Grace suggested. 'About to head up the Cape York Peninsular.'

Mitch squinted as he examined the map once more. 'I'd say you're dead right,' he admitted at last with a deep, weary sigh. They both looked out at the desolate expanse of savannah plain stretching before them. There was no evidence of human existence anywhere. No fence posts, no rooftops, not even a sign of cattle. 'How is anyone going to find us out here? This country is about as remote as it gets.'

'They won't,' Grace told him quietly.

Why didn't she feel more frightened? Their situation was desperate and yet somehow, even though her visit to the outback with the man she'd been determined to hate was turning into a worse nightmare than she could have ever predicted, she felt calm.

Almost safe.

Which was ridiculous given that Mitch didn't look at all relaxed or in control. Resting his elbows on his knees, he buried his face in his hands.

At that moment, a shadow crossed the sun and Grace looked up to see thousands of wild, swift-flying budgerigars free-wheeling across the bright sky. Little specks of green and yellow, they darted and danced agilely through the clear blue space, displaying the careless freedom of creatures who belonged to the natural environment.

Grace followed their movements. *We're alien invaders, out of our element. Displaced. And in great danger of perishing. We have none of the knowledge these wild things share.*

Mitch's hoarse voice invaded her reflections. 'Okay. I'm the boss, and I got us into this disaster. But I've considered our situation carefully and I'll get us out. This is what we've got to do.' He stood up and glared down at Grace, as if challenging her to defy him. His shoulders were squared and his jaw thrust forward belligerently. 'As I understand it, the golden rule when you're bushed is to stay with the vehicle.'

Grace frowned. 'In most circumstances,' she said slowly.

'In every case,' Mitch declared, scowling fiercely. 'It's your only hope of being found.'

'But...' Grace hesitated, and her brows drew low in a deep frown as she puzzled over how to handle this.

'I don't think I could take another of your "buts" right now, Grace.' He punched the air in a gesture of defiance and then his hands fell to his hips. He glared at her in angry silence. 'But I'm going to hear it anyway, so fire away.'

Grace rubbed her sweaty hands together nervously and cleared her throat. 'I think that the idea of staying put is very sensible when a car breaks down on a road, or some place where people are likely to come looking for you. Nine times out of ten it would be exactly the right thing to do. But our situation is different. No one-absolutely no one—knows where we are.'

Mitch didn't attempt to interrupt. He just continued to glower at her.

Swallowing, she pressed on. 'We told everyone in the office that we'd be away for five days, so they won't even *begin* to search for us till after that time is up. There's no food or water here, so we can't afford to stay put and just hope. I—I think we might have to work out a way to save ourselves.'

Mitch's hands clenched and he scowled with obvious annoyance, as if he wanted to flick her off the edge of the universe. Then he turned abruptly, marching away from her, his long legs taking enormous strides. Until suddenly, without warning, he spun back dramatically and his face was red—angry, dark red.

He reminded Grace of a cowboy in a shoot-out scene in a third-rate western. She half expected to see Mitch reach for his holster.

'You know what's the matter with you, Grace Robbins?' he bellowed.

'I'm *right*?' she shouted back.

'EVERY BLASTED TIME!'

She wanted to yell back at Mitch that he could take a flying leap, but his face suddenly softened into an unexpectedly boyish smile and the words died on her lips. He sauntered back towards her, his hands resting loosely on his hips. His smile lingered. 'Forgive me, Ms Robbins. You're too clever and chock-a-block with common sense for us to fight.' Reaching out, he took her hand. 'Honest, Grace, you're obviously the perfect assistant to be lost with in the outback.'

His gentleness, coming swift on the heels of his attack, floored her. This man sure knew how to calm ruffled feathers. She looked at her hand which had practically disappeared inside his strong grasp. 'If only I was also *willing*,' she muttered, snatching her hand away. And then she grimaced. He'd caught her off guard and now she'd let fly with a hopelessly stupid remark.

'Willing?' Mitch remained standing directly in front of her, a perplexed expression in his eyes as they gleamed from beneath thick lashes.

'Please, forget—forget I said that,' she stammered.

He smiled as he brushed her hair back from her cheek. 'A wild and willing Grace would be an unexpected bonus.' Then his face grew serious again and he dropped his hand to his side. 'But it won't get us out of here.'

There was nothing Grace could think of to say. Her mind was too busy cringing from her stupid gaffe.

'You think we should press on?' Mitch queried.

'We're—um—' Grace cleared her throat. 'We're—um, going to run out of water in less than a day if we stay here.'

Mitch looked again at the map. 'See this development road heading north? I'd say we're about forty kilometres away from it.'

'Yes,' Grace agreed. 'If we try to go back the way we came, we've got at least one hundred and fifty kilometres before we reach a road.'

'So that's settled. We'll push on and follow this northerly track before it gets too hot.'

Although it was mid-winter and the night had been cold, walking for hours under the full strength of the tropical sun soon produced thirst and sweat. Mitch was pleased that Grace could drape her jacket over her head to try to protect her face and bare shoulders from the unrelenting rays. There wasn't the slightest hint of a breeze.

And if they had read the map correctly they had many kilometres to walk. They could run out of food and water before they found the road.

When Grace turned, he was concerned to see how flushed her cheeks were. The symptoms of dehydration flashed through his head: dizziness, fatigue, loss of appetite.

'How much water do we have left?' she asked.

Nervously, he reached into the backpack he was carrying for her and pulled out the clear plastic bottle. 'About half.'

'Mmm. Better save it.'

'No. You have some.'

She didn't wait for a second invitation. 'Just need to wet my whistle,' she murmured, only taking a couple of sips. 'Your turn.'

But Mitch put the bottle back in the pack without taking any. Their lives depended on water, and he could last a little longer. After all, he'd got them into this.

He tried to shrug away the thought. Wallowing in guilt was a useless exercise. But he was very, very worried. Going even a day without water in this heat was perilous. Any longer and they could die. He and Grace wouldn't be the first to come to grief in the unforgiving outback. Australia's history was littered with such stories and, even now, there were tragic news items every year about people who perished terribly from lack of water.

He raised his hand to shade his eyes. 'We need to keep our eyes skinned for any clues that might lead us to water,' he said.

Wearily, Grace looked around her. 'Perhaps we should follow that animal track over there.'

'Perhaps…' mused Mitch. 'But I'd be happier to wait till we found a few more tracks. We need several tracks that are converging to lead us to water.'

She nodded. 'That makes sense.'

'Glad to have your approval, Ms Robbins,' he teased, although his interest in making even the weakest of jokes was rapidly diminishing.

They slogged on, too tired and downhearted to speak…hour followed weary hour.

Hot, tired, thirsty, hungry…

All around them the countryside shimmered under a sunburnt sky.

Eventually Mitch spoke. 'There's a bit of a ridge over there.' He pointed to their right.

Grace, who had been busy plodding with her head down, hadn't noticed the subtle change in the terrain. She'd been thinking about dying—wondering if she was going to die—out here with her boss. Already she felt weak and dizzy and her mind toyed with the question of whether it was easy to die of thirst. She didn't *want* to die, but what could she do about it? Grace had always imagined she would fight off death with every ounce of her will-power, and she was dismayed to find that now, when she most needed it, her natural determination and fighting spirit had evaporated as quickly as the light dew that had lain on the ground just before dawn.

'We might be able to save our legs and let our eyes do some work if we climb up there and have a good look around.' Mitch's suggestion broke through her cloud of dismal thoughts.

'Good idea,' she muttered, and hurried forward.

Mitch threw out a restraining hand to grab her elbow. 'No need to rush. We've plenty of time. Conserve your energy.'

'Whatever you say.' She was fast approaching the point where she didn't want to think any more. Exhausted and weak, she was quite happy to do as she was told.

When they reached the top of the ridge, the glare of the sun was so strong, Grace couldn't see anything at first. Mitch stood beside her, squinting at their surroundings, offering no comment. She rubbed a grimy hand over her eyes. 'What can you see?'

When there was no response from Mitch, Grace used her hands to shade her eyes and examine the view for herself. Her heart thumped. 'Oh, my... Oh, thank goodness,' she breathed.

They were standing on the top of an escarpment—a red slash of rock dropped down to a huge platform. And in the middle of the platform was a large pool of water carved out of the rock. Fringed by scraggy pandanus palms, no water had ever looked more wonderful.

Below that, there was another rocky drop. In the wet season, a waterfall would tumble over it to the plains below.

Mitch's voice was hesitant. 'You see what I see? It's not a mirage?'

Grace watched a black and white ibis dive into the pool, sending out circling ripples. 'No, it's not a mirage. It's—it's—oh, Mitch, we're not going to die. It's water! *It's water!*'

'We've been walking on a plateau.'

'And that's the coastal plain down there. And we've found *water*!'

'Eureka!' shouted Mitch, his eyes shining. He snatched up Grace in an excited hug and his arms welded her against his heated body. And, suddenly, she was shaking with silly tears springing into her eyes. It was exhaustion, of course—and aftershock.

Last night, when they had faced immediate danger, she'd been calm and in control. Now, when they'd found life-saving water and shade—maybe even food—Mitch's little show of jubilation was making her tremble like a frightened bandicoot.

He frowned at her and, with a lean finger, traced the path of a tear down her dust-streaked cheek. 'You've been incredibly brave,' he said gently. 'Just hold on for a little longer.'

Grace had never been so grateful of manly support. She sank against Mitch and his arms held her close, his chin resting on the top of her head. Hot, tired and dusty, she relaxed against his strength. How firm and strong he felt. His hand was stroking the back of her neck, slowly, soothingly.

She might have stayed there, relishing the sense of comfort and strength he gave, if her body hadn't betrayed her. Mitch's gentle touch kick-started every womanly part of her.

Never before had she been so acutely conscious of just how perfectly a man's hard muscles complemented a woman's yielding softness. The effect of the pressure of his lower body, tight against hers, caused her to wonder what she'd been doing all her life. Why hadn't any other man ever made her feel this sudden sunburst of wild longing?

She was quite definitely affected by the heat, she decided.

The heat—and the shock of her boss, Mitch Wentworth, handing out tenderness. They were a heady combination. No wonder she was a shivering mess.

Grace stiffened in his embrace and her chin lifted. 'Er…excuse me, Mr Wentworth,' she said primly. 'But you seem to have your arms around me.'

'Pardon?' Mitch looked puzzled. But he let her go quickly, both arms flinging wide. Grace felt his withdrawal more acutely than she would have liked.

'We have a deal,' she said unsteadily. 'No close encounters of the physical kind, except on request. Remember?'

His dark gaze locked with hers and Grace's throat constricted. In Mitch's eyes, shock and disbelief warred with something that must surely be contempt.

She looked away.

'Caught out on a technicality,' he drawled, before letting out a heavy sigh. Then he shook his head and released a half-hearted laugh. 'Okay. Let's take it slowly climbing down these rocks. We don't want to have an accident at this stage.' He shot her a wary glance. 'You might need to allow me to take your hand for the really steep bits.'

Luckily, their journey down the cliff was not too difficult. Although the orange sandstone was worn smooth, there were still footholds, carved over the centuries by wind, sand and water and, at times, they could hang onto the strong roots of fig trees which, miraculously, clung to the rock wall.

And Grace allowed Mitch to help her over the really difficult sections. With eyes downcast, she muttered her thanks.

When, at last, they reached the safety of the rocky platform, Grace stepped forward eagerly. The pool was cool, clear and sparkling. At one end it came hard up against the sandstone bluff and in the middle it spread out and formed a little curving shallow bay where lily pads floated serenely. In an overhanging branch, black cockatoos with their bright red flashes chattered while they kept guard.

Eden could not have looked more pristine or untouched. More inviting.

She dragged off her boots and rushed into the water fully clothed. The cockatoos and a pair of ibises took off with a wild flapping of wings.

And after tossing the backpack aside, Mitch followed her. Splashing and frolicking, they drank the clear, life-giving water with cupped hands like happy children on holidays.

'What's the verdict?' Mitch called, after his dark head, wet and sleek, surfaced some distance away.

'It's amazing.' She laughed back at him. 'If only we had food, I could settle in here.'

With slow, leisurely strokes, he swam closer. 'Don't talk about food,' he moaned. 'You'll set me fantasising about a sizzling, juicy barbecued steak.'

'With jacket potatoes,' added Grace, licking her lips.

'Pan-fried mushrooms.'

'A garden salad and a bread roll, fresh from the oven.'

'Stop it, woman!' groaned Mitch. 'A few minutes ago I was happy with water, but now I'm starving. Heck, I'm so ravenous I could eat a horse and chase the rider.'

'And for dessert there'd be hot apple crumble and—'

Grace didn't get to finish the sentence. Using his big hands as paddles to scoop up the water, Mitch started to swamp her mercilessly with a man-made tidal wave. 'Help!' she cried, gasping and laughing simultaneously. 'Stop splashing!'

'Do you promise to stop talking about food?'

'Yes.'

His hands stilled and Mitch stood knee-deep in the water facing her, laughing, panting, every line of his strongly muscled body outlined by the wet clinging shirt and jeans. Grace tried to drag her eyes away, but he was so darned beautiful. She stood there, drinking in each trim and taut detail.

And he was staring at her, too.

With a start, she realised that her body was even more distinctly revealed. Her stretch-knit top was every bit as wet and clinging as his clothes. She might as well be naked.

She folded her arms across her chest.

Slowly, Mitch waded towards her. When he was level, he paused. 'I'll stop looking at you, if you'll stop checking me out,' he said softly, a little breathlessly. 'Otherwise we'll end up back in the danger zone. Your no-go territory.'

Too late, Grace flicked her gaze away and, while her cheeks blazed, she made a pretence of studying the bright blue backdrop of sky.

'I made you a promise, Grace, but you've got to help. You can't look at a man like you want to peel his clothes off.' A puzzled smile hovered, lightening his gaze, twitching at his lips. 'Do you know what you want, Grace Robbins?'

'I certainly know what I *don't* want!' she bit back. She didn't want this growing need to touch him. And she certainly didn't want this strong desire to experience his touch, the comfort of his arms holding her, the tender thrill of his kiss.

His smile faded. 'Bully for you.'

'Actually,' she continued, with a defiant little lift of her chin, 'I haven't finished talking about food.'

'You don't say?'

'There's got to be food here, Mitch. You know—bush tucker. There's plenty of bird-life around. Perhaps there's fish?'

He nodded, surveying the pool through squinted eyes. 'And the holidays I spent in the bush when I was young might just come in useful after all.'

They lunched on the last shared muesli bar. Mitch stripped off his shirt and hung it over a nearby branch to dry. Grace sat on a rock with her back to that broad, bronzed body and she was grateful that the sun quickly dried her clothes. Afterwards, she decided to curl up in the shade of a clump of pandanus and rest. Sleep was what she needed and she didn't want to think about Mitch, or the possibility of finding the development road. She couldn't even bring herself to worry about food. She was completely exhausted.

Mitch watched her, curled in the shade, long lashes resting against the soft, slightly sunburnt curve of her cheek and her hair streaming out on the rock behind her. Her lissom loveliness was gut-wrenching.

But he knew this was no Sleeping Beauty lying around waiting for her prince to come. Grace Robbins would decide exactly when she wanted a man. And then she would have a detailed list of criteria the poor fellow would need to meet. No doubt she would put him through a series of stringent, secret tests.

She was just like those fairy-tale princesses, he decided, wryly acknowledging that only a movie maker with his head in the clouds would come up with such a comparison. She kept herself locked up tight in a tower. A tower made up of her own very clear expectations.

He remembered the sexy goddess in black lace, framed by Henry Aspinall's doorway, and frowned. Clearly Grace wrote her own rules—and broke them when it pleased her.

And the fact that he, Mitch Wentworth, wouldn't get past the first rung of any ladder leading to her tower was damned annoying.

CHAPTER SEVEN

GRACE WAS HUNGRY.

It was late in the day when she woke to gnawing hunger pangs. The rock where she slept was still warm from the sun, but the trees' shadows had lengthened—reaching across one end of the rock pool, making the water look dark and cool.

She struggled to remember how much they had left to eat. One apple! Heavens above, she didn't think she could last another night without more food than that. Where was Mitch? came her next thought.

A pair of rock wallabies moved soundlessly in a lazy, leisurely lope across the terrace. After they disappeared, heading down to the grassy plains below, she rose to her feet and scanned the area. Quite an assortment of birds seemed to be taking their evening drink at the rock pool. Dozens of small finches with bright rosy beaks and brilliant red blazes across their rumps were perched along the sandstone rim. They took dainty sips of water and tilted their heads back to swallow.

Not wanting to disturb them, Grace sat very still and continued to survey the area. Her forehead wrinkled in surprise. Mitch had been busy. A huge heap of firewood was piled on a sandy 'beach' at the edge of the little bay.

Eventually the birds left and she stood and wandered around the rocky platform that skirted the pool's perimeter. Her hair flapped about her face as a late afternoon breeze flicked it playfully. Next to the wood pile rested an old, blackened billycan. Where on earth had Mitch found that?

She looked around her, uneasy that she couldn't see him, and walked to the edge of the water, wondering if he was fishing or perhaps diving. Boy, she was hungry! In the water below her lay an unusual bundle of twigs held down by a rock. Frowning and curious, she stepped into the water, rolled the stone away with her toe and pulled the clump of twigs out. A sharp jab of pain shot through one finger. Screaming, she dropped the sticks.

'Grace, what is it?' From somewhere behind her, Mitch came running. He was slightly breathless when he reached her and grabbed her shoulders. 'Are you all right?'

'Something *bit* me.' She sucked at her throbbing finger, absurdly pleased by the concern evident in his expression.

'What was it?'

'I don't know. It was in that pile of sticks.'

'Oh.' Mitch's glance fell to the twigs she had dropped. A flicker of exasperation darkened his features. He reached down and, grasping the bundle carefully at one end, lifted it out of the water and examined it. 'Good one. I'd say you've just lost our dinner.'

'Our dinner? Oh, no! I couldn't have!'

''Fraid so. I'd say we had a crayfish in there. And this *pile of sticks* you just tipped upside down and destroyed was my carefully engineered, highly scientific crayfish trap.'

'You designed that bundle of sticks?'

'Of course I designed it. It's bushcraft perfected. And this trap has to be picked up very carefully or our precious meal gets clear away.' He muttered a soft curse. 'A fat, juicy freshwater crayfish would have been rather tasty roasted over the coals.'

'Ohh and I'm so hungry,' she moaned. 'How was I to know? It didn't look much like a trap.' Grace shrugged guiltily and pulled a grimacing face. 'But I'm sorry. Trust me to lose our dinner!'

Contrite, she watched Mitch shake his head as he spoke. 'What do they say about women and their relentless curiosity?'

A hot retort formed on her lips, but Grace managed to remain silent. At this particular point in time, hunger was more important than worn-out sexist battles.

Mitch's lips were also tightly clamped as he busily rearranged his trap. Grace watched as he retied one end of the sticks with a length of grass.

'What's that nut thing you're putting inside?'

'A crushed pandanus nut. That's the bait.'

'Oh, I see. So the crayfish crawls down this kind of funnel?'

'Yeah.'

'Do you think he's dumb enough to try it a second time?'

He lowered his trap into the water again and flashed her a brief grin as he repositioned the stone to weigh it down. 'I don't have much info on the IQ of the freshwater crayfish. I guess we'll just have to hope it's not too high.'

'I know that the memory span of a goldfish is three seconds.'

Mitch folded his arms across his chest and laughed. 'And I guess you read that somewhere.'

Grinning foolishly, Grace rubbed at her arms as the early evening breeze gusted over them. She knew they could expect the temperature to drop quite quickly as soon as the sun went down. 'You've collected plenty of firewood.'

'Yeah.' He nodded. 'We'll be more comfortable tonight. I remembered how the Aborigines do it. They build three fires and leave plenty of space to sleep in the middle.'

'To avoid scorching on one side and freezing on the other?'

His grin flowed over her. 'We'll be warm as toast.'

She gulped and dismissed thoughts of lying near Mitch on the soft sandy beach, clean from a swim in the rock pool and warmed by three fires. 'We'll be warm but hungry, thanks to me.'

He didn't answer that. 'I'll start building a fire here. Do you want to make one over there?'

Hoping to redeem herself after losing their meal, Grace built her fire very carefully, starting with small twigs and sticks and gradually adding bigger pieces of timber until she had a neat, solid-looking pyramid.

At last she looked up from her work. Mitch had built the other two fires, his methods more slapdash. Grace studied the stark differences between their efforts—his timber piles were thrown together with a kind of casual, rustic elegance and her trim, geometrically accurate affair looked ridiculously neat. She sighed.

When would she ever learn not to be so fussy?

Mitch eyed her handiwork with ill-concealed amusement and she was grateful he didn't take the opportunity to make fun of her. 'We'll use your fire as the cooking fire, and keep the others for warmth later on,' was all he said.

'How long will it take for the crayfish to try the bait again?'

He cocked his head to one side as if calculating his answer carefully. 'Better give him another hour. But we can always eat water lily tubers. They're supposed to be quite okay. Would you like to dig some up and boil them in this billy I found?'

'Yeah, sure thing,' she replied offhandedly, not prepared to admit that she didn't know how. *She didn't even know water lilies had tubers!*

Mitch tossed her the billycan and then strode off to the far side of the rock pool whistling an annoying, jaunty little tune.

Luckily, after she rolled her shorts up high and re-entered the water, Grace discovered that the tubers were exactly where one might expect them to be—at the base of the water lily plant. Pulling them up out of the mud was more difficult. They were very deeply embedded in the heavy silt in the bottom of the pool, but they came away eventually when she tugged with all her strength. Except that, as they finally left the clinging, squelchy silt, the force sent her tumbling backwards into the water.

'Darn it!'

Mitch returned at that moment to find her dripping wet, yet again, and floundering around in the shallows, trying to pick up the precious tubers she'd dropped as she'd collapsed. 'I'm okay!' she yelled at him before he could comment.

It was almost dark, and she couldn't see what he was carrying, but his arms were full. He seemed to shrug his acknowledgement and continued on towards the fire. With her bare toes, Grace located the smooth bulbs she'd dropped. She would never have forgiven herself if she'd lost their second course as well as the first.

By the time she'd washed the muddy tubers and filled the billycan with fresh water, Mitch had the fire started and was squatting in front of it. She shivered as she placed her contribution to the meal on the rock beside him.

Over his shoulder, his gaze assessed her. 'You're cold. You'd better get out of those wet things.'

Grace stiffened and her tongue seemed glued to the roof of her mouth. 'I—I'll be all right,' she muttered at last. Did he think she'd had a sudden personality transplant? There was no way she could strip off and parade around naked in front of him. 'The fire will soon dry me.'

'Not fast enough in this chilly night air,' he growled impatiently. Standing quickly, he tugged his shirt out of the waist of his jeans. The movement exposed a shadowing of hair that tapered down from his chest and turned Grace's insides to jelly. 'Here, wear this for a while. And we'll dry your clothes at one of the other fires.'

Despite her best intentions, Grace couldn't help staring as his well-developed shoulders, tinged ruddy by the firelight, emerged from the shirt. Soon the broad chest was fully exposed. And for Grace the cooling night air wasn't a problem at all. A heatwave was swamping her.

Flustered, she found the words to issue a protest. 'There's no need for you to give up your shirt. I have my leather jacket.'

Mitch tossed her the shirt. 'You can wear your jacket if you like, but it won't cover much.' He shrugged and grinned. 'Not that I would raise any objections.'

Grace pulled a face. He was dead right about the jacket. It was waist-length—hopelessly short.

'Now get over there behind the trees and get changed before I take those wet clothes off for you,' Mitch ordered.

She scurried obediently off into the dark grove of trees, quite certain that it was exasperation and not amusement that caused the fiery gleam in Mitch's eyes.

As she peeled off her wet shorts, she began to wish that she weren't so uptight about Mitch Wentworth. Here she was, stranded with him in the outback in the kind of clichéd fantasy situation most girls dreamed about. She should be deliriously excited. She was alone with a man whose looks alone could have won him the lead in a string of top-billing movies.

She wriggled out of her wet shirt. But he was her boss, for heaven's sake! An annoying, arrogant, pig-headed boss, she reminded herself. A devastatingly handsome, *bachelor* boss, another part of her brain argued.

Grace could imagine her workmate Maria's scornful expression when she heard that she had been alone in the bush with Mitch and had behaved like a terrified schoolgirl. Bare-breasted and shivering, she fished around in her backpack for the spare pair of knickers.

Something in the backpack moved.

Something round and smooth and long.

And *slithery*.

She dropped the bag. Screamed and screamed again, as she catapulted out of the trees. *'Snake! Help, Mitch! It's a snake!'*

He was beside her in a moment, holding a flaming branch above him like a torch.

'Did it bite you?'

She shook her head.

'Where is it?' he asked quickly.

Shuddering, Grace pointed to the grove of pandanus. 'In there. In my p-pack.'

Warily, with the burning torch in front, Mitch edged forward. 'I can see it. It's trying to get away as fast as it can. It's as frightened as you are, Grace, and it's out of your pack now and climbing that tree.' He stepped closer.

'Leave it alone! Keep away from it!' she shrieked.

'It's okay. It's a python!' He turned and grinned at her. 'It isn't deadly. Quite harmless.'

She stood behind him, her hands still shaking, desperately trying to hide her topless state. How was it that fate had delivered her, once again, into a situation that found her parading nearly naked in front of Mitch Wentworth?

'If we leave the snake alone and stay over by the fire, it will leave us alone.'

'You're—you're sure?'

'Absolutely. The dangerous ones don't climb trees.' He sent her another reassuring smile and his gaze dropped to her chest, but just as quickly he flicked his eyes back to his torch.

'M-my clothes,' she stammered as she tried, ineffectively, to simultaneously point at the abandoned huddle of garments and cover herself with her hands. 'They're—they're in there.'

'Okay. Keep your hair on. I'll get them for you.' Mitch rescued the backpack and his shirt, then went back for her wet clothes.

There was no way she would go back into the grove to change. She turned her back to Mitch. It didn't help that as she dragged his shirt over her head it smelled faintly of smoke and heated male. Its sleeves hung out over her hands and the tails finished halfway down her thighs. At least it covered her.

Grace felt calmer as she rolled the sleeves back, while Mitch discreetly carried her wet clothes over to the second fire he had lit, and spread them out on the rock to dry. She knew enough about snakes to know that Mitch was right. They would be perfectly safe if they stayed by the fire.

Mitch returned to crouch over his cooking. All around them, beyond their glowing fires, Grace could sense the silent, night-black bush reaching out to the distant, starry horizons.

They might have been the only two people on the planet.

'Why is it that women always look so much better in men's shirts than guys do?' he asked as she self-consciously made her way back to him. He poked casually at the coals with a long piece of wire and his gaze rested on her with unexpected appreciation as she neared him.

Tamping down the heady scamper of pleasure his words brought, she tried to ignore his gaze. 'I guess at least half the population, the female half, might not agree with you.' She wrinkled her nose and sniffed the night air hungrily as her growling stomach told her that something smelled *good*. 'What are you cooking?'

'Crayfish.'

'Wow! So the fellow I lost crawled back into your trap?'

He stood up. 'Actually, no.'

'But…how did you catch him?'

'Catch *them*,' he corrected.

'Excuse me?'

'The five other traps I set all worked famously. We're going to have a feast.'

Her jaw dropped open and she levelled a swift punch at Mitch's upper arm. 'You mean to say you set *five other traps*? And you didn't tell me? You beast! You let me think I'd lost our one and only chance for a feed? You *pig*!' She let fly with another right hook. Mitch didn't flinch. Grace did. His arm was as solid as a block of concrete and her hand hurt.

'You can't expect to know everything, Grace,' he drawled.

She sniffed haughtily and dropped to her haunches, making a pretence of examining the fire and her water lily tubers as they simmered in the billycan. She needed to concentrate on the food and forget about the obnoxious man and his beautiful, bare-chested body standing right behind her.

But the next moment he was crouching right beside her. Startled to find he'd moved so close, Grace nearly pitched forward into the fire.

'These shouldn't take very long.' Apparently unaware of her tension, Mitch rolled a crayfish over with the piece of blackened wire that he'd found.

'How will we break them open?' Her stomach was doing somersaults and she told herself it was the tempting aroma of roasting crayfish that caused the sensation.

'One thing I do have in my jeans is my trusty pocket knife,' Mitch informed her with a wide grin. He handed the knife to her. 'Here, give those lily bulbs a poke and see if they're cooked. I thinks our crays are ready.'

Everything was ready.

'Gourmet food in the bush.' Mitch grinned as he handed Grace her meal of succulent white crayfish and sliced water lily tubers on a strip of pandanus leaf.

If the smell was tantalising, the taste was pure heaven. 'Mmm… yummo,' she mumbled between mouthfuls.

They munched in the happy silence of people who had been truly hungry. But after he'd polished off two of the crayfish and half the tubers Mitch began to chat companionably. He brought up a range of topics, and Grace was surprised to discover that they both adored rainy days and loved reading autobiographies. And they shared a penchant for visiting museums, while they both hated pizza with too much cheese.

Grace revealed that she had an ambition to one day make a romance movie set in Thailand—an idea that intrigued Mitch. And he outlined for her his dream to eventually create a film about his great-grandmother, who had lived a life of incredible hardship, danger and courage as an early Australian outback pioneer.

And slowly, as Grace's hunger pangs diminished, the world began to seem a whole lot brighter.

'We've been very lucky.' Mitch's smile was wide, as if his own spirits were also lifting. He wiped sticky fingers on a piece of pandanus. 'We have food, shelter, water and warmth.'

'We just need to be rescued now.'

He looked at her sharply. 'You're in a hurry to be rescued?'

'Of course. Aren't you?' she asked, while her heart gave a strange little lurch.

'I guess so,' he said ambiguously as he broke open the last crayfish. 'But I don't know. I could do with a few days of enforced isolation in a remote little Eden like this. Life's pretty hectic out there in the real world. I rather fancy the idea of no deadlines. No phone calls...' He grinned again. 'We've got everything we want here—and, unlike in the movies, no one is shooting at us.'

Grace couldn't take her eyes from Mitch. He looked so happy, so relaxed and at peace with his simple surroundings—and amazingly sexy with his dark, rumpled hair and his eyes reflecting the fire's glow. And, if she were really honest, she had to admit that with each moment she spent alone with him he seemed to grow less and less like the bossy jerk she'd once thought him to be.

In fact, apart from his looks, he seemed to have very little in common with her old boyfriend, Roger. There had always been selfish elements to Roger's personality. But Mitch had been rather thoughtful...respecting her needs...keeping her spirits high... protecting her...

He was still smiling at her now and she sensed a happy glow beginning to make her feel fuzzy from the toes up.

A weird kind of excitement bubbled through her, as if something wonderful might be about to happen. It was just like the first time she'd sat in the movies, her nostrils filled with the hot, salty smell of popcorn while she'd perched on the edge of her seat and watched the heavy velvet curtains draw back.

Happiness swirled and floated all the way up through her body, till she was filled to the brim with a trembling sense of expectation.

The realisation hit her with the force of a meteor slamming into Earth. She *wanted Mitch to kiss her*! Needed him to kiss her.

Grace stopped eating. Perhaps she'd stopped breathing; she couldn't tell. All she knew was that this warm welling of emotion, this sudden longing for Mitch Wentworth, seemed to be the only right and certain thing in the universe.

She couldn't drag her mind away from how nice he'd been to her. She couldn't tear her eyes away from the way the fire highlighted his masculine beauty, creating sexy shadows, angles and planes.

And he was looking at her as if he sensed the reason for her sudden stillness. Could he hear the frenetic pounding of her heart? Her ragged breathing? What could she do about this dilemma? For Pete's sake, she had issued instructions that this man was not to touch her! And now she couldn't think of anything she wanted more than for him to take her into his arms.

She wanted to be held against that strong chest. She wanted to rest her cheek against that smooth shoulder while her nose and mouth nuzzled that brown neck. Most of all, she wanted to have his lips seek out hers.

This was so ridiculous! If she wanted him to kiss her, she would have to ask him. *Out loud!*

Her cheeks flamed as she pushed the empty crayfish shells aside and inched her bottom across the sand just a tiny notch closer to Mitch. The night air zinged with her tension and he didn't move a muscle; he didn't speak.

But he was looking straight at her.

The world around them grew very still and absolutely quiet—as if every stick and star, each rock and tree had become tense and taut in sympathy with Grace's longing.

Even the fire seemed to have stopped crackling.

Silence…silence…silence.

The night was so very hushed that Grace could not raise her voice above a whisper. 'I was wondering…' she mumbled.

Mitch leaned his glossy dark head a little closer to catch her words.

Breathless, she stared at the bronze curve of his shoulder and took a deep, heart-thumping breath. 'I was wondering if you might consider—' Oh, why was she so nervous? She was shaking. She couldn't do this.

'What was that, Grace? Consider?'

'Yes,' she squeaked.

'Consider what exactly?'

'Would you consider…?' Grace knew that if she looked into Mitch's eyes she would find them teasing her. So she stared instead at his strong and comforting chest. 'Consider breaking our contract. Do you *think*? Might you give some *thought*…?'

Closing her eyes, she cursed her exasperating shyness. This was absolutely the wrong way to go about seduction. She was way too tense. Any other girl would have flirted and joked with Mitch and together they would have 'fallen into' a kiss naturally and spontaneously, the way it happened in the movies.

The way it happened for every other couple in the whole world.

When she opened her eyes, Mitch was still waiting quietly and he was staring at her. He seemed to be taking deep, difficult breaths.

She realised she'd waited far too long to even try to finish her question. And now, when he looked at her like that—as if he was as tense as she was—there was no way she could find the words she needed. 'I'll rinse out the billy,' she blurted instead, and, grabbing the can, dashed to the edge of the rock pool.

She crouched on the sandy edge and noisily sloshed water into the billycan, breaking the watery reflection of the starry sky into tiny spots of dancing light while she willed herself to calm down.

For crying out loud, how could a woman of twenty-six have so much difficulty asking a man for a simple kiss? Could it have something to do with the fact that there was nothing simple about her boss's kisses? She felt a cringe of embarrassment as she remembered how she'd made such an almighty fuss last time he'd kissed her. Or perhaps it was that a kiss out here, between a man and a woman alone in the wilderness, would almost certainly lead to much, much more?

That thought had her jumping to her feet and shaking out the excess water from the billy. Nervously, she watched the ripples spread and flatten and she wondered what Mitch was thinking of her strange behaviour.

Her answer came with the slight crunch of footsteps in the sand behind her. Hairs lifted on the back of her neck. And her breath caught as his hands came to rest lightly on her shoulders.

Slowly his thumbs massaged her. 'Are you running away from me?'

She felt her shoulders being drawn back to rest against his warm, bare chest and shivers chased each other down her spine. Mitch's voice murmured in her ear. 'Were you wanting to ask me something, Grace?'

She nodded and he leaned even closer so that his stubble grazed her cheek. 'You were asking me to give some thought...'

Her body burned out of control. Shaking, she turned in his arms and his hands adjusted to the shift, still holding her against him. This man was absolutely irresistible and there was no longer anything she could do about it.

Her next words came of their own accord. 'I—I want you to kiss me.' Overcome by her temerity, her eyes flew shut.

And when he didn't answer she felt terrible. *Mitch didn't want to kiss her.*

Grateful for the darkness, Grace could feel blushes of embarrassment burning her cheeks. Her mind cringed. Mitch had kissed the world's sexiest women. Why would he want to kiss her? How could she ever have...?

Her frantic thoughts were invaded by the touch of a hand on her cheek.

She could feel Mitch's knuckles tracing twin lines from her ears to her lips. Her eyes shot open and he opened his hands to capture both sides of her face. And when she looked up Grace found in his gaze the same wild hunger she was feeling.

'You have the very best ideas, Grace Robbins,' he murmured.

'I don't think I've ever heard a suggestion that has interested me more.' His belt buckle nudged her stomach provocatively. 'I've been giving plenty of thought to kissing you.'

Unable to answer, she simply nodded.

And she trembled as his lips lowered towards hers. His warm, persuasive mouth roamed temptingly over Grace's parted lips and she released a tell-tale, eager little gasp. His hands shifted to her buttocks, lifting her tight against his hardness, while his tongue delved deep in her mouth, questing and promising, sending a slow-burning, languorous flame all the way through her.

She moaned softly, growing giddier, hotter, more carefree... more powerful than she'd ever felt before.

Queen of the Night.

Turning to liquid.

Floating on a cloud of heat.

It was a kiss she never wanted to end.

So when it did stop, when Mitch lifted his head, she felt robbed of something vital—like her lungs. He looked down at her from beneath heavy, lowered lids. 'I knew you were just as good at kissing as you are at everything else, Grace.'

Then why did you stop? she wanted to cry. She swallowed back a painful lump of disappointment. 'Will—will I need to offer an invitation for every kiss?'

'Oh, so you'd like more?'

She might die if there were no more!

She lifted her fingers to his lips and his eyes burned into hers as he kissed each finger slowly, one by one. Dreamily, she moved her hand higher and gasped as he licked the trembling palm. The feel of his tongue against her skin sent another molten wave of longing tumbling low inside her.

'No doubt about it, Mitch, I want more,' she whispered shakily.

'Thank heavens for that,' he growled. And, pulling her savagely against him, he crushed her mouth with a kiss that was as urgent as it was seeking, his lips and tongue totally wild as if he couldn't get enough of her.

CHAPTER EIGHT

MITCH KNEW THEY should have piled green leaves on their three fires to make three white plumes of smoke. That was the best way to send a distress signal in the remote outback. Any plane flying overhead would spot it and know at once that it was an SOS call.

But when the sun rolled over the horizon the next morning he had no thoughts of drawing attention to their plight. He didn't particularly want to be rescued. He lay watching the pink and grey streaks of another new day stretch across the heavens, and enjoyed the warmth of Grace's cheek as it rested against his shoulder.

With his finger, he traced the outline of her ear as she slept. This woman sure was a surprise package. Who would have known that being in the wilderness would strip every uptight, prim mouthed and pedantic little habit from her psyche, leaving her warm and lovely and totally unrestrained?

The thought of taking her back to the office and risking the chance that she would slip back behind the old, crusty camouflage was too depressing to consider.

Grace stirred against him, and her green eyes opened slowly. 'Good morning.' She smiled and, turning in his arms, she pressed her mouth to a hollow at the base of his throat.

Mitch groaned. To hell with planning a rescue!

He bent to taste Grace's sleepy, pouting lips and a low, growling sound rumbled in his throat. To hell with business. What could a man do when such a lovely woman stretched out her soft, feminine curves so temptingly beside him? For Pete's sake, who cared about budgets, or the clamour of casting agencies? He wanted to forget the pressure of projected deadlines. Surely losing himself in this woman was all that mattered.

'I think we should spend at least another day here before we push on,' he told Grace much later, after their morning dip in the pool. 'We need to recover from—our ordeal.'

She smiled a shy, knowing little smile, but she didn't object. And Mitch was happier than he had been for a long, long time.

They made the most of their day—capering like silly children in the sun-warmed water, laughing together as they collected more crayfish and water lily bulbs, or discussed their favourite movies and argued about those they hated.

And, more than once, they made love. Circled by clusters of ferns, the patch of green couch grass growing in the deep shade of the pandanus clump was, in Mitch's opinion, as romantic as any plush hotel suite.

And, at the end of the day, there was another night with Grace under the big outback skies and the silent vigil of a million stars.

But as the next morning dawned, Mitch had to face hard facts. They couldn't stay out here for ever. It was time to leave their sanctuary, even though the urge to hide from civilisation for even just a little longer was overwhelming.

His breath expelled on a long, heavy sigh. The old adage 'Time is money' was all too true. And, with most of his own personal fortune invested in the *New Tomorrow* project, money was a vital commodity. Rubbing his hand across the unfamiliar stubble of his four-day-old beard, Mitch knew that he couldn't afford to take too many business risks.

'We really should set off again today.'

Grace turned away quickly to hide her disappointment. She knew Mitch was right, but wondered if he hated the idea of leaving as much as she did.

'By my calculations,' Mitch continued, 'the road is only about another twenty to twenty-five kilometres away.'

'So we should have our breakfast, fill up our bottle as well as the billycan with fresh water, and head off towards the road,' she said, forcing any nuance of disappointment out of her voice.

'Once we reach the road, we're sure to be picked up.'

All morning, as they walked, clouds piled on the horizon in big, fluffy grey heaps.

'With a bit of luck, we'll get a storm this afternoon,' Mitch commented as, towards midday, they trudged across the coastal plains country.

'It would certainly be nice to get some relief from all this humidity,' Grace agreed.

He ran his sleeve across his brow, and then pointed some distance ahead. 'We should take a break when we get to that bunch of eucalyptus trees over there. It makes sense to spend the hottest part of the day resting in the shade.'

'I know all about you and what your idea of a rest in the shade entails, Mitch Wentworth.' She sent him a sultry, playful little smile.

He grinned back at her. 'I'm only thinking of what's best for you. It's common sense in the Tropics to take a siesta.'

A siesta with Mitch in another shady grove! Grace smiled again and prickles of pleasure broke out everywhere. How on earth had it happened that she was constantly thinking about making love when she was virtually lost in the middle of nowhere? Mitch had turned her into a wanton woman.

As her mind tussled with the challenge of finding a smart rejoinder, a distant rattle and throbbing caught her attention. 'What's that?' She cocked her ear towards the noise. 'I'm sure I can hear something. Like a motor.'

Spinning around, Mitch stood in silence, obviously straining his ears to listen. 'You're right. It's coming from behind us.'

'But there's no road there!' Grace frowned and peered back across the dusty plain they'd just crossed. What on earth could be coming from that direction? A station owner in a four-wheel drive?

In the distance, a dark blob was beginning to take shape. 'Oh, my goodness,' she breathed. The emerging form was nothing like what she expected. Instead of a battered but friendly cattleman's truck, a squat, sinister-looking, camouflaged vehicle rumbled towards them. 'Who on earth could *they* be?' she croaked.

She edged closer to Mitch. 'They've got guns. Have—have we been invaded or something?'

Mitch frowned, pulled a doubtful face and shook his head. 'They have two machine guns mounted on the cabin,' he commented as he squinted at them, 'but they don't seem to be ready for action.' He flashed her a tight smile, before screwing up his eyes to watch the approaching vehicle.

'But there's another gun!' she insisted, her voice sharp with fear. 'See the fellow riding on the bonnet—' She broke off on a note of sheer panic.

Mitch threw a comforting arm around her shaking shoulders. 'You've been watching too many movies, Grace.'

'Movies, Mr Director, can be very educational.'

Mitch granted her half a smile and he gave her shoulder a reassuring squeeze. 'I'll admit that fellow does have some kind of automatic weapon, but look, he's just got it slung over his shoulder. I don't think he intends to start shooting at us.'

But Grace wouldn't be mollified. How could Mitch stay so calm? For heaven's sake, strange soldiers wouldn't be travelling in this remote, northern part of the country unless something had gone seriously wrong.

'Mitch,' she whispered. 'They look so threatening. Could Australia have been invaded while we've been lost? We should have stayed at the rock pool.'

The roar of the vehicle grew louder as it neared them. Grace realised she was clutching Mitch's arm with the desperation of a victim of the *Titanic*. She was sure she was about to die. She would be shot or, at the very least, dragged away and raped before being murdered.

'I'm sure they're not aggressive,' Mitch muttered.

'Then why aren't you waving or acting friendly?'

'For heaven's sake, woman. Just let me deal with this.'

'Sure,' she fumed, with an impatient roll of her eyes skywards. Mitch was back in fearless leader mode. But perhaps that was just as well, she conceded as she cowered behind him and held her breath while the vehicle slowed to a halt.

Silently, the men scrambled out of the cabin and, with the menacing agility of a panther, the figure on the bonnet leaped to the ground.

Mitch was frowning.

Grace's heart thudded a deafening tattoo. Every one of these creatures was armed and their faces were smudged with green and black paint.

Out of the corner of her eye, she saw Mitch's puzzled expression melt slowly. And then she realised these men were all grinning broadly. An alert-looking fellow stepped forward and extended his hand to Mitch. 'Dr Livingstone, I presume?' he drawled with a distinctly Australian accent.

Mitch actually laughed as he shook the young man's hand heartily. 'G'day. Good to see you. Surely the Australian Army hasn't sent you looking for us?'

'Lieutenant Ripley,' the other fellow introduced himself, returning Mitch's handshake. 'We're a reconnaissance squad based in Townsville and we're up here on remote area exercises.' He nodded his head towards the fellow who'd been riding the bonnet. 'This is Freddie Day. He's our company's top tracker. We found a burnt-out vehicle early this morning—'

'That was ours,' Mitch interrupted.

'We know,' grinned Ripley. 'I decided it presented us with a pretty good challenge to test our squad's tracking abilities under real conditions. So here we are. Freddie's been following your tracks since then.'

'I'll be blowed; that's pretty quick work.' Mitch grinned back at them.

Grace sidled forward to take a closer look at their rescuers. Some were wearing floppy bush hats and two had heads covered by green bandannas that made them look like buccaneers, but now that she knew who they were she realised that none of them looked sinister.

Mitch completed the introductions. 'I'm Mitch Wentworth and this is Grace Robbins, my—' He flashed her a swift, secretive, almost possessive look that made her toes curl. 'Grace is my assistant. We left Townsville at the weekend and were checking out locations for Tropicana Films when we ran into trouble with the vehicle.'

'You did the right thing heading towards the coast,' Ripley said. 'That rock pool you found is the only water in about a fifty-kilometre radius of here.'

Mitch thumped Grace's shoulder and winked at her. 'That was Grace's bright idea. I wanted to stay with the vehicle.'

'Well done, ma'am. You saved your lives,' commented the man called Freddie Day. 'This was one of the few situations where staying with the vehicle would have been the wrong decision.' His face creased into a lazy, knowing smile and his eyes focused on Mitch. 'You had a cosy little campsite back at the rock pool.'

Grace had the awful feeling that this expert tracker, who had followed their trail so easily through such rugged terrain, would have taken one look at the imprint of their bodies where she and Mitch had slept and known exactly how *cosy* they had been.

Was she imagining it, or were all the soldiers exchanging covert glances and doing their best to hide knowing smirks?

Lieutenant Ripley held out a satellite phone to Mitch. 'Would you like to advise anyone of your whereabouts?'

'Yes, sure. Thanks, mate.' Mitch took the phone and strode some distance away to make his call. Grace watched him, noting his intense concentration as he spoke, the way he clutched the phone with one hand while gesticulating and explaining with the other, and she sensed him metamorphosing before her.

Turning back into her boss.

As one phone call was completed, he made another. And another. The soldiers, obviously uneasy about making polite conversation with her, chatted amongst themselves until Mitch was finished.

'We can take you both back to our base camp and then chopper you back to Townsville, if you like,' Ripley offered as Mitch returned.

'Wonderful.' Mitch held his hand out to Grace to help her up into the awkwardly high vehicle and she hesitated, staring at his sunburnt, outstretched hand.

They were going back.

Just like that. One minute they were about to make love in the outback in the shade of a clump of gum trees and the next they were heading back to Townsville.

To the office.

To their other world of phone calls and faxes, computer print-outs and inter-office memos, meetings and briefings…

Business! Other people. Other women.

She looked up at Mitch as she gave him her hand and his dark eyes probed her with a confusing intensity. In a worried daze, she climbed into the troop carrier and took the seat provided, her mind refusing to let go of an overwhelming sense of loss. She was being rescued, for heaven's sake. Why on earth did she feel so morbid?

She knew Mitch would tell her she was being silly, but she was quite, quite certain that it wasn't just the outback she was leaving. She was leaving behind the wonderful, astonishing thing that had happened to her and Mitch while they were lost.

Mitch swung into the seat beside her, and Lieutenant Ripley placed himself opposite. Two more men climbed in while the other soldiers seemed content to hang onto the outside. And, even before the vehicle roared forward once more, Mitch and Ripley began chatting like old friends.

While the men discussed the unit's recent involvement with the United Nations in Africa, Cambodia and Timor, Grace watched silently. Mitch seemed very at home. He was surprisingly knowledgeable about international affairs. She watched his relaxed smile and the genuine interest with which he listened to the other men. It was as if he'd known these strangers for years. It must be a blokey thing, she decided with a sigh.

He almost completely ignored her. Already it was hard to believe she had spent the past two days doing little else but make love with him. Why, just this morning, she had lain by the rock pool in his arms and he had kissed and caressed her and had murmured her name over and over as if he had been trying to fuse her identity with his. Several times she'd been on the brink of telling him how much his lovemaking meant to her.

How much *he* meant to her.

At the rock pool, she had *almost* allowed herself to think about *love*. Now, as they rattled across the stubbled plains, she thanked heavens that she hadn't said anything foolish about her feelings.

By the time they reached the base camp, Mitch was negotiating to use the army as extras and as advisors in the survival and battle scenes of *New Tomorrow*.

He flashed her an excited grin as he turned to her. 'Isn't this fantastic, Grace? Just what we need.'

'Great,' she agreed, with a forced smile. And, of course, it was. She wanted the very best for *New Tomorrow*, too. Until two days ago, the success of the company, and this film in particular, had been the central focus of her life.

For a brief moment in time, Mitch had caused a huge shift in her focus. But it was clear that, now she was returning to the real world, she would have to readjust her sights. In a few short hours they would be back in Townsville and she would be Ms Robbins, director's assistant.

And Mitch would be simply her boss.

Three hours later, the Black Hawk helicopter chugged and dipped in its descent to the helipad at Townsville's Lavarack Barracks, before finally settling on the ground. A huge metal door slid open, and Mitch stood, stretched and smiled down at Grace. She permitted herself the luxury of basking in that smile and allowed her gaze to linger for a moment on his delicious mouth and sexy brown eyes.

He placed a hand at her elbow. 'Ready to go?' he asked.

'Sure.' She swallowed back the painful lump in her throat as she allowed him to help her to her feet, and followed him out of the helicopter and down the short ladder. And she tried to shake off the heavy weight of her depression. These stinging eyes and the choky feeling in her throat were quite uncalled for. Ridiculous. She blinked and took in a deep breath.

Above them, the rotor blades stopped circling, and a predictable cluster of men in military fatigues stepped forward to greet them.

It was only as Grace's dusty walking boots hit the tarmac that she saw the woman. The woman with a heart-shaped face and eyes bigger than the Ross River Dam. The petite platinum-blonde in a hot-pink mini skirt and jacket with sheer black stockings and sin-fully high heeled shoes.

'Da-ar-arling.' Her voice and her clothes smacked of Hollywood as she tottered towards Mitch and launched herself into his arms. 'Are you okay, you poor, dear baby?'

CHAPTER NINE

MITCH LOOKED MOMENTARILY ambushed. 'Candy! I didn'—' His words were cut off as the woman rose onto tiptoes and smacked a noisy kiss on his mouth.

Grace's teeth clenched.

Candy lowered her heels to the ground and moaned, 'Where have you *been*, Mitch?'

He shook his head as he smiled back at her. 'I should have realised you'd be part of the welcoming party, when I heard you were in town.'

'You bad boy. Of course I had to come rushing straight out here to check for myself that you're okay.' She ran a possessive hand down his cheek and a heavy gold charm bracelet glinted in the sun. 'I've been so worried about you.'

Mitch frowned. 'But no one knew we were in any kind of trouble till I telephoned this morning.'

'Yes. But since *then*, baby. I've been going through all sorts of agony.' Her painted lips pouted.

Turning inside the tight circle of Candy's embrace, Mitch sent a quick smile Grace's way. 'We're well and quite fit, aren't we, Grace?'

'As a fiddle,' she agreed, her tone one hundred per cent acid.

Candy took a step back from Mitch, but left one arm draped

around his waist. Her round blue eyes narrowed as they confronted Grace.

And Grace was suddenly acutely conscious of her bedraggled appearance. She didn't need to see her reflection in any mirror. She could just imagine how she looked, with stringy, unbrushed hair, stained and considerably rumpled clothes and her face burnt by the sun.

The waiting military people stepped forward, introduced themselves, and Mitch thanked them for their help. During the exchange, Candy seemed to continue her study of Grace. She forced a smile that, in Grace's opinion, seemed as artificial as her hair colour.

'Mitch, baby, you must introduce me to your little secretary.'

Secretary! Silent rage bristled in her throat. Her work involved much more than secretarial duties, and she suspected Candy knew it.

She might have seethed and fumed some more if Mitch hadn't stepped away from Candy and reached for Grace's hand, drawing her closer.

'Candy, let me introduce the most brilliant assistant any director could ask for, Grace Robbins.'

The two women exchanged handshakes. Candy's hand was cool and limp and Grace decided that her thick black eyelashes were also fake.

'Grace,' Mitch continued, 'this is Candy Sorbell, the woman I most have to impress.'

'Oh?' Grace found it so hard to keep the coolness out of her voice.

'Oh, yes. She's the infamous tight-fisted finance executive from High Sierra Studios in L.A.'

'High Sierra?' Grace echoed. Film companies didn't come much bigger.

'Now, Mitch.' Candy pouted. 'I'm only tight-fisted if I'm not treated right.'

Mitch's chuckle was thin. Grace shivered.

'But let's not worry about that now,' Candy said, shaking her fist so the heavy charm bracelet jangled. 'You've been through a ghastly ordeal, you poor man, and you should be home in your hotel. I know exactly what you need. A nice hot bath, a decent meal and an early night. You should be tucked up in bed by—'

'Mitch,' Grace broke in quietly. 'Do you still have that phone? I'd like to organise a taxi.'

Mitch frowned. 'For you, Grace? There's no need. I'm sure Candy would be happy to give you a—'

'Oh, of course, we can do that for you, sweetie,' interrupted Candy with an enthusiastic grin that would have done a used-car salesman proud. She grabbed a mobile phone from her handbag. 'Here you are. Help yourself. That's very thoughtful of you to take a taxi home so I can hurry your poor boss straight off to his hotel.'

'Thanks,' muttered Grace.

'No,' interrupted Mitch sternly. 'We're not going to just leave Grace to make her own way home.'

Candy's eyebrows rose.

One of the army officers stepped forward and cleared his throat deferentially. 'We'd be only too happy to provide transport for Miss Robbins,' he said.

'Thank you so much.' Grace sent the man a warm smile, knowing that she couldn't take much more of Candy. The woman produced more gushing than the spas at Hot Springs. She turned to Mitch and hoped her voice sounded more steady than she felt. 'Please, go back to your hotel and get some—rest. I'll be absolutely fine.'

'I'm absolutely fine,' Grace repeated much later when an agitated Maria phoned her.

'You're sure you're okay? Not suffering from—um—exposure?'

Grace suppressed a sigh. Her exposed emotions had taken quite a battering, but she presumed Maria was referring to physical exposure to the elements in the harsh outback. 'We were lucky the tropical winters are so mild,' she explained. 'The middle of the day was pretty hot, but on the whole I haven't had any problems. And now I've had a lovely bath—the longest, hottest, sudsiest soak of my life. I'm shampooed and moisturised. I've put aloe vera on my sunburn, and I'm stretched out on the sofa with a lovely glass of chilled wine.' Grace took a deep swig of the wine. 'I feel great,' she lied.

'Okay, you've convinced me.' Maria laughed. 'I'm so relieved.'

There was a short silence. And Grace, feeling the kind of physical relaxation that comes from a hot bath, clean hair and weary muscles, snuggled lower on the sofa and took another sip of wine.

'So, come on, kiddo,' urged Maria. 'Spill the beans. Tell Aunt Maria all about it.'

Some of Grace's relaxation began to slip away. 'I've already told you everything about the accident and finding the rock pool. And then the army...'

'Yeah. But I want to know about the serious stuff.'

'Being lost had its serious moments.' She was hedging, aware that Maria had a nose for scandal as finely tuned as any member of the paparazzi's.

'Grace, are you stringing me along? You spent three days alone in the wilderness with the studliest of all studs. Come on,' she urged, her voice sounding as if she was going through some kind of endurance test. 'Give me just a hint.'

'Maria, there's nothing to hint about. We survived. We found water, and crayfish to eat.'

A swear word blasted from the other end of the line. 'Listen to me, Grace Robbins. If you haven't allowed yourself to experience the full force of Mitch Wentworth's—er—attention, you've— you've committed a crime against the feminine gender.'

'For crying out loud!'

'You got together with Mitch, didn't you? I can tell. He hit on you, Grace, and you succumbed.'

Grace felt cold wine trickling beneath the gaping neckline of her bathrobe and realised she was shaking. She set the wineglass on the floor beside her. *He hit on you and you succumbed.* Maria had smacked the bull's eye with her first shot. But how terribly basic and ordinary she made it sound!

And predictable. She'd fallen for Mitch just as she had feared she would. Mitch had only to...

Guiltily, Grace remembered that the situation was even worse than Maria had suggested. Mitch hadn't seduced her. *He hadn't lifted a finger!*

She had begged *him* to kiss her! And, of course, she had known exactly what would follow.

'I see.' Maria was purring into the phone. 'My dear girl, your silence is bellowing. All I can say is, good on you. And I'm emerald with envy.'

'No, Maria. You've got it wrong—'

There was a firm rat-a-tat on her door. 'Look, I have to go. There's someone at the door,' she added with relief.

'Sure there is,' grumbled Maria. 'And I came down in the last shower. Grace, you don't—'

Grace jumped to her feet and headed across the room, taking the cordless phone with her and frowning as Maria launched into another tirade. She swung the door open.

Mitch.

He stood there, clean and freshly shaven, in a white T-shirt that made his tan look darker than ever, smiling his lazy, heart-lurching smile, with his hands shoved into the pockets of his jeans. Questions about a certain blonde with a very sweet name flashed into Grace's head.

And out again.

'We have matters to discuss,' he said. His hands came out of his pockets and he drew her towards him, planting a warm, hungry kiss on her mouth.

The phone slipped to the floor and landed on Grace's doormat with a soft thud.

'Grace, are you there?'

Dimly, she was aware of Maria's frantic voice. But Mitch's mouth was demanding her attention—her undivided attention. She might have asked for that first kiss by the campfire, but now his kiss made all kinds of intimate requests. There was no doubting the urgent pleading of that tongue, seeking out hers, or that hard male body pressing itself firmly against her.

'Missed me?' he murmured against her ear.

'Oh, yes.' His skin smelled clean and just a little spicy, and it was warm and sensuous beneath her lips.

'You know, you have the sexiest mouth.' He nibbled at her full lower lip.

'Is that Mitch? Is he there with you now?' Maria's screech crackled at their feet.

'What the—?' Mitch looked just a little startled.

'Shh,' Grace warned, with a finger to her lips. She pointed to the phone on the mat and stooped to pick it up.

'Sorry, Maria,' she said into the receiver. 'My neighbour dropped in. She's—she's been looking after my goldfish. I had to—' Mitch nuzzled her neck, making it very difficult to keep the tremble out of her voice. 'When she handed over the tank, I dropped the phone.'

'Your neighbour? But I thought your neighbour was an old lady.'

Through the thin green silk of her robe, Mitch's hands traced Grace's backbone. They reached her bottom. For more reasons than one, sweat filmed her body. 'Ah, that's right, Maria. Mrs Nye lives next door. She's a real sweetie.'

'But I was sure I heard a man's voice. Grace, are you okay? You're kind of panting into the phone.'

The phone was snatched from Grace's hand. A strong masculine finger depressed a button.

And that was the end of Maria.

Grace stared at the phone as Mitch tossed it onto a large floor cushion. 'That was Maria Cavalero,' she cried. 'She will never forgive me for cutting her off. And the whole office will be buzzing with scandal tomorrow.'

He frowned. 'Why didn't you turn the darned phone off earlier?'

'You caught me by surprise.'

Mitch grinned slyly. 'I guess I did.'

'I wasn't expecting you, and I certainly didn't know you were going to start kissing me before you got through my front door.'

Lowering himself onto the sofa, he pulled Grace down to his lap. 'Just because we're back in civilisation doesn't mean we have to be civilised.'

'You're sure?' She smiled into his mouth as he nuzzled it against hers.

There was no answer. Just that mind-numbing, persuasive pressure of his mouth teasing hers. His hands nudging the silky robe from her shoulders. His breath catching as he found the soft curve of her breast. And his voice groaning her name.

'You'll have to help me make up some kind of convincing story to keep Maria quiet,' she murmured dreamily as wave upon dizzying wave of pleasure spread through her.

Mitch tensed in her arms. His head lifted, and he stared ahead bleakly. 'Cavalero's a motormouth?' he queried.

Startled by his abrupt mood change, Grace sat rather self-consciously on his lap. 'She has been known to gossip, but I'm sure Maria can be discreet,' she quickly amended, not wanting to get her friend into hot water. 'It's just that she loves romance. The faintest hint and she's—'

'Romance?' interrupted Mitch, frowning at her once more.

Grace slid from his lap to sit beside him on the sofa. Nervously she tucked stray strands of hair behind her ear. She was suddenly frightened by the wary darkness in his expression. 'I don't mean—I—I mean I'm not talking about *romantic* happy-ever-after romance. It's just that she's very into—you know—girl-guy stuff... hormonal activity,' she mumbled, embarrassed.

For a brief moment, Mitch's mouth twitched with amusement, but a more serious expression quickly replaced the bare glimmer of a smile. 'Actually, I came here tonight to sort out this employer-employee situation,' he said with a sigh.

'I see,' Grace said softly.

'Then somehow I got sidetracked,' he added with a wry grimace.

'You seem to make a habit of leaving the track, Mr Wentworth.' She sat very stiffly, quite certain that Mitch was going to explain, just as Roger had three years earlier, that their little affair, interlude, or whatever he might want to call it, was going to get in the way of business.

Wearily, Mitch leant his head back against the sofa, and the light from the nearby table-lamp played across his face. For the first time since he'd arrived, Grace saw the deep lines of exhaustion around his eyes and at the sides of his mouth.

His forehead wrinkled, creasing the lines more deeply. 'I like to think I'm a man who learns from his mistakes. Professionally,

I'm in a vulnerable position at the moment—putting all my eggs in one basket. I can't afford foolish slips.'

Foolish slips?

She was a foolish slip?

How could she prevent herself from weeping? If only she had trusted her initial instincts about her boss. Instead, she'd been swept away by his looks and his charm and she'd very nearly lost her heart in the process.

'You don't have to spell out how you want me to behave in the office,' she said carefully, her voice only just steady. 'I understand how complicated and inappropriate it would be if anyone suspected we had...been...been *involved*.'

He nodded, and Grace bit down hard on her lip. When he stared at her lip protruding from her clenched teeth, she had to turn away.

She had certainly been very, very naive. On the other hand, Mitch had simply stayed true to type. For a brief moment in the bush, the international playboy had dallied with a new playmate. She'd been the only available female at the time and, to make matters ten times worse, she'd thrown herself at him. It was as predictable as the changing of the seasons that he would have seized the opportunity to hone his sporting skills some more.

Feeling like a silly, witless Mitch Wentworth groupie, Grace inched away from him. He must never suspect that his lovemaking had been more wonderful than anything she'd ever known. And he must certainly never know that she had fancied herself in love with him. A man like Mitch didn't care for women who allowed their emotions to become entangled with their hormones.

Mitch switched his gaze to stare at her hand-woven rug as he spoke. 'This would all be so much easier if you weren't working for me. Office affairs are so darned inconvenient.'

Inconvenient? First she was a foolish slip, and now she was an inconvenience.

In a matter of seconds, Grace's swelling sense of misery dissolved and honest-to-goodness anger—her original feeling for this man—swiftly took its place. 'You've got a nerve,' she said. 'It would be a jolly sight more convenient for me if *you* weren't my *boss*!'

She jumped to her feet and crossed her arms belligerently over her chest. Her robe was gaping. Taking a moment to tug the neckline together, she re-crossed her arms. 'But I have no plans to go hunting for another job, *Mr* Wentworth.'

With a softly muttered curse, Mitch rose from the sofa, and Grace stepped back as his height unfurled before her. 'I'm not asking you to resign, Grace. I'm just acknowledging that we have a—potentially contentious situation at the office.'

'And you think rushing around to my flat tonight and kissing me in full public view on my front doorstep is the best way to solve it?'

Mitch's eyes widened and he scratched his head.

No, Grace tried to convince herself, *he does not look like a really cute little boy with a puzzle to solve.*

'I guess I hadn't considered that risk factor. But you said yourself that Maria Cavalero could cause problems.'

'And you said my working for you was a problem.'

'I was talking in general terms—the whole boss and employee scenario.'

Tapping her bare foot against the floor, Grace willed herself to stay calm and logical and to forget about how good it felt to be wrapped in his arms. She was fighting for her job now. 'If you are suggesting that my employment is a risk factor, you can think again. I love my work. It means everything to me.' She took a deep, rallying breath before she issued her ultimatum. 'I can manage quite nicely without your kisses, Mitch, but I can't give up my position at Tropicana Films.'

His eyes widened. For a second, Grace thought she saw a flicker of admiration, but she was too hurt and angry to stop and consider his reaction to her outburst.

'And I'd like you to leave now,' she added. 'We don't want anyone to think you'd lingered too long at my flat tonight.'

'Hold it, Grace. I think you're getting irrational about this. Don't get heated. I just wanted to—'

'Clear the air?' she supplied through gritted teeth as she sailed past him in the direction of her door. 'Consider the air clear, Mr Wentworth. And the slate's clean, too. No problem. All obstacles have been swept away. And you can make a fresh start in the morning with no nasty little innuendoes from me. I'll go back to work tomorrow as your assistant and—and—' she faltered for a moment '—I'll leave anything else to Candy Sorbell.'

'Candy? How does she come into this?'

Grace shook her head very slowly and sighed. 'Ask her. I'm sure she'll be only too happy to explain, and if you are still having difficulty understanding she can provide very helpful practical demonstrations.'

'Grace, for Pete's sake, I didn't come here to get you mad at me again.'

'I'm sure you didn't. That's why you were going to suggest I leave the company.' Choking down her fury, Grace flung her door open and with a dramatic gesture pointed the way down her front path.

Mitch stepped towards her. 'Grace, we can work something out.' He lifted a hand to her cheek.

But she flicked her face sideways so that no connection was made. 'I have the perfect solution,' she told him. 'If you're uncomfortable about our working relationship, why don't you go find yourself another film company to take over? Give Tropicana back to poor George Hervey. He didn't deserve to have the company he'd struggled to build up snatched away from him like *that*!' Her last words were accompanied by an angry snap of her fingers.

By the time she finished, she could see that Mitch was angry, too. His eyes were hard and glassy and his lips were compressed into a thin, pale line. His voice, when he spoke, was very low. 'If that's where you're coming from, then I'd be wasting my time trying to discuss any other point of view with you.'

Grace asked herself why his sudden acquiescence left her feeling as if she'd lost something. Surely this was a moment of victory?

Mitch dipped his head briefly in her direction and stepped past her out of the flat. 'I don't think there is anything helpful that can be added to this conversation. Goodnight.'

'Goodnight,' she whispered as he disappeared into the black of night. For a few moments longer, she could hear his footsteps ringing out his departure on the concrete driveway.

Then she shut her door and burst into tears.

CHAPTER TEN

MITCH LIFTED HIS wineglass to the light so he could examine the full-bodied red he'd ordered. It looked superb and, two sips later, he knew he'd made a wise choice. The Hunter Valley wine was dry and mellow—very good indeed.

Life was getting better by the minute.

Ever since Grace had accepted his invitation to dinner a short time earlier, he'd felt buoyed by a renewed sense of optimism. After last night, it was important to get this matter with her sorted out properly. The way things had ended up was totally unsatisfactory and he'd been rattled more than he cared to admit by her sudden, angry outburst.

But yesterday they'd been tired, their emotions overwrought on account of their ordeal.

They couldn't remain prickly and avoiding each other. It was an untenable working situation.

Tonight they could talk things over quietly and rationally.

Another sip of wine and Mitch congratulated himself on choosing the large and popular restaurant attached to the hotel where he was staying. To anyone inclined to speculate, it would look totally above board—a business meeting. He'd brought a pile of business papers and placed them on the table in front of him, to make that point clear.

But he was actually planning a very different discussion. He and Grace had some important bridges to build.

A jangle of jewellery and a cloud of exotic perfume interrupted his pleasant musings.

'Mitch! A working dinner and, darling, dining alone? We can't have that.' Candy Sorbell, in something orange, skin-tight and probably very expensive, dropped into the chair opposite him, apparently seeing no significance in the fact that his table was set for two.

'Good evening, Candy.' Mitch smiled politely, if not warmly.

'What are you drinking?' she asked loudly like a bright, annoying parrot.

He indicated the excellent wine.

'Nah.' Candy pulled a face. 'I need something that packs a punch.'

With a barely suppressed sigh, Mitch beckoned a waiter, and while the young man made his way to their table Candy prattled on. 'I decided to take a rain check on that concert, Mitch. I know you Australians have culture; you don't have to ram it down my throat.'

Mitch inclined his head with another polite smile. 'You're probably very tired.'

She leaned forward, offering him a generous view of her tanned cleavage before fixing him with her shrewd blue gaze. 'I've been expending a lot of energy trying to save your seat, Mitch. I talked to Joe again today. It was 6 a.m. in L.A. and he wasn't too happy, but it was the only time I could be sure of catching him. I was trying to get him to ease off on you for a few more days. Oh, an extra-dry martini, thanks, honey,' she added with a flutter of her eyelashes for the waiter. Then her expression hardened as she hissed at Mitch, 'I sure hope they know how to make a decent martini here.'

But Mitch didn't reply. He could see Grace standing in the restaurant's entrance, frowning as she looked in his direction.

He waved and tried to swallow away the sudden constriction in his throat. Grace was wearing a simple black and white striped dress that skimmed softly over her body, hinting at the perfection underneath. He sent her a smile.

Dimly, he heard Candy's voice. 'That's your little secretary, isn't it? What's she doing here?'

'She's joining me for dinner,' he muttered tersely out of the corner of his mouth.

'Oh, how quaint,' Candy murmured. 'It would be useful for me to get to know some more of your staff.'

The calculated, steely note in her voice sounded to Mitch like a definite warning.

Grace was grateful that the restaurant's receptionist was busy with a customer. She needed a moment to gather her wits and to figure out how it would look if she turned and walked straight back out of the hotel. The sight of Candy Sorbell, chatting so intimately with Mitch, ruined her appetite. And it prompted her to wonder what had happened to her brains in the past few days. Had she become so moronic that she'd imagined Mitch wanted to dine alone with her?

After last night?

Ever since he'd left her flat, she'd been unbearably miserable, and all day she'd known that she really needed to talk to him again. When his invitation had appeared amidst her e-mail messages, she'd mulled it over for some time. Eventually, she'd decided it was important to get things absolutely straight.

Glancing at his table again, she sighed. There'd be no straight talking here in this cosy little threesome. She reached into her purse for her car keys. It would be better if she left now. Candy wouldn't care. And Mitch...

Mitch, wearing a navy sports jacket and a snowy white shirt, was rising to his feet, his eyes fixed fiercely on her. Grace's heart melted at the intensity of his expression and her hesitation dissolved. The keys slid back into her purse.

He took a step towards her and, as if hypnotised by his dark gaze, she began to make her way across the room, weaving between the tables of chatting diners.

Halfway there, too late to turn back, she saw Candy reach out a suntanned, lean arm to grab Mitch's elbow. His attention caught, she was obviously urging him back into his seat and engaging him with animated conversation.

As she reached them, Grace's simmering emotions bubbled to quick anger.

Especially when Candy blithely ignored her and kept talking to Mitch as she waved a glass in one hand and rattled her bracelet. Mitch was giving strange sideways jerks of his head as he tried to break into the conversation and greet Grace.

'I keep telling Joe that anything you are excited about has to be a winner,' Candy was saying loudly. As she spoke, she stroked his arm, possessively, suggestively. 'I've worked with you before, darling, so I know just what you have to offer.'

Grace hovered.

Candy paused for breath and Mitch leapt to his feet. 'Grace, thanks for coming.' He held out his hand to take hers rather formally. 'Now,' he said solicitously, 'you take my chair and I'll grab a waiter to get us another and set an extra place.'

When these little formalities were attended to and the three sat facing each other, Mitch shot her a look loaded with meaning. 'Candy has rearranged her evening so that she's able to join us.'

'How nice.' Grace forced a smile and nodded to Candy. She always hated those awkward silences that sometimes followed introductions. But for the life of her she couldn't think of anything else to say. *Now what?*

And she was answered more quickly than she expected. 'This is just great to have you here,' over-enthused Candy. 'Mitch tells me you're such an efficient secretary. Did you bring a notebook and pencil? There might be a few points we raise tonight that Mitch will want jotted down.'

At what temperature did blood boil? Grace could hardly conceal her indignation. Her eyes shot sideways to Mitch and she was a little mollified by the shock and embarrassment she read in his expression.

'I doubt that will be necessary, Candy,' he responded quickly. 'Grace, let me pour you some of this delightful wine.'

But Grace's green eyes were not simply a genetic accident. A challenge had been laid and her chin lifted as she decided to play Candy's game. She always carried a small notepad and pen in her handbag and she retrieved them now, flipped the pad open to a clean page and sat with the pen poised. Baring her teeth at Candy, she said sweetly, 'Go ahead, Ms Sorbell. I'm all ready to take notes.'

'Ah, sure.' Candy looked just a little taken aback, but after a hefty swig of her martini she continued. 'That's good, thank you, dear. Now, Mitch. Where were we?'

'We were about to order dinner and we are going to leave business aside for a while,' Mitch said firmly. He picked up his own menu and began to study it assiduously.

With one eyebrow raised in a fretful arc, Candy shrugged unhappily and hastily scanned her menu. 'I'll just have a Caesar salad,' she muttered, and swung one foot impatiently while the others took their time choosing their meals.

As soon as the orders were placed, Mitch spoke, throwing a question casually onto the table and not aiming it at anyone in particular. 'I hear Magnetic Island is very pleasant and it's only a short ferry ride away from Townsville. Perhaps we should explore it on the weekend?'

'Haven't you two done enough exploring in the outdoors for this week?' snapped Candy. Her eyes slid to Grace. 'Poor Grace's nose couldn't take any more sun.'

Grace smiled thinly.

'Really, Mitch,' Candy hurried on. 'All this sightseeing, concerts, the theatre. I'm not here on holiday. We need to focus on business.' She leaned forward again, and Grace couldn't help wondering if the impressive cleavage was as fake as the hair colour and the eyelashes. 'And the message I bring from my company to you—'

'Just a minute.' Grace made a flurried display of taking up her notebook and pencil.

Mitch frowned and Candy stared at her coldly, but continued. 'This *New Tomorrow* project of yours is only going to work if you get High Sierra's backing. You really must settle the deal over a drink, tonight. Now.'

'I very much doubt that's possible,' Mitch replied smoothly.

Grace regarded the two of them. What on earth was she doing here? This was power play, and way out of her territory. Perhaps this dinner was a deliberate ploy of Mitch's to put her in her place? She looked at the pile of papers beside him.

How ridiculous that I've imagined an intimate dinner alone with him, holding hands across the table, drinking in his sexy smile. Making up...

Her pencil dug sharp, angry strokes onto the page.

Candy was getting heated. 'Are you playing games with me, Mitch? Look, if you come to the party, Joe's agreed. The money is yours, as long as you accept our terms. All we're asking is fifty-one per cent and exclusive world distribution rights.'

'Fifty-one per cent...' Grace parroted as she jotted down the figures. Candy glared at her, and Grace frowned at the page and stuck out her tongue as if concentrating on the task of note-taking were very difficult.

Mitch sighed in obvious irritation. 'You know I'm only prepared to offer twenty per cent. And then there are all your *other* conditions.' He shot an anxious glance towards Grace. 'They're too steep, Candy.'

Grace, feeling totally furious and very out of place, made some more noisy scribbles on the page. 'Would you like me to list those conditions?'

An angry red tinge crept along Mitch's cheekbones. He scowled at her. 'Grace, what on earth do you think you're doing? Don't be stupid.'

She blinked at him and then, fuming, rose to her feet, her anger giving the movement a surprising degree of majesty. 'On this occasion, I'm doing very little,' she replied icily.

Of all the arrogant men! There was only so much she could take. Not so long ago, Henry had called her stupid. And now Mitch. She admitted to many faults, but stupidity was not one of them.

As she stood there, her gaze darting from one to the other, Mitch's startled expression was too unsettling, so she addressed Candy. 'I'm sorry to leave you like this, but my understanding was that this evening was purely social.' Hardly believing her own actions, she tossed the notebook and pen onto the table in front of Candy. 'I'll leave these for you in case you *really do need* to make notes.'

With an abrupt about-turn, she hurried away, almost colliding with the waiter bringing their meals. Out of habit, she experienced a momentary pang of guilt about wasting the food she'd ordered. But then, she reminded herself, the people she was abandoning were not like her frugal parents. They handled multi-million-dollar deals without turning a hair and, at a pinch, they could manage to foot the bill for one small serving of satay beef with a green salad.

Mitch called her name, but she didn't look back. She dodged her way through the tables as annoying tears welled in her eyes and, by the time she reached the marbled expanse of the hotel foyer, her chin was trembling.

Behind her, there were hurried footsteps, but again she refused to turn around. Under no circumstances would she be coerced back to that table.

She sniffed and tossed her head defiantly high and sailed down the smooth, wide hotel steps, like Cinderella rushing from the ball. If Mitch had followed her, she didn't want to know about it. She continued on down the softly lit path, as it swept in a long curve past tropical palms and clumps of spider lilies, to the car park.

It was only as she reached her car that she realised there were no more footsteps. She looked behind her. No one was following.

And suddenly she was disappointed. An embarrassing sob erupted. *What had she been expecting? A fairy-tale reunion with Mitch under the tropical stars?*

Dream on.

Mitch was focused on money and movies. Power and fame. Not love.

Never love.

She wrenched her car door open, slumped into the driver's seat and slammed the door closed again. Never had she felt more alone and vulnerable. Up here in North Queensland, she was away from family and old friends and she'd fallen uselessly in love with her boss.

Her hands gripped the steering wheel and she rested her head against them. Her face felt hot and wet. Heavens above, what had happened to her? Until recently, she'd always stayed calm in the face of difficulty. She'd prided herself on her problem-solving ability and, at the very least, she'd thought she was mature enough to adjust to changing circumstances.

But the most recent major change in her working life—a new boss—had sent her to pieces. An emotional heap. She rubbed her eyes with clenched knuckles. Perhaps she would have to think about another job.

There was a sharp crack of shoes on the gravel outside. Startled, she peered into the darkness through tear-blurred eyes. Her door opened.

'Grace, what do you think you're playing at?' A furious Mitch bent down to glare at her.

No Prince Charming searching for his lost love. Just a very angry boss. Grace gulped back another sob and prayed that, in the dark, he couldn't see her tear-streaked face.

'What is it with you women?'

Wasn't he supposed to be an expert with women? 'I'm not *playing* at anything,' she cried. 'But I can't vouch for Candy Sorbell's motives.'

Mitch shook his head. 'Leave Candy out of this for the moment.'

'With pleasure.' *Whoosh.* She let out her breath. 'I thought, when you invited me to dinner, that you wanted to talk to me.'

Instead of replying, he sighed and leaned his back against the side of her car. He stared at the night sky. Grace waited for him to speak. She could hear, in the nearby marina, a motor boat's engine begin to chug and she saw the way the sea breeze lifted Mitch's dark hair.

It wasn't fair that, in the moonlight, he still looked like every woman's dream come true. How could a man be so confusingly arrogant and so dreamy at the same time?

'Of course I want to talk to you privately,' he said at last.

'Then what is Candy doing at our table? Why didn't you get rid of her?'

He shoved his hands deep into the pockets of his trousers. 'It's not that easy. I can't just send her packing.'

'You can't or you don't want to?' Grace's hands gripped the steering wheel once more.

'I can't and I'm not going to,' Mitch told her quietly. He turned and there was no smile, only a brooding frown.

Her bitter laugh sounded distinctly catty, but she couldn't help it. 'Are you and Candy Sorbell going to be the small print in the contract with High Sierra?'

'Now you're going too far.' His palm thumped into the side of the car. 'How did you dream up that crazy idea?'

Again, Grace laughed, but it trailed off into an uncertain little cough as she realised that she had steered this conversation into dangerous waters. Without even trying, she was slap bang in the middle of another argument with Mitch. And the tide of their angry feelings was so strong that she couldn't turn back. She didn't even have time to think out a way to direct herself onto safe ground.

Mitch lowered his head to speak softly through the open doorway. His voice was deep and persuasive. 'Come back and sweat it out for just a little longer, Grace. I'll try to get rid of Candy later.'

Incredulous, she stared at him, trying to understand. 'I don't believe I'm hearing this,' she said. 'If you were going to get rid of her, you could have done it half an hour ago.'

'You don't understand, Grace. If you value your job, you will come back with me now.'

Value her job? What on earth was going on? She should be panicking, but instead it was Mitch who looked distraught. This was too important to discuss from a sitting position. She swung her legs out of the car and jumped to her feet, her hands planting themselves on her hips to underline her indignation. 'My job depends on my going back to that table? To be put down by that witch?'

His dark eyes bored into hers. 'More or less.'

Why wasn't she terrified? Her work meant everything to her. Surely this should be a moment of pure dread? But all she could feel was hot, volcanic, exploding anger. 'If these are the new job specifications you and the delightful Candy have come up with, then it's time for me to make an important career move.'

'What are you talking about?'

'What am I talking about, Mitch? Do I have to spell it out? I'm resigning.'

Mitch paled. 'Please, Grace. Don't do this to me. I've got too much happening at present. My whole company's at risk. I don't think I have time to deal with your emotional outbursts as well.'

'You *rat!*' She was within a hair's breadth of slapping his face.

'Rat?' He had the nerve to look shocked. 'I'm a *rat?*'

First Roger, and now Mitch. She couldn't believe history was repeating itself. 'A shallow, materialistic, bully-boy rat.' The words flowed from the bitter resentment pouring through her. To hell with men! 'You couldn't care less about me, except as a useful—useful commodity.'

'Grace, don't overreact.' His hand reached out to her and she sprang back to avoid the contact.

Cruel memories of his hands on her skin and his passionate responses to her touch made her voice tremble. 'I believe my contract requires one month's notice. You've got it as from now.'

Blindly, she plunged back into the driver's seat, grabbed the door handle and yanked her door shut. She slammed it so savagely, she barely missed injuring Mitch.

'You don't understand...' he yelled.

Ignoring his protests, she angrily thrust her key into the ignition, jammed her foot on the accelerator and launched the gear lever into reverse. And as she screeched and roared out of the car park she had a brief glimpse of Mitch in her rearview mirror, looking chalky white and horrified.

Good, she told herself. We've finally set things straight.

CHAPTER ELEVEN

THE SEALED ENVELOPE, clearly identified by the jaunty green and aqua Tropicana logo, was waiting on Grace's desk when she returned from morning tea. She had been expecting Mitch's response to her letter of resignation, but that didn't stop her stomach from tightening when she saw it sitting there. Since she'd roared out of the hotel car park a few days ago, her insides had been twisted into permanent knots and now the strong coffee she'd just drunk churned unpleasantly.

With trembling hands, she reached for the envelope and slit it with her paper knife. When she extracted its contents, her hand shook so badly, she couldn't read the words on the page.

This is ridiculous. She closed her eyes and took a deep breath. Just read the letter and then you can get on with your life!

She placed the paper on her desk, lowered herself into her chair, and slowly spread the single page out flat. Then she read it through carefully.

Tropicana Films
Northtown Centre
Flinders Mall
July 8th
Dear Ms Robbins,

As you requested, I am responding to your letter of resignation with a written reply. I also note that your decision to leave this company is unconditional in that you are not prepared to discuss any counter-offers for the retention of your services.

Naturally, I have no alternative but to accept your resignation. However, I do so most reluctantly. You are aware of the terms of your contract, which require four weeks' notice by either party. It is my wish, as Managing Director, that you continue your duties until August 6th.

As you know, the future of *New Tomorrow* will be decided within the next few weeks and it is imperative that all staff engaged on this vital project apply themselves totally to their immediate tasks in a completely professional manner.

Your work as Executive Assistant to the Managing Director has, until your sudden and untimely resignation, always been of the highest professional standard and I need you to maintain this level of commitment in the next four weeks before you leave us.

Yours faithfully,

M.J. Wentworth

Mitchell J. Wentworth

Managing Director

She read it through twice, one hand over her mouth and the other pressed hard against her pounding chest. So this was it. The end of the job she cherished.

And goodbye to the man she'd been foolish enough to imagine she loved.

Her eyes closed to squeeze back the threat of tears, but images of a glowing campfire, a canopy of outback stars and a sexy, masculine smile invaded her mind. Grace pressed her lips together to hold back a bitter sob. She hurt so much, she wanted to run away. Now. To get out of the office. Out of North Queensland. Anywhere, as long as she was able to cut free.

'But he won't let me leave,' she whispered to the empty office. 'Not yet. I have to stay here four more weeks.'

Four weeks! How could she bear it? She had expected that Mitch would have been eager to let her go. She'd half expected him to demand that she clear her desk that very minute.

A tap on her door sent her spinning around.

Maria hovered in the office doorway, her arms full of papers and her eyes wide with concern. 'I was just bringing those printouts you asked for,' she said uncertainly.

Grace sniffed and blinked, hoping her face showed no sign of tears. 'That's great. Thanks.' She held out one hand for the papers and tried to cover Mitch's letter with the other, but she knew she'd been caught out.

'You've heard from the boss, haven't you?' came her friend's predictable query.

Grace nodded. 'He won't let me go straight away. I have to work out the four weeks of my notice.'

'The insensitive brute!' Maria accompanied her outburst with a thump of her fist as she dropped the printouts onto Grace's desk.

'He paid me some kind of back-handed compliment about my professionalism,' explained Grace, feeling strengthened by Maria's support, but then her face crumpled. 'He wasn't too worried about being professional when we were…'

'When you were playing Swiss Family Robinson with him up in the Gulf country?' supplied Maria. 'No need to blush and look embarrassed, Grace. I'm sure Mr. W. is too much temptation for any woman. Even you. What I don't understand is why you two came back fighting. Or is it just that your return coincided with Ms Sorbell's arrival?'

Grace sighed. She couldn't deny that Candy was a part, or perhaps the whole of her problem. 'Mitch doesn't give a hoot for me as a person. He just wants me as someone who has a finger on all the important pulses. You know—logistics, locations—all the things I was putting into place before he arrived.'

Feeling strengthened by her growing anger, Grace picked up the memo she'd received from Mitch the previous day, outlining tasks to be completed. She shook it at Maria. 'If it's professionalism he wants, he'll get four weeks of professionalism like he's never seen before. If this project falls over, it won't be because of anything I've done; it'll be because Mitch Wentworth's ego is too big.'

'Way to go,' cheered Maria. 'You show him. He'll certainly get a shock when he tries to replace you.'

'I doubt it.' Grace sighed, slumping back into her chair and fingering Mitch's letter. She began folding it into a tiny wad.

Maria backed towards the door. 'He's so tied up with his Candy stick, he wouldn't have a clue what you've put in place. All the details about the army, the accommodation for the cast and crew, caterers, charter flights, helicopters. The poor fool doesn't know it, but after you leave, Grace, our mighty Mitch Wentworth is going to find himself standing in the middle of an empty set with a puzzled look, scratching his cute behind.'

'Miss Cavalero?'

The jaws of both women dropped in the direction of their knees as a dark, masculine shape filled the doorway. Maria's face raced through three shades of red till it reached purple. 'M-Mr Wentworth?' she stammered.

With his mouth clenched in a grim, tight line, Mitch inclined his head ever so slightly in the direction of his office down the corridor. 'A word, please.'

'Yes, sir.'

'In my office. I'll be with you in a moment.'

Maria shot a guilty glance in Grace's direction and backed out of the room. Before she scurried down the corridor, she paused behind Mitch's back and gestured a throat-slitting motion with her hand.

Under other circumstances, Grace might have been tempted to smile at her friend's antics, but not when Mitch remained in her office, stern-faced and bristling with tension.

'I need a list of all the contacts we have with the region's top business operators,' he ordered tersely.

'That won't take long,' Grace replied, making a supreme effort to keep her voice businesslike. 'I have them all on file.'

She expected him to nod curtly and leave her. When he remained standing beside her chair, his unsmiling eyes resting on her, Grace pressed shaking fingers to her lips.

Mitch spoke softly. 'I'm completely tied up with a number of financial negotiations at present, but when these matters are settled we need to talk.'

She gulped. 'To discuss the arrival of the cast and the first shooting sessions?'

Mitch sighed and ran impatient fingers through his hair. 'No, Grace, it wasn't the movie business that I wanted to discuss.'

'Oh?' For just a second or two, she saw a flash of pain in his dark, stormy eyes. Her heart exploded as his gaze held hers. Surely she only imagined that Mitch looked hurt and lonely?

Without warning, his hand reached out to cup her chin and his head lowered until his mouth pressed urgently against hers. It was the shortest, hottest, most breathtaking kiss she'd ever experienced. 'We have other unfinished business,' he muttered heatedly into her ear. His thumb stroked her throat just once, and her skin flamed at his touch.

Then Mitch turned abruptly and was gone.

Grace did her level best to forget about that high-voltage kiss over the days that followed, but in spite of her efforts unexpected memories of the heated pressure of his mouth against hers would jump out and torment her. Then other taunting memories would follow.

Blast the man! If Mitch thought he could accept her resignation and still take liberties with her body, he was in for a surprise! She kept herself busy, convinced that hard work was the only thing between her sanity and a nervous breakdown. It helped that she saw very little of her boss. He and Candy and, on occasion, the company's accountant seemed to be involved in endless discussions behind firmly closed doors.

During the day, Grace coped by working flat out at the office, and in the evening she voraciously read overseas tourist brochures. What she needed, as soon as she was released from this job, was to get as far away as possible from Mitchell J. Wentworth.

The more inaccessible and remote the destinations, the more they interested her. Places like the Himalayas, Scotland's Orkney Isles or a trip up the Amazon had distinct appeal. But after a week of avid reading she was depressed to realise that these far-flung places might be no help at all.

When she sat at her desk and reflected that the attraction of these locations lay in their beautiful natural environments, Grace was plagued by a fresh crop of paralysing doubts. Wouldn't it be terrible if she travelled all the way across the globe only to spend her time thinking about some place else—an isolated spot with wide open skies and a pool carved out of a rocky platform?

A corner of her mouth curled in self-ridicule.

Perhaps she should find a big city to hide in. Buenos Aires? Tokyo? New York? But there was every chance that her memories would follow her there, too. Would she jump out of her skin every time she saw a tall, dark and handsome man?

A clinking of jewellery nearby brought Grace out of her daydream. The sound of Candy's bracelet was now infamous throughout the building. Only yesterday Maria had commented that the rattling charms warned everybody of her approach in much the same manner as the ticking clock swallowed by the crocodile in *Peter Pan.*

As the sound came closer, Grace looked up from her desk to see Candy sailing through her doorway, bringing a cloud of perfume with her. 'I've just popped in to say goodbye,' she said, helping herself to a chair.

Grace's eyes widened as she swung round to face Candy. 'Oh, really? I had no idea you were leaving already.' She was also very surprised that this high flier would bother to deliver a personal farewell to her.

'I've been here over a week, honey.' Candy crossed one shapely leg over the other and began to swing her foot. 'And I've completed my business.'

'And it was successful?' Grace queried, although she hardly expected Candy to take her into her confidence at this late stage.

The other woman's eyes glazed over and her leg stopped swinging. For a moment she looked as wooden as a mannequin in a shop window. Then she flashed Grace an ultra bright smile. 'In business terms, it was a complete and unmitigated failure.'

'A failure?' echoed Grace with a frown. 'I don't understand.'

'It's quite simple. Apart from the personal pleasure of—' she offered a simpering smile '—of catching up with our mutual friend, Mitch, my trip here has been a fiasco. Your darling boss has been playing financial games with me and he won. I lost. End of story.'

As Candy's leg began its imitation of a pendulum once more, Grace's heartbeats picked up pace. 'I'm still confused. I guess this

means High Sierra won't be giving Tropicana any financial backing. How does that make Mitch a winner?'

Candy leaned forward conspiratorially. 'Because he snaffled a
better deal, Gracie. He's been putting together some other negotiations behind my back, and now he's played his trump card. He's
getting all the funds he wants from the Queensland Film Commission.'

'Wow! That's fantastic!' For a reckless moment, Grace forgot
completely that she wasn't part of this company's future. All she
could think of was how relieved Mitch would be to have the rest
of the money he needed, and on his terms.

Candy nodded glumly. 'The Commission has agreed to give
Tropicana the additional finance plus plenty of help with promo-
tion. Understandably, they are excited about a blockbuster Australian movie filmed on location in North Queensland.'

'I guess so,' Grace agreed, but she was feeling utterly miserable again. She had to face the reality that the person who took her
place would inherit a really exciting job.

Candy jumped to her feet and began to pace the room. 'I tried
to tell my boss at High Sierra he was crazy holding out for fifty-
one per cent, when all Mitch wanted to negotiate was twenty. I
did my best to convince Joe that Mitch is no fool and that we'd be
better off grabbing the twenty per cent because it would be twenty
per cent of a big winner.'

'I'm surprised that you're taking the time to tell me all this. You
know I won't be sticking with this project, don't you? I've handed
in my resignation.'

'Yeah.' The other woman stopped pacing and stood squarely in
the centre of the room with her feet apart, eyeing Grace. 'And I
just wanted to say I think you're very wise to leave this company.'

A confusing heat crept into Grace's cheeks. Why should Candy
applaud her leaving a winning project? Unless… 'Why should you
care where I work?' she challenged.

Crossing her arms across her chest, Candy narrowed her eyes.
'We gals have got to stick together.'

'I see,' murmured Grace doubtfully. What she actually suspected
was that Candy had a king-size crush on Mitch. The American

had made no secret of her admiration for their wonder-boy boss. The whole office knew about it. Grace toyed with a pen on her desk. 'Am I also to understand that you might—*care*—for Mr Wentworth?'

With an exasperated sigh, Candy plonked herself back into the chair opposite Grace, crossed her legs and began the swinging once more. 'I'll be brutally frank with you, Gracie.'

Ouch! People usually used that term when they wanted to say something hurtful.

'Mitch Wentworth and I go back a long way.' Candy blew out air in the same way a smoker expels smoke from a cigarette.

What had happened to her own ability to breathe? Grace wondered. Her chest was painfully tight.

'We've always had a special—*understanding*,' continued Candy.

Unable to look at Candy, Grace made a show of studying her fingernails. She couldn't let the other woman see how much her words hurt. Her voice wobbled as she snapped a hasty retort. 'This special relationship you claim to have didn't help you secure the deal.'

Candy released a self-mocking little chuckle. 'Business and personal affairs are not good bedmates. But you'd understand that, wouldn't you, Gracie?'

Feeling as if she'd just stepped off a rollercoaster, Grace struggled to take in the implications of Candy's question. The floor beneath her seemed to sway and lurch. 'Mitch and I aren't having—'

'Hold it right there, honey. Don't protest too much. I've seen the way you look at your boss. And remember, I've known the dear boy for a long, long time. I understand his little *weaknesses*.' Candy's swinging foot stopped in mid-air and she used it to point at Grace. 'Don't think I blame you for making the most of a golden opportunity.'

'What on earth do you mean?'

'Getting yourself lost with Mitch in the bush. That was cute, real cute.'

Horrified by what Candy was implying, Grace jumped to her feet. 'You think I planned that? Risked my life just to—just to—'

'Climb into the sack with a babe like Mitch?' Candy favoured Grace with a knowing smirk. 'It was worth it, wasn't it, Gracie?'

Her fist clenched and, for an insane moment, Grace could feel it landing on Candy Sorbell's pert nose with a satisfying crunch. Struggling to keep her voice steady, she replied, 'What are you hoping to achieve by trying to dig up this dirt?'

The other woman's eyebrow arched. 'Why, honey, I'm offering you some sisterly advice.' She got up, crossed the room and placed both hands on Grace's shoulders, shaking her gently. 'However *sweet* Mitch was when you guys were alone in the outback, he's shown his true feelings for you by accepting your resignation without so much as a whimper. Don't waste any energy hankering after the man, my dear. I bet he was something else out there in the back of beyond, but, believe me, it was a flash in the pan.'

As if she sensed Grace's fury, Candy moved away, but hovered in the office doorway. 'Most of the women Mitch dates have the shelf-life of a punnet of fresh strawberries. Honestly, sweetheart, he wouldn't settle seriously for a quiet little thing like you. So, congratulations, you're doing the right thing by getting clear away.'

With another jangle of her jewellery, Candy left, and Grace lowered herself stiffly into her chair, staring into space.

Her ears recorded the sound of Candy's high heels tapping their exit along the corridor and somewhere a telephone was ringing. But echoing over and over in Grace's head were the words Candy had uttered: 'He wouldn't settle seriously for a quiet little thing like you.'

She knew it was true. It was what she'd told herself many times. Despite everything that had happened at the rock pool, Mitch didn't care about her as a person. He'd proved that by dropping her and turning to Candy, without so much as a backward glance. All he wanted from her now was a highly efficient assistant with a finger on all the important pulses.

And, while she knew she could search the world over without finding another man capable of capturing her heart and soul as completely as he had, Grace was just as aware that replacing her was a cinch for Mitch.

All he had to do was advertise her position in one of the country's major newspapers.

CHAPTER TWELVE

GRACE WAS EMOTIONALLY exhausted when she dragged herself back to her office the next morning. What had appalled her and kept her awake all night was the dreadful sense of revisiting the past—discovering all over again her unerring talent for falling in love with rats.

For the past week, while she'd worried about Mitch's interest in Candy, she'd been sick with misery. But a stubborn part of her mind had clung to the fragile hope that perhaps she'd imagined everything wrongly. Perhaps Mitch was only humouring Candy in order to clinch the deal. But yesterday Candy had spelt out just how *intimate* she and Mitch had been, and that was unbearable.

For just a moment she'd been tempted to disregard Candy's claims as jealous gossip, but three-year-old memories brought her back to reality. All the pain came flooding back. She had been so sure Roger loved her, yet he'd had no compunction about flinging her aside in his rush to scale the heady heights of business. Now she'd learned her lesson. She'd been taken in once by a handsome, sexy, successful man who'd left her feeling used and crushed. She wasn't going to let it happen again.

The sound of impatient footsteps forced her to lift her head and she groaned softly when she saw the current rat in her life marching stiffly through her doorway.

'Grace,' Mitch barked.

She felt like suggesting he get lost again—*permanently* this time—but, to her chagrin, Grace found her heart beginning to thump and she was jumping to attention. 'Yes, Mr Wentworth?'

He frowned and repeated, '*Grace,*' clearly emphasising his use of her first name, 'can we try again for dinner?'

The sheaf of papers she was holding fluttered to the floor with a soft swish, like pigeons landing. 'Oh, no,' she whispered, and bent to retrieve them.

A firm hand on her arm stopped her. 'I'll get them.' Mitch snatched the papers together impatiently and tossed them onto her desk. 'Well?'

'Dinner? Mitch, for heaven's sake, whatever for?'

Mitch gaped at her as if he couldn't believe what he'd heard. 'I had this weird idea that we could sit at a table and cut up food with a knife and fork. Then, after an amount of chewing and swallowing, I'd expect digestion to take place. The idea—'

'Sarcasm doesn't suit you,' she cut in, wishing she could sit down. Any minute now her knees would give way.

'No? I'm sorry, but I've had an awful week and I find your question frustrating. Why on earth wouldn't we have dinner? We need to talk.'

Grace noticed then how pale and drawn Mitch looked, and a painful lump clogged her throat. Trying to conceal her shaking hands, she folded her arms tightly across her chest. 'Mitch, I—' she struggled to reply '—I'm leaving soon. Do you really think it's wise for us to get together again?'

His expression softened slightly. 'I am sure it would be very unwise if we were to part without a decent chance to discuss—everything.'

Oh, why was she so weak? She could think of nothing nicer than going out to dinner with him. An image of Mitch, escorting her through an elegant restaurant to an intimate table for two danced through her imagination. She could picture him looking dark and dashing, pulling out her chair for her, smiling at her as they surveyed the menu together.

Grace pressed her lips together tightly to hold back the urge to accept his invitation. And she forced her mind to focus on the pain of Candy's revelations.

'I'm told there's an interesting garden restaurant in South Townsville,' he continued. 'I know the nights are cool, but it's still pleasant enough to eat outdoors. Will you join me tomorrow evening?'

'I—I'm busy tomorrow evening—it's late-night shopping.'

Mitch shoved his hands in his pockets and rocked on his heels. 'You'll have to come up with a better excuse than that.'

'Mitch, I don't think we should.'

'You've got to come out with me, Grace. I know it's unfortunate that I had to wait till Candy left.'

Good grief! How could he talk so calmly to her about Candy? He must have had his conscience surgically removed. She swung her head away and stared fiercely at her filing cabinet and tried counting to ten. 'You want me to take over where Ms Sorbell left off?'

'Pardon?'

Drawing in a deep breath, she swivelled back to face him. 'There's absolutely nothing personal left for us to discuss.'

He opened his mouth to protest, but she rushed on, not giving him a chance to hurt her even more. 'And, in case you've forgotten, I've resigned. I'm giving you another three weeks of professionalism and then I'm out of here.' With a grand sweeping gesture she pointed to the door. '*And* I very much doubt that dinner with you would aid my digestion.'

Mitch shook his head, clearly puzzled. 'What's going on here? Why are you so hung up about Candy?'

Hung up? His liaison with another woman was a minor issue?

The man had the moral habits of a rabbit! With every ounce of will-power, Grace ignored his question. 'I saw something come through on a fax yesterday afternoon about the launch of *New Tomorrow* being brought forward.'

'Grace, don't change the subject.'

'Is that correct? The State Minister for Tourism and the Arts will be in town next Thursday?'

'Damn it, Grace!'

Inhaling a deep breath, she forced herself to calm down. 'Mitch, I have nothing of a personal nature I wish to discuss with you.'

His hands rose as if he was about to grip her shoulders. For agonising moments, he stood facing her, his hands inches from connection.

'If I have to get a launch together in just a few days,' she continued, her voice tight with the effort to sound businesslike, 'I need to find out exactly what has to be done.'

For a long, breathless silence, Mitch stood still as stone and stared at her, then he sighed heavily and dropped his gaze to the grey carpet on her office floor. One hand kneaded his forehead as if he had a headache.

After more moments of silence, he looked up again and spoke. 'Okay, Grace, if this is the way you want it, I'll play it your way for now. The government has come through with the funding we need and the Minister doesn't want to miss the chance to promote his generosity before the media. So yes, we should launch the project while he's here.'

She swallowed, trying to shift the heavy lump of hopelessness lodged in her throat. She felt as if she'd swallowed a golf ball. 'It will be quite a challenge to pull all that together by next Thursday.'

Mitch nodded his agreement. 'I know, but the Minister's press staff are looking after notifying the media. We just have to throw together an invitation list for local VIPs and tee up a suitable venue.'

'Are you bringing up any of the cast?' It was hard to believe she could do this—keep talking about business while her heart was slowly breaking up, chunk by bleeding chunk.

'Of course, we definitely need our stars. They'll draw plenty of attention.'

'It'll be tricky, but I think we should just be able to pull a function like that together in time,' she told him, but she was speaking on automatic pilot, as if her head and her heart were disconnected.

'I'm sure you'll do an excellent job as always, Grace.' Mitch took three steps towards the door and turned. 'Thank you.'

She moved over to her desk, as if she expected him to head off and leave her to get on with her work now the discussion was over.

But he remained there, watching her. 'Grace, whatever you might have heard about me or decided about me, I'm actually not—'

'You want the invitations sent out first thing this morning?'

His splayed hand thumped her office wall. 'What are you made of, woman? Petrified wood?'

If only she were! She lifted her chin and told him boldly, 'I'm one hundred per cent old-fashioned common sense.'

At that, Mitch muttered a curse and strode out of the room.

And after he left, Grace stared at the empty doorway, feeling numb, as if her entire body had been anaesthetised from the eyebrows down. Why was Mitch so angry? How could he possibly expect her to go out to dinner with him and, presumably, take up where Candy left off? He knew she wasn't the type for a casual on-again, off-again affair.

How long she stood there she wasn't sure, but she was still in exactly the same position when Mitch came charging back.

'Here's the list of people we need to fly in for the launch.' He thrust a sheet of paper under her nose.

'Great. Thanks,' she replied dully, while her eyes skimmed the names listed in his spiky handwriting. One name jumped out at her. '*George Hervey?* You're inviting him?'

'Yeah. Your old mentor and number one fan. Surely you haven't got a problem with *that*?'

Horrified, she shook the page at Mitch. 'Of course I have. You can't invite George. It would be awful for him.'

He stared at her with the same stunned expression he might have worn if she'd accused him of kidnapping Santa Claus. 'Why shouldn't George be part of the celebration?'

'For heaven's sake, Mitch! How could you be so mean? Why do you have to rub poor George's nose in your own success?'

Bursting with moral indignation, Grace threw her hands in the air. How could Mitch be so insensitive? 'Wasn't it bad enough that you railroaded your way into the company with your bully-boy take-over bid? You threw George out to pasture. At the very least you could leave him in peace.'

'Grace, I will not be yelled at.'

She blinked as she realised just how loud her voice had become, and dropped her tone several decibels. 'George treated me almost like a daughter. Can't you see how terrible this would be for the poor man?'

Talk about coming back to earth! With the speed of a pricked party balloon, her very last, fragile hope about Mitch's integrity lay, deflated and shrivelled, at her feet. It was one thing for him to flit from woman to woman as the fancy took him, but how could he be so mean-spirited? How could he invite the man whose business he'd commandeered to witness his own hour of triumph?

Mitch was looking thunderous. 'I guess it's fair to say that, in your opinion, I've made an error of judgement.'

Grace whirled around. 'I'm completely shocked.'

'George doesn't have to accept the invitation.'

'Of course he does. He has his pride.' She stared at the ceiling, shaking her head. 'But I can't understand you, Mitch. You're either totally vindictive and egotistical or completely insensitive. Either way, you're not the kind of man I could ever lo—' Just in time she clamped her mouth shut.

'What was that, Grace? Were you about to mention—*love*?' He stepped towards her, his intense gaze lancing her, stripping away the protective shield of her anger.

Grace gulped, squirming under his probing stare, and she tried to pretend she hadn't heard that word, but she knew her cheeks were blazing.

'Were you about to admit—' His voice cracked dangerously '—that you—that we have something special going?'

She shook her head. 'I—I—' Totally flustered, she attacked from a different angle. 'What is it with men? Why do you all have to be so—so vicious? You seem to relish waging corporate warfare.'

But for some reason, Mitch wasn't glaring at her any more. He relaxed against her filing cabinet and folded his arms casually across his chest. 'So you think we're all brutes in suits?'

In desperation, her voice rose again. 'You bought out this company and now you want to parade poor old George like some kind of battle trophy.'

'Another male strikes a blow for his own ego?' suggested Mitch with the hint of a smile.

'How can you joke about this? It's disastrous.'

What was so disastrous was the obvious fact that Mitch was just as selfish as she had always feared.

'Hang on, Grace, I think you have a rather personalised view of disaster.' The old teasing glint was back in Mitch's eyes. He glanced at his watch. 'Look, I really don't have time to argue the toss with you. I have a corporation or two to raid.'

She sniffed at his flippant rejection of her well-placed criticism.

'So,' he continued, 'I'll leave you to issue George Hervey with an invitation, and, as you have such a special relationship with the dear fellow and you're so worried about his fragile ego, if he accepts, I want *you* to be his personal escort at the launch.'

Without so much as a by-your-leave, Mitch strode swiftly out of her office once more. Grace didn't close her mouth until some time after he had left.

CHAPTER THIRTEEN

CHAMPAGNE CORKS POPPED. Glasses clinked and cameras flashed.

Beneath feathery palm trees, laughter and light-hearted chatter floated on the warm, tropical winter air as guests met and mingled at the poolside reception area.

The launch of *New Tomorrow* was in full swing.

At the entry to the hotel's pool area, Grace acted as hostess, greeting guests and handing out promotional packages. The celebrity stars had arrived and were being fussed over by the local mayor and other city dignitaries.

Out of the corner of her eye, she watched Mitch circulating, soaking up the back-slaps and the hearty congratulations and smiling charmingly at the furiously batting feminine eyelashes. In his sleek suit, crisp shirt and silk tie, he was looking his corporate best.

Almost all the region's top business people had turned up, but, to Grace's relief, although George Hervey had accepted the invitation, he had not made an appearance. Perhaps he'd changed his mind.

She could almost relax.

Checking her watch, she reassured herself that everything was running to schedule. Waiters circulated with huge silver platters offering a range of cheeses and dainty seafood combinations served on water crackers. A suitably eager pack of journalists and photographers panted around the speakers' podium, angling their cameras and thrusting their microphones forward.

Finally, the Minister, looking as dignified and pompous as an opera star about to burst into his favourite aria, moved onto the podium to address the crowd. 'The making of *New Tomorrow* is a sound investment for the people of this state,' he boomed, and his arm extended to acknowledge Mitch, who had joined him.

'This project is a fine example of the great partnership that can be achieved between our government and the private sector.'

In the manner of all politicians, phrases glowing with promise rolled off his tongue and his florid face deepened in colour as he warmed to his topic.

Grace circled around the edge of the crowd, checking that all was well. Drinks waiters were standing by, ready to top up people's glasses for the toasts. And as soon as the speeches were over, hot savouries would be served. Everything seemed in order.

Except her. She longed to escape. What she wanted most was to hang a sign around her neck stating, 'Out of order' or 'Gone fishing'.

If only she could vanish. This revelry was proving much more of an ordeal than she had anticipated. She was the only person present who had nothing to celebrate. Before the first scene of this movie could be shot, she would be gone.

Luckily, over the past week, since she'd discovered just exactly what kind of corporate commando Mitch was, she had hardly seen him.

Everyone in the company had been swarming frantically backwards and forwards, from one task to the next, like distracted ants. Mitch's casual assumption that a launch could be pulled together in a matter of days without much disruption had been another example of his supreme arrogance.

But they had done it. The launch was happening.

And with that behind them she would be able to say goodbye to Tropicana Films and Mitchell J. Wentworth once and for all.

But the prospect of leaving still hurt.

Coming to terms with the realisation that she had pegged Mitch correctly from the start was the hardest lesson of her life. Perhaps one day she would be able to rid herself of this gnawing sense of loss. One day her head would find a way to teach her heart to stop pounding whenever he or his company or his movies were mentioned.

She could rationalise it all in her mind. The facts spoke for themselves. Mitch was so handsome, charming and sexy that he could believe his own hype and forget about the feelings of others. But when would her heart accept this reality? When would she be able to forget about the other, tender and tantalising side of Mitch? When…?

'Grace!'

Someone whispering her name brought her swivelling around, and her old boss's kind and familiar face came into focus. 'George!'

'How are you, my dear?'

Looking more frail than she remembered, the elderly and balding George Hervey flung a fatherly arm around her shoulders and gave her a peck on the cheek.

'It's so good to see you,' she whispered. 'I thought you'd changed your mind about coming.'

'Plane was delayed taking off from Mascot,' George explained. 'What's this fellow rambling on about?' He squinted towards the Minister on the podium. 'Let's get out of here and you can tell me your news. I never did like political speeches.' George took Grace's hand and drew her towards a door leading out of the pool area.

Happy to escape, she followed without a murmur. And, as they hurried away, George said, 'You're looking more beautiful than ever, Grace. Working for Mitch must agree with you.'

How courageous this man is, she thought. Here he is, cut to the core over his loss of Tropicana Films, and he takes time to pay me compliments. All her protective instincts sprang into high gear. And, once the glass doors cut them off from the crowd, she turned to her old friend. 'George, you're a brave man.'

'I am?' he replied with a puzzled smile.

'Of course you are. I couldn't believe Mitch made you come here today. And I don't blame you at all for wanting to escape the celebrations. All that chest-beating and trumpet-blowing. It's offensive.'

'Some of the speeches can be tedious,' George agreed. 'But I'll go back out there when Mitch talks. I want to hear what he has to say.'

'Oh, no, you don't.'

'Why not? Have you heard Mitch speak? I can't imagine he would be boring.'

'But it will be so painful for you, George.'

George looked puzzled. 'My dear, I'm feeling perfectly well. I'm quite fit actually, even if I do look a bit decrepit.'

'Oh, I don't mean physically painful. I mean emotionally...' Grace brought her hand to her heart. 'You must be feeling so hurt—so distressed and—and resentful.'

'You're confusing me, Grace. Come and sit down.'

They headed for some deep cane chairs in the hotel foyer.

'Can I get you something to drink—a cup of tea, perhaps?' she asked.

'No, no. I'll eat and drink my fill when I go back out there in a minute. Now, tell me how things are going for you.'

Grace tossed a grand gesture in the direction of the celebrations beyond the huge wall of glass. 'Tropicana is the name on everyone's lips!'

George leaned forward. 'But how are you, Grace? Are you happy?'

Hesitating to tell too much, she twisted her hands together. 'I wish I was still working for you,' she said at last. When she looked up, she was surprised to see George looking pale and anxious.

'But, my dear, you wouldn't have a job.'

Grace frowned. 'What are you talking about?'

'There'd be no Tropicana Films.'

'That's rubbish.'

George took off his glasses and polished them with his handkerchief. He blinked myopically at Grace. 'I was sure the news would have filtered through by now—about the mess I made of the company.'

'M-m-mess?'

'A dreadful mess, my dear. I made some extremely unwise decisions and managed to let Tropicana fall into bad shape. Very bad shape indeed. If it wasn't for Mitch Wentworth rescuing the company when it was on the verge of bankruptcy, there would be no Tropicana Films.'

At Grace's gasp of astonishment, he patted her hand and nodded. 'The dear boy took a huge gamble and invested his life's savings to bale me out.'

'But he…but he…' She groped for words with the desperation of someone drowning, but was forced to give up. 'You were *happy* for him to take over?'

'Deliriously.' George replaced his spectacles and his blue eyes blazed with certainty. 'I was facing financial ruin and the threat of a poverty-stricken old age. I'm indebted to Mitch and I'm just so relieved that it looks like he'll make a go of it.'

She stared back at George, shaking her head. 'But why didn't he explain all that to me? He's known all along that I believed he'd bullied you into selling out.'

'He never said anything?'

Grace shook her head again. She felt confused, guilty…ill.

'I guess he didn't want to broadcast my failure. He's a gentleman, Grace.'

'No, he's not,' she retorted automatically. 'He can't be. He…'

George looked a little shamefaced. 'I'm really sorry I didn't explain all this to you at the time. But a man has his pride. You looked up to me, and I'm afraid I was rather weak. I took the coward's way out and just crept quietly away. I didn't want to see your disappointment.'

'Oh, George.' Grace left her chair and stooped to give him a hug. 'I wouldn't have thought any the worse of you.' She sighed heavily. 'But I might have thought just a little more highly of my new boss.'

George patted her arm. 'It's a pity that you and he haven't hit it off. I've been nursing a secret fantasy that you two are a perfect match.'

'Really? What a ridiculous notion.' Grace could feel a blush coming on. Quickly, she tried to change the subject. 'You said you wanted to hear Mitch's speech. Perhaps you'd better go back.'

George's news had rocked her completely. Needing a chance to take it all in, she dragged him out of his chair and almost pushed him towards the pool area.

She desperately wanted time to think.

As she watched George go, Grace felt all at sea. Disoriented. It was as if her understanding of north and south, right and wrong, truth and falsehood had broken loose—leaving her to drift without a chart.

Mitch's take-over had been a rescue?

She remembered his stunned expression when she'd harangued him mercilessly about his mistreatment of George.

The male corporate raider was a gentleman?

She stood stiffly, watching through the glass, following George's stooped figure as he mingled with the crowd. And in the distance she could see Mitch at the microphone, smiling, waving his hand to acknowledge the applause. She watched the guests raise their glasses...heard the faint cheers...saw the cameras flashing...saw Mitch smiling...felt tears slide down her cheeks.

Don't get too sentimental, a warning inner voice whispered. *Remember Candy.*

But somehow Candy's accusations had a hollow ring to them now. Mitch had always claimed bewilderment whenever she'd dropped hints about Candy.

Perhaps...

Grabbing tissues from her shoulder bag, she mopped at her face and began to walk forward slowly.

Perhaps...

She had to speak to him.

Predictably, by the time Grace drew near to Mitch, he was surrounded by a throng of well-wishers, who had rushed forward to shake his hand.

Standing to one side, she waited quietly, watching him while her heart raced. She watched him deliver his killer charm as effortlessly as he might spread jam on toast. A little lopsided smile here, a twinkle of the eye there. A polite laugh for one man's joke, concentrated attention for another's more serious comments.

Then he saw her.

Her chest tightened unbearably as his dark eyes locked onto hers.

The group clustered around him continued to gush and chatter, but Mitch stared straight at Grace. For a brief second, his eyes wandered vaguely to a woman who was trying to ask him a question, but Grace saw him offer an excuse.

As he continued to watch her closely, Mitch separated from the crowd and made his way towards her.

Her heart drummed.

'You were wanting to speak to me?' he asked.

CHAPTER FOURTEEN

NOW HER KNEES knocked together. She needed to run into Mitch's arms. To apologise—to ask a thousand questions.

He was so tall, so dangerously, dreamily beautiful.

Single-handed, he'd rescued Tropicana Films.

'I—I need to speak to you about one of the guests, Mr Wentworth,' she said, in the most businesslike voice she could manage.

Mitch glanced at a gaggle of bystanders, queuing to meet him. 'Right now, Ms Robbins?'

'If you'd be so kind.' She tried to keep her face impassive, but was defeated by the fat tear that filled her right eye.

He frowned. And, for a heart-wrenching moment, he hesitated and glanced again at the throng waiting to speak to him. And she imagined he was considering refusing her request. But then he turned politely to the line of people gathered behind him. 'If you'll excuse me,' he murmured, 'I need to consult with my executive assistant.'

Grace saw a waiter coming from the kitchen with a fresh plate of crispy Chinese chicken wings. She beckoned to him. 'These people are hungry,' she said, indicating the group Mitch had been speaking to, and he hastily moved to serve them. Fortunately they murmured appreciatively.

Stepping towards Grace, Mitch placed a hand at the small of her back and steered her away from the crowd.

'Can we go somewhere private?' she asked, then bit her lip anxiously.

His eyes widened with surprise, but to her relief he nodded and turned towards the far end of the pool. As they walked, his hand stayed at her back and she sensed its warmth through the fine linen of her blouse.

He didn't speak till they reached a rectangle of grass screened off from the crowds by clusters of golden cane palms.

Suddenly hopelessly nervous, Grace came to an abrupt halt. She turned to stare at the peaceful view across Cleveland Bay. In the distance, she could make out the faint blue humps of the Palm Islands.

Mitch spoke quietly. 'You implied you have something important to discuss?'

She sucked in a deep breath of sea air, searching for a way to voice what needed to be said—that she'd been wrong about him and that she was sorry. 'I—I think I owe you an apology.'

Her words were gabbled and for a moment he looked startled. Then his hands rose to rest on his hips, pushing aside the elegant Italian suit coat. 'Do you, now?' His jaw relaxed and his face broke into a slow, teasing smile. 'Have you encountered the first step in my five-point plan?'

'The problem is,' Grace rushed on, shifting her line of sight from the gleam in his eye to a cloud drifting across the patch of afternoon sky beyond his right shoulder, 'I've kept thinking of you as...' She paused. 'Five-point-plan? What are you talking about?'

'I'll explain in due course. A man has to take precautions with you, Grace. But don't get sidetracked. You were talking about an apology. I'm intrigued.'

Grace squirmed, suddenly wary about baring her soul if Mitch still had something up his sleeve. 'But what's this five-point-plan?'

His head was cocked to one side, his expression bemused. 'My, my, you *are* impatient.'

'You've presented me with a puzzle, and I have one of those minds that likes to work things out.'

Mitch folded his arms across his chest and looked infuriatingly relaxed. 'It's the downside of being born with a brain. Now, let me hear why you dragged me away from my guests.'

'Oh,' she said, taking a deep breath. 'I've been talking to George Hervey.'

He regarded her steadily, but remained silent.

Her mouth twisted with the effort to hold back her nervousness. 'I think you knew that if George came here I would find out you didn't bulldoze him out of the way. That I've been holding a grudge against you—based on—not knowing the truth.'

Mitch's eyes glowed.

'What I'm trying to say is, I'm so sorry, Mitch. I was so rude to you. But how was I to know that you aren't a—a—?'

'A gold-plated rat?'

'Oh, Mitch.' Another tear rolled down her cheek.

With a soft sound, he reached out and gently traced the tear's path. 'I was certainly gambling on the fact that if you had a chance to speak to George, an intelligent woman like you could be trusted to put two and two together,' he murmured.

'And come up with point-number-one in this plan of yours?' she asked, curving her cheek closer into his touch.

He drew her nearer and chuckled as he lowered his face to hers. 'Yes, my clever Grace. That's exactly what I hoped.'

She shivered deliciously as their lips met.

There was an embarrassed cough behind them. 'Mr Wentworth?'

Mitch's head jerked back. 'What is it?'

'Er—the Minister will be leaving shortly, sir. He has another meeting to attend.'

'Yes, of course.' Mitch sighed. He looked at his watch. 'All right. I'm coming. Give me two minutes.'

As soon as the messenger had gone, Grace whispered, 'Two minutes? There are so many things I need to ask you.' You could start with *Candy*, a warning voice niggled. But Grace didn't want to spoil this moment. Not when Mitch's dark eyes were sending her so many silent promises.

'I'm all ears. Fire away with your questions,' he said.

'We couldn't possibly get through points two to five in two minutes.'

He brushed his lips across her forehead. 'Patience, Grace.'

'I'm running out of patience,' she breathed.

'We don't want to rush something that's vitally important to get right.' He smiled and trailed slow, seductive kisses down her cheek. 'Will you promise not to disappear if I ask you to give me another hour? And then we'll discuss these matters in minute detail.' He sighed. 'But at the moment there are still a lot of people expecting to talk to me.'

Somehow she forced herself to reply. 'I suppose I could wait just a little longer.'

'I hope *I* can,' he murmured, dropping one last kiss behind her ear. 'And you'll promise to hang around?'

'Of course.'

They rejoined the crowd and, very quickly, Mitch was absorbed once more into the enthusiastic mood of the launch.

As soon as the Minister had been farewelled, Grace popped some snacks onto a plate for Mitch which he accepted with thanks and a wink, before continuing to discuss the brilliant quality of the natural light in North Queensland with a group of cameramen.

How can he stay so composed? she wondered as she mingled and chatted and tried to talk sense. She found it enormously difficult to concentrate on what people were saying. Especially as the whole time she conversed she was aware of Mitch, head and shoulders above the crowd.

He kept catching her eye and sending her knowing, secretive smiles. And each time her insides rippled with delight. But the ordeal of keeping up appearances for sixty long minutes was exhausting.

Eventually, as the sun began to dip into the sea, Maria appeared at her elbow. 'Grace, this arrived for you.' From behind her back, her friend produced a huge bouquet of flowers—beautiful native Australian wildflowers: wattles and banksias, grevilleas and wild irises.

Grace stared at the arrangement. 'They're beautiful. Are you sure they're for me and not for one of the stars?' she asked.

Maria shook her head. 'The fellow who delivered them insisted that they're for you. But the card's weird. No name on it. Just says "Point number two".'

'Oh,' Grace gasped.

'Oh?' queried Maria, studying her shrewdly. 'So you know who they're from?'

'Um, I have a fair idea.'

'Our esteemed boss tickling your fancy again?'

When Grace didn't answer, Maria added with a knowing smile, 'I have inside information that tells me things are looking good for you, Grace. But look at you! You're already bursting with... something.'

Grace smiled. It was no use trying to fool Maria. 'I was hoping it wasn't too obvious, but I'm so worked up, I feel like I'm about to explode.'

Maria cast a quick glance at her friend and then at the assembled guests. 'Can I suggest you implode? It's not as messy, and these people are all dressed up in their best bibs and tuckers.'

The two women burst into a fit of giggles.

For Grace, it was a relief to let off some of her pent-up emotion. Every part of her longed for Mitch, and yet she didn't know if she should dare to hope. All they really had between them were a few blissful days in the outback. Since then they'd done nothing but fight. And then, of course, there was the Candy factor.

'There's George Hervey,' commented Maria.

On the far side of the pool, Mitch and George were deep in conversation. And, as Grace watched, George gave Mitch a hearty pat on the back and the two men shook hands. There was a great deal of nodding and grinning and even some outright laughter. They were clearly on very good terms.

'Unless my eyes are deceiving me, our Mr W. can't be quite the black-hearted invader we imagined,' commented Maria.

Grace quickly explained what George had told her.

'Phew!' Maria whistled, before giving Grace a not-so-gentle

shove. 'What are you waiting for? Get over there. This party's about to fold very soon anyway.'

Grace didn't need any further encouragement. Mitch was checking his watch and looking in her direction.

They exchanged cautious smiles and began to walk towards each other.

'Has anyone ever told you how stunning you look? How you stand out in a crowd?' he asked as they met.

'Thanks for the flowers, Mitch.'

He grinned and, heedless of curious stares, shot a possessive arm around her shoulders. 'That restaurant I mentioned last week,' he said, 'I have a booking for this evening. Will you join me for dinner?'

'Tonight?' She looked around at the scattered remaining guests, the attendants now clearing away wine and food. A waiter was chasing paper serviettes that had been caught by a gust of sea air and now danced towards the pool. She waved a hand at the scene. 'In the midst of all this, you found time to make a booking?'

'And order flowers. That nosy little workmate of yours—the one with the big mouth. She has her moments of efficiency.'

'Maria?' Grace felt her own mouth drop open and she swung round to see Maria speeding through a side door.

'So you'll come?'

She couldn't bear to refuse. 'Is this point number three?'

His face broke into a slow, teasing smile. 'I didn't realise you suffered from such a burning curiosity. Is this Pandora complex of yours a new development?'

She suppressed a sigh, feeling on such tenterhooks, she didn't know whether to laugh or cry. By accepting his flowers, by going out with Mitch, she was risking being hurt one more time. Could she bear it if everything fell apart now?

'Let's go,' Mitch urged.

She hesitated. 'Shouldn't I help with farewelling people?'

'No,' he answered succinctly. 'Maria and her crew are doing a fine job.'

'What about George? I'm afraid I haven't looked after him as well as you ordered.'

'George is fine. The Mayor's wife has invited him home for dinner.'

'Oh, how nice,' murmured Grace. Her mouth opened ready for another protest—but it was difficult to find something else to protest about.

With a finger pressed under her chin, Mitch nudged her lips together again. 'My beautiful Grace, forget George Hervey,' he whispered. 'Forget Maria. I want you to concentrate all your attention on me.'

Eyes brimming suddenly, she gave up and nodded her willingness.

He offered her his elbow. Obediently she threaded her arm through his, and together they hurried to the car park where Mitch's car waited.

They were the first diners to arrive at the old worker's cottage that had been restored and transformed into a restaurant. The sun was just setting as Grace and Mitch were led down a narrow brick path to the back garden.

A table in a secluded corner, under a spreading sea almond tree, was reserved for them. From the branches above hung bud lights fashioned into the shape of stars. Even though it wasn't completely dark, they looked very pretty, and Grace couldn't hide her delight.

'This is just lovely—quite enchanting,' she commented as soon as they were seated.

Mitch grinned. 'I thought it might be a little different.' He looked at her across the table and Grace knew from the appreciative glimmer in his eyes and the warmth of his smile that he was enjoying what he saw.

She wondered what they were going to talk about. Were they here, as she hoped, to build bridges?

'Do you realise this is our first official date?' Mitch asked.

'I guess so,' she answered softly, and his words increased her shyness. Carefully, she unfolded the starched serviette and spread it over her lap, wiping her damp palms as she did so.

He smiled. 'You know, with your tawny hair and natural tan, you make me think of a lioness—a proud and very lovely lioness.'

Grace had to smile. 'My star sign is Leo. Maybe that has something to do with it.'

'Leo? That would make your birthday some time soon, wouldn't it?'

'Yes,' she replied, feeling suddenly very awkward. 'August 6th, to be exact.'

A dark shadow dimmed Mitch's smile. 'The day you finish with the company,' he said softly.

'Life's full of little ironies,' she quipped, amazed at the steadiness in her voice.

The waiter arrived with a jug of iced water and the menus, and Grace was grateful for the distraction. She would be able to fill in some time choosing her meal. Now that she had the chance to fire questions at Mitch, to find out exactly where she stood, she was reluctant to probe.

The truth might hurt.

In the few minutes since they'd arrived, night had fallen and another group of diners entered the garden, chatting happily. Her eyes scanned the menu choices, and her hand flew to her mouth. Only one item was listed.

Roasted freshwater crayfish and sautéed water lily bulbs served on a fresh pandanus leaf.

Grace stared in silence at the page before her and her heart hammered loudly as she dragged her eyes past Mitch to the multiple loops of starry lights shimmering above them.

Her head spun.

'Grace, are you all right?' Mitch reached across the table and cupped her shaking hand in both of his.

She tried to speak, but she couldn't. *Crayfish, water lilies, stars! What was going on here?* Tears welled, blurring her vision and blocking her throat.

'I know it's a bit theatrical of me,' Mitch said with a sheepish grin.

Grace managed to clear her throat. 'It certainly is,' she croaked, pointing to the menu and then to the stars above. 'Things like this are only supposed to happen in the movies.'

His fingers played with her hand. 'I wanted to find a way to take us back.'

'Back to the rock pool?'

'To when things were right between us.'

She watched as his strong brown fingers gently massaged her hand, while her heart jigged at a rickety pace. 'Out there...things... between us were very...*right*, weren't they?' she asked hesitantly.

'Couldn't have been *righter*.' He grinned, and Grace found it impossible not to smile back. He lifted her hand to his lips and her spine tingled deliciously as his mouth met her fingertips. 'When we were out there, we were able to forget about the outside world. We had no external pressures...'

'Apart from the pressure of survival,' Grace reminded him.

'Of course. And we shouldn't underestimate that we were in real danger. But, apart from that, the wilderness stripped us of all our emotional baggage, didn't it?'

Grace nodded. How could she not agree? She'd been a completely different person in the outback. So many times since they'd returned, she'd wondered if that had been the *real* Grace.

'We had no past, the future was in doubt, we had virtually no possessions,' he continued. 'We were just two people dealing with an ever-present danger. It's the kind of situation that brings out the best and the worst in people.' He squeezed her hand. 'And with us it was the best that came out. The very best.'

'And the office brings out the worst?' She couldn't help asking as she remembered how every time he'd tried to talk to her lately they'd ended up fighting.

'I wouldn't say that,' Mitch replied thoughtfully. 'I think what went wrong was the rapid transition back. We didn't get a chance to adjust. When that army patrol turned up out of the blue, everything finished so abruptly. One minute we were about to make love, and the next we were winging our way back to Townsville in a Black Hawk.'

She noticed that he didn't mention the minor detail of Candy's intrusion into their lives.

'So what I propose,' he said, keeping her hand firmly in his, 'is that tonight we try to cheat time.' Mitch's mouth quirked into a crooked smile and Grace realised, with an overwhelming rush of affection, that he was nervous. 'We should imagine we are still at our outback rock pool, and we can talk about how we want to continue from there. We should forget about anything that has happened since then.'

Grace lowered her eyes from the intensity of his gaze. 'I'm leaving town, Mitch. How can we forget that I'm going away?'

'We just put it out of our minds for now.' He reached out and snapped his fingers near her ear. 'Abracadabra. We've gone back in time. Remember?'

'I'll try,' she whispered.

Mitch added, 'I think you'll find the crayfish and water lilies are prepared in a more inventive manner than we managed out in the bush.'

'I'm looking forward to it.' Grace sent him a newly determined and almost optimistic smile. 'And this restaurant put on a special menu just for us?'

'Just for you and me, Grace. Consider yourself a celebrity.'

The meal was delicious. Mitch had already selected a very classy wine to accompany their food. The crayfish was served with a delicate pesto sauce and the water lilies were roasted with garlic and mushrooms. These were accompanied by a tasty side dish of carrots and green beans in a bush honey glaze.

While they ate, they carefully talked about the future as if there were no clouds on the horizon. They talked about *New Tomorrow*, about the location decisions, about how Mitch had first come up with the idea and what he hoped to achieve. It was all very pleasant.

Very safe.

But, while they waited for their desserts of exotic tropical fruit and ice cream drizzled with mango liqueur, Mitch reached out to take Grace's hand once more. He opened his mouth to speak and then seemed to lose confidence.

Surprised, she felt a sympathetic thrill bring goose bumps out on her arms. Even before Mitch spoke again, she knew he wanted to divert the conversation down a more serious path, and her heart began to pump painfully.

'Something happened to me in the outback,' he said at last, his dark eyes regarding her tenderly. 'It's never happened before.'

'Never?' she whispered.

He shook his head and his smile was actually shy. 'I've never fallen bang flat on my face into—into such emotional overload before.'

Their desserts arrived while Grace assimilated this admission. Once the waiter had gone, she commented, 'This—this overload occurrence—doesn't sound like a very pleasant experience.'

Mitch put down his spoon. 'Grace, falling for you has to be the ultimate of all experiences I can expect in this lifetime.'

Her cheeks blazed.

'The painfully unpleasant part has been the aftermath. The way I made such a crazy mess of everything—and then received your resignation.'

She made a fuss of stirring her fruits into her ice cream while her mind and heart whizzed and thumped in dizzying confusion.

'All that stuff that's been written about unrequited love. It's actually worse than the poets make out.' While he spoke, Mitch switched to staring fiercely at the urn of ferns beside her, but now his eyes swung back to her. 'And I find it particularly painful when, deep down, I believe you really do care.'

Grace stabbed at her plate, but suddenly she couldn't see the fruit. 'You—' She gulped. 'That night in my flat, you said loving— I mean—being romantically attached to me—was inconvenient.'

'I said a lot of rubbish.'

'And what about...?'

His eyes speared hers. 'What about...what?'

Oh, why did she have so much difficulty asking questions... asking for kisses...asking about Candy...?

'Candy!' she burst out at last. 'What about Candy?' Her question seemed to hang in the air. And her heart beat so loudly, its sound filled her eardrums.

He frowned. 'Just what is it about Candy that has you so upset?'

Her mouth gaped. 'Everything!' she cried. Then she hurried on, 'No, if I'm honest, it's just one thing. The fact that you and she have a special *understanding.*'

'She told you that?'

Grace nodded. 'I couldn't stand thinking of you—of the two of you—'

'She claimed we were sleeping together?'

She shot him a challenging glare. 'She sure implied that.'

Mitch's fingers drummed on the tabletop. 'I can't believe you listened to her. How could you believe that?'

'Why shouldn't I?'

'Because I never gave you any reason to believe it.'

'Oh?' Grace gulped. She could think of several times Mitch had allowed Candy to drape herself all over him. Several days he'd spent closeted with her in his office. Several nights he'd spent in the same hotel as her.

Still, she had to admit, there was no real evidence.

'I didn't touch the woman. Yeah, she made a play for me, but I don't think I even gave her a peck on the cheek. I swear it.' His thoughtful gaze held hers, but then dropped as he picked up his wineglass and carefully placed it at another spot on the table, as if he were moving a chess piece. He stared at the glass as he spoke. 'You know she made it a condition of the finance that I get rid of you?'

'What?' The blood rushed into Grace's cheeks.

'I wouldn't hear of it, of course.'

'But, Mitch, you could have lost everything.'

Lost everything!

His company, his project, his dreams! *Everything!* Stunned, Grace stared at him, her own words echoing over and over in her head. He would have sacrificed all that *for her*!

'I couldn't let you go.'

'Oh, no,' groaned Grace. 'And then I resigned anyhow.' Her guilty eyes grew round as another thought struck. 'That night I resigned...you wanted to me to come back to dinner at the hotel, hoping I'd suss Candy out and—and find a way to support you.'

Grace couldn't bear thinking about how she'd let Mitch down, how she'd roared out of that car park without giving him a chance to explain, how she'd handed in that primly worded, watertight resignation...had refused to talk...

His soft words broke through her remorse. 'We've got to forget all that now. All I want to think about tonight is you, my sweet girl. About us. Ever since we got back to town, it's been like there was a part of me that was missing. The most vital part.'

His astonishing words flowed into her, bringing with them a flood of warmth and well-being. 'I've been an absolute mess, too,' she whispered, and her admission seemed to set something free inside her. It was as if all the pieces of her disintegrating heart were being drawn together and were settling back into place.

'Let's get out of here,' urged Mitch, scraping back his chair as he jumped to his feet. 'We have some serious catching up to do.'

The waiter was approaching their table with a tray holding coffee and chocolates. Mitch quickly explained that they were leaving and asked for the bill instead and, as soon as he had dealt with it, he bundled Grace ahead of him out of the restaurant. His car was parked only a few metres away.

'Now, where was I?' he murmured, gathering her into his arms as he leaned back against the car door, pulling her with him.

'You were going to kiss me?' she asked breathlessly.

'Just a moment,' he teased in a throaty whisper. His lips moved slowly up her neck to linger along her jawline. 'It's my turn to ask for a kiss.'

In a sensuous haze, she lifted her arms to circle his neck. Slowly, she repeated his action, moving her lips along his jaw and nibbling gently. 'You can start asking any time you like.'

As kisses went, it eclipsed all the others. Shameless desire ricocheted through Grace with the lightning pace of a laser. In seconds she was trembling with need. 'Take me home quickly, Mitch,' she pleaded.

'Try stopping me.'

They reached her flat in record time and tumbled out of the car in a laughing, eager scurry. Mitch kissed her again at the front door and, once inside, he clasped her to him with a groan of raw passion.

'Grace, you've no idea...'

'Shush,' she whispered against his cheek and, taking him by the hand, she led him across her lounge room.

'Hold on, sweetheart.' His arms came round her, halting her progress. He held her against him and lifted her hair away from her face, tucking it behind one ear. 'Any minute now I'm going

to totally lose my head, but there's something I want to say first.'
He kissed her exposed ear, then smiled at her.

By the soft light of a table-lamp, she could see the tender warmth
in his eyes, the slight tremor at the corner of his mouth. Her heart
sky-rocketed.

'I need to tell you about…' he murmured roughly, but then his
words died as his lips grazed hers, once, twice, and with his body
he steered her to the sofa. He pulled her down beside him for a
kiss that was deep and hungry and urgent—as if he needed her
more than oxygen.

And, when he finally pulled away, she cried, 'Don't stop!'

'I thought you wanted to know about points four and five.'

'I thought you'd started.'

Her eyes were held by his suddenly serious expression. 'Not
quite.' He held her close and ordered softly, 'Ms Robbins, I'm
going to explain these points very clearly and I will expect you to
take in every detail.'

Taking her hands in his, he stroked with his thumbs the faint
blue veins just beneath the skin of her wrists. 'First, don't ever let
anything or anyone like Candy get in our way again.'

She nodded, and sobbed happy tears. 'I'm sorry, Mitch. I was
too willing to misjudge you. I was so sure you were prepared to
do anything to achieve business success.'

'What you must realise is that I love you, Grace,' he said softly,
just a little shyly. 'And this is a first for me. I've never felt this way
about anybody. I love your mind, your body—every tiny, wonderful thing about—'

She couldn't resist throwing her arms about his neck and crushing his lips with hers. 'Oh, Mitch,' she cried. 'Oh, Mitch. I'm so
happy. I can't believe this.'

'You'd better believe it,' he said, pressing a warning finger to
her mouth. 'And you must promise me that you won't be afraid
to ask me anything. Come to me with every doubt. I—I want to
share my life with you.'

Tears poured down Grace's cheeks and burned her throat. She
couldn't speak, but she leaned her face against his and kissed Mitch
with happy little kisses.

His hands came up to cradle her head and he returned her kiss with breathtaking reverence. When at last he lifted his face from hers, he smiled. 'I'm afraid I can't promise you wealth. Tropicana Films might end up successful, but that's in the lap of the gods at this stage. All I can offer you is my love and my life, but I am hoping that will be enough to convince you that we should be married.'

She swiped at her tears and smiled through her sniffles.

'So this is my fourth point. Will you marry me?'

'I have a point to make, too.'

'You'll marry me?'

'Just a minute, Mitch,' she said gently. 'Now you're the impatient one.'

'No doubt about that. Come on, put me out of my misery.'

'I just want to make it clear that I love you too, Mitch. I'm sorry for the kind of tantrums that prompted me to resign. I want to tell you I'd stay here to be with you without the job. I might love my work, but I know now that I love you more.'

'Thank God,' breathed Mitch. 'But you've kind of stolen my thunder. The last point I planned to demand was that a condition of our marriage involved throwing that resignation out the window. Do you think you could handle having me as your boss and your husband?'

'I actually think we make a pretty good team.' Grace knew her smile was a mile wide.

'Unless, of course, you want to get straight into babies and all that scene,' Mitch hastily corrected.

Grace snuggled up close to her man—her sweet gentleman disguised as a seriously sexy, A-grade hunk. 'I'll tell you exactly what I want, Mr W.' She looked him straight in the eye as she spoke. 'I want to make love with you, and I want to marry you, Mitch, my darling. And in between I want to work with you and make movies with you and, one day in the future, I want to make babies with you.' She ticked off her five fingers as she made each point. 'That's the order I have in mind. How does it sound to you?'

Mitch lined his hand up with hers, palm to palm, finger to finger. 'That sounds like the perfect five-point plan to me.'

EPILOGUE

BIG NIGHT AT THE OSCARS
FOR AUSSIES

GLAMOUR ABOUNDED AT this year's Oscars; however, *MOVIE MAG'S* Bridget Winter reports that the Australian contingent from *New Tomorrow* stole the show.

Waiting fans, who had already seen quite a few celebrities make their way down the famous red carpet, erupted when Mitch Wentworth arrived. Tall and rugged in a sleek Armani tuxedo, Mitch looked more like a film star than the producer-director of *New Tomorrow*.

Arm in arm with Mitch was his truly radiant wife of three years, Grace Robbins, and she looked totally stunning in a sea-green body net dusted with seed-pearls. Most of the media contingent agreed that her outfit was by far the most arresting and attractive of the evening.

In fact, Mitch and Grace stole the spotlight from the stars.

Grace's gown will be auctioned to raise money for charity, and bidding is expected to reach tens of thousands.

But the most excited and confused man in the Dorothy Chandler Pavilion was surprise Oscar winner Henry Aspinall, who has been flooded with offers from other Hollywood movie-makers since scoring his award for Most Creative Use of New Technology.

During his emotional acceptance speech, Henry paid tribute to his boss, Mitch Wentworth, thanking him for seeing the amazing potential in his original computer graphics.

Looking like an absent-minded professor who'd stumbled into the Awards Night by mistake, Henry had a permanent attachment in the form of High Sierra's ever-present Candy Sorbell.

After the huge box office success of *New Tomorrow*, Wentworth and crew are now filming a romance set in Thailand from a script written by his talented wife.

Hollywood rumour says these two are inseparable, and it seems that working side by side must agree with them. Grace and Mitch Wentworth have that very special aura which suggests they enjoy the kind of happily ever after the rest of us usually only find at the movies.

* * * * *

Outback Baby

For Lucy Francesca, who was born into our family
at the time this story was coming to life.

CHAPTER ONE

WHEN GEMMA HEARD the pounding on her front door, she knew something was desperately wrong. Startled, she hurried to answer it, hardly expecting to find her best friend on her doorstep, clutching her ten-month-old daughter to her chest as if the baby were a life-preserver.

'I need your help, Gemma. Are you terribly busy?'

Shocked by the fear in her friend's eyes, Gemma slipped a reassuring arm around her shoulders. 'Bel, you know I'm never too busy for you. Come in and tell me what's wrong.'

Isobel stepped into the flat with a shaky sigh and hefted baby Mollie higher on her hip. Her eyes darted to the pile of paperwork on Gemma's dining table. 'Oh, you *are* busy. I'm sorry.'

'Don't worry about this mess.' With a quick dismissive gesture, Gemma gathered up the designs she'd just finished and slipped them into a manila folder. For the moment she would have to put aside her own panic about deadlines and the need to dash this marketing brochure to the printers this afternoon. Isobel was obviously besieged by much more serious problems. 'How can I help?'

To Gemma's horror, Isobel's normally serene face crumpled and tears spilled onto her cheeks. 'It's Dave.'

'Dave? Has something happened in Africa?' Two months earlier, Isobel's husband Dave had been seconded by an Australian aid agency to sink wells in Somalia.

Isobel hugged Mollie even closer and rested a trembling chin on the baby's curly head. 'It's so sudden, it's terrible. He's being held hostage. I'm sure it's all some awful mistake, but rebels are involved.' She drew a deep shuddering breath, clearly trying to suppress the urge to burst into full-scale crying.

'I can't believe it,' Gemma whispered, gripping her friend's cold fingers while she gaped at her.

Surely this sort of thing didn't happen to ordinary people? Not to easygoing, cheerful Dave Jardine?

She groped for the right words and gave up the struggle. 'I'm so sorry. This is terrible. Poor Dave.' The thought of her childhood friend—the boy she'd grown up with in the bush—facing armed rebels was appalling. How could his wife bear it? She stared helplessly at Isobel's white face and whispered, 'What can we do?'

'I'm going to him,' Isobel answered with a determined lift of her chin.

'*You're* going to Africa?' Gemma pulled out another chair and sat down swiftly. This second shock was almost worse than the first. 'What can you do?' she asked at last.

'Apparently I'm the only one who can do anything,' Isobel explained with wide, frightened eyes. 'Because I'm Dave's wife, the people at the Australian Embassy think I can help. Dave's there for humanitarian reasons and they think the rebels are more likely to respond if we work on the family angle.'

'Oh, Isobel, how brave of you!!' Gemma jumped up again and hugged her. 'Lucky Dave to have such a wonderful wife.' She smiled wistfully. 'Love and the kind of marriage that you guys have—it's—it's *amazing*!' For Gemma it was beyond imagining. With a short burst of pride, she remembered that she shared responsibility for this wonderful partnership by introducing Isobel and Dave during their university days.

Her gaze dropped to the innocent baby perched happily on her mother's lap. 'You couldn't dream of taking little Mollie into a dangerous situation like that?'

'No, of course I couldn't.' Isobel sighed and pressed her lips to her daughter's chubby cheek. 'I can't bear the thought of leaving her behind, but that's where you come in, Gem. I've an enormous favour to ask.'

'Of course—I'll do anything.' Gemma did her best to ignore the nervous knot tightening in her stomach as her mind raced.

'I'm sorry I didn't ring you first to warn you, but I knew you were going to be home and…' Isobel's voice trailed away as she looked at her friend hopefully.

'Just tell me how I can help.'

'I was hoping you could mind Mollie for me.'

Gemma gulped. While she adored Mollie, she knew absolutely zilch about caring for babies. She pressed her lips tightly together before she verbalised any of the sudden doubts that swamped her. Of course she could mind a baby. Millions of women all over the world had been doing it for centuries without turning a hair. 'I'd love to have her,' she said with a bright smile.

Isobel reached out and squeezed Gemma's hand. 'I'm sorry I've dumped this on you at such short notice, but I wouldn't trust anyone else to look after my little girl. My parents are on holiday in Spain, as you know. Dave's father is too old—and it has to be someone I know well. Someone who cares about Mollie. Not a nanny I've never met. Honestly, Gem, you're my best friend and, working from home as you do, I couldn't think of anyone better.'

'I'm flattered that you trust me,' Gemma responded warmly, but she couldn't help adding, 'You do realise, don't you, that I—I don't have much experience with babies. Actually—I don't have *any* experience with them.'

'Oh, Gemma, you've been around Mollie heaps. And you'll be amazed how it all comes so instinctively. I'm sure you're a natural!' She gave her daughter a motherly hug. 'And Mollie's really quite a good little poppet.'

'Of course,' Gemma responded quickly, not wanting to alarm her friend. 'She's a darling.' When she thought about Dave's desperate plight and Isobel's brave decision to go to Africa, Gemma knew she could hardly make a fuss about caring for one perfectly harmless and tiny human being.

Her friend's grey eyes brightened. 'Don't worry,' she said, 'I've rung Max. I'm sure he'll be happy to help you any way he can.'

'*Max?*' Gemma had been playing with Mollie's pink toes, but at the mention of Dave's older brother Max, her head jerked up. 'I won't need any help from *him*!'

To her annoyance, Gemma's heart began a fretful pounding.

Since she'd been six years old, Max Jardine had always managed to get under her skin. When they were teenagers, Gemma had never been able to understand why the girls in the outback town of Goodbye Creek, where she and the Jardine boys had gone to school, had scored Max a 'hunk factor' of ten. They had raved about his well-toned body and dark good looks.

'But you've seriously overlooked his personality defects,' she'd pointed out.

'What defects?' the girls had scoffed.

And Gemma had rolled her eyes in disgust. She was well-acquainted with his faults. She'd spent half her childhood on the Jardine's property, camping and canoeing or horse-riding with Dave, and Max had always been in the background, treating her like a bad smell that hung around his brother.

In the years since she'd left the outback she'd only seen Max a handful of times, but nothing had changed. He still looked on her as a lower life-form. She shook her head. 'Max Jardine would know even less than I do about caring for a baby.'

Isobel was regarding Gemma strangely. 'I didn't realise you were so touchy about Max.'

'I'm not *touchy* about him,' Gemma snapped.

Isobel's eyebrows rose. 'If you say so.'

'It's just that I fail to see how a man who spends his whole life marooned in the outback like a hermit with only cattle for company could be any use when it comes to minding Mollie.'

'Maybe you're right,' Isobel agreed cautiously. 'But let's not forget that Max *is* Dave's brother. I had to let him know what had happened.'

Gemma could hardly deny that, but it didn't help her to feel any better. 'How did he react?' she asked warily.

'Actually, I couldn't speak to him directly. There was no answer when I rang through to the property this morning, so I left a message on his answering machine. He must be out in the bush mustering or maybe fencing, so I simply explained what I was going to do.'

'And you told him I would be taking care of Mollie?'

'I said that was my plan.'

'I see.'

Gemma decided there and then that if Max Jardine knew she'd been asked to care for Mollie, she would mind this baby as expertly as a triple-certificated nanny. This wasn't just a case of helping out her best friend. She didn't want to give Mollie's grumpy Uncle Max one tiny chance to criticise her.

Exactly why Gemma cared about Max's opinion was an issue she didn't have time to consider now. She was too busy worrying about how she could mind Mollie *and* carry on her business.

But she would find a way. She might collapse in the attempt, but she would give it her best shot.

Lifting Mollie from Isobel's arms, Gemma cuddled her close. The baby girl was soft and warm and smelt delicious. 'Tell me everything I need to know about our little darling.'

'Oh, Gem. I'm so relieved. I knew I could depend on you.' Isobel let out a relieved sigh. 'I can give you everything you'll need for Mollie. In fact, my bag's packed and I have it all in the car.'

'You mean you're heading off today?'

'It's important that I get to Dave as fast as I can. I'll get Mollie's things for you now.'

'Sure,' Gemma replied, more confidently than she felt. 'You get the baby gear and I'll make us some coffee.'

By the time she'd drunk her coffee, Gemma's mind was reeling. She had three closely written pages of detailed instructions about caring for Mollie. At the outset, Isobel had said minding a baby was simple, but Mollie came with more operating instructions than a state-of-the-art computer.

How could one little scrap require so much work? And how, she wondered, after she'd waved goodbye to Isobel, could she suddenly manage Mollie and her business? She looked at the pink and white bundle in her arms and tried to suppress a surge of alarm. She had immediate deadlines to meet and there was the constant need to drum up new clients.

Mollie's round little eyes stared solemnly up at her, reminding Gemma of an unblinking owl. Her heart melted. 'Kiddo, it's
just you and me now. And we're not going to let this lick us.' She
dropped a quick kiss on Mollie's curly head. Then she walked
briskly back up the path to her flat, determined to tackle this task
in as businesslike a fashion as possible.

A swish of tyres behind her brought her spinning around. In
her driveway, a taxi was pulling up and a tall, rangy figure leapt
from the passenger's seat.

Max Jardine!

*How in tarnation had he got from Western Queensland to Bris-
bane so quickly?*

'Gemma!' Max barked as he swung open her front gate and
strode towards her. His piercing blue eyes were fixed on Mollie.
'Where's Isobel?'

'Hello, Max. Nice to see you, too,' Gemma replied coolly while
her heart thudded. Max switched his gaze to her and he glared as
ferociously as a headmaster scowling at an unmanageable pupil.
Suddenly, she felt extremely self-conscious—as if her skirt was too
short, her black stockings too sheer, or her platform heels too high.
No matter how much decorum she'd acquired over the years, this
older brother of Dave's always, always, *always* made her feel like
a silly little girl. 'How did you get here so quickly?' she demanded.

'I flew. I got in early this morning from checking out the back
country and found Isobel's message on the answering machine.'

Gemma remembered that she'd been told Max had invested in
his own light aircraft.

'Well, Isobel's already left for Eagle Farm airport. You probably passed her.'

Max grimaced. 'So she's going ahead with this madcap scheme?'

'Yes, she's a very determined woman.' Gemma hugged Mollie
a little closer. Faced by this angry maelstrom of a man, she found
the baby's warmth and softness reassuring.

Cursing, Max ran impatient fingers through his dark brown hair.
'I should be the one chasing across the world after Dave.'

Gemma smacked a hand to her forehead, pantomime-style, and
beamed at him. 'What a brilliant idea! Why didn't Isobel or I think

of that? You're the obvious choice. You're Dave's brother. You're family but, even better, you're a man. You could spare Isobel the danger and Isobel—' Gemma felt a heady rush of excitement and relief as the next point sank in '—and Isobel could continue to care for Mollie.'

'So you don't want to look after the baby?'

'I—I didn't say that.' Her sense of relief plummeted. She and Max had hardly been talking for thirty seconds and already he'd found a way to put her down. 'Of course I'm happy to mind her, but could you really go to Africa? Do you have your passport with you?'

'Don't you think I haven't tried to go?' Max glared back at her. 'Foreign Affairs quickly knocked me back. They told me in no uncertain terms to stay out of it. Isobel is Dave's next of kin and they want the wifely touch to try to appeal on humanitarian grounds. Apparently, that's much more likely to get Dave released. I'm not happy, but I'm not going to muddy the water.'

Gemma's shoulders sagged. 'I suppose that's wise. It does sound like a touchy situation.'

Max merely grunted. He moved up the path towards her and she found herself backing away from his determined stride. Some women had been heard to comment that now he'd reached thirty Max was even more good-looking than he'd been in his teens, but none of them had enticed him into marriage and Gemma knew why. His personality hadn't improved one jot.

'Who decided that you should be taking care of the baby?' he drawled.

She squared her shoulders. 'Her mother is absolutely certain that I am the perfect choice.'

A sudden wind gusted across the garden and Gemma ducked her head to protect Mollie, so she missed seeing his reaction. But she didn't miss the sound of her front door slamming shut. Horrified, she whirled around. *Dammit!* Now she was stranded on her own front path with a baby in her arms and Max Jardine glowering at her.

He looked in the direction of her door. 'You're not locked out, are you?'

She fumbled around in her pockets, knowing that it was useless and that her keys were still hanging on a little brass hook in her kitchen. 'Yes,' she replied through gritted teeth.

'You can't get in the back way?'

'No. I made sure I closed my back door because I was worried about my neighbour's cat and...the baby.'

For a fraction of a second, she almost thought he smiled at her. 'So it's a case of climbing through a window.'

Gemma looked at her windows. It had been windy all day and the only one she'd left open was in her bedroom.

'I can get through there in a flash,' Max offered.

She pictured him swinging his riding boots and his long, jeans-clad legs over the sill, squeezing past the big bed that almost filled her small room—seeing the muddle of books, perfume and make-up on her bedside table and the underwear she'd left in a jumble on the end of the bed.

For some silly reason, she felt ridiculously flustered at the mere thought of Max seeing her private domain. 'It's OK,' she said quickly. 'I'll go. I—I know my way around.'

This time he was definitely smiling. His blue eyes danced as they rested first on Mollie in her arms and then on her short skirt. 'If you insist on getting in there yourself, let me at least help.' He held out his arms for Mollie.

Oh, Lord! What was worse? Did she want Max Jardine prowling around her bedroom, or Max, with Mollie in one arm, helping her up to her window and watching her skirt hike over her hips as she clambered through? Damn the man! Why did his presence always rock her so badly? This was hardly a life-threatening situation and yet she was feeling completely rattled.

'I guess you've got the longer legs. You'd better do the climbing,' she muttered ungraciously.

'OK,' he agreed easily, and in no time he had disappeared.

She saw her lace curtain snag as Max moved past it and she wondered what he thought of the ridiculously huge bed that dominated her tiny bedroom. She had taken the flat because it came fully furnished and the rent was cheap, considering how closely it was situated to the central business district. Most tenants, she assumed, would consider the king-size bed a bonus, but it was rather more than she needed.

The front door swung open.

'Miss Brown, Miss Mollie,' Max welcomed them with a deep bow.

'Thanks,' Gemma replied stiffly as she sailed past him into her flat with her head high. At the entrance to her lounge room, she paused and eyed him coolly, feeling uncomfortably more like the guest than the hostess. To right matters she added, 'I take it you've come to visit us?'

'We've got to work out what's best for this little one.'

Gemma sighed. She sensed combat ahead of her and here she was, facing the enemy without any time to construct a battle plan. The whole business of getting into the flat had set her off on the wrong foot. 'Isobel has already decided what's best for her daughter,' she told him haughtily. 'Don't forget this baby's mother is my best friend.'

'And this baby is my niece,' Max growled.

What would poor little Mollie think, if she could understand the way they were bickering over her?

Max moved away and she grimaced as he surveyed her lounge room. Its appearance had deteriorated somewhat now that Mollie's gear was piled in the middle of the carpet. Out of the corner of her eye, she noted Max's brows pull into a frown as he studied the mountain of equipment. There were numerous toys, a collapsible cot, a car seat, pram and playpen, not to mention enough clothes to dress an entire kindergarten.

His gaze also took in the piles of pamphlets and boxes Gemma had 'filed' on her sofa. Her computer and more paperwork covered the small dining table.

'There'll be much more room when I move the baby's gear into the bedroom,' she explained hastily.

Max cracked half a grin. 'Which bedroom would that be?'

'M-mine.'

'How many bedrooms do you have?'

Why her cheeks should flame at such a straightforward question was beyond her. 'Just—just the one,' she stammered.

Max stood staring at her with his hands on his hips, shaking his head as if he hadn't heard her properly. 'You're going to put all this gear in that miniature bedroom I just came through?'

'Some of it,' she mumbled.

'You'll need to buy a smaller bed.'

Gemma wouldn't give into his provocation by responding to that comment. To her further annoyance, he turned and sauntered around her compact kitchen, then back to the lounge and dining area, silently, grimly inspecting every detail. Her dwelling seemed smaller than ever with his large frame invading the space. Finally, he swivelled back to face her. And for an unnecessarily long moment, his disturbing blue eyes rested on her.

At last he spoke very quietly. 'It can't be done, Gemma. You can't take care of Mollie here in this shoebox.'

'Of course I can. Isobel has total faith in me.'

'Isobel is desperate.'

Gemma told herself she should expect a hurtful jab like this from Max and she resolved not to let him intimidate her. She matched his challenging gaze with a scornful glare. 'Isobel wasn't so desperate that she'd risk her baby's welfare. She has complete trust in my ability to care for Mollie.'

His eyes narrowed as he stared thoughtfully at the toes of his leather riding boots.

'Why don't you?' she challenged.

His head came up slowly, but he didn't speak.

'Why don't you trust me, Max?'

Before he replied, he thrust his hands deep into the pockets of his faded jeans. 'I'm sure you have good intentions, Gemma. But I keep remembering...' His Adam's apple moved up and down rapidly.

When he paused, Gemma rushed to defend herself. 'I doubt that you've noticed, but I'm not a little kid any more.'

This time his mouth curved into a relaxed smile and his amused blue gaze rested on her for an uncomfortable length of time before he spoke. 'Believe me, kiddo, I've noticed how grown-up you look these days.'

No amount of willpower could prevent Gemma's blushes. She ducked her face behind Mollie's golden curls.

'But what I'm remembering is your reaction at the hospital when Mollie was born,' he continued. 'You told us all very loudly that you were allergic to babies. You wouldn't touch her for fear she would break.'

Gemma tried valiantly to suppress a gasp of dismay. 'Newborn babies don't count,' she muttered defensively. 'Everyone's nervous about holding them. I love Mollie now.'

'But you said you were going to wait till she was old enough to—what was it? Take shopping? I think you were planning to teach her how to buy shoes and where to get the very best coffee in town.'

Stunned, Gemma stared at Max. The man had the memory of an elephant! She had only dim recollections of this conversation. How on earth did he retain such insignificant details? He must make a habit of hoarding up ammunition like this to fire when it most hurt.

'OK, I was scared of Mollie at first,' she admitted. 'I'd never been in close contact with such a tiny new baby before, but I—I've adjusted. Mollie and I get on famously now.'

At that moment, Mollie wriggled restlessly in Gemma's arms and uttered a little cry of protest. Gemma stared helplessly at the squirming baby. *Just whose side was this kid on?* She tried to jiggle Mollie on her hip. She'd seen Isobel do it many times and it always seemed to work.

'I take it,' added Max, 'you're going to *try* to play nursemaid and carry on a business as well?'

'Of course. It shouldn't be a problem.' It was the worst possible moment for Mollie to let out an ear-splitting wail, but she did. Her little face turned deep pink, her bottom lip wobbled and she sobbed desperately. Feeling totally threatened, Gemma quickly placed the baby on the floor at her feet. To her surprise, Mollie stopped crying almost immediately. She sat there quietly and began to suck her fist.

'Look at that,' Gemma beamed, feeling a whole lot better. 'I won't have to cart her around every minute of the day. I'll be able to sit her in her playpen surrounded by toys and get on with my work.'

Max's expression softened for a moment as he watched his niece, but when his gaze reached Gemma again, he scowled, shook his head and shoved his hands deeper in the pockets of his jeans. 'I'm not going to allow her to stay here, Gemma.'

'I beg your pardon?' *Not going to allow her? Could she be hearing this?* Gemma had always wondered what people meant when they described hackles rising on the backs of their necks. Now she knew.

'You heard me. I'm not going to abandon my niece.'

'*Abandon* her?' she echoed. 'How dare you insinuate that leaving her with me is the same as abandoning her?'

'Don't take it personally, Gem.'

The relaxed way Max leaned back against her kitchen bench doubled Gemma's anger.

'How on earth am I supposed to take it?'

'This is a family matter. You know the old saying about blood being thicker than water. A friend can't be expected to take on such responsibility.'

'For crying out loud, I'm more than a friend,' Gemma cried. 'I'm Mollie's godmother!' But as the words left her lips, she realised they weren't much help. This man, this enemy, this ogre— was poor Mollie's godfather.

'How on earth are *you* going to look after Mollie?' Gemma challenged before Max could respond. 'You've no women on your property and only a handful of ringers. I doubt they'll be much help.'

'I'll hire a nanny, of course. Someone with the very best training.'

She made an exaggerated show of rolling her eyes in disgust. 'If Isobel wanted a nanny for Mollie, she could have hired one herself. The poor woman doesn't know how long she's going to be away and she wants someone she knows, someone who really cares about her baby, not a stranger who happens to have official qualifications.'

Max sighed and ran long fingers through his hair as he stared at the waxed tiles on Gemma's kitchen floor. 'Isobel said she didn't want a nanny?'

'Yes,' she replied firmly.

'OK,' he said at last. With another deeper sigh, his head flicked sideways and his eyes locked onto hers. 'You and I are both Mollie's godparents, so we should make this a shared responsibility.'

CHAPTER TWO

'WHAT EXACTLY DO you mean?' Gemma asked, appalled by what Max seemed to be suggesting.

'We're both the baby's godparents. So we look after her.' His eyes revealed the briefest twinkle. *'Together.'*

She knew her mouth was gaping. 'You and me?' she gasped.

'Yeah.'

'But we can't.'

'Why not?'

'It—it's not necessary. Being a godparent is simply a gesture of intent.'

Resting his hands on the counter top, Max leaned forward. 'You can't have it both ways, Gemma. Either being Mollie's godmother is a good reason for you to take care of her, or it isn't.'

She knew she was losing ground fast. Apparently Max had been honing his skills as a bush lawyer. She ran frantic fingers through her short, dark hair. 'But it doesn't mean we're obliged to— For crying out loud, Max, that doesn't mean we have to actually do anything *parental* together.'

Max's eyes teased her. 'It's the only sensible solution. You and Mollie should come and stay on Goodbye Creek Station until Isobel returns. That way we can share the load. It's called co-operation.'

Her stomach lurched as if she were coming down in a very fast elevator. 'Co-operation, my foot!' she said at last. 'How much co-operation are *you* planning to contribute? I'm the one who'll have to make all the sacrifices. Why should *I* give up everything here to head off into the bush and stay with you?'

'Because, as I've already explained,' Max said, with exaggerated patience, 'we need to share this responsibility. That way we can both get on with our work commitments.' He pointed to the pamphlets and papers on her sofa. 'I imagine it will be much easier for you to bring your stuff to Goodbye Creek and to carry on your business from there, than for me to bring thousands of head of cattle down to this, er—cosy little suburban flat.'

He was so smug and sure of himself, Gemma wanted to thump him. She was beginning to feel cornered. 'It won't work.'

'I think it's a compromise that has distinct possibilities.'

If only she could tell him she was far too busy—booked up to organise half a dozen events—but even if she did tell such a lie, she was sure he would find a way to use it against her. Instead she glared at him. 'We'll spend the whole time fighting!'

He pretended to be shocked by her words. 'Why on earth should we do that?'

Gemma groaned. '*Maxwell T.* Jardine, I don't believe I'm hearing this. We would fight, for the simple reason that we have never agreed about anything. Haven't you noticed the only thing we have in common is that we both breathe oxygen? We can't stand each other!'

Just to prove how utterly detestable he was, Max burst out laughing.

Gemma gave in to her anger. She smashed her fist onto the counter. 'What's so funny?' she yelled.

'Oh, Gemma,' he chuckled. 'You certainly are all grown up now, aren't you?'

Choking, she gasped and spluttered. Trust Max to point out that she wasn't nearly as sophisticated and worldly wise as she liked to think she was. She had a sneaking suspicion that she might never become mature and discerning. It was her long-term ambition to become cool and detached—especially when this man was around doing his best to flummox her.

For a brief moment, Max's expression softened. Then he stepped around the counter and towards her. Gemma wished he wouldn't. When he rested his strong, warm hands on both her shoulders, her nerves were way too strained to cope.

'*Gemma Elizabeth* Brown,' he said, his voice low and gravelly.

Her eyes widened at his use of her middle name. She hadn't even realised he knew it.

'We agree on the most important thing.'

She could feel the heat of his hands as they held her. Her lungs appeared to be malfunctioning, but Max didn't notice, he just kept on talking.

'We agree that Mollie deserves very good care and, on this occasion, I think most definitely, we *do* have to do something together.' His eyes flashed as he added, 'Something *parental*. You're right, we'll probably fight like cats and dogs, but we'll manage somehow—for Mollie's sake. On our own, we'd both have major difficulties looking after the poor little kid properly, wouldn't we?'

She allowed her gaze to meet those deep blue eyes, those disturbing blue eyes, and Gemma felt less sure of her line of argument.

'Together, we stand a fair chance of success—both for Mollie and our work.'

What he proposed was unthinkable! She couldn't let this happen. How on earth could she live with Max while he inspected her babysitting skills? She'd be a dithering mess. Holy smoke, he'd be checking up on her every minute of the day and he would soon discover she knew absolutely zero about babies.

Gemma felt as if she'd stepped aside and become a spectator of this discussion. Incredibly, she realised she was nodding, accepting Max's terms.

If only she could remember exactly when Max had turned their battle to his advantage, but she had loosened her grip on this whole scene. She'd lost sight of her counter-argument.

'I'll do my fair share,' Max added. 'I'll give Mollie her tucker or bathe her, or whatever's necessary. We can work out some sort of roster if you like.'

She passed a dazed hand across her eyes. Never in her wildest dreams had she pictured this rough-riding cattleman in a hands-on relationship with a baby. She tried to visualise him attending to Mollie, but her musings were interrupted by the telephone.

'Oh, heavens! That's probably the printers.' Gemma had almost forgotten her current project and her deadline this afternoon. 'I have to get some pamphlet designs to them before five o'clock.' She glared fiercely at Max as she hurried to the phone.

'Hello, Gemma Brown speaking.'

A woman's voice reached her. 'Gemma, Sue Easton from Over the Page. I was wondering...'

The printers were chasing her copy. Gemma reassured the woman that everything was ready and she would be at their office shortly. As she spoke, she heard Mollie begin to cry behind her and she was acutely aware of Max moving quietly in the flat.

Mollie's wails ceased abruptly and by the time Gemma put the receiver down and turned to face Max again, she was startled to find him perched on the arm of her sofa and jogging the delighted baby on his knee.

He looked very pleased with himself. 'See? You can't manage without me, can you? I'll mind this little possum while you do whatever running around you need to this afternoon.'

'Thanks,' she replied uncertainly.

'And after that,' he said with confident assurance, 'we can plan your move to Goodbye Creek. I'll book into a pub tonight and we can head off first thing in the morning.'

As he continued to favour both Gemma and Mollie with a look of smug satisfaction, the baby's face turned red and Gemma noticed that she seemed to be concentrating very hard.

'Oh-oh.' Max's confident grin slipped. Cautiously, he lifted Mollie away from his knee.

'Has she dirtied her nappy?' asked Gemma.

'I—I think so.'

At the sight of his sudden dismay, Gemma felt an urge to grin, but she managed to keep a straight face. 'Thanks so much, Max. It would be great if you could watch Mollie for half an hour or so. I do have several errands to run—especially if I'm moving house. Let me show you where the clean nappies are...' She rummaged in the pile of things Isobel had left and produced a freshly folded nappy and a container of baby wipes and, with a deadpan expression, handed them to him. 'These are what you need.'

'You're running out on me at a moment like this?' he asked, clearly horrified. By now he was holding Mollie at arm's length.

'I'm sorry,' Gemma murmured sweetly, 'but I really do have important deadlines to meet. You'll be fine.' She gathered up her designs and her handbag and rushed out her front door.

'He thinks he's such a hotshot babysitter, he can manage this one,' she muttered under her breath.

But she wished she didn't feel quite so guilty about deserting him.

The next day, when Max piloted their plane over the vast property that made up Goodbye Creek Station, Gemma was stunned by the unexpected flood of homesickness that swept through her. It was five years since she'd been back, but she knew the Jardine family holding almost as well as she knew the township of Goodbye Creek, where her own home had been. Her parents had owned a stock and station agency in the town. They had sold up and moved to the coast about the same time she'd gone away to university.

Now, she and Max were flying back, the plane stacked carefully with the baby's gear. Max explained that he had a well-equipped study complete with an up-to-the-minute computer and a fax machine, so Gemma only needed to bring her clothes, a box of computer disks and her paperwork.

They'd left Brisbane just as dawn broke and during the five-hour flight Mollie had alternated between napping and waking for little snacks and drinks. Gemma had kept her entertained with picture books and games of 'This little pig went to market'.

Max had chatted very politely about the weather and the scenery beneath them, but it occurred to Gemma that he was behaving more like a newly introduced acquaintance than someone who had known her for more than twenty years. But now, as heart-wrenchingly familiar red soil plains unfolded below, she felt edgy, knowing that once they landed their shared past could no longer be ignored.

Wriggling forward in her seat, she peered eagerly through the windscreen, wondering why the sight of dry, grassy paddocks and straggly stands of eucalypts should make her feel so soppy and sentimental. Way below, she could recognise the signs of spring merging into summer. Early wet season storms had brought bright green new growth and purple and yellow wild flowers were poking up through the grass.

Max's flight-path followed the course of the old creek that had given its name to the district and Gemma noted that water was already flowing down its entire length. She could make out the shallow, rocky stretch of rapids and finally the deeper section they called Big Bend.

Fringed by majestic paperbarks, this cool, shady pool had been a favourite spot for childhood picnics. At the age of ten, Gemma had rocketed in a tractor tube right through the rapids as far as the Big Bend. She'd been so proud of herself and Dave had been lavish with his praise.

'You're as good as a boy,' he'd shouted. 'You made it the whole way without squealing once. Max, isn't she great?'

But Max, of course, had merely grunted and looked bored.

As they neared the homestead, her sense of nostalgia increased.

'Nearly home,' said Max, with a contented little smile, as he worked the controls to increase their angle of descent.

First came the stockyards and the corrugated iron roofs under which hay bales would be stacked to protect them from the rain. Then she could see the smaller, original holding yard, made of old timbers weathered to a silvery grey and built in the rustic post and rail design that had been around since the pioneering days.

Gemma glanced at Mollie dozing in her little safety seat beside her. 'Has Mollie been out here before?' she asked.

'No,' admitted Max. 'This will be the first time she's set foot on Jardine soil. It's a significant moment.' He made a sweeping gesture with his arm. 'All this is her inheritance.'

'Unless you have children of your own,' Gemma said softly. 'I guess then they would all be shareholders.'

He turned and their eyes met. His blue gaze held a disquieting mixture of uncertainty and bitterness. 'Yeah,' he said, and then jerked his head back to the front. 'There's always that possibility.'

They swooped a little lower and the familiar sight of the muddy dam dotted with black ducks and the rusty metal skeleton of the old windmill standing sentry nearby made her feel ridiculously emotional. She blinked her eyes to clear the misted view. In her imagination, she could hear the squeak and clank of the old windmill as it slowly pumped water to the drinking troughs.

Within seconds she was exclaiming. 'Max, my goodness! You've installed a satellite dish.'

'Got to keep up with technology.'

Their plane continued its descent and he nodded to their right, past the machinery sheds and workshops. 'I've put in some new windmills, too. That one over there has a solar panel and an electric pump.'

'Is it better than the old one?' she asked, doubtfully eyeing the shiny modern equipment.

'Too right. Before, it was always a case of no breeze, no water. Now we can get a constant flow if we need it.'

But the biggest surprise came as they made the final dip towards the airstrip, when Gemma saw the homestead, which for as long as she could remember had been a comfortable but shabby timber home with peeling paint and vine-covered wrap-around verandahs.

'Wow!' Her breath exhaled slowly as she absorbed the changes. Max's home was now a showplace. 'What have you done to the house?' she asked.

He was concentrating on making an initial swoop over the strip to clear the ground of horses and birds before attempting a landing. 'Painted it,' he muttered tersely as he swung the plane around to double back for the approach.

Below them, skittish horses cantered out of their way and a flock of cockatoos, feeding on grass seed, lifted their wings to disperse like so many pieces of white paper caught in a wind gust. The plane plunged lower and finally touched down on the gravel runway.

'What a difference,' Gemma exclaimed, still staring at Max's house, amazed by the transformation. The homestead's timber walls were now painted a pretty powder blue, the iron roof was a clean, crisp silver and all the trims and the lattice on the verandahs were gleaming white.

As they taxied down the short airstrip, Max shot her a cautious glance. 'You like it?'

'It's beautiful, Max. I had no idea the old place could look so lovely.' She was startled to see an unexpected red tinge creep along his cheekbones. 'Who did the job for you?'

'Did it myself,' he muttered. 'During the dry season, of course.' Another shock.

As the plane came to a standstill, Gemma assimilated this news and sat quietly, thinking about the lonely weeks Max must have spent on the task. The life of an outback cattleman was solitary and hard and the men who survived it were tough, complex creatures. And they didn't come much more complicated than Max, she thought with a wry grimace. 'It's fantastic,' she told him with genuine warmth. 'You've done an amazing job.'

He looked embarrassed and she realised he was probably more used to her scorn than her praise. She allowed herself a private smile as she thought about that. They were probably both much more comfortable fighting than co-operating.

An old utility truck had been left at the end of the runway and Gemma and Max were kept busy for the next ten minutes, transferring Mollie and the gear into the vehicle. Even though it was only a few hundred metres to the homestead, there was too much to lug such a distance.

It was late morning. The sun was already high overhead and very hot and so, by the time they reached the kitchen, a cool drink was the first priority. Gemma found Mollie's little feeding cup, while Max swung his fridge door open and grabbed a jug of iced water.

Just before he closed the fridge, he paused to survey its contents and frowned. 'I might have to stock up on a few things from town,' he commented before filling a glass and handing it to Gemma. 'I'm afraid I wasn't expecting you and I haven't got the kind of fancy things that women like for breakfast. I'm still a steak and eggs man myself.'

Gemma's eyes widened. 'How do you know what women like for breakfast?' The question was out before she really thought through what she was saying. She'd always pictured Max as a crusty bachelor living the life of a lonely recluse in the back of beyond.

Max went very still and she cringed with sudden shame as she recognised just how rude and downright stupid her query sounded. How on earth could she retract her words?

Before any bright ideas struck, he spun around, and the glance he sent her way was tinged with wry amusement.

Had she left her brains in Brisbane? Of course this man would have attracted and entertained women. He was quite well off and had the kind of rugged and rangy masculinity that swarms of women hunted down. Unlike her, they'd be willing to overlook his gruffness.

She knew by the heat in her cheeks that her embarrassment was obvious, but she was also just as sure Max wouldn't miss an opportunity to make her suffer further for her foolishness.

'Now let me see.' He cocked his head to the ceiling as if considering her question. 'How is it that I know so much about women's breakfast habits?'

His eyes narrowed as if he was giving this matter his undivided attention. 'I think I probably picked up some pointers—like women's belief in the importance of orange juice—from all those television advertisements.'

Totally flustered and unable to think of an appropriate retort, Gemma concentrated very carefully on holding Mollie's cup at just the right angle for her to drink easily.

'But it beats me if I can remember just how I uncovered the mysterious feminine desire to dine first thing in the morning on low-fat yoghurt and muesli. That really has me stumped.' Relaxing back in a wooden kitchen chair, he joined his hands behind his head with elbows pointing to the ceiling. 'I guess I found out about European women's predilection for coffee and croissants from some foreign movie.'

'For heaven's sake,' Gemma growled at him. 'Good luck to any long-suffering woman who's had breakfast with you. The poor thing would need a ton of luck and a truckload of tolerance to put up with your chauvinism.'

He took a deep swig of iced water and chuckled. 'I'd say you're probably right.' Setting the glass back on the table, he grinned at her. 'You'll be able to find out tomorrow morning, won't you?'

'I think I could do without your early-morning charm,' she sniffed. 'And Mollie and I will have soft boiled eggs and toast soldiers for our breakfast.'

She turned away from his mocking grin and made a fuss of Mollie. But it was difficult to stop her mind from dwelling on the unexplored area of this conversation—the particular circumstances that led to a woman sharing breakfast with Max.

They didn't bear thinking about.

And yet, in spite of her efforts to ignore such offensive details, an unbidden picture planted itself firmly in Gemma's mind. A vision of a lamp-lit bedroom—with cool, white sheets—and Max's brown, muscle-packed back encircled by softly rounded, pale and feminine arms. A night of intimacy...

She felt an unpleasant wave of panic.

Would Max Jardine be charming in the company of other women?

Surely not.

'Do you have any bananas?' she asked, in a desperate bid to change the subject and to rid herself of these extremely unsettling thoughts. 'I—I could mash one for Mollie's lunch while you set up her cot.'

His eyes surveyed the kitchen. 'No bananas, I'm afraid. You might have to give her some of the tinned stuff we brought with us. I'll take a run into town first thing tomorrow morning. We should make up a shopping list.'

Gemma was so grateful they were no longer talking about Max's women that she spent the afternoon being particularly obliging and co-operative. Max made cold roast beef sandwiches for their lunch and they ate them at a table on the side verandah and washed them down with huge mugs of strong tea while Mollie played with her blocks on the floor nearby. Out in the paddocks the white cockatoos screeched raucous greetings as they returned to the grass seed to feed.

Then, after lunch, as Max had never bothered with a housekeeper, together they dusted and vacuumed spare rooms for her and Mollie's use. They set up Mollie's folding cot and her other equipment in a bedroom on the cool side of the house, with doors opening onto the verandah.

Gemma's bedroom was right next door. She had stayed in it before—a pretty room, very feminine, with pink and white curtains and a white candlewick bedspread on the old-fashioned iron bed. The bed-ends were decorated with shiny brass knobs and pretty pieces of porcelain painted with rosebuds.

She was startled to see a silver-framed photo of Dave and herself on the mahogany dressing table. It had been taken five years ago—in the days before Dave met Isobel—when Gemma was eighteen and she and Dave had still been 'going together'. Their liaison had been a casual arrangement that they'd drifted into as they grew older. She'd come back from university for his twenty-first birthday.

In the photo, they were dancing. Dave, dressed in a formal dinner suit, was laughing, and she was smiling at the camera and looking very pleased with herself in a pale blue evening gown with thin straps, a fitted bodice and a softly floating, long skirt. There were tiny white flowers dotted through her dark brown hair. At the time, she'd thought she looked very romantic.

Now she shuddered as a painful memory forced itself on her.

The night of Dave's party had ended with a shameful and embarrassing incident. A scene she had worked desperately hard to forget over the years. Surely Max had wanted to forget it, too? At the time he had been as upset as she was about what happened.

Shaking, she turned to him now. 'Why didn't you throw this old photo away?'

Max set down her suitcase, straightened and frowned in its direction. An unreadable emotion flashed in his eyes and his mouth tightened. After a moment, he said with a shrug, 'Didn't cross my mind.'

Rigid with tension, it took Gemma a moment or two to take in his words. Then relief flooded her. He must have forgotten what had happened that night! Either that or the incident that had caused her so much grief over the years had never really bothered him. Gemma forced herself to shrug as nonchalantly as he had. 'Fair enough,' she said.

She knew she should be relieved, but it took some time for her to feel calm again and to convince herself that she was happy with his detached reaction.

By evening, they had worked out how to barricade off the section of the verandah adjacent to the study, so that Mollie could have a safe area to crawl and play while Gemma worked. Gemma had unpacked her clothes and had showered to wash off the dust from her journey. She'd bathed the baby girl in the old claw-foot tub in the main bathroom and fed her mashed vegetables. Max had ambled down to one of the ringers' huts to discuss station matters and explain about his visitors.

When he returned, he fixed a simple supper of steaks and salad while Gemma gave Mollie her bottle and settled her for sleep.

Everything went like clockwork. Gemma couldn't believe how obliging Mollie was and how conciliatory Max had been. She was beginning to feel calm and confident and even optimistic about the whole venture. Surely this mood wouldn't last?

They ate together, and their steaks were followed by a simple, no-frills dessert of chocolate chip ice cream and tinned apricots. Then coffee. They chatted about people they both knew from around the district and Max was a surprisingly entertaining host— slipping humorous anecdotes and juicy titbits of gossip into the conversation.

As he drained the last of his coffee, he put his cup down and leaned back in his chair. 'I should have offered you a nightcap. Would you like a liqueur or brandy?'

She shook her head. 'No, thank you. I'm quite tired, but you have one.'

'Not tonight.' He looked at her thoughtfully. 'You haven't told me anything about the trip you made to England after university.'

'I didn't think you'd be interested,' she answered stiffly.

His eyebrows rose the tiniest fraction. 'I don't need a travelogue, but I'd like to know whether you found what you were looking for.'

The coffee cup in Gemma's hand rattled against its saucer. 'I went to London for two years' work experience.'

After a little, Max said, 'I suspected you were running away.'

He'd dropped the charm and reverted to Big Brother mode and

Gemma's sense of relaxation was falling away at breakneck speed. She should have known the truce had been too good to last. 'What would I have been running away from?'

He frowned. 'You and Dave were so close for so many years. Everyone in the district thought of you as a couple.'

'Yes, but I'm sure everyone knew it wasn't serious.' She was stunned to think that Max might have thought she'd been pining after Dave. 'Heavens, Max, Dave and I just sort of hung out together out of habit. I mean—being with him was always fun and sweet and everything, but when we parted it was quite painless and definitely for the best.' She added quietly, 'There was something missing in our relationship.'

Heat leapt into her cheeks. She didn't add that there had seemed to be something missing in every relationship she'd attempted. Gemma had a dreadful suspicion that there was something missing in her own personality. She feared she just wasn't suited to romance. No matter how handsome and charming and eager to please her the young men she'd met had been, none of then had ever once made her feel giddily, genuinely in love. Not the kind of love she was hoping to find.

'You thought you would find that missing *something*…in London?' Max's eyes were lit with a puzzling intensity.

Blue fire.

The way their gaze locked onto hers robbed her breath. This man of all people shouldn't be asking her such questions.

'No, I wasn't hoping for that,' she said at last, and prayed that he couldn't guess she was lying through her teeth.

'No suave English gentleman swept you off your feet?'

It was time to finish this conversation. Gemma didn't like it at all. She especially didn't like the way her heart began beat so frantically when Max looked at her.

Unless she put an end to this now, she might end up admitting to him that although she'd met plenty of nice young men, none of them had captured her heart. And the very last thing Gemma wanted was for him to continue this line of questioning and uncover her embarrassing secret.

None of her family or friends knew the truth about her love life.

Or rather her lack of a love life. Gemma was quite certain that she was the only twenty-three-year-old female outside a nunnery who was still a virgin.

She lifted her chin to what she hoped was a challenging angle. 'There were several men,' she told him. 'But, Max, you're not *my* big brother. I'm not giving you an itemised account and you don't need to keep watch over me. It's none of your business how many men I've met or—or how many affairs I've had.' Pushing back her chair, she jumped to her feet. 'I haven't asked you one tiny question about your breakfast companions.'

He stood also and looked down at her from his menacing height. 'What would you like to know?' he asked while a poorly suppressed grin tugged at the corners of his mouth.

'I have absolutely no interest in your philanderings.' She spun on her heel and began to stomp away from the table. Then she stopped abruptly, remembering her manners. 'I'll help you clear the table and tidy the kitchen,' she mumbled.

'Thank you, Gemma,' he replied with a studied politeness that annoyed her.

In silence they worked, Max gathering up the plates and cutlery, Gemma collecting the cups, place mats and serviettes. Together they walked into the kitchen and set their things down at the sink. They both reached for the tap at the same time. Their hands connected.

As if she'd been burnt, Gemma snatched her hand away from the contact, but Max's reaction was just as quick and he caught her fingers in his strong grasp.

His thumb stroked her skin once, twice…and she felt her blood stirring in response. Her hand trembled.

She wanted to pull away, but she was too fascinated by her body's astonishing reaction. Never had she felt so unsettled, so fired up by a man's simple touch. She didn't dare look at Max. She stood by the sink, mesmerised by the sight of her slim white hand in his large, suntanned grip. She could see little hairs on the back of his hand, bleached to gold by the sun. A faint trace of the fresh, lemon-scented soap he'd used in the shower still clung to his skin and his work-roughened thumb continued to move slowly over her hand, making her feel shivery and breathless.

'Gem.' His gruff voice barely reached her over the savage drum-beat in her ears.

She couldn't move, couldn't speak.

'Gemma,' he said again, and his other hand reached under her chin, forcing her head up until their eyes met. Max was looking as startled as she felt. His breathing sounded just as hectic.

When his fingers began to trace ever so gently the outline of her face, she could feel her skin flame at his touch.

'Gemma Brown,' he whispered, 'whether you like it or not, I'm going to keep watching you…just like I always have.'

And the moment was spoiled. Gemma was embarrassingly disappointed.

'For Pete's sake!' she exclaimed, wrenching her hand out of his grasp and pulling right away from him. She was fearfully angry with him and she wasn't quite sure why. 'You are not my brother, my bodyguard or my guardian angel!' For a dreadful moment she thought she might burst into tears. 'Go paint some more walls. Get a life, Max, and leave me to get on with mine!'

This time she didn't care about good manners. Gemma rushed out of the kitchen and left him with the dirty dishes.

CHAPTER THREE

THE GRIMY DISHES were still sitting on the counter top waiting to be washed when Gemma walked into the kitchen the next morning. Added to last night's pile were an extra-greasy frying pan, a mug and more plates—things Max must have used for his breakfast before he headed off at sunrise.

'Who does he think he is?' she asked Mollie as she surveyed the dreary mess. Mollie merely whimpered and rubbed her face against Gemma's shoulder. She'd been restless during the night and still seemed rather fragile this morning. Having slept very fitfully, Gemma wasn't feeling too chipper either. In their own separate ways, both Max and Mollie Jardine had kept her tossing and turning for hours.

She set Mollie down on the floor while she hunted through Max's cupboards for a saucepan to boil their eggs, but Mollie began to cry almost as soon as Gemma walked away from her.

'Aren't you going to let me do anything this morning?' Gemma sighed. She tried to cheer the baby up with clucking noises while she set about making their breakfast.

After popping two eggs into a pot of water, she slid bread into the toaster and boiled the kettle for a mug of tea for herself. The phone rang. Gemma glanced at Mollie, who was still making miserable little whimpers and she deliberated whether she should let the answering machine deal with the call. Then, having second thoughts, she handed the baby a saucepan lid, hoping it would keep her happy while she dashed to the phone.

The call was from Brisbane—the printers were wanting to clarify some final details about the pamphlet—so Gemma was glad she'd answered. But when she returned to the kitchen, her heart sank.

Max stood in the middle of the room, with his hands on his hips, staring in dismay at Mollie, who was howling loudly and banging the saucepan lid on the floor in time to her wails.

She dashed into the room and swept the baby into her arms. 'Why didn't you pick her up?' she challenged Max, deciding to attack him before he could begin to accuse her of neglect.

But he clearly didn't react well to being scolded. His eyes narrowed. 'Where were you?' he asked.

'Where was *I*?' She knew she sounded shrewish, but was too frazzled to care. 'After pacing the floorboards all night, trying to calm your niece, I was answering an important business call. Where were *you*?'

'I've had one or two things to attend to,' he snapped. 'I need to talk to my men—delegate more jobs now that I have other responsibilities.'

'Who are you trying to kid?' Gemma cut in. 'You wouldn't recognise a responsibility if it was formally introduced to you. Who rocked Mollie back to sleep when she wouldn't settle last night? Me! Who waltzed off this morning without a care in the world and left the kitchen covered in grease? You did!'

'I'm sorry you had a bad night,' he replied with annoying composure, 'but calm down, Gemma.' He reached over and lifted the miserable Mollie from her arms. 'I had every intention of doing the dishes—same as I always do them-at lunchtime.'

'Lunchtime?'

Gemma might have launched into another tirade, but she noticed that Max's nose had begun to twitch. Was he feeling angry or just very guilty? Neither of the above, she realised with dismay as the acrid smell of smoke reached her.

'It seems you've burnt the toast,' he said quietly.

Black smoke billowed from the corner of the kitchen and Max, with Mollie on one hip, lunged across the room, switched the toaster off and flung its doors open.

Wasn't it just typical of this man? Gemma thought as she watched him. He could buy himself a smart little plane, a satellite dish and a fancy computer and still not have progressed to a pop-up toaster.

On the stove, the eggs were boiling so rapidly they rattled against the saucepan. 'Oh, blast! They'll be hard-boiled!' she wailed. This was definitely *not* her morning.

She snatched the saucepan from the stove, thumped it into the sink, then whirled around to glare at Max. He was nuzzling Mollie's tummy with his nose and making her laugh.

Laugh! Out loud!

Proper chuckles!

Gemma could feel her bottom lip drooping into a pout. How dared Mollie be so sweet and responsive to Max when she was the one who'd lost all the sleep? She sagged against the kitchen bench and, with a self-pitying sigh, folded her arms across her chest.

Max glanced at her. 'I'll take her out to see the puppies and give you some space to have another go at cooking breakfast,' he suggested.

She drew in a deep breath and nodded. Some peace and quiet, some space...that was what she needed...

And yet she felt strangely abandoned watching Max take Mollie outside—as if they belonged together and she was the outsider. He carried her so easily, without any sense of awkwardness. He would make a good father... She found herself wondering how many of Max's breakfast companions had been hoping to marry him, to have him father their children.

Groaning at the stupid direction of her thoughts, Gemma picked up the blackened pieces of toast and, with grimly compressed lips, tossed them into the bin before setting out to remake breakfast.

By the time Max and Mollie returned, she had set the little table on the verandah and her breakfast and Mollie's were ready. She had decided against eggs after all and had made Mollie some porridge, settling for tea and toast for herself. And she'd assumed Max might want some more to eat so had made extra for him.

'Thanks,' he said as he settled Mollie on his lap and proceeded to feed her milky porridge with a tiny spoon.

'We could do with a high chair. It would make mealtimes much easier,' Gemma commented as Max intercepted Mollie's plump little hand before she could dunk it into the porridge bowl.

'I'll add it to my shopping list, but I'm not sure if Goodbye Creek runs to high chairs.'

'So you're going into town this morning?'

He nodded. 'Want to come?'

Gemma hesitated and took a sip of tea, shocked by her ready willingness to accept his offer. The idea of going to town with Max seemed more appealing than she could have thought possible. Her mind ran ahead of her, wondering what she might wear.

He was looking at her thoughtfully. 'Of course, you might appreciate some time to set up your office. I could take Mollie with me and get her out of your hair for the morning, while you get your business sorted out. It's a hot day for travelling and seeing you've had a rough night...'

Gemma placed her mug carefully back on the table. What on earth was wrong with her? Max Jardine was offering to get out of her way. She should be celebrating. This time yesterday she would have *paid* him to stay away.

His suggestion that she take the morning to reorganise her business was so brimming with common sense that she couldn't refuse without looking foolish. So why on earth did it make her feel downright miserable? Her tiredness had to be the answer—plus the fact that she had already grown so attached to Mollie that she hated to be parted from her.

'A morning to myself would be great,' she told Max brightly. 'You finish your toast and I'll go clean up Mollie and make up an extra bottle for you to take.'

'Better give me some extra clothes for her, too,' Max said as she stood to go. 'We might be some time.'

They were gone for most of the day. Many, many times Gemma went to the front verandah to peer down the dirt track, searching for the cloud of red dust on the horizon that would tell her the truck was returning. She hadn't the courage to tell Max that there wasn't much work on her books at present. He already had a low enough opinion of her without adding fuel to his fire.

But by ten o'clock in the morning she'd finished her work and she spent the rest of the day roaming restlessly around the house.

After lunch, she washed and dried all the dishes, vowing that she would have to change some of Max's bachelor habits. Then she set a sprinkler on the front lawn and picked some flowers from the old rambling garden that Max's grandmother had established many, many years ago. Exotic-smelling white gardenias, roses in two shades of pink and some yellow crucifix orchids.

After arranging the flowers in a crystal vase on the hall table, she piled a blue bowl with tangy bush lemons and set it on the kitchen dresser, then brought in Mollie's washing from the line, folded it and put it away.

By mid-afternoon, Gemma wondered if she should start thinking about the evening meal, but decided to wait and see what Max had bought.

At about four, a trail of dust signalled their return at last. Trying not to hurry, she made her way through the house to greet them, unable to disguise her pleasure when they pulled up near the kitchen door.

Max grinned at her as he swung his long frame down from the driver's seat and her heart gave a silly little lurch. He held a finger to his lips. 'Mollie's asleep,' he whispered. 'I'll try to get her out without disturbing her.'

Expertly, he unbuckled Mollie's car seat and lifted her gently out of the truck. In his strong arms, the baby girl looked comfortable and safe and Gemma's throat constricted painfully. The combined effect of Max's surprisingly tender manner as he handled his little niece and the way his usually grim gaze softened when he looked at her lying asleep in his arms upset her.

He hunched one broad shoulder forward to accommodate the little head covered in damp curls and the thoughtful gesture touched her deeply. But Gemma didn't want her emotions to be touched— such reactions were out of order and made her distinctly uncomfortable.

She felt better when she set about the businesslike task of un-loading groceries and carting them through to the kitchen.

'How was town?' she asked when Max joined her.

'Same as always.' He shrugged. 'Mollie caused quite a stir.'

'I guess babies are a bit of a rarity out this way.'

He nodded and continued the unloading without further com-ment. He brought in a rather battered-looking high chair, which he proudly announced he'd found in the secondhand shop, and then he carried through an Esky full of cold goods and began to load the freezer with more tubs of chocolate chip ice cream and pack-ets of frozen corn cobs and peas.

At last he looked up. 'Get plenty of work done while we were away?'

'Oh,' Gemma replied, with a vague wave of her hand, 'yes—heaps.'

'Mollie's been awake for most of the day. So many people wanted to make a fuss of her. I'd say she needs a good sleep now.'

'I guess so,' Gemma agreed. With a plastic scoop, she trans-ferred sugar from a huge hessian bag into an old-fashioned metal canister. 'Would you like some afternoon tea?'

He glanced at his watch. 'I should mosey on down to the ring-ers' place and have something there. I need to know if Chad and Dingo were able to fix the pump on the five-mile bore.'

With that, he reached for the Akubra hat hanging on a nail near the back door and was gone.

Gemma clamped the lid down tight on the sugar canister, lugged the bag into the pantry, then sat down at the kitchen table and propped up her chin with her hand. She stayed there staring at the door where Max had disappeared. The clock on the wall ticked loudly.

Running her fingers through her short hair, she let out a long sigh. A gloomy sense of depression settled on her, like a thick, suffocating fog.

Just why she felt so low was a puzzle.

She knew she should be delighted with how well this whole babysitting business was progressing. Instead of snarling at her and constantly annoying her, Max was keeping his criticisms to a minimum and, for the most part, he was being polite. If she over-looked the matter of the washing up, he was going out of his way to be co-operative. And instead of hanging around and making her nervous all day long, he was giving her space. He much preferred the company of his ringers to hers.

Was she imagining it, she wondered, or was he actually avoiding her?

Why should it matter?

The blast of a car horn sounded outside. A visitor. Gemma jumped to her feet and hurried down the hallway to find a dusty sedan pulling up at the front of the homestead. The driver's door swung open and a woman with a mass of bright red hair emerged. As Gemma watched, she opened the back of her car and, when she leaned in to retrieve something, the denim of her jeans stretched sinfully over well-rounded buttocks.

Gemma's eyebrows rose. Their visitor was wearing a sheer white blouse through which her lacy bra was clearly visible. It was tucked into the tightest jeans she'd ever seen.

'Yoo-hoo! Maxie!' the woman called as she straightened again. In one hand she was holding what looked like a casserole dish wrapped in a tea towel. She slammed her car door shut and began to sashay on very high heels towards the stairs.

Was this one of the breakfast ladies?

Gemma found herself studying the woman very carefully. Her age, she guessed, would be just the other side of thirty, and there was really only one word to describe her figure—curvaceous. On a highway, such curves would come with a sign warning danger. Except, Gemma noted grimly, these curves came in all the right places—exactly where men were supposed to want them.

Lucky Max.

When she saw Gemma standing on the verandah, the visitor paused.

'Hi,' Gemma called.

'Hello,' came the cautious reply. It was very clear to Gemma that the woman was shocked to see her there. She stood staring, her eyes popping and her carefully painted mouth wide open.

After an uncomfortable stretch of silence, Gemma asked, 'Are you looking for Max?'

'Yes… I am…' The visitor tossed her mane of gleaming red hair, like an animal preparing for a battle.

Gemma pointed to the dirt track leading away from the homestead and towards the ringers' huts. 'He's down there.'

'With Dingo?'

She nodded. 'I'm sure you're welcome to go on over, if you want to see him.' Coming down the steps, she held out her hand. 'Or perhaps I can help you?'

A petulant frown marred the woman's otherwise pretty features. 'I don't know,' she muttered. 'You see, I was expecting…' She fiddled with the tea towel that covered the container she was holding. Her fingernails were very long and painted to match her hair. 'I thought…' Then, with an embarrassed shrug, she shoved the covered dish towards Gemma. 'Here, you might as well take this. It's a casserole. I didn't know there was a woman here, though. You see, I thought Max was trying to look after the little baby on his own and I figured he might need a hand.'

Gemma offered the woman her sweetest smile. 'How kind of you, but I don't know if I should accept this meal. That's why I'm here. To help Max out. We're caring for Mollie together.'

'I wonder why Max didn't mention you.'

Gemma shrugged. She'd been wondering the same thing.

'You're not from round these parts, are you?'

'Not any more, but I grew up out here. I'm Gemma Brown. An old friend of…of the family and I'm the baby's godmother.' She extended her hand.

It was accepted reluctantly. 'Sharon Foster. I own Sharon's Hair Affair, the beauty salon in town. Max dropped by this morning.'

'Nice to meet you, Sharon. He just…dropped by…did he?'

'He was tickled pink to show off the kid.'

Gemma struggled to imagine Max in a beauty salon, surrounded by women all fussing over Mollie. 'Can I offer you a cup of tea or coffee, or a cold drink?'

Sharon shook her head and she gave Gemma the distinct impression that she'd choke on anything she gave her. 'No. I'll be right, thanks.'

'And you're sure you don't want to see Max?'

There was a long moment of hesitation during which Gemma was subjected to a lengthy scrutiny. Eventually Sharon made up her mind. 'No. No, I won't bother him. Look, you might as well keep the casserole. There's only enough for two.'

'Thank you.'

'It's beef stroganoff.' Sharon looked smug. 'I know it's Max's favourite.'

'Really?' Gemma murmured with teeth clenched in a grimacing smile. 'You're so thoughtful. I'm sure he'll just gobble it up. What a pity you can't wait to see him after coming so far out of your way.' She knew the drive from town took at least an hour. Now this woman faced the long, dusty drive back.

'Yeah, well... Might see you some time,' Sharon said uncertainly and without the slightest effort at sincerity. She turned and tottered back to the car. Her departure was accompanied by a slamming of doors and a roaring acceleration down the track.

As Gemma walked back into the house, trying not to think about other times Max and Sharon Foster had shared beef stroganoff, she heard the unmistakable sounds of Mollie waking. She hurried to attend to her and had just finished changing her nappy when the phone rang. Balancing Mollie on her hip, she dashed to answer it.

'Hello, Goodbye Creek Station.'

'Er...hello,' replied a woman's voice. 'Do I have the right number? Is that the Jardines' place?'

'Yes.'

'*Max* Jardine's?'

'Yes, that's right. Were you wanting to speak to Max?'

'Oh...er, yes, please.'

'I'm sorry. He isn't in at the moment. Can I take a message.'

'Excuse me, but who is this?'

'Gemma Brown. I'm...a... I'm looking after Max's niece.'

'Oh! *Oh*... I see. I didn't realise he'd hired a nanny.' The feminine voice was mellow and sophisticated.

Gemma resisted the urge to let out a loud, exasperated sigh.

'He didn't actually hire me. I'm a close family friend—Mollie's godmother.'

'I see,' the caller said again, with less enthusiasm.

'Can I be of any help?'

'Uh...this is just a social call, really. I met little Mollie in town this morning. Max dropped past my surgery to say hello.'

'He took Mollie to a doctor's surgery?' Alarmed, Gemma took another look at the baby in her arms. She seemed healthy enough. 'Was there something wrong with her? Max didn't mention any problems.'

'Oh, no. It wasn't a professional visit. We're just...' The caller paused to indulge in a self-conscious little laugh. 'Max and I are just good friends. And he was so excited about his little niece, he just had to show her to me.'

'I'm sorry, I didn't catch your name.'

'I'm Helena Roberts-Jones, the local GP.'

The hairdresser, the doctor... With a nasty blaze of anger, Gemma wondered how many more of Max's women she would have to deal with.

'I'll tell Max you called,' she said in saccharine tones. 'It's good to know there's medical help nearby if we need it—especially with a baby in the house.'

'Thank you,' came the subdued reply. 'Goodbye, Gemma. Perhaps we'll meet up some time?'

'That would be nice.'

'Oh, one more thing,' Helena Roberts-Jones purred. 'Could you do me a tiny favour?'

'I—I guess so.'

'Could you please check with Max if he needs me to order him a dinner suit for the Mungulla Ball?'

'Sure. With pleasure,' muttered Gemma.

She dropped the receiver in its cradle and, with teeth clamped together, made her way to the kitchen, to find Mollie a drink. 'Who'll be next, Moll?' she asked the innocent baby in her arms. 'The local schoolmarm?' Luckily, Mollie wasn't perturbed by her godmother's tension. She simply chuckled and played with the gold chain at Gemma's neck.

With Sharon's casserole safely deposited in a slow oven, Gemma wandered through to the large and comfortable lounge room and settled on the softly carpeted floor to play with Mollie and try to forget about Max's harem. Not that she really cared how many of the local females he courted, she told herself.

But she did object to being thrust into the role of his social secretary.

Nevertheless, she was surprised and a little taken aback by the interest of these women. Yesterday, when the little issue of breakfast had arisen, Gemma had decided Max was teasing her. But now she wasn't quite so sure. In spite of the comments various women had made from time to time about his looks, she'd never really thought of him as a ladies' man. Surely he was too stern and aloof?

For the next half-hour, Gemma lolled on the lounge room carpet and built towers out of blocks for Mollie to knock over. And she played peek-a-boo using a huge velvet cushion. Each time she reappeared from behind the soft blue cushion, the baby squealed with delight.

'Someone's having fun,' came a deeply masculine voice.

Gemma lowered the cushion to find two dusty riding boots in front of her. She looked up.

'Boo,' grinned Max.

'Good evening,' she replied primly. She didn't enjoy finding herself kneeling at Max Jardine's feet. She struggled to stand.

'Don't let me spoil the fun,' he said. 'Stay there. I'm going to crack open a beer. Would you like a drink?'

About to snap back with a negative reply, Gemma thought better of it. Her nerves were feeling distinctly frazzled. 'Yes, I'll have a beer, too.'

'Right you are.'

When he returned with two long glasses of icy cold beer, she left the floor and sat on one of the chintz-covered armchairs. Max relaxed into a deep chair opposite her and stretched his long legs in front of him. Mollie crawled over to him and patted his leg happily. He lifted her with one hand onto his knee. She crowed with delight.

Gemma hunted for something to say. She wanted to let off steam about Max's callers, but decided this was an occasion when she should put into practice her intentions to stay calm and collected. If she made a fuss, Max might think she cared about his women for the wrong reasons. 'Is the bore fixed?' she asked.

'Yes. Chad and Dingo are handy blokes to have around.' He took a long, thirsty swig of beer. 'You can meet them tomorrow night. They always come up here on Friday nights. I cook a roast and we have a few beers. Nothing flash, of course. As you know, social life in the bush is fairly quiet.'

Gemma felt her plans to be calm and uncritical flying out of the window. '*Quiet?*' she repeated. 'You surprise me, Max. From what I can see, your social life seems rather lively.'

'It does?'

'I mean if we start with the Breakfast Club...'

Max straightened and almost dropped Mollie off his knee. 'I beg your pardon?'

'Your lady friends. Your *breakfast* companions.'

'Gemma, what the hell are you talking about?'

'How about I start with Sharon Foster? Helena Roberts-Jones?'

He stared at her, obviously taken aback. Then he set Mollie back on the floor and downed his beer in one long gulp. 'Have you been spying on me or something?'

'She shot him a searing look. 'I don't need to go searching for your women, Max. I've been beating them off with a stick all afternoon.'

'The hell you have. What do you mean?'

'There have been phone calls, casseroles, visitors in see-through blouses and skin-tight jeans.'

He had the grace to frown and look confused as if she were talking in a foreign language. 'What on earth are you raving on about?'

'Ever since you came home from town there's been an endless stream of women callers.'

'Really?'

'Definitely. You and Mollie sure made a big impression this morning.'

'I must admit, I couldn't believe the way everyone carried on.'

'Well, you tried hard enough to get their attention...calling in at the beauty salon…dropping in on the lady doctor… I guess we'll hear from the school teacher next.'

At that very moment, the phone on the little side table rang.

'It'll be for you,' Gemma growled.

Max looked at the telephone as if it were a venomous snake about to bite him. Gingerly, he lifted the receiver.

'Jardine speaking.'

As he listened to his caller, a red flush flared in his cheeks. 'Susan? What a…surprise.' His hand fiddled with the collar of his shirt, as if it was too tight. 'A *nice* surprise, of course.' He turned, so that he was no longer facing Gemma. 'That's very thoughtful of you, Susan. *Tonight?* Well, actually, I think…'

Gemma picked up Mollie and, with a grim little smile, quietly left the room.

CHAPTER FOUR

FROM OUTSIDE THE lounge room, Gemma could still hear Max's low coaxing tones as he murmured into the phone. He seemed to be placating his caller's ruffled feathers. But, not wanting to eavesdrop on his conversation with Susan—the schoolmarm or librarian, or whoever she was—Gemma shut the elegant French doors which separated the lounge and dining areas.

She decided to do justice to Sharon Foster's meal by setting the table in the formal dining room, so she carried Mollie and her high chair through from the kitchen. In the linen cupboard, she found a delicate white lace tablecloth, which she spread over the polished timber table. As a centrepiece, Gemma set the vase of flowers she'd arranged earlier in the afternoon and two silver candlesticks holding slim, pale blue candles.

After a moment's hesitation, she approached the magnificent English oak sideboard and discovered a set of very good quality silverware and an exquisite blue and white Wedgwood dinner service.

'It's a pity to have all this going to waste,' she told Mollie.

She finished setting the table, lit the candles and stepped back to observe her work with a critical eye. The overall effect was surprisingly pretty.

By the time Max sauntered through the French doors, Mollie was halfway through her meal. He and Susan had had a jolly long phone call, Gemma thought grumpily.

'You'll be happy to know that Susan isn't a school teacher,' he announced, before nonchalantly shoving his hands in the pockets of his jeans and rocking back on his heels. 'She's the post mistress.'

Blast him! It was only because she knew the quality of the tableware that Gemma resisted the temptation to bang something. She squared her shoulders and eyed him with as much haughty disdain as she could muster. 'I don't care if the entire Australian women's basketball team are interested in you. They can phone you—or drop by—as often as they like. Just as long as I don't have to keep taking their calls.'

'I'm sorry you've had to deal with this.' His attention was caught by the dimmed lights and the table. He eyed the candles with deep suspicion. 'Are we—am *I* expecting company?'

Gemma suppressed a smile. 'No, but we have something special for dinner, so I thought I should make an effort. Can you finish feeding Mollie while I fetch our food?'

'Sure.'

As she moved away, Max called after her. 'You might be interested to know that I put a call through to the embassy in Somalia as well. I managed to speak to Isobel.'

Poor Isobel! Guiltily, Gemma turned back. 'That's wonderful. How is she? Has she seen Dave?' How could she have become so caught up in her own grumbles about Max that, for a moment, she'd almost forgotten about her friends' horrendous situation?

'Actually, she sounded very tired and depressed. She's only just arrived in Somalia, so she hasn't been able to see Dave yet. There's a certain amount of red tape to get through first.' His mouth twisted into a half-hearted smile. 'I did my best to cheer her up.'

Gemma stepped towards him and rested her hand on his arm. He was standing with a spoonful of Mollie's dinner in one hand and her bowl in the other. At Gemma's touch, he froze. 'I'm sure she loved hearing from you. Don't worry about Dave,' she said gently. 'I have every faith that he will be OK.'

'Yeah, of course.' He nodded before continuing to spoon food into Mollie's waiting mouth with the precision of an expert.

'How did Isobel take the news about our decision to share minding Mollie?'

'Her initial reaction was stunned disbelief.'

'I'll bet it was. She knows I—I—well, she knows you and I aren't soul mates.'

Max grunted. 'Once she got over the first shock, she seemed to warm to the idea. And the Embassy have given Isobel an e-mail address, so we'll be able to keep her posted about how Mollie's doing and she'll keep us up to date as well.'

'That's great.'

When she returned from the kitchen with two plates of Sharon's beef stroganoff and a rusk for Mollie to chew on, Max sniffed appreciatively. 'Smells good.'

'You should enjoy this. It's a very special treat.'

'It is?'

She smiled sweetly. 'You don't recognise this tasty dish?'

Lifting a tentative forkful of the beef and mushroom mixture, he tasted it, chewed carefully and swallowed. He looked puzzled. 'I'm not totally familiar with the flavour. It's rather fancier than my usual meals.'

'Oh? Surely Sharon's not mistaken? She assured me this was your favourite.'

Max seemed to choke a little and reached for his water glass. 'My favourite?'

'Yes,' Gemma replied with a devilish sense of satisfaction. 'Sharon Foster cooked this for us with her own two hands—well, if I'm honest, it wasn't meant for *us* exactly—I'm sure she didn't plan for me to be enjoying her culinary efforts.'

He chewed thoughtfully. 'She's a good cook, isn't she? This is very tasty.'

Gemma wasn't going to give him satisfaction by admitting anything of the sort. 'After poor Sharon drove all the way out here this afternoon, I thought the least I could do was go to the trouble of setting the table nicely with candles and flowers. I've tried to reproduce the evening just how she would have wanted it for you.'

'Gemma,' Max asked, not trying to hide the glitter of scepticism in his eyes, 'are you being catty?'

Her cheeks grew uncomfortably warm. Trust Max to try to turn this situation against her. She took another mouthful of beef to give herself time to think of an answer.

He watched her obvious discomfort. 'I think I detect a little of the green-eyed monster.'

'Why on earth would I be jealous?' she exploded. 'That's utter nonsense, Max.'

'I'm relieved to hear it.'

Her hands clenched tightly in her lap. *Damn him!* How on earth could Max even begin to think that she was jealous of his women? Why, she was downright sorry for them. Wasting their feelings on a grumpy recluse like him. If the poor deluded souls were hoping to trap him into marriage, they had Gemma's heartfelt sympathy.

She glared at him. 'Isn't it enough that you have Sharon, Helena *and* Susan all panting after you? Surely you don't expect me to go weak-kneed as well?'

He frowned and Gemma was forced to lower her own eyes, so that she didn't have to meet his piercing gaze. To her intense dismay, when he looked at her like that, she felt goose bumps forming on her arms. Surely he wasn't remembering that long ago time? A time that she'd rather forget.

His voice cut into her thoughts. 'So I'm safe from your affection. That's a weight off my mind.'

She wasn't looking at him, but she could tell by the sudden wariness in his tone that he was as uncomfortable talking about such matters as she was.

'You're very safe, Max. As far as I'm concerned, you've about as much sex appeal as toenail clippings!' She refused to look up.

'Oh, well,' he said with an exaggerated sigh. 'I guess three women out of four is not a bad score for a bloke from the bush.' Suddenly, the tension left his voice. 'Seriously, Gemma, it's not really all that surprising that Mollie's stirred up all this feminine interest.'

Her head shot up again. 'Only you could blame a stampede of women to your door on a helpless baby.' She glanced at Mollie innocently chewing on her rusk and rubbing moist crumbs all over her chubby, little face. 'You should be ashamed of yourself,' she cried. 'This *feminine interest* has nothing to do with Mollie.'

He smiled slowly. 'I must admit I didn't think about any repercussions when I headed for town. I just wanted to show off Dave's little daughter, but I should have gone to Helena first. She would have been able to warn me.'

'*Warn you?*'

'About the effects of a bachelor and a baby on women. Apparently most women find it a pretty heady combination.'

'Oh?'

'Yeah. Didn't you know? A fellow with a baby is a real chick magnet.'

'*Chick* magnet?'

'That's what Helena told me.'

'That doesn't sound like the scientific terminology you'd expect from a doctor.'

'I wasn't visiting Helena for medical advice. She and I—'

'I know, I know,' Gemma cut in coldly. 'You're just good friends.'

'That's exactly right.' He shrugged and held out his hands, palms up, as if pleading innocence. 'Anyway, it seems that lots of females happen to find a single bloke with a baby kind of…irresistible, although you've remained quite untouched.'

Her chair scraped loudly against the polished timber floor as she jumped to her feet. 'That's because I've been overexposed to the single bloke in question. I'm sure the dear doctor would classify me as a hardened case.'

She made a fuss of wiping Mollie's face and forced a hard edge of sarcasm into her voice. 'It's just as well some of us are immune to your fatal charms, Mr Jardine. Half the women in the district have started behaving foolishly—throwing themselves all over you.' For a shocking moment she hesitated as an unwanted memory taunted her again. Her eyes caught his and she blushed before hurrying on. 'We—we can't let the entire Australian outback come to a grinding halt.'

Lifting Mollie out of the high chair, she dropped a light kiss on her head. 'I'm going to fix this little girl's bottle.'

At the dining room doorway she turned to face Max, still sitting at the table, a bemused expression on his face. 'By the way, I mustn't forget to give you a message from your *very* good friend,

Dr Roberts-Jones. She must have been so busy imparting all that helpful information, she forgot to ask you if you need to hire a formal dinner suit for the Mungulla Ball. You are to let her know if you want one.'

She dashed away without waiting to hear his answer.

The next day, Gemma was spared an overdose of Max's company. He was busy with station matters all morning and he charged in at lunchtime with instructions for roasting the large piece of beef he'd extracted from the cold room the night before.

'The ringers will start dropping by around sunset, but they won't expect to eat straight away. Make sure there are plenty of potatoes,' he called as he raced off, leaving the fly-screen door to bang behind him and without so much as a passing glance at the pile of dirty dishes in the sink.

Scant minutes later, he dashed back and popped his head through the door again. 'Oh, and there's a Pommy Jackaroo joining us tonight. He's been working on Mungulla, but he's shown a flair for horse work, so I'm using him here for a few weeks.' His eyes darted to the sink and he hesitated, then sent her the grin of naughty schoolboy, who hadn't done his homework. 'Mind if I skip sink duty just this once?'

When he looked at her like that, Gemma felt a weird little pain in her chest. 'I hope you have a very good excuse.'

'This Pom and I are pretty busy trying to break in some extra horses. We're going to need more mounts this season because after the rain there's so much feed on the ground. It'll be dangerous using motorbikes for cattle work.'

Giving an exaggerated sigh, she held out her hands. 'If I get dishpan hands, you can pay for my next manicure.'

He touched one of her hands with his rough fingers and winked. 'If I speak to her extra nicely, Sharon might give you a slap-up manicure for free.' Then he dashed away again before she could reply.

At a quarter to six, shortly before sunset, Gemma heard Max's footsteps re-enter the house and head for the bathroom. She checked the oven. Assuming that the men would want to sit and enjoy a few beers before they ate, everything was coming along nicely. She'd added carrots, pumpkin and onions as well as the mandatory potatoes to the baking tray and she'd unearthed a deep-dish apple pie from the depths of the freezer.

For the occasion, she'd set the dining table again with the good china and silver and she'd dressed Mollie in a pretty little pink and white dress. Gemma had thought about dressing up, but understood enough about outback ways to know that this evening would be a casual affair. Nevertheless, she'd exchanged her usual cotton sun-dress for a pair of tailored white jeans and a sleeveless red silk shirt.

She was rather looking forward to the evening ahead. In the past she had enjoyed similar times, when she'd sat on the verandah, watching the sun go down and the stars come out, and listened to background drone of cicadas while the men swapped jokes and yarns about the bush. The men in the outback were always great story-tellers. If the jokes became a bit rough, they would apologise to her, but they never made her feel unwelcome.

'The roast smells great.' Max came into the kitchen, with his hair wet from the shower and slicked back. He was still buttoning his light-blue cotton shirt and hadn't yet tucked it into his jeans. He smelled clean and spicy—the kind of smell that made Gemma's feeble brain think about getting closer.

Horrified by her reaction, she turned and took several steps clear away from him.

'Hey,' he said, watching her walk, 'you look…you…look… Do you think you should be wearing jeans like that when there'll be so many fellows around?'

'What's wrong with my jeans?'

'Well there's nothing *wrong* with them, exactly. That's the problem. They're just right. They look terrific. But you'll give these blokes ideas.'

'What kind of ideas?' she asked, pretending innocence.

'They might think you're—available.'

Feeling emboldened by his apparent discomfort, Gemma folded her arms and cocked her head to one side as she eyed him steadily. 'I had no idea I was *un*available.'

Max scratched his exposed chest and looked at her with a puzzled frown.

'What have you told them about me?' she persisted.

'Nothing. Absolutely nothing. Well—' He fiddled with one of his shirt buttons and Gemma wished he would hurry and get the shirt done up. She didn't need to see that broad, brown chest and those sleek, sculpted muscles. He cleared his throat. 'I've told them—just in case they got the wrong idea, you see—I've explained that you and I are not an item.'

'I—I'm very glad they understand that,' she muttered while she hunted noisily through the saucepan cupboard to find a pot for boiling beans.

'But, unfortunately, they didn't really believe me.'

She found a suitable pot and thumped it down on the counter top. 'Well, what would they expect, Max? You have so many women who *are*—items. I suppose they've seen me about the place and leapt to a very logical conclusion.'

'Gemma, I think you might have been getting the wrong idea about me. I'm no lady-killer.'

Slowly and deliberately, he tucked the shirt tails into his jeans and Gemma swung her glance to the floor. It unnerved her to see him doing intimate things like that. The movements emphasised his manliness—the pleasing angle his body made as it tapered from his shoulders through to his hips—and it made her forget his problem personality. If she didn't rein in her thoughts right now, she might be lining up with Susan, Sharon and Helena.

'I never suspected that you *killed* ladies, ' she hissed, waving the saucepan at him.

'You're deliberately misunderstanding me.'

'I'm deliberately telling you to get out of here. Go play host while I—'

'While you play Cinderella? No way.' He stepped closer and grabbed her hand as it gripped the saucepan handle. 'We're partners, remember? I don't want you stuck in the kitchen like a meek little servant.'

If she were honest, it wasn't a role she fancied, either.

'Let's take Mollie and go out on the verandah and relax with a well-earned drink.'

When she followed Max outside, Gemma was relieved to find that the ringers, Chad and Dingo and a young apprentice they called Squirt, were just arriving. They all had a distinctly scrubbed-up look about them and reeked of after-shave, and they looked a little shy and awkward while Max made the introductions and handed round beer stubbies in polystyrene holders.

Gemma was contemplating breaking the ice with a question about their day, when another man appeared around the corner of the homestead and made his way onto the verandah. She knew at once that he must be the Pommy Jackaroo.

As he approached, his body silhouetted against the setting sun, he seemed to her to be every inch an Englishman. She watched him come closer and she could see that his skin had been burnt a ruddy brown in the outback, but his neat, light-brown hair, grey-blue eyes and dignified bearing marked him as coming from the same mould as many of the nicer young men she had met in London.

Max introduced the newcomer to Gemma as Simon Fox and he watched warily as the young man returned her greeting. Gemma couldn't help noting the way Max's eyes darkened while Simon's lit with appreciation as they exchanged a firm handshake. She was impressed when the young Englishman took the trouble to show polite attention to Mollie, who was sitting on Gemma's lap, blissfully sucking her toes.

Once Simon had accepted a beer and lowered his length into a low-slung squatter's chair, the conversation soon settled into a leisurely discussion of the importance of a good stock horse. Gemma listened with interest to the men's thoughts about the comparable benefits of motorbikes over horses for station work.

'There are plenty of places where a good stock horse will beat a motorbike hands down any day,' affirmed Dingo. 'For starters, there are far too many hills and gullies to the north of here for a motorbike and you'll always need a good horse for mustering and yard work.'

For a moment Gemma stopped listening as she thought about her own experiences in the bush and the excitement of a good muster. The smell of dust and the thrill of thundering hooves as her horse tore over the red soil plains. The heart-stopping danger as she watched the men catch and throw bullocks. And then there was the intense satisfaction of being part of a fast-paced, energetic team during yard work, when they branded, ear-tagged and vaccinated each beast inside a minute.

All through her high school years, when the wet season finished and the mustering began, Gemma had never missed the chance to join the team on Goodbye Creek station.

'You can't beat a horse for walking cattle and holding them,' she heard Chad drawl, before taking a deep thirsty swig at his beer.

She turned to Simon. 'And I understand you're something of an expert with horses?'

'I seem to have a bit of a knack,' he agreed modestly.

They exchanged friendly smiles.

'He's not too bad for a Pommy Jackaroo,' chipped in Dingo with a sly grin.

'Have you been in Australia very long?'

'Eighteen months. And that's too long, as far as my family are concerned,' he explained with a laugh.

'I guess they're missing you.'

'My father thinks I've done enough adventuring around the antipodes and it's time to come home and be of some use to the family.'

'They're farmers?' Gemma asked with genuine interest. Out of the corner of her eye, she sensed Max shifting restlessly on his chair.

'How's that roast?' he asked suddenly. ' You'll need to get the beans on by now, won't you?'

Lord, the man was a spoilsport! Gemma felt her anger flaring. For the first time since she'd arrived at Goodbye Creek someone was treating her like a human being and she was having a normal conversation that had nothing to do with babies, hormones or other people's love lives. She was tempted to tell Max to check his own roast, like he did every other Friday night when she wasn't there, but the men were all looking at her with an expectant air.

If she gave their boss a piece of her mind, she knew they would either be shocked to the soles of their riding boots, or they would assume she and Max had an 'understanding'—and that, married or not, she was his 'missus'.

That was the last thing she wanted them to think, so she rose and meekly handed Mollie over while she went to the kitchen to check the meal.

The roast was fine, the beans boiled beautifully and the rest of the evening went without a hitch. And after they had eaten and were replete with good food and fine wine, everyone moved back to the verandah. Gemma felt completely relaxed for the first time since she'd arrived at Goodbye Creek. Jokes and yarns were swapped, accompanied by the occasional slapping at a mosquito or the clink of glasses as they downed a nightcap.

After the men eventually left, she checked on Mollie and came back into the kitchen to find Max up to his elbows in hot sudsy water, tackling the washing-up straight away, rather than leaving it till the next day. Surprised, she took up a tea towel and quietly worked beside him.

She found it safer to look at the view through the window over the sink than to watch his strong hands gleaming with soapy water, or his muscular arms with shirt sleeves rolled back. Outside, the moon was hanging high in the sky like a shiny saucepan lid. Bathed in its light, the paddocks looked pale and silvery. From down near the creek, she could hear a lone curlew calling.

She found herself thinking again about how much she loved the bush and how, at one time, ages ago, she had never expected to leave it. Now, the bush still felt like home—as if she belonged. And yet, any day soon, she hoped to hear from Isobel that Dave was safe and then they would be coming back for Mollie. Handing Mollie back to her mother meant returning to Brisbane.

Leaving the bush.

And Max.

'How long are you going to spend drying that one plate?'

His voice penetrated her cloud of thoughts and Gemma realised she'd been standing in a daze for ages and there was no more room on the dish rack. Hastily, she dumped the plate she'd polished bone dry and grabbed another.

Max shook his head in mock exasperation then picked up the baking dish and scratched at a blackened patch with the steel wool pad. 'Thanks for tonight,' he said. 'It's nice for a change to have the little feminine touches that I kind of gloss over, like flowers on the table, red wine, gravy...and apple pie.'

She smiled at him, and thought how different he looked when he wasn't frowning at her. She was beginning to understand why some women were attracted to Max. Well, lots of women, she had to admit. There were odd moments when he let his charm shine through—even for her.

And those charming moments had been getting to her recently, so that she'd found herself thinking about them when he was away during the day. She'd even thought about what it would be like when he really turned on the charm. The effect would probably be quite stunning.

Heart-stopping.

She wondered why he hadn't married. There didn't seem to be a shortage of volunteers for the job. Now that Dave was carving a different career path for himself, Max could do with someone to help him run the household as well as the property. When she thought about the amount of renovating he'd done in recent years, she realised that he'd been working extremely hard.

Surely it was a too much for one man to manage on his own?

She stood side by side with him, drying several more plates, and realised that a week ago she would never have dreamed of connecting Max and marriage.

'You and the Pommy Jackaroo seemed to hit it off,' he said, after they'd worked together some time. His blue eyes met hers, glanced away and met again, before he went back to scrubbing fiercely at the bottom of the blackened baking dish.

'Yes. He's a nice young fellow, isn't he?'

'"A nice young fellow,"' Max scoffed. 'You sound like somebody's grandmother.' He shot her a sceptical grimace. 'You two seemed to be cooking up something when he was in the kitchen helping you with dessert.'

She should have known that her eagle-eyed overseer wouldn't miss a trick. 'Actually,' she said quickly, deciding not to beat around the bush, 'Simon has asked me to go with him to the Mungulla Ball.'

Max's scrubbing movements stilled. 'The sneaky devil.' He let the baking dish slide beneath the suds as he rose to his full height and stared down at her. 'And you explained why you couldn't oblige, didn't you?'

Gemma lifted her chin. 'I certainly did not.'

'You didn't?' He let out a mirthless huff. 'For heaven's sake, Gemma, you'll have to explain to him first thing tomorrow that you can't go.'

'No way!' she cried defensively. ' I really want to go to that ball. It's for Ruth and Tom Neville's tenth wedding anniversary. You're going with Helena, aren't you?'

'She spoke to me about it weeks ago. I accepted before—before I knew about Dave—otherwise I would have—'

For several heartbeats, Gemma waited for him to finish the sentence, but it seemed he'd changed his mind. He was concentrating on rinsing the baking dish with fresh, hot water.

After the silence went on too long, she answered back. 'Well, Simon couldn't speak to me about it weeks ago. We only met tonight.'

'Exactly. That's my point. You hardly know the man.'

Gemma shook her damp tea towel at him. 'Max, can I remind once again that you are not *my* big brother? You don't have to worry about me. I really don't need you to vet my dates.'

'What about your other responsibilities? What about Mollie?'

'For Pete's sake!' For the second time tonight she felt like Cinderella. This time she was fighting for her right to go to the ball. 'Don't try to use Mollie as an excuse, Max. You know as well as I do that babies and children go to balls out here. You, Dave and I cut our teeth on outback balls. The Nevilles will have plenty of rooms set aside for the little ones to sleep in.'

Max eased his weight back against the sink with his hands folded across his chest and eyed her thoughtfully.

'I'm going, Max,' she challenged, stepping forward and jabbing a finger into his hard chest. 'And, what's more, I'm going to have the time of my life.'

He clasped her fingers in a hand that was warm and damp from washing up.

Something drastic happened to Gemma's ability to breathe. Max was holding her hand against his chest and, Lord help her, she was thinking how interesting it would be if he kept on hauling her closer.

His eyes were so very blue when they were this close. 'You've always been a mouthy little shrimp,' he said while his thumb massaged her fingers, her hand, her wrist. 'Have you any idea how you look when you're all fired up like that?'

His question hung in the silent room.

'No,' she whispered breathlessly.

Had she risen on tiptoes? Or was Max leaning closer? They seemed to be almost touching. What an incredible mouth he had. So sexy. 'How do I look, Max?'

'Definitely kissable,' he said in a voice that sounded half trapped in his throat.

Heaven help her! It was what she wanted him to say and what he mustn't say. His lips were on her forehead. She could feel them caressing her with their soft, warm pressure. His arms were coming round her and they felt sensational and she knew that any minute now his lips would seek hers.

But—but this was all wrong!

This was *Max!*

She knew that she couldn't let him kiss her!

Just in time, she struggled out of his embrace and staggered backwards across the kitchen, her breathing ragged, painful, panting.

Max stood, still as a rock, with his back to the sink and his arms hanging empty at his sides. He regarded her with a steady, unsmiling gaze.

'You mustn't kiss me, Max.'

'No?'

Desperately, she shook her head.

'You're saving yourself for the Pommy Jackaroo?'

She didn't know what else to say, couldn't think how else to answer. 'I guess I am.'

At that, his face hardened into a blank mask. 'Then I wish you good luck.' He nodded curtly. 'And goodnight, Gemma.'

'Goodnight,' she echoed as he strode slowly out of the room.

Her shoulders sagged as she sank onto a kitchen chair. So close. She'd almost let Max kiss her.

But Gemma knew for certain that to kiss Max Jardine was to book a passage on the *Titanic*. She must make sure that he never tried to kiss her again.

CHAPTER FIVE

'I'M AFRAID I don't stock much formal wear.' Jessie Block, the stout and rather worried-looking owner of Goodbye Creek's one and only dress shop, shook her head gloomily. 'And I've almost nothing in your size, Gemma.'

With eyes the colour of faded denim, she studied Gemma and frowned.

'I'm too small?'

'Too small and too young,' sighed Jessie. 'All the young people get their clothes when they go to the city, or they have them sent out.'

'I haven't time to have anything sent out.'

It was already Wednesday, just a few days before the ball, but it was the first day Max had been free to babysit so that Gemma could escape into town to find something to wear. She'd known that at this late stage the chances of finding something suitable in a tiny outpost like Goodbye Creek were almost nil. She stared at the racks of Jessie's frocks and suppressed a grimace. They were mostly florals and prints in fabrics, styles and sizes suitable for the most conservative and matronly of souls.

She would just have to stick to the basic black that she'd thrown into her bag at the last minute. It had served her faithfully many times in the past and, while it was no longer the height of fashion and it definitely wasn't a ball gown, it would do at a pinch.

Jessie was rummaging around, shuffling coat hangers and desperately pulling out the most unlikely offerings. 'I'm sorry,' she said, as Gemma shook her head at a lime-green and feathered concoction. 'I really don't think I'm going to be able to help you.'

'That's OK,' Gemma reassured her. 'It was a stab in the dark thinking I might find something at this late stage.'

'What a pity.'

'Thanks for going to so much trouble.' Gemma slipped the strap of her bag back over her shoulder and turned to leave the shop.

'Wait a minute!' Jessie exclaimed. 'I've just remembered something. It's right at the back because it's never been suitable—' She darted excitedly to a rack at the back of the shop and hunted through a row of tired and outdated-looking clothes covered with plastic film. 'I'm sure it's still here,' she muttered.

But Gemma had resigned herself to wearing her black and she had no faith whatever in anything Jessie might unearth. 'Please, don't go to any more bother.'

'It's no bother,' came the predictable reply.

Gemma hovered near the doorway. Already she was thinking about what else she wanted to buy while she was in town. More formula for Mollie, a new toothbrush, some fresh oranges…

'Eureka!' shrieked Jessie. She charged back to Gemma, reverently holding a dusty plastic bag in front of her as if she were offering the Holy Grail. 'I'm sure it's your size,' she beamed.

As Jessie peeled away the plastic cover, Gemma eyed the garment dubiously. There seemed to be nothing of it. It looked more like a bundle of spangled cobwebs than a dress.

'It looks much better on,' urged Jessie.

It would need to.

'You'll try it?'

'Is it my size?'

Jessie nodded enthusiastically and led the way to the curtained cubicle at the back of the shop. 'Sing out if you need a hand,' she called as she drew the curtain closed.

Gemma was no longer in the mood for trying on clothes. Her eagerness had faded soon after she saw what was available. She was sure this dress would be no more suitable than the others. But, to please Jessie, she wriggled out of the trouser suit she'd worn into town and reached for the coat hanger.

The dress was so soft and shapeless Gemma took a few minutes to work out the front from the back and how exactly to put it on. Eventually, she slipped the cobweb-fine garment over her head. One arm slid into a slim, fitted sleeve while the other stayed bare as the dress slid over her breasts, past her waist and hips to skim her ankles. She took a deep breath and looked in the mirror.

And took another, sharper breath—more like a gasp.

'How are you going, dear?' Jessie called through the curtain.

'I'm almost ready,' Gemma replied. She needed a moment to examine the dress without Jessie fussing around her. She had to get used to the idea that this garment suited her. Suited her? It was amazing. When Cinderella's fairy godmother had waved her wand, she couldn't have achieved a more magical transformation.

The off-one-shoulder gown was soft and clinging and fitted her perfectly. Silvery blue, it looked as if it had been spun out of moonshine—and the sparkle it put into Gemma's light-blue eyes was quite amazing. She reached up and fluffed her short dark hair and, as she moved, she noticed long slits up each side of the skirt. 'Good, it will be suitable for dancing,' she said softly.

'What's that, dear?'

Time to put Jessie out of her misery. Drawing back the curtain, Gemma did an excited little spin. She was feeling great! 'What do you think?'

'Oh, my dear! Oh, Gemma! I knew it would be perfect!' Jessie circled around her, sighing with delight. 'You'll blow Max away with this!'

'Do you think so?'

'Oh, yes, love.'

Something nasty, like an electric shock zapped through Gemma. She clapped her hand to her mouth and wished with everything she had that she could take back this silly conversation. 'It's not what Max thinks that counts,' she hastily corrected. 'I'm not going to the ball with Max.'

Her words echoed over and over in her head. *I'm not going to the ball with Max.* And her sense of happiness and excitement drifted away, heading straight for the ground like dying autumn leaves.

Gemma covered her face with her hands and gave a little shake. This was so silly. She'd known all along she wasn't going with Max. So why had she been thinking about him when she first saw her reflection in the mirror?

'I'm going to the ball with Simon Fox,' she explained, looking Jessie squarely in the eye.

'Oh?' Jessie looked puzzled. 'Is he from around these parts, dear?'

'Yes.' Gemma laughed. 'Surely you've heard about the Pommy Jackaroo?'

'Oh, yes. Of course.' Jessie looked exceedingly embarrassed. 'I'm sorry. I just thought with you staying out at the Jardines' place to look after the baby and all—'

'Max is taking Dr Roberts-Jones.'

'Oh, I see.'

Gemma was startled by how forlorn Jessie looked. 'But I'm still going to buy this dress, Jessie. How much is it?'

The shopkeeper named a ridiculously cheap price. 'It's old stock,' she explained. 'And I'll never be able to sell it to anyone else.'

Once Gemma was back into her street clothes and the dress was paid for and carefully wrapped in lavender tissue paper, she found it easier to shrug off her sense of depression. Lately, she'd been letting herself get tied up in knots about Max. At night, she kept dreaming about him and the way he'd told her she looked kiss-able. What she had to remind herself, in the broad, bright light of day, was that Max had a string of women he told things like that.

And he would be taking one of them to the ball.

Besides, she might as well be positive. There was a very good chance that Simon Fox would find her kissable, too, and that was preferable any day to being kissed by Max Jardine.

But although Gemma gave an outward appearance of calm over the next few days, by the time Saturday, the day of the ball, arrived, she was as keyed up as a teenager on her first date.

Simon, Max, Mollie and Gemma had arranged to travel together to Mungulla and meet Helena there. All their party clothes were packed carefully into one suit pack, while in the back of the four-wheel drive they loaded tents and swags for sleeping plus Mollie's folding cot.

Gemma knew from past experience that many revellers would stay up and party all night, progressing straight from dancing and drinking to the recovery breakfast in the morning. But she was most definitely planning to pitch a tent down by the creek and catch a few hours' rest before breakfast and the long, dusty drive home the next day.

On the journey, Gemma stayed in the back of the cabin with Mollie, while the men sat in front, but she was determined not to be left out of the conversation. She wanted to get to know her partner better before she found herself dancing in his arms all evening, and besides, there was so much to discuss about London.

Simon knew most of the pubs and restaurants she had frequented while she lived there and they had also seen many of the same shows. Their discussion warmed up as they threw around names like Notting Hill Gate and Richmond Park and Simon grew quite animated. As they chatted, Max sat in grim, jaw-clenched silence, gripping the steering wheel with whitened knuckles.

His moodiness reminded Gemma of the Max of old, the Max who'd looked down on her girlhood friendship with Dave, and it made her more determined than ever to find Simon utterly fascinating.

They turned off the bitumen highway and rattled over the gravel road that led into Mungulla station, past pale, grassy paddocks dotted with skinny gum trees and sleek, grey-coated Brahman cattle.

Simon turned back to Gemma. 'What a pity we didn't cross paths while you were in London. I could have taken you down to our farm in Devon.'

'Devon!' she exclaimed. 'I *loved* Devon. It would be wonderful to—'

Crunch! At that moment, the vehicle swerved and hit an enormous pothole. Gemma was thrown against the door. Mollie woke up and began to cry and Simon, who had only just managed to hold himself upright, turned smartly to the front again.

Gemma glanced suspiciously at Max's stiff back and her eyes

caught his narrowed gaze in the rear vision mirror. She had the distinct impression that he'd hit that pothole in a deliberate attempt to stop their conversation. But if he thought he could prevent her from spending an enjoyable evening with Simon, he was going to be disappointed.

The sun was slipping low towards the distant rim of blue hills by the time they reached Mungulla. Many people had arrived ahead of them and their vehicles were parked in the shade of the huge paperbarks lining the crest of the bank that ran down to the creek. Trestle tables and chairs were set out on the stretch of lawn in front of the long, low homestead and in one corner a timber floor had been constructed for dancing. The African Tulip trees that framed the lawn were strung with lights.

'This is going to look absolutely gorgeous once it's properly dark,' Gemma said as she took in all the preparations.

They climbed out of the car and stretched their cramped legs.

Simon touched Gemma's arm and asked in his usual gentlemanly manner, 'Can I help you with Mollie's things?'

'She'll be right, mate,' cut in Max. He wrenched open the back door of his vehicle and tossed Simon a folded canvas tent. His actions were so rough that the Englishman grunted as he caught the heavy bundle. 'Do us a favour and set this up somewhere,' Max ordered. 'I'll look after the rest.'

He gathered up Mollie's equipment and headed for the homestead. Gemma hurried after him, Mollie in her arms. 'I hope you're not going to spoil this evening by being rude to Simon,' she hissed through gritted teeth.

'Wouldn't dream of it,' he replied.

'Huh!' Gemma huffed. 'You almost winded him when you flung that heavy tent in his stomach.'

Max stopped in his tracks and stared at Gemma. With his spare hand, he pushed his broad-brimmed hat back and scratched his head. 'For crying out loud, Gemma. The man's out here to be toughened up. Of course he can catch a tent without flinching. How on earth do you think he manages to stay on a bucking horse or throw a bullock?'

Gemma's upper lip curled. 'I'm not talking about Simon's

strength or lack of it. I'm talking about *your* behaviour. You just remember to mind your manners.'

'There's nothing wrong with my manners.'

'Let's hope not. I'd appreciate it if you were nice to my partner this evening. That way we'll all be able to have a pleasant time.'

He grunted. 'You'll be very sweet to Helena, of course.'

'Of course.'

Their hostess Ruth Neville greeted them with excited hugs and showed them where to set up Mollie's cot. By the time that was organised, the sun was almost set and guests, dressed in their finery, were starting to drift out of the homestead and out of the tents to gather on the lawn.

'Better get into our party clobber,' Max said. 'Let's hope the Pommy Jackaroo has the tent up. Do you want to get changed first?'

'No. You two fellows will be faster than me,' Gemma replied quickly.

While the men changed, she sat on the cool creek bank and tried to concentrate on the tranquillity of the bush and the creek below, but, to her annoyance, her imagination kept intruding, seriously disturbing her quest for peace and inner calm. No matter how hard she tried, she couldn't eliminate the pictures of Max that kept flashing through her mind. She tried to focus on Simon, her neat and personable partner.

Instead, Gemma found tempting visions taunting her... Visions of Max, only metres away, dressing inside the tent. She could picture his strong brown back and tightly toned buttocks as he shed his jeans and work shirt... The play of muscles in his chest as he raised his arms to haul a clean shirt over his head...the sideways jerking movement of his neck as he did up the tiny button at his collar and knotted his tie.

She had never seen Max do any of these things, so it was entirely disconcerting that her imagination could present such clear and detailed pictures.

'All done, Gemma. Your turn.'

The men emerged from the tent. Two handsome fellows looking their dashing best in sleek dark suits with gleaming white shirts and elegant black bow ties. Gemma smiled at Simon and tried to stifle any sense of comparison. Who cared if Max was taller, darker, broader-shouldered or had bluer eyes and a fuller, sexier mouth?

Simon was nice-looking, charming and polite—the kind of gentleman her mother had told her to look out for—the perfect partner for such an enchanting evening.

'You both look absolutely splendid,' she told them as she scrambled to her feet, and she sent Simon another encouraging smile.

'Don't take too long,' Max urged. 'We're getting thirsty.'

'I don't mind waiting for Gemma if you want to go ahead, Max,' Simon offered.

'No,' came the abrupt reply, accompanied by a frown. 'We may as well all go up together.'

As she slipped into the tent, Gemma grinned back at them. 'I don't have any problem zips, so I won't need any help with changing.'

'We weren't getting our hopes up,' Max drawled in reply.

Without a full-length mirror, Gemma had to hope that her dress was straight. The men had left a small lantern burning in a corner of the tent, and as darkness was encroaching very swiftly she needed its light to help her apply make-up while she peered into the minuscule mirror of her compact.

Given the limitations of her situation, she found complicated make-up difficult, but she was determined to make her appearance more dramatic than her usual casual look. Quickly she applied eye-shadow, mascara, a dusting of blush on her cheeks and lipstick. There wasn't much more she could do with her short, dark hair than run a little styling mousse through it with her fingers, so that it separated into feathery wisps.

Finally, she was satisfied and she slipped out of the tent. 'Hope I haven't taken too long.'

The men had been standing with their backs to her, looking at something on the far side of the creek. As she called to them they turned simultaneously and she felt self-conscious standing there before them in her new, dramatic, softly clinging gown.

Simon grinned broadly. 'My goodness,' he breathed. 'You look absolutely gorgeous.'

Max gave a very good impression of someone who had been shot by a stun gun. The shocked expression on his face sent Gemma's heart thumping and her knees to water. She reached for one of the tent's guy ropes to steady herself.

To her relief, he seemed to recover in a moment or two, but he walked towards her, smiling a strange, sadly lopsided little smile. 'We're waiting for Gemma Brown. Have you seen her?'

Gemma felt dizzy when he looked at her like that. She wondered how on earth he expected her to answer. 'She ran away with a gypsy,' she whispered and, blinking back silly tears, she dashed past Max to Simon.

Looping her arm through the Englishman's, she beamed up at him. 'Let's party, Mr Fox!'

'At once, Miss Brown!'

The trio crossed the stretch of paddock between the creek and the homestead and joined the revellers. A tall, willowy woman with auburn hair drawn back into a neat chignon separated from one of the groups and seemed to glide towards them, her pale, slender arms extended to Max.

Helena Roberts-Jones.

Dressed in an elegant cream chiffon gown and draped in pearls. Her attire toned perfectly with her titian colouring. 'Max, darling.'

'Helena.'

They embraced with a gentle, refined hug.

'So glad you were able to get away at last.'

'Yes,' Helena replied. 'I sent up a very demanding prayer—more of an order, really. No babies are allowed to be born tonight. No one's allowed to get appendicitis—or any other kind of illness, for that matter.'

'I'm sure no one would dare,' Max reassured her. With a hand at her elbow, he turned her to meet Gemma and Simon.

'Oh,' Helena said when she was introduced to Gemma. 'So you're the young lady I spoke to on the phone—the nanny who's been staying with Max.' Her eyes widened. 'You sounded younger on the phone.'

'She usually *looks* much younger, too,' Max commented dryly.

'Oh, well,' shrugged Helena with a self-conscious little laugh, 'it's amazing what can be done with make-up.'

Gemma didn't appreciate Helena's attempt at a snub, but she had to admit that Max's partner was beautiful and exceedingly elegant. How good Helena and Max look together, she thought with an unexpected pang of dismay.

But this was not jealousy! She couldn't possibly be jealous. She didn't care what kind of women Max dated. It was wonderful that he and Helena were perfect for each other. They looked like people in an advertisement for something expensive—an exclusive restaurant, perhaps. He was the ruggedly handsome, worldly wise man and she his beautiful, steady, capable wife.

A girl approached their group with a tray of champagne cocktails and they all took a slim glass flute and toasted each other. Soon people from other groups, mainly friends from neighbouring properties, joined their little circle and more introductions were made. Several people who had known Gemma when she was growing up in the district greeted her as an old friend. A silver platter of delicious savouries came their way.

Night fell swiftly and completely while Gemma and Simon discussed stock horses with a cattleman who had travelled all the way from Julia Creek. The lights in the trees and the floodlights for the dance area came on, creating dazzling spots of colour and intimate shadowy areas around the garden.

An old friend Gemma had known since schooldays claimed her, and by the time she glanced back to where Max and Helena had been standing, they had disappeared.

After a time, Simon walked towards her. 'Would you like to dance?'

She looked across to the makeshift dance floor. Only a few couples were gyrating to taped music. She preferred to dance on a crowded floor.

'Apparently the band should be here by now,' Simon explained. 'I think Max has gone down the track a bit to see if they made it across the creek.'

'Helena went with him?' Gemma couldn't help asking.

'I'm not sure.' Simon took her hand and led her to the dance floor.

He held her companionably close without any tasteless groping and he moved smoothly in time to the music, guiding her expertly around the floor. Gemma couldn't help admiring Simon. He was one of those rare gems—a capable, resilient worker in the bush and a socially adept gentleman. She wished she felt more excited to be with him.

After the first bracket of songs finished, they stood together on the dance floor waiting for someone to change the tape. 'You're looking very beautiful tonight, Gemma. The belle of the ball, I'm sure.'

'Thank you.' She accepted his praise with a slight bow of her head and wished that his opinion meant more to her.

When the music started up again, there was a little cheer from the crowd on the dance floor. It was a slow romantic number and once more Simon took her in his arms.

'Do you mind being labelled the Pommy Jackaroo?' she asked.

He laughed. 'I was a bit taken aback at first, but I know now that it's used with grudging respect. It means I may be a bit wet behind the ears—'

'But you're still a likeable sort of bloke.'

He looked into her eyes, as if searching for an answer to a question he hadn't asked. 'Something like that.' After a few more laps around the floor, he asked, 'I understand you grew up in these parts?'

'Yes, that's right.'

'But you don't talk about it much.'

Gemma grimaced. 'Everyone around here knows my life story. You can't keep any secrets in the outback.'

He smiled. 'I've discovered that.'

They swirled past another dancing couple.

'So you already know all about me?'

He looked a trifle embarrassed and slowed his pace till they were merely shuffling together. 'I know that everyone in the district expected you to pair up with Max's kid brother Dave, but you didn't. And now you're back here with his daughter.'

'My goodness,' Gemma groaned. 'When you put it like that it sounds highly suspect, doesn't it?'

She quickly explained that she and Dave had never been serious and told him about Dave and Isobel in Africa, and she was startled by the relief that shone in Simon's eyes when he heard her version of the situation. His hand at her waist tightened its hold and Gemma drew in her breath to keep her body from touching his. She stared sadly at the star-studded sky over his shoulder and knew with a terrible certainty that tonight wasn't going to be the dazzling evening she had hoped for.

The setting had all the right ingredients. Above them arched the huge outback sky, like an enormous dome lined with black velvet and studded with diamonds. Every so often, the familiar, heartwarming call of black cockatoos came floating up from the trees along the creek. All around them happy, hard-working people were enjoying one of the rare opportunities life in the bush afforded to dress up to the nines, kick up one's heels and have a good time.

This should be a night to remember. She wanted so much to enjoy herself with Simon.

But she had run slap bang into her same old, same old problem...

It didn't seen to matter how many likeable and charming men she met. When they got interested in her and their ideas turned to romance, she wanted to back off.

The bracket of songs finished, and Gemma opted for another drink. Simon fetched it for her and they went to join a group sitting at a table near the sunken fish pond. A little fountain played in the middle of the pond, its soft splashing sounds making a comforting backdrop. But Simon sat close beside her with an arm draped over her shoulders and several times, as they chatted, she found him looking at her, an intense spark burning in his eyes.

She set her glass down on the table. 'I'd like to go and check on Mollie,' she murmured, and, stood quickly. She hurried away before he could reply. Across the lawn she sped, holding her dress away from the dew-covered grass.

In the bedroom off the side verandah, Mollie was sleeping like an angel, but Gemma stayed watching over her for some time. There was a soft night-light in the room and she could see the little golden head, the thick dark lashes lying against her soft cheeks, one pink starfish hand resting on top of the patchwork quilt and the other cuddling a tiny pink rabbit. What a darling little girl she was.

It occurred to Gemma that she was doing rather a good job of looking after Isobel and Dave's baby—and she was enjoying it, too. That was totally unexpected. She leaned across the cot and whispered a prayer for the safety of little Mollie's parents and she wondered if she would ever have a baby of her own. Not if she continued to run away from every man who ever looked twice at her, she thought with a sigh.

A mirror on the opposite wall caught her attention. She saw the reflection of her lovely gown and couldn't help admiring its colour—the pale, silvery blue of moonlight. As she stared at the mirror she saw a dark shape move behind her on the verandah. But there was no sound and she reasoned that it must have been a shrub being blown by the wind.

But a second later she was gripping the railing of Mollie's cot with a shaking hand.

Images of a shadowy figure...a pale, blue dress and...a darkened verandah...dropped into her mind as if somebody was slipping slides into a projector.

Déjà vu.

It had happened before.

This scene, these images... A party on a night like this...a dress this colour...

And the photograph Max still kept on the dressing table in her room.

CHAPTER SIX

GEMMA SLID HER arms along the cot's wooden railing until her fingers interlaced. She lowered her burning face to rest on her hands. Every detail of the memory of that night replayed once more in her mind. Piece by relentless piece.

Five years earlier, when she was eighteen, she had come home from university for Dave's twenty-first birthday party. The Jardines had invited nearly everyone in the district to a huge celebration at the Goodbye Creek homestead.

That evening Gemma had had the time of her life in her lovely new dress—her first formal evening gown—pale blue with tiny straps, a figure-hugging bodice and a dreamy, floating skirt.

It had been a hot night, but she had danced and danced in her new silver sandals and drunk rather too much champagne. She'd stood by Dave as he'd cut his birthday cake and, in front of all the guests, he had kissed her. This had been greeted by a rousing chorus of cheers and loud cat-calls. And, while his father had made a speech, Dave had flung a possessive arm around her shoulders.

By midnight, after she'd given every second dance to Dave and divided up the others between the eager young men from the district, Gemma had been exhausted and just a little dizzy. When the band had finally stopped for a well-earned break, she had been relieved that her dancing partner, the head stockman from Acacia Downs, was happy to rejoin his mates around the beer keg.

Gemma had dashed away to hunt down some cool lemonade and a quiet spot to catch her breath.

She had found just what she needed at one end of the verandah, an old rattan lounge chair lined with ancient patchworked cushions and screened from the party by a vine-covered lattice. Gratefully she'd collapsed into it, flinging one leg over the chair's arm while she sipped her icy lemonade and not caring one jot that it was an unladylike pose. Hot and sticky, she had tried to fan herself with her hand.

'Oh, boy,' she murmured softly. 'What a great party.'

She wondered where Dave had got to, but wasn't too worried. There were so many people about; he could be anywhere. The ice clinked as she drained the lemonade and she placed the glass on the wooden floor beside her. Releasing a deep sigh of satisfaction, she slipped off her sandals and wriggled her aching feet. Already she was feeling much better.

A soft sound behind her brought her curling around in the chair to peer into the shadows.

Someone was there. A man, leaning against the verandah railing and, like her, enjoying a moment of peace. She was sure she recognised the familiar silhouette.

'Dave?'

The answer reached her soft and low from the shadows. 'Hi, Gemma.'

In a flash, she was out of the chair and closing the distance between them. Standing high on her bare toes, she threw her arms around his neck and dropped a carefree, happy little kiss on his lips.

Of course, he kissed her back.

And she knew at that moment this man wasn't Dave.

She should have pulled away! Of course she should have. Especially when the dreadful truth dawned.

The man she was kissing was Max.

But a part of her, some dreadful, shameless part of her, didn't care! From the moment Max's mouth landed hotly on hers Gemma couldn't help herself. His kiss was so exciting, so intensely arousing, all she worried about was that he might stop.

She felt as if she'd stepped through a door straight into woman-hood. She didn't know if it was the champagne or the hot night, the moonlight, or a taste of midnight madness, but in a heartbeat she and Max were exchanging kisses more breathtaking than any-thing she'd experienced before. Kissing Dave had been nice, but now something seriously sexy was happening.

She had no idea tasting and touching could drive her so wild. His mouth was hot and demanding as his tongue sought hers, making ripple after ripple of shocking, heated pleasure flood through her. For the first time in her life she knew why people made so much fuss about making love.

At first she looped her hands around his neck, but soon they were straying restlessly through his thick hair and across his shoul-ders, and, under her seeking fingers, she could feel the roll and flex of his hard muscles as he tugged her closer.

Then his hands began to move. Her skin sizzled as slowly, lazily, he made teasing trails from her waist, up her sides to her breasts. Cascades of sensation streamed through her and she heard a soft moan drifting from her lips.

Next moment she was pushing her breasts into the willing heat of his hands, wishing she could tear away the filmy fabric of her gown. It didn't matter that this man usually regarded her with dis-dain. Right now, she didn't want anything between her skin and his daring touch. An astonishing, warm and pulsing hunger fanned through her. And she realised that she wanted to give herself to him. Wanted him to possess her completely.

Willed him to take her.

'Oh, please, please,' she whispered.

He gave a gruff cry of protest, but still held her close, burying his face in her neck.

Having no experience and very little skill, Gemma responded purely by instinct, urging him with her body to understand her need. This astonishing need she'd never felt before. Boldly, she pressed herself into him, standing on tiptoe to nudge his lower body with hers, thrusting her swelling breasts against him, taking his face between her hands and covering his mouth and jaw with more eager, hungry kisses. 'Please make love to me.'

'Oh, God.' Max went very still. His harsh breaths as he dragged air into his lungs were the only indication he hadn't turned to stone. 'I'm so sorry, Gemma.'

At the sound of his voice the spell was broken—shattered into a thousand accusations.

Shaking, Gemma backed away from him, her hands tightly clasped at the neckline of her dress.

In stunned disbelief at what she'd done, she watched as Max raised an arm and drew it across his forehead, as if trying to clear his brain of what had just happened.

She was dazed, numb with shock, unable to speak.

How could she have done all that? With Max?

He was still in darkness, so she couldn't see the expression on his face, but she could see the slump in his shoulders, and the way his head hung low. She could tell that he was as horrified as she was by what they'd just shared.

The tears came as she edged further away from him. Her vision blurred so that his dark form swam against the night sky. *How on earth had it happened?* She'd been in darkened corners with Dave before now and she'd never behaved like that.

Dave had never been like that!

This knowledge was too awful to bear. It sent her scurrying down the verandah, without stopping for her sandals. She ran into her bedroom and stayed in the silent house for the rest of the night, while the party continued outside.

When Dave came looking for her, Gemma pretended to be asleep. She wanted to tell him what had happened, to say that it was a mistake, that she was sorry. But the admission was too terrible. The words remained locked in her throat.

So instead of unburdening her guilt when Dave stood in her doorway, she closed her eyes and made her breathing regular and deep. After some time, she heard his footsteps echo as they moved away down the verandah and into the warm night.

She would never speak about what had happened to anyone.

The next morning Dave expressed puzzlement over her early departure from the party and she told him she'd had a headache from too much champagne. After that little lie, there was no way she could try to explain what had really happened. In the daylight, it seemed even harder to understand how she could ever have allowed herself to behave like that.

And, of course, she could never bring herself to speak to Max about it.

For the next few days, he was away on some remote part of the property. 'Checking boundaries,' someone told her.

Two days later, just before she returned to the city, a slightly nervous Dave asked her if they could 'have a bit of a chat' and the outcome was his suggestion that perhaps he and Gemma shouldn't feel too committed to each other just because they'd been friends since forever.

Her guilty heart reacted wildly. *Had Max spoken to Dave?*

But he seemed to be thinking on a different tangent. 'I know everyone around here has always expected that one day we'd be a couple, but, hell, Gemma, I'm sorry, but I think we maybe need some space—a chance to meet a few more people.'

Once she got over the shock of Dave's suggestion, Gemma adjusted to it rather quickly.

Dave continued, 'You see, we're only young, and I'm not sure we've got everything happening the way it's supposed to for people who eventually get hitched. Maybe we never will.'

She looked hard at him then, and realised that a part of her had always known she and Dave could never be more than friends. 'I know what you mean,' she whispered, and her cheeks flamed as she remembered the shameful way she'd behaved in Max's arms.

'You're sure you understand?' he asked, his sense of relief making his eyes shine.

'There's supposed to be more than friendship—something a bit more—cataclysmic.'

'Cata-what?' Dave sounded puzzled, but then he grinned ruefully. 'You mean fireworks, the earth moving—that sort of thing?'

Suddenly embarrassed, Gemma simply nodded.

Dave leaned over and brushed her cheek affectionately with his knuckles. 'We've been the very best of mates, Gem. I'm sure we always will be.'

She was surprised how easily she'd got used to the idea of part-ing with Dave but, although she'd learned a thing or two about 'chemistry' on the night of the party, she couldn't let herself think that this willingness to separate from one brother had anything to do with how she felt about the other.

Max returned to the homestead the afternoon before she was to go back to Brisbane and he tried, just once, to speak to her.

She was taking a final walk along the tree-shaded track by the creek and had stopped to sit on a flat granite boulder to watch electric-blue dragonflies chase each other across the sunlit water. The sound of a twig snapping alerted her that someone was coming, and when she looked up she saw Max's tall figure striding towards her through the trees.

Alarmed, she jumped to her feet, and was poised for flight when his voice reached her.

'Gemma!'

Her face flamed with embarrassment and she felt sick.

'Gemma,' he called again, his long strides bringing him very close now. 'We need to talk.'

She didn't want to speak to him, couldn't bear to discuss that kiss. Talking about it would only make everything they had done all too shamefully real. The horrid truth, that she had offered herself in a wild fit of passion to Max, of all people, was terrifying. She couldn't deal with it.

She wouldn't let him near.

Running away felt foolish, but Gemma had to flee that scene. Like a hunted rabbit she darted off, not following the track, but ducking and diving through the undergrowth. To her relief, Max didn't follow her. She imagined it was beneath his dignity to scramble after her through the scratchy acacia scrub and lantana.

By the time she reached the homestead, breathless and panting, she'd decided that the only way she could ever face the rest of her life was to behave as if the incident had never happened.

She'd done her best to keep that memory locked away ever since. In her mind she'd pictured herself forcing the regrettable interlude into an ugly little padlocked box, and whenever it tried to haunt her she would visualise the lid snapping tight and the fat key turning in the lock, holding the horrible memory inside. And for long stretches of time it had worked. She'd been able to forget about the kiss and get on with her life. But every so often the memory caught her by surprise.

Like tonight…when once more she wore a dress of pale, pale blue and knew that, behind her, a man waited in the dark.

Gemma raised her head and the shadowy shape on the verandah behind her moved. She watched the reflection in the mirror and saw Max step forward until he was framed by the doorway. A wall light outside made his dark hair shine, but cast shadows lower on his face. Hardly daring to breathe, she remained very still with her back to him.

'Everything OK?' he asked softly, coming closer. He stopped just behind her, looking over her shoulder at the sleeping baby girl.

She turned, ever so slightly, in his direction. 'She's sleeping like an angel,' she whispered.

He was so close she could feel his warmth at her back, the stirring of his breath against her hair when he murmured, 'She's cute, isn't she?'

His hand touched her bare shoulder and she jumped.

'Come outside,' he said close to her ear.

Knowing she couldn't spend the rest of the evening watching a baby sleep, she followed him—after a slight hesitation. As she did, she sent up a frantic prayer that, after all these years, Max had forgotten that terrible incident.

On the verandah again, he paused, and she was so nervous she rushed to speak, to fill in the moments that must follow with safe, harmless chatter. 'Did you find the band?'

'Yes.' He cocked his head in the direction of the party. 'They're a group of townies and so they're not used to driving in the bush. They tried to take that bend just before the creek far too quickly and their van ended up in a ditch.'

'Goodness—was anyone hurt?'

'No, they were very lucky. The singer has a sprained wrist, but Helena's attending to it.'

'Poor Helena. She hasn't been able to keep her night free of medical duties after all.'

'She's used to it.'

'Will they still play for the dancing?'

'Sure. They're setting up now.'

'Great,' she said, extra brightly. She stepped quickly away from him. 'Then let's go. We'd better find our partners and dance the night away with them.'

'Hold it, Gemma.' His hand reached out and caught hers.

Just like that—her fingers were linked with his. Such a flimsy trap and yet, for the life of her, she couldn't pull away. 'What—do you want?' The words felt squeezed from her throat.

'I want to tell you how lovely you look tonight.'

The moon, spilling through the shubbery, illuminated his face and Gemma saw a startling tenderness that made her want to weep.

'Thank you,' she whispered.

'Are you enjoying yourself?'

'Of course. I'm having the time of my life. It's a wonderful party.'

He gave her a look that said he didn't believe her, but he grinned anyway and said, 'Glad you're having a good time. It would be a pity to waste this stunning dress.' He touched her skin, just above the sloping neckline of her gown, and she was sure her heart stilled.

In the burning silence, he whispered, 'You've grown up, Gem.'

Tears welled in her throat, making it hard to reply. 'What—what did you expect?'

'Oh, I expected something quite spectacular.' The skin around his eyes creased as he smiled.

This conversation was dangerous, but she was mesmerised by his voice, deep, yet rough around the edges, as if his throat felt as choked as hers. She couldn't drag herself away, despite the embarrassing memories still hot in her thoughts.

As if sensing her confusion, Max took both her hands in his and pulled her towards him. 'Now that you're so grown-up, I think it's time we talked about a little matter that we should have discussed long ago—five years ago.'

'No, Max, no!' She hated the sudden note of panic in her voice.

'The night of Dave's twenty-first.'

'Don't do this,' she pleaded, trying to pull her hands from his.

This was exactly what mustn't happen. Remembering was one thing, but she couldn't talk about that night now any more easily than she could then. It was much better to go on pretending they'd both forgotten.

The light in his eyes dimmed. 'You're frightened?'

She gave a tiny nod and looked away, unable to meet the directness of his gaze. 'It's not worth dredging up the past, Max.'

'You don't want to hear my apology?'

'*Your* apology?' *He thought he was to blame?* Through brimming tears, she dragged her eyes back to meet his.

'Hell, Gemma, don't sound so surprised. I knew exactly who was in my arms that night, but you thought it was Dave. I deceived you and I've had to live with the weight of that deception all these years. I cheated you *and* my brother.'

'Oh, Max.' She couldn't stop the tears from flowing and she lunged forward. His strong arms come round her and she sank against him, burying her face in his chest.

'Damn it,' he murmured as he stroked the back of her neck. 'I've been worried sick that you'd been traumatised by this whole business.'

The full-blown remorse she heard in his voice shocked her. On that night all those years ago, when her sense of guilt had coiled through her like a hissing, striking serpent, she hadn't stopped to consider that Max might be feeling guilty. She had always been quite certain that she was the evil one. She was the sinner.

Far worse than Eve in the Garden of Eden.

The biblical Eve had simply held out a piece of fruit to Adam, but Gemma had hurled herself into Max's arms, rubbed her body all over him and pleaded with him to make love to her.

Oh, Lord.

And now he was claiming the guilt. When all along she'd known it was Max she was kissing...

In the distant garden, a guitarist from the band twanged a few notes and she could hear the singer clearing his throat into the mike. 'One, two, three, testing...testing...'

As these ordinary, familiar sounds reached her from the party, from the ordinary, familiar world beyond the verandah, Gemma felt she was emerging from a dream. It was as if everything that had happened in her life so far had been leading her to this point and as if her entire future might well be shaped by her next move.

It was time to be honest with Max.

She knew that if she were as adult as Max assumed her to be she would let him off the hook. Any mature woman in her situation would admit that she'd known exactly which brother she was kissing that night, and then she might even let him know that she was quite interested in kissing him again and see what he had to say about that.

That was probably what most well-adjusted women would do.

Or she could play the part of the outraged virgin, grudgingly accepting his apology while struggling out of his arms.

That would be childish and deceitful but, then again, she'd practised being a coward for five years now.

Or there was one other way...

CHAPTER SEVEN

LIFTING HER FACE from his dampened shirt front, Gemma swiped at her tears and sniffed. 'For heaven's sake, Max,' she began in a shaky, high-pitched voice. 'Don't torture yourself with a guilt trip about some little old kiss that happened five years ago. That's ancient history. I haven't been worrying about it. I haven't given it a moment's thought.'

'You haven't?' He looked so disbelieving she found it hard to meet his gaze. His hand reached out and with his fingertips he touched her wet cheek. 'If that's so, why all these tears?' His attempt at a laugh fell short of the mark. 'And why do I look like I've spilled drink all down my shirt?'

'I'm sorry about that,' she said, seeing the damage her tears and her mascara had done. 'I'll get something to mop you up.' She turned, about to dash away, but he grabbed her arm and swung her back.

'Hey, not so fast, Gemma Brown.'

And she wished, oh, how she wished that she wasn't back so close to him again. Any minute now she would be doing a repeat performance—reaching up on her tiptoes, throwing her arms around Max Jardine's neck and kissing him till morning. Her stomach flipped at the thought.

She forced the tremors out of her voice. 'You had something else you wanted to say?'

His sad and thoughtful expression as his gaze rested on her made her feel he understood more about what she hadn't been saying than what she'd actually said. Eventually, he broke the silence. 'So that was just some little old kiss, was it?'

Her palms were sweating and, instinctively, she rubbed them down her thighs, but when his gaze lingered there, she hastily clasped her hands in front of her. 'I'm surprised that a man who has, at the very least, *three* women currently panting after him, would give one little kiss a second thought.'

He emitted a strange little grunt, and a moment later his hands were gripping her shoulders, holding her squarely in front of him. His eyes glinted fiercely. 'What if I *have* thought about that night—more than once or twice? What if I think we should try to lay this ghost?' His head dipped closer and she felt dizzy with longing. 'How about we try that little old kiss again, Gemma, and you can show me that I'm forgiven?'

Gemma's heartbeats thundered in her ears. Her weak and foolish body wanted to be in Max's arms again and to experience that passionate mouth locked with hers! But she couldn't bear to make a fool of herself again. 'There—there's nothing to forgive,' she stammered.

'That's not what your tears tell me.' His lips lowered to kiss her bare shoulder and, in spite of her caution, Gemma arched her neck sideways, offering an inviting path for him to follow all the way to her mouth. Already her senses anticipated the moment when his lips reached hers.

'I'm so glad you've grown up, Gemma,' he murmured, his breath hot against her skin. 'You smell wonderful. Feel so womanly, so soft.'

Oh, Lord. His mouth was too close. She needed him.

'Five years is a long time between kisses,' he whispered.

And at that moment she discovered just how immature and unsophisticated she still was. While her body yearned to be seduced, her mind succumbed to panic.

'Max, wait a minute.' Pushing against his chest with both hands, she broke his hold and stepped back. 'This is—this is all wrong!'

His hands rose in a gesture of helplessness. 'It feels all wrong to you?'

One part of her wanted to admit that being in his arms felt every kind of wonderful, but instead she rattled off a string of desperate excuses. 'It doesn't matter how it feels. I know it's wrong. You don't love me.' Her voice broke a little to make that admission, but she hurried on. 'I'm sorry if you got the wrong impression about me five years ago. I'm not free and easy with my—with my—'

Her eyes fixed on his exquisite mouth and for a breathless moment she couldn't continue, couldn't remember exactly what she was protesting about. She struggled to focus on the world beyond this verandah—the guests in the garden, the sleeping baby nearby. 'The point is—I came out here at your insistence to look after Mollie, not to be your—your mistress.'

'Mistress?' he repeated, his brows frowning low over amused eyes.

'Your imagination's running away on you, Gemma. There's a hell of a jump from one little kiss to…everything a mistress has to offer.'

Oh, Lord! And didn't she know it? It was a jump she'd never made. Fierce blushes burned in her cheeks. His words embarrassed her, angered her, *hurt* her! Smouldering, Gemma drew further away, wrenching her shoulders back and pointing in the direction of the party. 'That's exactly why you should get back out there to Helena.'

He remained standing before her in silence, as if he needed time to adjust to what she was saying.

'How can you kiss me when Helena's waiting?'

'That's a very good question.' Max watched her face carefully. 'Think about it.'

But she couldn't think about it. Not when her brain was seized by mind-numbing confusion. 'And Simon will be dreadfully worried about me. Any minute now he'll turn up here looking for me. How can you think about kissing me again? This is just as bad as last time. Don't forget I came to this ball at the invitation of another man.'

'Huh,' muttered Max. 'Of course, we wouldn't want His British Highness to find you in a compromising clinch.'

'Certainly not!' she hissed. 'And if you're any sort of a man—any sort of *gentleman*—you wouldn't have tried this a second time!'

He let out a loud, weary sigh. 'You're so right. You'd better get back to the party.'

'I intend to.'

As she turned to go, he called, 'So, Gemma, have we sorted things out?'

She looked back at him over her shoulder as he stood there with an arm outstretched, and it took all her will power not to run back and have him hold her again.

'You're fine about—about everything?'

'Absolutely everything, Max.'

She turned quickly again before the stupid tears threatened and she hurried down the steps into the garden. Never had she felt so confused—bewildered by her own feelings and by Max's behaviour. How could he want to dally with her and exchange a few kisses when he had Helena waiting nearby?

Think about it, he'd said. But what conclusion could she come to other than the fact that Max could kiss any number of women at the drop of a hat? Did he fancy himself as some kind of outback Don Juan?

Grateful for the subdued lighting in the garden, she dabbed at her wet face with a handkerchief and, as she threaded her way through the laughing guests, she vowed to find the Pommy Jackaroo and be very, very nice to him for the rest of the evening.

The band, eager to make up for lost time, played loudly and energetically into the early hours of the morning. Their singer, thanks to Helena's expert attention, seemed to have recovered from his ordeal and crooned seductively while nursing his arm in a sling.

Gemma danced with Simon, or sat with him and listened to his stories about adjusting to the life in the outback, and, once or twice, she allowed him to kiss her. They were very nice kisses. Like Simon himself. Skilful, practised, not too demanding—and yet hinting that he would be keen to demand a great deal more if she showed the right response.

When Gemma couldn't dredge up the appropriate response, she felt very depressed. Her partner remained charming and polite. But as the evening wore on, pretending to be even vaguely interested in him became more and more difficult.

And there were only so many times she could check on Mollie as an excuse to get away.

When she wasn't dancing, Gemma tried desperately to avoid watching Helena in Max's arms as they glided elegantly around the dance floor, but she didn't miss the touching moments of intimacy the other couple shared. She saw how Helena dropped her head onto Max's broad shoulder as they danced and the way she smiled up into his eyes as if she adored him. And she noted the possessive way Max held her close, his hand cradling her sleek hip. *The two-timing rat!*

As Gemma sat watching the dancers and twisting the stem of her champagne flute between anxious fingers, she reflected guiltily on her feeble response to Simon's romantic efforts. It was the same pattern all over again. The same sense of something missing that had dogged all her relationships with men.

She caught sight of Max's rugged profile dipping courteously towards Helena as she whispered something in his ear.

And suddenly Gemma was shaking, feeling ill, as a terrible realisation flooded her thoughts. She tried to hold back the knowledge that pounded in her head. *My dilemma is Max's fault. I've been in love with him for five years.*

Damn his sexy eyes!

Every man she'd met, since that night five years ago, had only been able to offer a pale shadow of what Max had given her. His kisses and caresses had stirred and aroused her beyond her wildest imaginings. Dave had simply been the first in a series of young men who had found a disappointing response when they'd tried to kiss Gemma.

And it was all because of Max.

He had given her a taste of a different kind of loving.

And, by doing so when he had no real interest in her except as someone to tease and spar with, he had wrecked her chances of happiness.

From beneath wet lashes, she stole another surreptitious glance at Max and Helena. They had stopped dancing and were laughing over a joke told by their host, Tom Neville. Helena's arm was draped casually around Max's neck and she nestled her beautifully groomed head against him. When she laughed, she buried her face in his chest.

Gemma dragged her gaze elsewhere, before she made a fool of herself by crying openly. It was so painful to finally accept the fact that after she'd tasted Max's brand of lovemaking *she* had never been satisfied with anyone else.

But if she wanted him now, she would have to take her place in the line-up beside a string of other women.

By one a.m., Gemma couldn't take any more. She was too emotionally drained to keep pretending enjoyment and too exhausted to dance another step, so she flopped back into another chair and smiled apologetically at Simon. 'I'm absolutely pooped,' she told him. 'And I know Mollie is going to wake at the crack of dawn, so I'm going to call it a night.'

He jumped to his feet. 'I'll walk you down to the tent.'

'Thank you.' An expectant gleam in his eyes made her hesitate. 'Um—don't rush, Simon. I'll make one final check on Mollie first.'

Feeling foolish, she dashed towards the homestead again. To her left, she could see a couple of teenagers emerging from the darkness at the edge of the lawn, the boy swaggered slightly and the girl was trying to look super-cool as she combed tousled hair with her fingers. They seemed to take a little fumble in the shadows in their stride. Was she the only person who remained scarred for life by that kind of experience?

'Gemma.'

As she reached the foot of the stairs, Max's voice called from behind. She hesitated, not sure if she could face him again, but eventually she turned around.

He was alone. Tall, dark, handsome in his debonair tuxedo, and alone. In the moonlight, his hair looked soft and exceedingly touchable. Gemma clenched her fists as if to ward off his spell-binding impact.

'Are you going back to the tent now?' he asked.

'Yes,' she replied coldly. *Did he have to check on her every move?* She couldn't help snapping back with, 'What's it to you?'

Max cleared his throat. 'My things are in the tent,' he said, glaring at her as if she were planning a string of shocking crimes. 'Could you toss my swag and my clothes out before you and, er— the Pommy Jackaroo—I'm sorry, you and *Simon* settle in there?'

Highly embarrassed, she let her eyes dart away.

'I presume you two want the tent to yourselves,' Max drawled. His words were accompanied by a loud yawn, as if he found the whole subject tedious.

'N-no,' she stammered. 'Don't worry about that.'

'Don't worry about what, exactly?'

Gemma was sure he was being deliberately obtuse. 'We—Simon and I won't need the tent.'

'I beg your pardon?'

'We're not looking for privacy.'

'You won't be needing the tent to yourselves?'

She huffed out an angry sigh. 'You're not hard of hearing, Max. You heard me the first time.' Looking up at the cloudless night sky, she added, 'It's a beautiful night. We can sleep under the stars in our swags.' She forced a face-splitting smile his way. 'And leave the tent for you and Helena.'

To her surprise, his confident gaze dropped and, with his hands in his pockets, he shuffled his shiny black dress shoes in the dewy grass. 'Helena's been offered a comfortable bed up in the home-stead.' He looked up again and grinned at her, a surprisingly shy grin. 'You know how highly respected doctors are in the bush. Her hostess can't let her rough it with the common folk.'

'Of course,' Gemma responded, and a silly little laugh escaped as she tried to cover her highly unsuitable sense of relief. 'I'm sure the poor darling's exhausted and needs her—her rest.' She hesi-tated. 'In that case, I guess we three can all share the tent.'

He looked startled by her suggestion. His throat worked. 'No, you're right. It's a clear night. I'd prefer to sleep under the stars myself.'

She followed his gaze up to the heavens. The silhouette of a huge bird, probably a tawny owl, was winging its way to the east, with the Southern Cross as its backdrop. Her comment came spontaneously. 'I love these big outback skies.'

'Yeah? I guess you'll miss them when you go back?' He looked unusually ill-at-ease, as if this was a question he hadn't meant to ask.

'Definitely.' She nodded and wrapped her arms around herself, wishing he would leave her.

Standing here with him again—alone—she felt far too vulnerable. She dropped her gaze, afraid that if he looked into her eyes he would discover the bitter home truths she'd had to face up to this evening.

She didn't want him to guess the awesome power he had over her.

For another thirty seconds she hovered on the bottom step, embarrassed and lost for words, and then she turned abruptly and hurried up the steps that led to Mollie's room.

'Just throw my things out of the tent anyway,' Max called after her. 'I might see this party through till dawn yet... And, Gemma?'

At the top of the steps she paused, but there was no way she could look back. She stood with her back rigid, but her ears were straining to catch his words.

His voice drifted up to her, low and gentle as a lullaby. 'Sleep tight.'

When she told Simon that she wanted to sleep outside, he was a little surprised and, she suspected, disappointed.

'That's what everyone does,' she replied with what she hoped passed for wide-eyed innocence. 'We get changed in the tents and use them for storage, but why waste a wonderful night stuck under canvas when you could be out here?' She flung her arms wide to take in the warm night, the silver-speckled sky, the creek bank and the bush beyond.

Simon scratched his head as he surveyed the scene. Other visitors were settling for the night. Some dark humps suggested people already asleep under the stars. In other areas people were sitting on their swags still chatting and laughing quietly. Further along the bank a group had lit a small camp fire and were gathered in a circle, spinning more yarns and tossing back more drinks. But from one or two tents nearby she could hear rustling, suppressed giggles and sultry murmurs. There was no doubting what was happening in there.

Simon stepped towards Gemma and said in a quiet voice, 'I had something a little cosier in mind.'

With her hands clasped in front of her, Gemma turned to face him. 'Not this time, Simon. But thank you for a lovely evening. I've thoroughly enjoyed myself.'

His face tightened. 'Do you really mean that?'

'Of course I do. I've never had a more charming or attentive escort. And there's absolutely no doubt that you can out-dance Aussie blokes.'

He was silent and she knew that he'd hoped to be more than her dancing partner. She saw a little flash of hurt in his eyes and, because she could offer him no comfort, she hurried into the tent to change before dragging her swag out onto the grass.

When she finally settled for sleep, Gemma was grateful for her emotional and physical exhaustion. To her surprise, she slept soundly and the next morning, although she was still very tired, she woke out of habit around dawn to find Max lying only a few metres away, curled on his side. She felt a familiar pain in her chest as she stole a secretive look at him sleeping there, his mouth open just a little, so she could hear the soft hush of his breathing. Simon was on the other side—sound asleep on his back with one hand flung over his eyes.

As quietly as she could, Gemma scrambled out of the swag and made her way down the bracken-covered bank to the creek where she planned to wash her face. White mist trailed softly over the surface of the water like a bridal veil. Early mornings were her favourite time in the bush. She perched at the water's edge, enjoying the almost spiritual silence broken every so often by the occasional lilting songs of magpies or the cheeky chatter of budgerigars and honeyeaters.

Dipping her hands into the chill, clear creek, she splashed her face. *Oh, Lord*, she thought as the refreshing water hit her cheeks. *I love it out here.* She tipped her head back and stared at the crisscross of leafy green branches above her. Through them she could see patches of sky. Although it was early morning, the heavens were already bright blue—blue as Max's eyes.

I don't want to go back to Brisbane.

The thought bounced into her mind and wouldn't budge. The longer she sat there, the more she was sure of it. Ever since she'd come back, her heart had been remembering and absorbing the things she loved most about the bush and now it ached for this tough, uncivilised country. And this yearning had nothing to do with a certain tough, uncivilised cattleman.

She whispered a wish that she could stay.

So many times in her teens she'd paddled a canoe down this creek, sliding silently under the willow-like branches close to the dank, brown banks. Behind the curtain of green lace, she'd stayed in the shaded, totally private world for hours, watching till a water rat came slinking out of its home beneath the tangled roots of a paperbark. She would throw leaves and sticks onto the water, knowing such movements would bring black bream darting out from beneath logs to snap at the surface in the hope of finding a juicy insect. Sometimes a long-necked tortoise would poke its little head out of the water and stare at her with yellow eyes.

All her life she had known and loved this creek, this district. It was in her blood and the thought of leaving it again brought a pain like a heavy fist gripping tightly in her chest. The first time she'd left had been important. She'd needed to discover the world beyond this little corner of the outback. But now she'd been away and seen what the rest of the world had to offer, and suddenly she knew with absolute certainty this was where she wanted to be.

It made no sense, of course. Her work belonged in the city and she needed to get back there as soon as she could.

And, even more importantly, she needed to forget about Max.

Hanging around would only make things far worse—rub salt in the freshly opened wound.

With a sad sigh, Gemma turned away from the creek and, after slipping into the tent to tidy herself, she hurried up to the homestead, knowing there was every chance that Mollie would be awake by now. In the garden, there were several others up and about already and some stalwart party animals, who had obviously stayed up all night and were flopped in chairs in one corner, looking a touch the worse for wear. Their host was lighting the barbecue in preparation for the recovery breakfast and he gave Gemma a good-natured wave as she passed.

Mollie was wide awake when Gemma entered her room. Wide awake and beaming with a big surprise.

'Good heavens!' Gemma cried as she dashed towards the cot. 'Mollie, you clever little muffin! You're standing up!'

The baby gurgled at her, obviously very proud of herself as she stood, clinging to the cot railing and peering over the top. Gemma hugged her and smothered her with kisses. 'You clever, clever little girl. Fancy standing up all by yourself. Oh, what will Mummy and Daddy think? And Uncle Max?'

This news was too good to keep to herself. Gemma ran to the doorway. How weird that she should feel so madly excited! She had to fetch Max. 'Stay there, darling. Don't move!' she called to Mollie before racing along the verandah and flying across the lawn, down to the creek bank.

'Max! Max!' she called, but when her cries were met by groans from sleeping forms in nearby swags, she knelt beside him and shook his shoulder, whispering, 'Max! Wake up! Come and take a look at Mollie!'

'What's wrong?' Max shot out of the swag and shoved aside the tumble of hair in his eyes. 'Gemma! What is it?' Wearing nothing but jeans, he looked as wild and ready for action as a Hollywood hero.

'It's all right, Max.' Gemma touched his arm, but when he looked down at her hand on his skin, she drew back again. 'Mollie's standing up!'

He frowned as he took in her news. Then his jaw dropped. 'She is?' His face creased into a grin. 'That's fantastic!'

'Come and see for yourself.'

She tugged at his elbow.

Together they raced back to the homestead. Max took the steps two at a time and reached Mollie before Gemma but, to her relief, the baby was still performing her clever act, standing with her little hands clutching the rail and crowing proudly as she bobbed up and down on unsteady legs.

'What a little champion!' he laughed, skipping around the cot and looking proud as punch as if somehow he'd achieved this small miracle himself. He grinned smugly at Gemma. 'If she's true blue Jardine stock, we'll be watching her standing up today and riding a pony tomorrow.'

Gemma laughed. 'Give the poor girl a break.'

'No fear,' responded Max. 'We'll have her running to meet her parents.'

'Is everything all right?'

A cool voice in the doorway brought them swinging around. Helena, looking pale without her make-up, but ultra-elegant in a classically tailored white silk dressing gown, leaned against the door post and peered in at them uncertainly. 'There seemed to be a commotion.' Her eyes darted suspiciously from Max's half-dressed state to Gemma and back again.

'Just a little celebration,' Max explained. He stepped aside and made a deep bow, sweeping one arm in Mollie's direction like a ring master in a circus announcing the star act. 'Mollie Jardine has joined the rest of the human race. Drum roll, please. May I present one small lady, who is now *standing upright*!'

Helena looked at Max as if she suspected he'd lost his marbles. 'From all the panic, I thought at the very least she'd developed measles. It's been going around. How old is she, anyway?'

Max beamed back at her and announced in the same grandiose manner, 'A mere *ten months*!'

Rolling her eyes to the ceiling, Helena muttered tersely, 'What's all the fuss? It's about time. Some babies are already walking at this age.'

Gemma found herself watching this little exchange with interest. From the way Max's face closed up, she could tell that he was miffed by Helena's snub and Helena was clearly much less impressed by his interest in Mollie than she had seemed when she'd telephoned after his trip to town. Had there been a lover's tiff?

'I'd say our clever little girl needs rescuing,' she said quickly, stepping forward and lifting Mollie out of the cot. 'She's learned to pull herself up, but I don't think she knows how to let go again yet, and she definitely needs a nappy change.'

'And you need to go back to the tent and get properly dressed,' Helena told Max, taking in the details of his exposed muscles and unshaven jaw with a puzzling, displeased frown.

As Helena turned away and drifted back down the verandah, Gemma set about changing Mollie. Then she took her down to the roomy Mungulla kitchen to fix her some breakfast.

By the time she emerged into the garden to join in the adults' breakfast, guests were making their selections from the mountain of food spread beside the barbecue. Crispy homemade sausages shared pride of place beside fried eggs, onions, tomatoes and mushrooms as well as baskets of freshly baked damper and a choice of bush honey, golden syrup or mango jam to spread on it. And, of course, there was plenty of good strong billy tea to wash it down.

Max had already piled his plate and offered to take Mollie while he ate picnic-style under one of the shady wattles. As he sat cross-legged, the baby happily practised her new standing skills, one hand gripping his jeans tightly. In her other chubby fist she clutched a wedge of his damper, which she was allowing a cheeky magpie to peck at.

Helena, looking immaculate in a neatly pressed white linen shirt and slacks, moved next to Gemma and Simon as they loaded their plates.

'You slept well?' she asked them solicitously.

Gemma's eyes flicked to her right to meet Helena's steady gaze. 'Not so well as you did, I'm sure. The ground was rather lumpy.'

'It was a warm night,' Helena responded. 'Must have been a little close in the tent.'

Gemma concentrated hard on spearing a juicy sausage. Helena's unexpected concern made her edgy.

'Oh, we weren't in the tent,' Simon hastily intervened. He shook his head. 'I can't understand why Australians love to abandon perfectly good tents to sleep out in the open.'

Helena's impeccable eyebrows rose as she stared at Gemma. 'So you and Max were outside, then?'

'And Simon, of course,' Gemma added.

'One big happy family,' Simon elaborated dryly.

'Oh, I see. The three of you.' Helena seemed extraordinarily delighted by this news and her reaction puzzled Gemma some more. What on earth did the other woman think had been happening down in the tents?

When they all settled to eat their breakfast, Helena seemed much more relaxed and prepared to take a renewed interest in Mollie's feats, but there was a tangible air of tension between Max and Simon.

It seemed to Gemma, as she munched on her tasty sausage, that the men had been involved in some kind of argument while she'd been giving Mollie her breakfast. Last week they'd carried on as if they were great mates—the best horse-breaking team in the state—and now they could barely speak to each other.

And the situation hadn't improved by the time they'd finished eating, thanked their hosts and made their farewells before rattling back along the track from Mungulla to Goodbye Creek. It was a solemn and silent journey. Perhaps they were just tired, Gemma decided, but the tension was still there. Nobody seemed interested in talking.

Occasionally, when another car passed in the opposite direction, Max would raise a finger or two, or perhaps his entire hand from the steering wheel.

Gemma whispered to Simon, 'That's known as the *outback salute*. Watch how many fingers he raises and you'll be able to gauge how well he knows the other driver.'

But Max glared at her so fiercely that she and Simon exchanged guilty looks and reverted to uncomfortable silence.

As if in sympathy with their bleak mood, storm clouds gathered ahead of them like huge black and purple bruises. But while weather would usually be a subject of intense discussion for people who worked the land, they all stared through the dusty windscreen at the threatening storm but no one commented. They were wrapped in their own grim thoughts.

The skies opened before they reached home, turning the dirt road to slippery red mud in a matter of minutes. They dropped Simon off at the ringers' hut and after a muttered, businesslike exchange between the jackaroo and Max, they drove on to the homestead. When they clambered out of the car, Max tried to protect Mollie by holding her inside his shirt, but the heavy rain poured straight through the fine cotton.

'I'll dry her off quickly,' Gemma offered when they hurried inside. In no time, she had fetched a thick, fluffy towel and rubbed Mollie warm and dry. She changed her into fresh clean clothes.

Max stepped into the room. His gaze took in Gemma's wet hair and saturated T-shirt and skirt. The temperature had dropped with the rain and she was shivering slightly. 'You need a warm shower,' he said softly.

'I do indeed.' She looked down and was embarrassed to discover how thoroughly transparent her white shirt was now that it was wet. 'I look like Sharon Foster.'

His face broke into a slow, sexy smile. 'Not a chance, Gemma.'

She bit her lip. Of course her curves were nowhere near as magnificent as Sharon's.

'Off you go,' he urged. 'I'll keep an eye on Mollie.'

When she emerged from her shower, dressed in jeans and a red gingham shirt with her hair towelled dry into a cap of wispy curls, Gemma found Max with Mollie on his lap, sitting at the computer in his study. He looked up at her and his face was flooded with joy. 'There's an e-mail message from Isobel. She and Dave are on their way home.' His mouth curved into an enormous grin.

She'd never seen him look like that. Excited, relieved. He looked even happier than he had this morning over Mollie's accomplishments.

His enthusiasm was infectious. 'That's wonderful!' she cried.

'Mollie, Mummy and Daddy are coming home!' She turned back to Max. 'I take it Dave's OK?'

'As far as I can tell he's fine. Isobel hasn't given too many details. Have a look at her message for yourself.'

Over his bare shoulder, Gemma peered at the computer screen.

Hi Max and Gem,

Great news, guys. Dave has been released. I actually got to touch him and hold him this morning. You've absolutely no idea how happy I am. We're flying out tomorrow! And we'll be with you guys the day after.

Can't wait to get home to see our little Cuddlepie.

We owe you two so much. Please give Mollie heaps of hugs and kisses and, hey, hug each other, too. You're both angels.

Much love,

Bel, who is heading off to buy Dave some shaving gear. My face is scratched to bits already!

'I'm so happy for them,' she breathed.

Max reached for her hand and gave it a gentle squeeze. 'I've given Mollie her hug.'

She stared at him, her heart jumping. *Oh, and now you'd like yours?* she tried to ask, but no words would emerge.

It should have been so easy to step towards him and give him a swift friendly hug. Except Gemma knew that, from her point of view, the minute she put her arms around Max all thoughts of friendship would fly out the window.

So instead of offering a casual reply, she stood there tongue-tied and pretended she didn't know what he was implying.

The expectant light in Max's eyes died. He dropped her hand. 'You should be extra pleased. This means your ordeal's over, Gemma. In a couple of days you'll be free to go back to Brisbane.'

CHAPTER EIGHT

DISAPPOINTMENT SPIKED GEMMA'S chest. Only a short time ago she would have been glad to escape, but now, even if she ignored the confusing jumble of feelings she had for Max, the thought of leaving Goodbye Creek so soon filled her with despair.

How awful to feel a sense of destiny and connection to this place when, in reality, she didn't belong here any more than Simon, the Pommy Jackaroo.

Max was watching her thoughtfully. 'That's what you want, isn't it? To get back to Brisbane as fast as you can?'

She had to press her fingers into the top of his desk to stop their tremble. 'Actually—I—I've been thinking I might be able to drum up a bit of work out here.'

He shook his head as if he hadn't heard her correctly. 'Station work?' he asked cautiously.

'No, something along the lines of what I do in the city—events co-ordination, promotions—that sort of thing.'

The idea, that had been sitting in the back of Gemma's head for days now, was so vague and nebulous she felt silly speaking about it.

Max popped Mollie on the floor and she crawled off eagerly to investigate the sand-filled door stopper. He straightened slowly and frowned at Gemma. 'What on earth are you going to find out here that you could promote to the public? Fresh air?'

'I've been thinking about the township,' she said hesitantly. 'When I was shopping the other day, I was shocked by how badly Goodbye Creek's gone downhill in the past few years. So many people have left and no newcomers have replaced them. Max, it's practically a ghost town.'

He picked up a pen on his desk and rolled it between thumb and fingers. 'You have heard about the rural recession, haven't you?'

'Of course. I know lots of people, including my own family, have headed for the city in droves, but it seems such a pity. There are still folks who have lived out here all their lives and who want to go on staying here. This town is where they belong. And the people on the properties—like you—all need towns for decent supplies. The cities on the coast are too far away.'

'What exactly do you have in mind?'

'I haven't thought it through properly yet.' She turned away to avoid his scrutiny. It was too hard to think when she could see those piercing blue eyes fixed on her. 'But there must be a way to attract people back to Goodbye Creek.'

'Tourists?'

'They would be a start,' she said carefully. 'And if the tourists brought in money to boost the economy, more people would want to stay here. The first settlers came to the district because there was gold in the creek. Perhaps I could do some research into those times.' As she spoke, Gemma could feel her enthusiasm gaining momentum. 'There must have been bushrangers. They're colourful characters. I'm sure I could come up with some great ideas to generate fresh interest. '

Max leaned forward and placed the pen carefully on the varnished timber surface. He rested his elbow on the desk, dropped his head and kneaded the bridge of his nose. Finally he looked up at her. 'I can't believe you're serious about this.'

His rejection of her idea was so genuine, so complete, it struck her like a physical blow. The old rage she'd felt towards Max so many times in the past surged through her, but she sensed that if she threw a tantrum now she might as well kiss her fledgling project goodbye.

'Max, give me a break. I respect your understanding of the cattle industry. I'll admit you can brand and muster cattle, yard them and sell them as well as anyone—better than most. But you don't know the first thing about my line of work.'

'Fill me in.'

'What's the use?' she fired back, hands on hips. 'You would only take extraordinary delight in pointing out the error of my ways. Forget, it, Max. I should never have mentioned my idea. I said it's still in the very early stages.'

He hitched himself out of the chair and stood before her, feet planted wide apart and shoulders back, his face a grim challenge. 'Does your interest in staying out here have anything to do with a young gentleman from England?'

Whoosh! Gemma exhaled air with the speed of a punctured tyre. She gaped at Max. His question had caught her totally unprepared. Did he really care if she had a special interest in Simon, or was he simply playing his favourite game-finding ways to annoy her and boss her around?

She folded her arms across her chest and tapped a foot as her mind whirred in a frantic effort to come up with a suitable answer. Blast him! Why should she lay her cards on the table when she had absolutely no idea what games he was playing in *his* private life?

She would leave Max guessing. 'What does my interest in Simon have to do with you?'

His face tightened. 'I happen to be his current employer.'

'Surely that doesn't give you the right to know about his—um— personal affairs.'

'But I happen to have information that could make you change your mind about staying.'

Gemma swallowed hard, totally unsure where this conversation was heading. 'How do you mean?'

'If you are planning to hang around in the hope of seeing more of our Pommy Jackaroo, you could be sadly disappointed.'

'Why?'

'He won't be here. He's heading off tomorrow to take part of the herd to my new holding up near Wild River and he'll be gone for at least three weeks.'

'Wild River!' Her anger had been simmering. Now it boiled over.

Gemma could see in a flash that Max was deliberately sending Simon north to get him away from her. He'd probably given the jackaroo his marching orders before breakfast this morning. No doubt it had brought on the tension between them.

She wasn't in love with the Englishman, but that didn't matter. What mattered was that Max was interfering in her life. Acting out the nosy big brother role just as he always had.

'Why the blazes are you sending him way up there?' she shouted.

'The Wild River property needs restocking and I can't get road trains in. It's too remote.'

'But why send Simon? Why not one of the ringers?'

The question seemed to annoy him, and he scowled at her. Some emotion she couldn't read burned in his eyes. 'He'll take Squirt with him and a couple of contract musterers.'

'It's a rotten thing to do, Max.'

His mouth tightened into a grim line and his voice grew very quiet. 'So you do care for him?'

'I thought Simon was here to work with the horses. I thought he was some kind of expert,' she snapped back, knowing she had deliberately avoided answering his question.

Max looked a little flushed around the neck, but his eyes were hard as flint. 'He's a good rider. That means he'll make a good drover. And anyway, he's out here to see the countryside.' Impatience sharpened his voice. 'I'm giving him an excellent opportunity to see some more of it.'

'Sure. The most desolate and toughest territory possible.'

'It's going to be tough, but it'll be character-building.'

Her chin jutted defiantly. 'Simon doesn't need *you* to build his character. His character is quite fine already.' Her anger sent her marching across the room. She came to a halt in front of the window and stood with her back to him. When she spoke, she tossed the words over her shoulder. 'But there's someone else around here who definitely needs his character improved.'

Glaring through the window, she could see that the rain had stopped. The leaves of a hibiscus bush looked shiny and washed clean and its large scarlet flowers were heavy and drooping. The warm and musty smell of dampened earth came to her on a soft breeze. Behind her, she could hear Max's fingers drumming. A threatening, ominous beat. He was angry with her.

Too bad. She was angry with him. He had interfered in her life, scolded her and bossed her one too many times. What was sauce for the goose was most definitely sauce for the gander. She wasn't about to apologise.

But life was so unfair!

If only she could turn off her feelings. Max was the last man in the world she wanted to fall in love with, and yet it was hard to be in the same room with him without making a detailed, lingering study of the way he carried himself confidently and proudly, of the easy, untapped strength in his movements and the distracting attractiveness of his smile. And after last night it was impossible to stop her mind from revisiting old memories of his sensuous mouth, his slow, teasing hands, his devastating kisses.

Slowly she picked up Mollie's favourite toy—a stacking set of bright plastic rings—and she took it to her. 'I'm sure you're tired of pounding that doorstop,' she said to the baby girl. Without looking at Max again, she crouched down beside Mollie and began to play with her, but as she made herself comfortable on the carpet her eye was caught by the title of a book on the shelf beside her. *The Golden Years.* It was a history of gold mining in Queensland.

Curious, she picked it up and glanced cautiously at Max. 'This could have the kind of information I need.'

He was still leaning against the desk as if lost in thought and he frowned again. 'So you really meant it—about researching the district and wanting to revitalise the town single-handed?'

'I'm not so dewy-eyed that I think I can do it totally on my own.'

'But you want to stay on—after Dave and Isobel collect Mollie?'

'I don't know, Max. Perhaps it is a silly idea.'

'Now that you know Mr Fox won't be here.'

'For heaven's sake, no! Leave Simon out of it. If I had more time, or if I'd started earlier, I might have been able to find out how viable my ideas are. But as things stand, I really only have tomorrow to check things out. I can't do much in one day.'

'You could at least put out a few feelers.'

His reply startled her. 'You think it's worth it?'

'I wouldn't have a clue, Gemma. But if you've only got this afternoon and tomorrow, then you may as well make the most of the time left.'

He walked across to the bookshelf and crouched down, running a tanned finger along the spines as he scanned the titles. 'There are a few more history books here that might be useful.' Pulling a thick book from the shelf, he handed it to her. 'How about we make ourselves a sandwich lunch and then we can both spend a quiet Sunday afternoon doing a spot of research?'

Gemma got up off her knees, clutching the two books to her chest. 'You mean it, Max?'

'No. I was only joking. I'd much rather do my accounts.' He relieved her of one of the books and began to thumb through it idly. 'Of course I mean it. There's not much point in your going to town tomorrow with high-flying ideas and no facts to back them up. That's like firing blanks. You need some decent ammunition.'

They spent the most unexpectedly pleasant afternoon. Gemma had to keep pinching herself. There was no fighting, no tension between them, just a calm sense of something that felt remarkably like companionship. Outside, the rain started falling softly again, its pattering on the tin roof providing a soothing lullaby. Mollie ate her lunch and drank her milk and curled up on a cushion on the floor for an afternoon nap.

On the carpet nearby, Gemma sprawled on her side, slowly munching corned beef and tomato sauce sandwiches while she read the history books and took notes.

Max kicked off his boots and lounged in an old leather armchair also reading, his feet, in thick socks, crossed at the ankles. When he found something he thought might be of interest, he read it aloud to Gemma. They discussed its relevance and sometimes she took notes.

'I think you'll want this,' he said, sitting up straighter. 'There *was* a well-known bushranger in the district.'

'Really? I hope he has an interesting name—like Thunderbolt.'

'How does Captain Firelight sound? That's what he was known as, but I'm afraid his real name was Frederick Flagg.'

Gemma rolled onto her back, propping herself up with her elbows. 'Captain Firelight sounds OK. Yeah. It sounds good. What did he do?'

Max scanned the page. 'He was attracted here by the gold—obviously. He was the usual bush larrikin—bailed up the stage coaches when they were heading back to the coast full of gold.' He read half a page further, then looked up at her and beamed. 'Freddie Firelight was in the bar at the local pub when the troopers tried to snaffle him, but, because he'd shouted drinks for the entire bar, all the locals wanted to protect him. In a final bid for freedom, he jumped out a side window and the troopers fired shots after him. The bullets went right through the pub's wall.'

'Wow!' laughed Gemma. 'Did he get away?'

'No. Eventually they ran him down.'

'If only those bullet holes were still in the old pub wall,' she sighed, but then she looked up at Max, her eyes bright with growing excitement. 'If we could reproduce a few authentic touches, I could convince a city TV crew that it would be worth covering a story like that.'

From his chair on the other side of the room, Max grinned at her. 'You look so pretty when you get all excited like that. Your eyes light up and you—you just glow.'

His words shocked her. And she saw a softness in his eyes that did crazy things to her chest. She could feel her heart beginning to pound hysterically and her face growing bright and hot.

Don't get fired up, she warned herself. *He just dropped a casual comment. Doesn't mean anything. Not a thing.*

But she was feeling very confused. This afternoon Max had been acting as if he'd been through some kind of metamorphosis. Like a toad turning into a prince. Converting from big brother mode to friendship—perhaps a close friendship. No lectures. No reprimands or scowls. Instead he'd showered her with warm and friendly smiles. Making her feel respected and liked.

And now this compliment...

Confused and blushing, not daring to allow herself even a shred of hope that he suddenly cared for her, Gemma glanced at her watch. 'Goodness, look at the time,' she blustered. 'We've let Mollie sleep for far too long and now we'll never get her back to sleep tonight.'

'Better wake her.' Max padded across the room in his navy blue socks and stood beside her, looking down at Mollie. 'You think she looks like a Jardine?'

Still feeling flustered by Max, Gemma pretended to study the sleeping baby carefully. Washed in late-afternoon sunlight, Mollie's golden curls, long lashes, and plump, dimpled face looked totally angelic. 'She's far too pretty to look anything like you or Dave,' she teased. 'I'm sure she must take after Isobel's side of the family. Wait a minute,' she added with an impish grin as Mollie frowned in her sleep. 'Look at that frown. Now that's a definite Jardine feature.'

'Cheeky minx.' He cuffed a feather-light brush to the side of her head and for a moment afterwards his hand lingered, as if he wanted to test the texture of her dark hair, rolling it softly between fingers and thumb.

And when his hand stayed there, just that shade too long, the impulse to lean her head into the curve of his palm was overpowering. Gemma closed her eyes as she pictured what might happen next. With just one tiny movement she could turn ever so slightly and rub her cheek against him—an innocent enough movement, like a cat wanting to be stroked.

And then she could kiss his fondling fingers...

But, of course, she didn't have the courage.

Would never have the nerve to do any such thing.

Instead, Gemma bent forward, away from his touch, and gave the sleeping baby a gentle shake. 'Time to wake up, little girl,' she murmured.

Behind her, Max straightened, yawned and stretched his arms high, as if he hadn't noticed the tension that zinged between them only seconds before. 'It's stopped raining,' he commented. 'I'll take her for a walk. I need to have a quick look around the place and check up on what the men have been up to while we've been away.'

On the floor, Mollie stirred and rolled over at top speed, her little eyes wide, instantly awake and alert, ready for action.

'Oh,' groaned Gemma. 'Wouldn't you just love to be able to wake up that easily.'

'You don't seem to have too much trouble. You were up with the birds this morning,' Max responded quickly.

Gemma shrugged the comment away. She was in no mood to expand on her own habits of sleeping and waking. Right now, she was quite certain that talking casually to Max about practices even vaguely associated with bedrooms would send her into an absolute dithering mess.

'I'll get her a clean nappy,' she muttered. After she'd returned, and had watched him change the baby with the speed of an expert, she said to him, 'While you're gone, I'll have a think about what I can cook for dinner.'

'Right you are,' agreed Max, and he sat a delighted Mollie high on his shoulders and headed out of the room, whistling 'Molly Malone' slightly off-key.

After they left, Gemma felt more confused than ever. Did she sense a slight shift in the way Max regarded her? Was it her imagination running away again? Perhaps he was still playing the big brother role. Or was he? The way he looked at her this afternoon. So sad sometimes. As if there was so much more he wanted to say. As if he was holding something back.

'You're dreaming, Gemma Brown,' she told herself. 'Concentrate on food.'

Needing a distraction, she decided to try to cook something different. Max was a surprisingly good cook, but he tended to produce rather conservative meals. Time to spice up the menu, Gemma told herself as she surveyed the pantry shelves. There was a tin of red kidney beans and another of tomato soup. She knew there was some minced beef in the fridge and capsicums growing in the vegetable garden, so she could make chilli con carne, if only Max kept chilli powder.

But his supply of herbs and spices was severely limited.

'No wonder this man is so set in his ways,' she grumbled to herself as an exhaustive search of the pantry proved fruitless. 'He doesn't have enough spice in his diet.' Setting the ingredients on the kitchen counter top, she went into the garden, wondering if an extra red capsicum could make up for the lack of chilli.

She left the house and crossed the wet grass to Max's vegetable garden and the smell of damp soil filled her nostrils. Rejuvenated by the storm and sparkling with rain drops, the plants looked fresh and thriving. But although the rain had stopped for now, the grey sky seemed to press low towards the earth like a heavy, wet blanket. The air closed around her, warm and oppressive. In the distance, thunder still rumbled, threatening another storm.

Gemma walked slowly between the dripping rows of tomatoes, lettuce, capsicums and carrots, enjoying the distillation of scents that hovered around her—the sharp tang of tomato leaves as she brushed past, the sweet crush of garlic chives beneath her feet and the earthy warmth of damp soil.

She bent to pick a beautiful, shiny red capsicum and noticed a fat grasshopper munching on a lettuce in the row behind. Lunging forward, she swiped at it and almost lost her balance. But as she dipped and swayed for a moment, she saw a little bush that had been hidden from view before.

It was covered with tiny red chillies.

'Excellent!' she cried triumphantly. And, as they were very small, she picked five. Now, when she hurried back to the kitchen, she was satisfied that she would be able to give Max a meal to remember.

Everything was simmering nicely and Gemma was boiling water for rice to accompany the meal when she heard the creak of the screen door opening. She turned, to see Simon stepping inside.

'That smells wonderful,' the Englishman said, drawing in a deep breath.

Tucking a wing of hair behind her ear, Gemma smiled at him. 'Hi, Simon.' She wondered if he had come to say goodbye. 'Would you like to join us for dinner?'

He rolled his eyes and laughed wryly. 'Thanks. But I wouldn't dare.'

She frowned. 'For heaven's sake, what do you mean?'

'Not worth upsetting the boss.'

'Good grief, why should that upset him? You're not letting Max intimidate you, are you?'

He folded his arms across his chest and his grey eyes regarded her steadily. ' I don't think it's worth rousing his temper. I'd prefer to restrict any wrestling I have to do to cattle.'

'Wrestling?' Gemma stopped stirring and rested the wooden spoon across the top of the saucepan. 'Are things that bad between you and Max?'

He shrugged. 'I think everything will be fine once I'm out of the way.'

'What on earth have you done to get in his bad books?'

His face twisted into a grim smile. 'Gemma, how can you ask?'

Fine hairs lifted on the back of her neck. 'I—I don't understand,' she replied, annoyed by the way her voice cracked.

'No, I don't think you do.' He looked down at the wide brimmed hat in his hand and fiddled with the brim. 'Sometimes it's like that.' He sighed. 'People can't see what's right in front of their noses.'

'Simon, please!' Gemma shook her head at him. 'What are you trying to say?'

His mouth tilted into a bemused, wistful smile. 'It's not for me to say much at all, Gemma.' He touched her cheek briefly. 'Except goodbye and good luck. I'm actually looking forward to seeing the country up north—the big crocodiles and all the bird life in the Gulf. But I'll be heading home after I finish this trip to Wild River.' He moved back to the doorway. 'Perhaps I could offer just one tiny spot of advice.'

Flustered, Gemma took up the wooden spoon again and gave the meal some unnecessary pokes. She shot a sideways glance to Simon. 'I'm listening.'

'I think you're searching for your own special slice of happiness.'

She frowned at him. 'Isn't everyone?'

'Sure. But some find it closer to home than others.'

Then he turned swiftly and was gone, out through the door into the purple twilight, before she could recover enough to say goodbye.

Suddenly she felt overwhelmed, as if her emotions had been stirred as thoroughly as the chilli con carne. Gemma's eyes filled with tears. Surely Simon wasn't implying that Max could make her happy?

How could that be?

A tear rolled down her nose and was in danger of dropping into the cooking pot. She wiped it with the back of her hand. How could she be happy with a man who already had Helena, Sharon and Susan and heaven knows who else? Being part of a harem was definitely not Gemma's idea of happiness.

She sniffed away another tear that threatened to fall. What puzzled her was how Simon could possibly guess her feelings for Max. It had only been last night that she'd discovered these emotions for herself. Surely her feelings didn't show?

She covered her face with her hands. If Simon had read her heart, could Max also tell how she felt? Was her face a dead giveaway?

Max's whistle just outside jolted her out of her musings. Gemma grabbed a tea towel and scrubbed at her tear streaked face only seconds before the flyscreen door swung open.

His dark hair had been whipped by the wind, so that some fell over his forehead. His cheeks and eyes were glowing. With Mollie in his arms, he looked incredibly happy—wonderful.

Oh, heaven, what could she do about this? She loved this man. And she could no longer tell whether it had happened last night, this afternoon, or perhaps a long time ago, but at some point in time her instinctive need for his physical embrace had expanded into a stronger need for so much more.

She had a sneaking feeling she was *properly* in love.

The real thing. Wanting the give and take of day to day living, yearning to share his burdens. The kind of loving that led to a lasting commitment.

A lifetime together.

She shook her head and threw back her shoulders. Enough of such nonsense. She had no chance of a life-long love with Max Jardine. She had more chance of waking in the morning to discover he'd turned into a frog!

He grinned at her. 'Mollie and I have quacked at the ducks on the dam,' he announced with a chuckle. 'And we've let the chickens out for their green pick. The dogs have been fed and—' He sniffed and looked eagerly towards the cooking pot. 'I'm famished. What's for—' Stopping mid-sentence, he stared hard at Gemma. 'What's the matter?'

She gulped. 'Nothing. I'm fine.'

'You don't look fine. You look all blotchy and red eyed, like you've been—' His eyes narrowed. 'Gemma, I saw the Pommy Jackaroo moseying over this way before. Has he been upsetting you?'

'No,' she answered hastily. 'Certainly not.'

His jaw clenched. 'And now you're heartbroken—because he's going away.'

'No, of course not. It's—it's the chillies. They made my eyes water when I cut them up.'

He frowned. 'Chillies?'

'Yes. Our dinner. Chilli con carne,' she announced proudly. 'Have you had it before?'

He eyed the cooking pot again and asked with a teasing grin, 'What is it with women and foreign tucker? First we had Sharon's beef stroganoff and now you've got this chilli con carne?'

Tossing the wooden spoon back into the pot, she glared at him, hands on hips. The last thing Gemma needed this evening was to be compared with Sharon Foster. She had absolutely no desire to be reminded that Max had a string of women. 'A varied diet is essential to a healthy body and mind and eating corned beef or steak six nights a week and roast beef on the seventh hardly amounts to variety.'

For a moment his face set into stubborn, defensive lines and Gemma expected an argument, but, to her surprise, Max dipped his head respectfully. 'I beg your pardon, Gemma. I'm sure your chilli dish is delicious. Is there time to give Mollie a quick bath before you serve up?'

'Of course,' she muttered.

And she banged things around in the kitchen as she heated Mollie's dinner and set the table for their meal. There would be no extra fuss tonight—plain thick white china and battered old cutlery and eating at the scrubbed pine kitchen table.

By the time she had things ready, Max had come back with Mollie smelling sweetly of baby powder and looking shining clean and more cherubic than ever in a fresh white nightie. Gemma couldn't help picturing him with a baby of his own, bringing her up in this home that he'd worked hard to make nice and on this land he'd worked hard to tame. It wouldn't be an easy life. His children would have to learn to work hard too and to entertain themselves. And to take the lean years with the good.

But it could be quite, quite wonderful.

She took a deep breath as he sat Mollie in her high chair in front of her bowl of beef broth and mashed vegetables. Gemma set two loaded plates on the table and took her place beside Mollie. 'Don't wait for me,' she said as she spooned some vegetables into the baby's mouth.

'Thanks. I am feeling rather peckish.'

Out of the corner of her eye, she saw Max dip his fork and take a hungry, man-sized helping of food. Then she heard his gasp and the clatter of his fork as he dropped it. Gemma watched, horrified, as he jumped to his feet, spluttering with his hand clutched to his throat. Then he dashed across the room to the sink, grabbed a glass from the dish drainer, filled it with water and gulped it down. This action was followed by another glass of water.

'Max! What's the matter?'

'Bloody hell! What the heck did you put in that?' he wheezed. 'It's lethal.'

Gemma stood and nervously crossed the kitchen. 'Are you all right?'

'I'm not sure,' he said, filling the glass for the third time.

'Perhaps those chillies were hotter than I realised.'

'Where'd you get them from?'

'Your garden.'

'*My* garden? I don't grow chillies.'

'Yes, you do.' She looked away from his glare. 'Perhaps the seeds were dropped by birds.'

'Did you taste this stuff while you were making it?'

'No. I've made it lots of times before, but I must admit I usually use dried chilli powder.' What she couldn't admit was she'd been so busy thinking about *him* that she hadn't really focused on the meal. She'd been working on automatic pilot, her mind in the clouds.

He shook his head. 'I defy any man to eat that stuff.'

Her fragile emotions, already strained to the limit, threatened to give way. 'Perhaps I could pick the chillies out?'

Max shook his head. 'Don't bother. I guess I'll have to make some more corned beef sandwiches.'

'Or get Sharon to make you a decent meal,' Gemma couldn't help shouting at him. Her lower lip trembled. 'I don't suppose *she* ever makes mistakes.'

'Don't be childish.'

Gemma closed her eyes to hold back the tears. Here she was once again, feeling immature and useless. Why did she always make a fool of herself around this man? It seemed that although she was twenty-three he would probably never think of her as anything but an annoying, half-witted kid. No wonder he always adopted the big brother role with her.

At least he seemed to recover from his gastronomic ordeal fairly quickly. Gemma kept her mouth tightly shut as she removed the plates of food and fed Mollie while Max made a pile of sandwiches.

She was relieved that he didn't continue to tease or lecture her.

'Well, Mollie,' he said, handing her a crust to munch on, 'two more sleeps and your mum and dad will be home.'

'I suppose she remembers them,' Gemma commented.

Max's eyes widened. 'I hadn't even thought about that. Surely she won't have forgotten her mother? It hasn't been that long.'

'How do you feel about handing her back?'

He didn't answer straight away, but just sat there staring at Mollie, his jaw propped on an upturned palm. 'I can't wait for both of you to leave,' he said at last. 'You know what a reclusive old bachelor I am. It's time I had this place to myself again. It's been overrun with females.'

She wondered if he was bluffing, trying to cover how he really felt. But after tonight's effort, perhaps he meant it.

'I guess you're hoping I don't have too much success in town tomorrow,' she said. 'You won't be happy if the locals are enthusiastic about the "Welcome to Goodbye Creek" festival I'm planning.'

He took a long sip of tea and, when he set the mug down, his eyes held hers. 'I'll reserve my judgement till we see what tomorrow brings.'

She dropped her gaze and paid careful attention to the geometric pattern of the blue and white tablecloth. 'If people want me to go ahead with the project, I'll find somewhere to stay in town. I wouldn't want to be a bother to you.' She felt braver after she'd said that, as if she could almost believe it.

'That's fine,' he said softly.

Again, stupid tears threatened. She jumped up and began to clear the table, hoping all the time that Max might reach over and touch her, tell her he was joking and he didn't want her to go. But he didn't move and didn't speak. He simply sat staring at Mollie. Looking sad.

CHAPTER NINE

GEMMA'S DAY IN town didn't go quite the way she'd planned.

Mid-afternoon found her slouched in a corner of the waiting room of the Goodbye Creek Police Station, hot, hungry, completely frustrated and more than a little embarrassed.

Last night's disaster with the chillies paled to insignificance beside today's effort. At least Max hadn't been there to make matters worse.

'Gemma, what's happened?'

Oh, cripes! Gemma swivelled around to find Max shoving his shoulder against the glass doors of the waiting room and dashing towards her with Mollie in his arms. He almost skidded to a halt.

'Are you all right?' He looked breathless and anxious and her heart developed a strange version of a quickstep as she jumped to her feet.

'I'm OK, Max.'

Panting, he stared at her. 'You're sure?'

'Sure I'm sure. I'm just being held for questioning.'

'What in the blazes is going on?'

'They're talking to the publican, Mick Laver, now.' She chewed her lip. 'How did you know I was here?'

As soon as he'd established that she was in one piece, Max switched from simply staring at Gemma to skewering her with his very best, no-holds-barred glare. With his free hand, he raked his hair wildly. 'I had a phone call from Susan.'

'The *post mistress*? What did she tell you?'

'She left a message to say there'd been a shooting at the pub and that the police had carted you and Mick Laver away.'

'Oh, I see.' *Good one, Susan*, Gemma muttered to herself. She could have done without the helpful intervention of another of Max's women. 'I'm sorry you had to find out like that.'

'What the hell's been happening, Gemma? Who's been shot?'

'No one's been shot.'

'No?' He was breathing deeply, as if he'd run all the miles into town, but any concern he'd shown when he'd arrived seemed to be churning into anger.

Wincing at the sight of him returning to full scowl mode, Gemma twisted her hands together nervously and struggled to find a way to calm him. 'It's a pity you've been dragged into this. But there's nothing to worry about.'

'All I want is an explanation! You come into town today to discuss a little business and the next thing I know you're heading for jail!'

'It's not that bad,' she said, trying to sound much calmer than she felt. 'Here, let me take Mollie. You look like you're about to drop her.'

Max seemed to have to drag his attention back to the baby in his arms, as if he'd forgotten her existence. 'Er—thanks,' he said, looking and sounding hassled.

'If you'll come and sit here, I'll explain what happened.'

He handed the baby to Gemma and their eyes met. She gulped. *Good grief! He looked angry enough to start hurling furniture around.* 'Don't worry,' she hastened to reassure him. 'Nobody's been hurt. It's all a storm in a teacup.'

He seemed reluctant to sit, as if he would prefer to pace the room like a caged tiger, but when Gemma returned to her seat and waited for him he eventually joined her, although he kept his hands on his thighs, clenching and unclenching them restlessly.

Mollie sneezed and Gemma searched for a tissue.

'I got the impression you'd been shot,' he snapped.

'If I'd been shot,' she told him testily, 'they would have taken me to the medical centre, not the police station.'

'I've already been there.' He jumped to his feet again and spun on his heel, striding to the far wall and back.

She concentrated very hard on wiping the baby's nose.

From the far side of the room he fumed, 'I'm waiting for a decent explanation, Gemma.'

Here he was again—acting like her big brother, or, worse still, her sergeant major. 'I'm beginning to wish I had an *indecent* explanation,' she snapped. 'If I'd done something sordid you could really have an excuse to sound off, but all I was doing was trying to help your struggling old town.'

For just a second his grim mask slipped. 'Something *sordid*, Gem? Let's not get melodramatic.'

Gemma groaned. 'If anyone is indulging in melodrama, it's you, Max. Now do you want to hear what happened, or do you want to make a spectacle of yourself?'

He looked at her sharply. 'I imagine you've created a big enough spectacle for both of us.' He approached her once more and took a seat again. In a more controlled voice he asked, 'For the last time, what happened?'

'Not a lot really,' she told him with a shaky attempt at a smile. 'My plans started out well. I told Mick Laver at the pub about my background in promotions and my idea for a "Welcome to Goodbye Creek" festival and he was mad keen on the idea.' Wrapping her arms around Mollie, she held the baby closer. 'I explained to him how I wanted to promote the town and how important the pub used to be in the gold rush days. And he was totally fired up! So I went on to tell him about the shoot-out between Captain Firelight and the troopers and he was furious that he'd renovated the place and puttied up the original bullet holes. And that's when he had his brainwave.'

Max shook his head. 'Mick's famous for having bright ideas that backfire.'

'You might have warned me.'

He didn't reply to that—just waited for her to continue.

'Well, he had a ripper of an idea today. He decided to shoot some fresh bullet holes.'

'What? Through the pub wall?' Max asked incredulously.

Gemma nodded. 'Spot on. Before I could stop him, he whipped out the rifle he keeps under the counter near the till, and—Kapow! Kapow! Goodbye Creek pub has two new holes in its wall.'

'Of all the hare-brained schemes...' Max whistled through his teeth.

'I had no idea he would get so carried away,' Gemma added defensively.

'You obviously got him over-excited. What did you do? Suggest there'd be unlimited publicity, crowds of tourists clamouring for drinks at his pub? Tell him Goodbye Creek will be a boom town again?'

'*I* got him excited?' Gemma shouted in frustration. 'That's rich! You can't blame his actions on me.'

He shook his head. 'You should have taken things more slowly and you certainly shouldn't have put yourself at risk like that when—when I—when your main responsibility is Mollie.'

She sprang to her feet. 'We're supposed to be sharing the care of Mollie and I'm sure I've held up my part of the bargain. I only asked for one day.'

'Yeah. I let you out of my sight for *one* day and you end up in all this mess.'

There was only so much of this Gemma could take. 'Max, do you know what your problem is?' In her arms, Mollie coughed and let out a little whimper. Gemma forgot she was about to accuse Max of egomania and shot him a worried glance. 'Do you think she's getting a cold? She did get soaked through in that storm yesterday.'

He frowned and looked a touch shamefaced. 'I don't know,' he muttered. 'I think she might have been coughing a bit earlier in the day, but she's been eating well.' He touched Mollie's plump little knee. 'Don't you dare get sick on us now, possum. Your mum and dad arrive home tomorrow and we want you firing on all cylinders.' He glanced at Gemma again. 'If there's no real problem here, why all the fuss? Why are you still being held ?'

Gemma shrugged and rolled her eyes. 'There's a police inspector in town and he made the local sergeant extra nervous. When they heard the shots, they both came bursting into the pub with their pistols drawn.'

'Sounds like everybody's been over-reacting,' Max replied.

'Especially you!' Gemma retorted, but at that moment Mollie whimpered and gave another little cough and suddenly she was more worried about the baby than Max. 'Perhaps you'd better take Mollie home again. I'll be back as soon as I can.'

Max studied Mollie, and on cue she offered him one of her sunshiny smiles. 'She doesn't look too bad,' he said. 'I'd like to speak to Dan Kelly first, just to know there won't be any problems.'

'Max, won't you ever learn to trust me to sort out my own life?'

What a dangerous question! Gemma was glad that before he could answer a door in the opposite wall opened and a uniformed man and Mick Laver, the publican, came out.

The policeman nodded at Max. 'She's free to go,' he said straight away. 'We've sorted out this scallywag and don't plan to press any charges.'

About time! thought Gemma, just a little miffed that the sergeant was talking about her to Max as if she were a minor. She'd wasted the best part of the afternoon sweating it out in this grimy, boring waiting room and she hadn't made it even halfway through the list of things she'd hoped to achieve today.

But Max was shaking the sergeant's hand, smiling and thanking him as if the man had done him a good turn. He turned to Gemma. 'Let's go. Do you want to bring Mollie home with you? Your vehicle has the proper seat for her.'

Gemma frowned. 'I'd been hoping to stay in town a bit longer. There are still a lot of people I need to talk to.'

Sergeant Kelly squinted at her while he pushed his police cap to the back of his head and scratched his grey curly hair. 'You'll be making sure the little baby travels in the regulation safety seat, won't you, Miss Brown?'

Gemma smiled sweetly at him. 'Of course, sergeant.' She could argue this one with Max when they got outside.

Mollie coughed again and the cough had a raspy edge to it.

Gemma felt faint stirrings of alarm. 'I'll come now,' she decided quickly. 'The Goodbye Creek Festival is not as important as our little girl.'

As she rattled through the bush on the trip home, Gemma toyed with the notion that Max had been so angry because he cared about her. It was a comforting thought—but not something she could dwell on. She was growing more worried about Mollie. Her coughs were getting worse and she seemed fretful—quite unlike her usually sunny self. The very last thing she wanted was for Isobel and Dave to come home, eager to see their little daughter, and to find her sick. Until now the babysitting project had gone so well!

Clutching the steering wheel, Gemma felt Mollie's forehead with her free hand. She didn't feel hot. Surely that was a good sign? Suddenly, she felt totally inadequate again. Caring for a healthy baby was one thing, but what did she do if Mollie got sick?

When they returned home, Max's reaction, as soon as he heard Mollie's worsening cough, was to ring Helena at the medical centre straight away, but she was out on an urgent call.

'I guess we'll just have to keep her comfortable,' suggested Gemma. 'Do you have any eucalyptus oil? We could rub her chest with it.'

Max fetched the oil, while Gemma changed Mollie into her nightgown. Together they stared down at the baby lying on the change table, looking so frighteningly quiet as Gemma rubbed her little chest. Although she didn't look ill, there was none of her usual bounce, no chuckles when Gemma gave her ribs a tickle.

Together they fed her, rocked her and put her to bed and, to their dismay, Mollie went to sleep quickly, as if she were quite exhausted. They looked at each other, their eyes wide with despair.

'Now what do we do?' Gemma asked Max, as he stood at the end of the cot with a clean nappy draped over one shoulder and Mollie's empty bottle in his hand. 'Watch over her?'

'Perhaps all she needs is a good night's sleep,' he suggested. But he looked wretched with worry. 'We should get ourselves something to eat and then we can check on her again.'

They ate a scratch meal in the kitchen. In silence. Instead of chatting eagerly about Isobel and Dave's arrival in the morning, they both avoided the subject, just as they avoided any further discussion of her disastrous day in town. Gemma was concentrating on Mollie, willing her to get better quickly. Halfway through the meal, Max got up and turned the radio on, as if he needed to be distracted from his own thoughts, and they continued eating while listening to a summary of a cricket test match between England and Australia, but neither took much notice of the score.

While Gemma dished out their second course of cheese and crackers with the fresh grapes she'd bought in town, Max went back to Mollie's room to check her again. He returned looking sombre and sat down heavily. 'She's still asleep, but I'm afraid the coughing hasn't stopped.'

He looked so miserable that Gemma felt the urge to cheer him up. The radio wasn't helping. The cricket broadcast had finished and a symphony orchestra had begun to play something sad and slow. 'We mustn't sit here being morbid,' she cajoled. 'Surely we can do something to lift our spirits—but I'm hopeless at telling jokes. I can never remember the punch line. Um—perhaps we could try a game of I Spy?'

His eyes widened. 'I Spy?' Putting down the cheese knife, Max propped his chin in one hand and frowned, as if giving the matter careful thought. Finally he favoured her with a slow grin and his eyes danced with tolerant amusement. 'And what exactly do you spy, Gemma?'

Feeling very tense, and just a little ridiculous, she began self-consciously to recite the childish chant. 'I spy with my little eye—' She paused and looked around the kitchen, hunting for something interesting. 'Something beginning with s.'

'Spider?' he suggested quickly.

'Where?' Gemma jumped out of her chair and scanned the room frantically. Spiders were the one form of wildlife she hated. But she it didn't take her long to realise that she'd been tricked. 'Play fair, Max,' she warned as she sat down again. 'There aren't any spiders.'

'OK.' He grinned. 'I'll try again. Something beginning with s.' He glanced at the dresser and a photograph taken of his grandfather during the war. 'Could it be soldier?'

Her fist thumped the table top. 'You must be a mind-reader.'

'Didn't you know I read minds as a sideline?' As he said this, Max rose to his feet slowly and moved around the corner of the table to her. His eyes were no longer smiling, but fixed steadily on hers. He reached for her hand. 'How about you, Gem? Can you read minds? Tell me what I am thinking about.'

Instinctively, she knew that he wanted to kiss her, but for the life of her she couldn't answer him. Her chest swelled with a rush of emotion as she allowed him to pull her out of her chair. They stood together, their gazes locked, their eyes asking silent questions.

And offering silent answers.

He cradled her close. Then lowered his face. She felt his delicious mouth moving over hers, warm and seeking, teasing her lips apart, felt his stubbled jaw graze her cheek and felt his strong hands holding her body against him.

And this time Gemma didn't panic.

She nestled closer, needing the reassurance and compassion of his arms. Understanding his anxiety about Mollie, she wanted to offer him her comfort in return.

This was a very different kiss from the one they had shared five years earlier. This time there was no urgent, desperate passion. This time Max was offering her a gift of tenderness and Gemma could feel his caring and warmth seeping into her. She had no idea kissing a man could feel so sweet—so right—like a blessing. She knew in her heart that it was good. Was meant to be.

They kissed and kissed some more, his mouth moving slowly, slowly over hers, tasting her, delving to explore her inner secrets. Sending her dizzy. Their bodies pressed closer, without haste, but showing each other, in every way they knew, that they yearned for an even closer intimacy.

A happy tear seeped from under her eyelashes and Max kissed it away. 'Little Gem,' he murmured, 'thank you for trying to cheer me up. You've no idea—'

The sound of slow hand-clapping startled them. Clap...clap... clap.

Gemma jerked her head sideways to discover Helena Roberts-Jones, leaning against the kitchen doorway. Her eyes were wide with embarrassment and a disconcerted smile twisted her mouth, distorting her usually attractive appearance. 'Well, my goodness,' she remarked, lowering her hands to her hips. 'How touching. How deeply touching.'

Stunned, Gemma stood ramrod-still, waiting for Max to release her, to say something, but he seemed as stupefied as she felt. She was aware of how moist and rosy her lips must look, but resisted the impulse to wipe her mouth with the back of her hand. It was too late to remove any evidence.

Finally Max dropped his hands to his sides and cleared his throat. 'Ah—Helena. I've been trying to reach you.'

'So I noticed.'

'No, seriously.' He stepped towards her. 'We're worried about Mollie.'

'You don't say?'

Guiltily, Gemma stood beside the kitchen table watching Max, not daring to speak.

'You can't have been too worried,' Helena told him frostily. 'I've been knocking on the front door for some time, but there was no answer, so I let myself in. If I'd been one or two minutes later, I might have really embarrassed us all.'

From Mollie's bedroom nearby came a little wail and a cough.

'That's the baby,' said Max.

'Oh, I'd never have guessed.' Helena rolled her eyes.

Max glared at her. 'Can't you be professional about this?'

She glared back. 'I was being *mega* professional, Max. I got a message that you were trying to contact me about a medical problem so, as I've been over at the Pearsons', because all four of their kids are down with the measles and the littlest one is really sick, I thought I'd call in here on my way home.'

'Thanks, Helena. We really appreciate it. I mean it. And we *are* really concerned about Mollie.'

Helena's face settled back into its mask of professional composure. 'What's the matter with her?'

'She's coughing a lot.'

'And she's listless,' Gemma added. 'But I don't think she has a fever.'

'I'd better take a look at her,' Helena said in her businesslike, matter-of-fact manner. She picked up her bag from the floor and moved towards the bedroom. Max followed. Mollie was still crying.

'Can I make you some coffee?' Gemma called after them.

'Thanks,' Helena replied grimly, and Gemma gathered up the dirty plates and cutlery from the table and carried them to the sink.

Surely Mollie couldn't have measles? There'd been a dreadful epidemic the year before. She remembered reading in the papers that children had died. Gemma's lower teeth nervously nibbled her upper lip as she switched on the kettle and spooned coffee into three mugs, placing them on a tray along with a little milk jug and sugar basin. As she poured steaming water into the mugs, her mind was completely taken up with her concern for Mollie. The Pearson children lived on the neighbouring property.

She hunted in the pantry for a packet of biscuits and wondered if Helena needed something more substantial to eat. But she found it difficult to concentrate on practicalities when her mind was focused on picturing the doctor in the bedroom examining Mollie. *What had she discovered?*

And, as well as her fear, she also had Max's kiss to think about. But that was something beautiful and precious that she must tuck away safely for now. Later she would think about it, savour it. Wonder about it. But even now, while she worried about Mollie and squirmed with embarrassment at the way Helena had caught them 'in the act', the impact of the kiss stayed with her, giving her an underlying sense of promise—like a talisman.

Finding the biscuits at last, she piled them onto a plate and carried the loaded tray through to the lounge room. Helena and Max were coming down the hall from Mollie's room, talking softly. They looked up when they saw Gemma.

'What's the verdict?' she asked nervously.

Helena tucked a stethoscope into her bag. 'I don't think there's too much to worry about,' she said. 'No measles symptoms at this stage. Her throat looks rather red, but I hesitate to prescribe antibiotics. Max and I have given her some baby painkiller. That might make her feel more comfortable.'

'Otherwise we continue as we have,' Max added, with a reassuring wink for Gemma.

Helena nodded. 'And keep in touch with me if you have more concerns.'

'I must say I'm relieved that it doesn't seem serious!' Gemma placed the tray carefully on the coffee table. 'This parenting business is nerve-racking.'

As she eased herself onto a sofa, Helena shot her a wry smirk. 'Parents are the bane of my life.'

'You look tired, Helena.' Max handed her a mug of coffee. Gemma noticed that he added milk and one sugar. He knew exactly how Helena took her coffee.

'It goes with the territory.'

'You've chosen a hard life as a rural doctor in outback Queensland,' Gemma suggested with as much sympathy as she could muster.

Taking a deep draught of her coffee, Helena shrugged. 'You're lucky to be going back to the city in a day or two.' She swung a sultry glance Max's way. 'Nobody out here has it easy. Look at our dear boy, Max. He has to be a Jack-of-all-trades. Cattlemen have to be able to do everything with little or no help—one minute they're fixing a broken-down motorbike in the middle of nowhere and next they're spaying heifers.' Her affectionate smile as she looked at him transformed her face.

Gemma felt her own smile growing a little stiff. 'You're both heroes.'

'We certainly are.' Sarcasm underscored Helena's voice as she put her coffee cup back on the tray. She pushed herself to her feet. 'But if I'm going to stay heroic I'd better make tracks.'

Max stepped forward gallantly. 'I'll see you out.'

'Thanks.' She scooped up her doctor's bag with one hand and looped her free arm through his. 'Bye, Gemma,' she called over her shoulder. 'Don't worry too much about that little baby. But I've given Max strict instructions to call me if he's at all concerned.'

Gemma offered an ineffectual wave to their retreating backs. The two walked with their heads leaning together, talking earnestly. For Gemma, it was like being back at the ball. Once again, she was struck by how good this couple looked together. Both were tall and handsome, strong characters—confident of their place in the world—*at ease with their sexuality.* They would make an excellent partnership. A perfect match.

What was a little kiss beside all that?

She stared down at her coffee. The mug was half full, but her stomach churned at the thought of drinking any more. Fifteen minutes earlier, in Max's arms, she'd been on cloud nine. Her heart had been full to bursting with happiness and—and what she'd thought was love. Max had held her so tenderly, kissed her so intimately, murmured her name…

Now, she'd come to her senses. She'd come hurtling back to earth with an almighty, heartbreaking thud. And the truth was as sharp and clear as an outback winter's morning. All that had happened this evening was that she'd joined the ranks as one of Max Jardine's women.

CHAPTER TEN

GEMMA HURRIED THROUGH the washing-up, while her mind boiled. She wanted to have everything done and to be out of the kitchen before Max returned. *No, she didn't!*

What if he acted indifferently, as if their kiss had never happened? *What if he wanted to continue where they'd left off?*

Her head spun. Her eyes burned.

Not for a moment did she question whether she loved Max. But when it came to his feelings for her, the questions were endless.

And they began with...what about... Helena? Sharon? Susan?

Did he kiss them as tenderly, as lovingly as he'd kissed her? Surely not.

Her mind seemed like a candy floss machine, going round and round, spinning out questions like pieces of sugary floss, only to have them dissolve as soon as she tried to catch hold of the answers.

By the time she'd washed the few dishes and wiped down the bench tops, Max had not returned. Gemma blacked out images of the two of them saying farewell outside by concentrating her thoughts on Mollie. The baby was the only member of the Jardine family she should worry about tonight. She turned out the light in the kitchen and hurried down the hall to her bedroom. By opening the French doors between hers and Mollie's rooms, she would have more chance of hearing her. And as she hastily prepared for sleep she prayed for a peaceful night and that she would find Mollie much better in the morning.

She woke with a fright, sitting bolt upright in bed, clutching the sheet and trembling in the dark with an unknown fear. Then it came to her. The horrible noise that had been haunting her dreams. A hoarse, brassy cough followed by a harsh, high-pitched wheezing sound. And then little cries.

Mollie!!

She leapt out of bed and dashed to the cot. Mollie sounded much worse. Gemma's heart crashed crazily against her ribs as she lifted the little form in its white cotton nightdress out of the cot and clasped the baby to her. Up close, the coughing and wheezing sounded horrifying. 'Oh, little girl,' Gemma whispered. 'What's happened to you? Oh, Lord! What are we going to do?'

Without a moment's hesitation, she rushed with Mollie in her arms down the hall to Max's room. He was already awake and swinging his long legs from beneath the sheets. Shuttered moonlight striped the room, showing up the deep distress in his face.

'She's worse?' was his immediate question.

Sick with fear, Gemma nodded. 'She sounds terrible, Max. I think she's having trouble breathing.'

'God, no.'

For a moment they both stood in petrified silence, listening to the dreadful barking and wheezing noises coming from Mollie.

'I'll ring Helena,' Max said immediately.

'I'll rub some more eucalyptus oil on her. It's all I can think of to do.' *Oh, Isobel,* Gemma thought as she hurried back to Mollie's room. *I'm so sorry. I've tried to take care of your little girl. Oh, God! I can't bear this!*

Mollie gave a little whimper.

'There, there, sweetheart,' Gemma crooned as she changed the baby's nappy and rubbed her chest. 'You'll be all right. The doctor will tell us what to do.'

She heard Max's step on the floorboards behind her.

'No luck,' he muttered with a curse. 'I can't get an answer. I rang

Helena's home number and the medical centre. Nobody's answering. I don't know what the hell's going on.'

'What are we going to do?' Gemma's question emerged as a terrified whisper.

Max took a deep, agonised breath and groaned. He looked away and crossed his arms over his bare chest. 'I haven't got a damn clue,' he muttered harshly. 'I'll just have to keep trying to get through to someone.'

'Perhaps we could ring one of the women on another property? Someone who's had children.'

Max grunted his disapproval. 'We don't want old wives' tales. We want proper medical attention.' He spun on his bare heel. 'And it's no use jumping in a vehicle and rushing into town if Helena's not there. She's the only doctor for two hundred kilometres. I'm going to keep on that darn phone until I get some answers.'

With her heart thumping in terror, Gemma watched him race back to the telephone in the kitchen, his retreating back, brown and sleek above long blue and white striped pyjama pants. He pinned so much faith on Helena. *Only Helena had the answers!* She pressed her lips to Mollie's soft cheek. 'There's got to be some other way to get help,' she whispered.

Mollie seemed less distressed in her arms, so Gemma walked her up and down the darkened hallway. The only light came from patches of lamplight spilling through bedroom doorways. As she walked, up and down, up and down, she crooned soft songs—snippets of pop tunes, nursery rhymes, lullabies—whatever soothing bits and pieces came into her head. She had no idea what the baby thought of them, but they helped, just a little, to make Gemma feel calmer.

But the coughing and the nasty, frightening wheezing sound continued.

Gemma passed the door to the study. The curtains weren't drawn in that room and the moonlight sent its blue light tumbling through the window and across the carpet. Hoping a glimpse of the outside world and the serene bush might give her some kind of comfort, she moved into the room and crossed to the window, her bare feet cushioned by the velvet-soft carpet.

But, outside, the darkened clumps of trees and the vista of paddocks painted in pale moonshine seemed remote—unfriendly and unhelpful. She turned away quickly before useless tears could form. Now was not a time to give in to her fears. She had to be strong for Mollie. With her back to the window, she faced the rows and rows of books on the opposite wall. And they seemed to be staring back at her, voicing silent accusations.

'I wonder,' she whispered to Mollie and stepped forward. 'This library is old and extensive. I wonder if there would be such a thing as a book on baby care.' Spurred by a burst of fresh hope, she snapped on the light and squinted at the sudden brightness.

While clucking soothing noises to Mollie, her eyes hungrily raced along the titles, searching, searching... There were countless books on animal husbandry and farm management, international markets and economics, action-adventure novels and spy thrillers—the kind of collection she would expect a man like Max to have. This was useless. How could she expect him to have a book on baby care?

Deeply disappointed, she sank into Max's leather armchair, hoping against hope that any minute now he would come racing back with good news. She saw his computer sitting on the desk and thought of the last happy e-mail they'd received from Isobel. Good heavens! It was after midnight. Isobel and Dave were arriving later this very day. And to find Mollie like *this*!

She jumped to her feet again. Where was Max? She couldn't bear being alone with Mollie any longer.

As she raised her hand to flick off the light switch, she saw it. A shabby old book with a peeling paper dust jacket shoved sideways on top of some others. The word 'baby' in the title caught her eye. 'Please, please,' she whispered as she pulled the book out from where it was tightly wedged. She read the title. *Caring for your baby. The first three years.*

Trembling and anxious, Gemma lowered herself back into the armchair. She settled Mollie over one shoulder and, with a frenzied sense of desperation, read down the list of contents. There was a section on illnesses. Thank heavens!

Max burst into the room, his eyes wild and despairing. 'I finally got through to the medical centre! There's been a bad smash on the highway. Helena was called out there, of course. Now she's riding in the ambulance trying to stabilise someone in a critical condition while they travel to Mt Isa hospital.'

'She won't be able to help us?'

Max shook his head and slammed one balled fist into the other. 'I can't believe this! Who'd live in the bush? What a disaster!' He stepped closer and uncurled his hand to cup Mollie's head. 'How's our little one?'

Gemma didn't need to answer. Mollie's distress was all too evident. She sighed. 'I'm afraid she's much the same. It's awful, Max.' She held out the book. 'But I've found this old book on childcare. I'm hoping I might find something in here to help.'

With a hopeless kind of gesture, he scowled. 'I wouldn't hold out too much hope. That looks like it came out of the Ark. It must have been Mum's or perhaps even my grandmother's. I'm going to get back on that phone and try the Flying Doctors. There's got to be someone, *somewhere* who can help us.'

This time Gemma didn't watch him go, she was too busy reading. In spite of his doubts about the book, she wanted desperately to find something helpful. She quickly reached the section on coughs and colds. Running her finger down the page, she scanned the text, looking for a description that fitted Mollie's terrible dry, barking cough and wheeze. And then she found it.

Croup. Gemma read through the section again. Yes, that had to be it. The symptoms sounded exactly like Mollie's. Feeling elated, sick and scared, she read on. The book stated, of course, to call your doctor immediately if you thought your child had croup. She felt her stomach contract. 'What else? What else?' she whispered desperately. There was a paragraph or two about cold steam humidifiers. She and Max had as much chance of finding one of them as finding the doctor in a hurry. Finally, at the bottom of the article, was a last-ditch suggestion.

Take your baby into the bathroom, close the door and run hot water in the bathtub or run a hot shower. The heat will steam up the room. The moist air should rapidly improve the baby's breathing.

Right! Gemma jumped to her feet. This was something she could do. And it sounded safe enough, no matter what was actually wrong with Mollie. She charged out of the room and down the hall to the bathroom.

Eager for as much steam as possible, she wrapped Mollie carefully in a towel and laid her on the bath mat while she turned on the taps in both the shower and the bath. Then she sat on the floor with her back to the white tiled wall and nursed Mollie, while the bathroom began to fill up with steam.

And that was where Max found them twenty minutes later.

He banged loudly on the door. 'Gemma, are you in there?'

'Yes,' she called. 'Come in.'

He flung the door open and charged in, then came to an abrupt halt. Through the steam, he peered at her. 'I finally got through to someone at Flying Doctor Base,' he began, but stopped and dropped to his knees beside her. 'How's Mollie?'

'She's heaps better,' Gemma told him. 'She's gone to sleep and she's breathing easily again. It's amazing the way the steam's helped. Like a miracle.'

'Wow,' he replied, the word drawn out on a long sigh. He swivelled so that his back was against the wall and he slid his length down until he sat next to her. Just for a moment, he dropped his head sideways to rest on hers. 'I eventually got through to a nursing sister at the base who suggested doing exactly this. She said it should work if it wasn't a really serious case of croup.'

'I'd hate to see a serious case.' Gemma felt his head lift away again and she turned to look at him. His blue eyes were only inches from her and his body and hers were touching at the shoulders; the rest of his bare torso was a whisker's distance. She became conscious of her tongue running slowly over her lips.

'Thank goodness it worked. Thanks so much, Gem. You did all this on your own while I rushed around like a demented, headless chook.'

'I'm just so glad it worked,' she replied drowsily, her eyes mesmerised by the steamy sheen forming on his skin.

He took a deep breath and looked down at Mollie lying asleep in her arms. Her little chest rose and fell in its usual regular rhythm and her breathing seemed soft and even. Lowering his head, Max dropped a light kiss on the downy head. 'Don't frighten me like that, ever again,' he told the sleeping Mollie. Then his eyes met Gemma's.

His expression was so intense Gemma felt tiny pinpricks of tension break out on her arms and her back—all over her body. His Adam's apple moved up and down and he attempted a very wobbly smile. 'Do you think—?' he began, then cleared his throat. 'Is there any chance—?' His hand came up to touch her hair, damp from the steam-filled room.

Slowly he traced the outline of her face, the soft curve of her cheek, the rounded, perky chin. His thumb rubbed her lower lip. He seemed suddenly shy. Gemma knew that he was thinking about another kiss. She was absolutely certain she wanted to kiss him back. What was stopping him?

'Why don't you just say it, Max?'

'Say what?'

'Whatever it is you're trying so hard to get out.'

His hand rested lightly against her cheek. 'Later,' he whispered, and looked again at the sleeping Mollie. 'Now's not the right time.'

But Gemma thought this was a perfect time for getting closer to Max. She turned her face to his and lifted her lips. Every cell in her body screamed out for him to kiss her.

And, to her infinite relief, he did. Holding the sides of her face in his big hands, he kissed her deeply, daringly. With his tongue and his lips Max showed her exactly what had been left unsaid moments before and Gemma almost dropped Mollie, her body felt so limp and melting.

Between kisses, she gasped, 'I see what you mean.'

'What's that?' he asked, kissing her neck, her eyelids, her shoulder.

'Now isn't a good time. I'm either going to drop Mollie or squash her.'

'Here, let me take her.' Max lifted the sleeping baby gently out of Gemma's arms and slowly stood up. 'Do you think it would be OK to put her back to bed now?'

'Yes. I guess so.' Gemma replied, feeling lonely without his arms around her. 'She hasn't coughed for quite some time.'

He cocked his head towards the shower. 'I'd say we're about to run out of hot water anyhow. You turn off the taps and I'll take Mollie through to her room.'

In a daze of awakened desire, Gemma turned off the taps, hung up the bath towels and switched off the bathroom light. She padded down the hall to Mollie's room, but it was empty. Her room was empty, too. Puzzled, she stepped back into the hall and made her way down the passage to Max's bedroom.

He was lying on his huge bed with Mollie cradled in the crook of one arm and he sent Gemma a tummy-flipping grin as he patted the mattress on the other side of the baby. 'I've decided we should keep her with us for the rest of the night.'

'With—with *us*? You mean *me, too*? Here with you? And her?'

'I do.' He smiled. 'You have any objections?'

'Ah—I—I don't suppose so. I mean, I haven't—' Gemma gulped and stood shyly at the end of his bed, keeping her eyes lowered, unable to return his gaze. But looking downwards merely showed her the state of her nightdress. After half an hour in a steamy bathroom, the fine, pale pink cotton clung to her every curve. Self-consciously, she lifted her arms and crossed them over her chest, then took two steps forward.

Every part of her wanted to be there on the bed with Max. If he made love to her the way he kissed her, she was quite sure there could be nothing more beautiful in the whole world—but vestiges of the old fear clung. He knew so much and she knew so little...

Then again, she reasoned, Max could hardly hope to ravish her if Mollie was there with them...

Hesitantly, she lowered herself onto the mattress and the three of them lay on the wide, king-sized bed with its crisp, clean, white sheets—Max and Gemma with little Mollie sleeping soundly and peacefully between them. The tiny warm body close to hers was very reassuring.

She felt his hand touch her shoulder. He began to massage it slowly. 'Relax, Gemma. You're exhausted. You need to sleep.'

She rolled over and stared at him, wondering if she'd heard him correctly. Up close, against the pillow, he looked divine. 'You want to go to *sleep*?'

'It's what most people do at this time of night, especially when they've been through what we've just experienced and have a sick baby to care for.'

'Oh,' Gemma said softly, not sure if she was relieved or disappointed. 'Of course.'

'Did you think I was going to use innocent little Mollie as bait to lure you into my bed and then have my wicked way with you?'

'No, not really,' she lied.

He leaned closer and murmured in her ear, his voice rumbling and shockingly sexy, 'I'm sure I can find a much better way to tempt you to sleep with me, Gemma.'

She was sure he could, too. He'd put in a pretty good effort in the bathroom when he'd kissed the living daylights out of her. Just remembering sent her nerves a-tingle. But what she should get off her chest now, she decided, as she lay only a short distance from him, was a confession about how inexperienced she was in these bedroom matters.

'Max,' she said, lying stiffly, not looking at him and pulling the sheet up to her chin. She stared at the delicate blue ceiling, groping for the right words. But the perfect words wouldn't come, so there was nothing for it but to head straight to the heart of the matter. 'Do—do you know much about virgins?'

His silent response was no help at all. Gemma still couldn't bring herself to look at him. She didn't want to read his reaction to her admission. All too often in the past those blue eyes had dismissed her or mocked her.

'Did you hear me?' she asked a crack in the ceiling.

'I heard you, Gem, but I hardly know how to answer.' She sensed rather than saw him turn his head in her direction. 'Is this question intended to launch a discussion about my personal life, or a general chat about today's society, or is it perhaps scientific? Are you wanting a biological definition of virginity?'

A hot blush crept up her neck and into her cheeks. 'It—it's purely a social issue,' she said, her eyes still avoiding contact with his. 'I mean, these days, apparently many girls lose their virginity at an early age.'

'Yes,' he replied cautiously.

'But that's only *many*, Max. There is still a large group of perfectly normal, healthy and well-adjusted young women who—'

'Why on earth are we talking about this subject now, at this time of night?'

Couldn't he guess?

Perhaps not, she thought with alarm, when she remembered how she'd behaved every time Max had kissed her.

Out of the corner of her eye, she admired the play of muscles in his back as he reached over and switched off the lamp on the bedside table. Then, in the dark, she felt the mattress give as he leaned over Mollie towards her. His warm, sensuous lips brushed hers and then pressed her eyelids closed. 'Stop fretting and go to sleep, Gemma.' He kissed her mouth again—an undemanding, affectionate, goodnight kiss.

She felt amazingly relaxed, considering she was in a man's bed for the first time in her life.

'Just count yourself lucky this little angel is lying between us,' he murmured, dropping more kisses onto her bare shoulder. 'I promise you won't escape me so easily next time.'

Next time?

It was a thought that should have kept her wide awake, but as Gemma lay there, cuddled close to Mollie, with Max's dark shape nearby, a feeling of peace and a sense of rightness settled over her, and she yawned, blissfully happy. Through the dark, she whispered to him, 'So you don't mind, Max?'

'Mind what?' he mumbled sleepily.

'That I haven't...ever...' She couldn't bring herself to finish the sentence, but Max didn't help. He remained completely silent. Gemma figured the penny had dropped. He was probably

shocked that the girl who'd acted like a brazen hussy in his arms
at the age of eighteen was trying to claim she was still a virgin
five years later.

She felt compelled to try to explain. 'Actually, the reason I've
never—um—never made love has something to do with you.'

Abruptly, he rolled onto to his side and propped himself on one
elbow. Through the dark, she could feel his eyes staring fiercely
at her. 'Then you'd better tell me.'

'You kissed me a long time ago—that night of Dave's party,
when I was eighteen.'

'Yes,' he said quietly and she could hear the tension in his voice.

'You spoiled me for any other man, Max.'

'Oh, God,' she heard him moan, and he flopped back onto the
bed and lay staring at the ceiling, his hands clasped beneath his
head.

He sounded so upset; she wished desperately that she'd never
started this ridiculous conversation. They were both exhausted.
She should have taken his advice and gone to sleep. Now her
clumsy admission had completely spoiled the happy contentment
of a few moments ago. The last thing a man like Max would want
to discuss with a woman in his bed would be the details of her in-
experience with men.

As if to prove her right, he rose swiftly from the bed and headed
straight for the door opening onto the verandah.

'Where are you going?'

'I've got to do some thinking,' he replied gruffly. 'And I can't
do it lying in bed next to you.' Then he disappeared into the night.

CHAPTER ELEVEN

TEARS STREAMED DOWN Gemma's face as she lay wretchedly awake beside the soundly sleeping baby. She wanted so badly to go after Max. If only she hadn't been so desperate to off-load her confession! She'd made everything between them so much more complicated.

Complicated? She'd ruined everything!

A few hours ago, Max had been kissing her as if he thought the world was about to end! 'Just count yourself lucky this little angel is lying between us,' he'd said. 'I promise you won't escape me so easily next time.'

But then she'd made a first-class fool of herself—blaming Max for her virginity—burdening him with her hang-ups—and now there would be no next time. Tomorrow, as soon as Mollie was safely handed over to Isobel and Dave, he would bundle her onto a plane and get her out of the district as fast as he could.

Lord! When would she ever learn to play it cool? If she hadn't shot her mouth off, Max would be sleeping peacefully beside her now instead of prowling angrily through the dim, dark depths of the house.

It wasn't until the grim, grey dawn light began to creep into the room that the tears and her exhaustion took their toll and she drifted miserably off to sleep...

She woke late to find bright sunshine spinning through the slats in the timber louvers and striping the honey-toned floorboards of Max's bedroom. Yawning and stretching, she rolled over. *Mollie was gone!* Frantically, she pushed herself onto her elbows as the events of the night came back to her. With them came a new rush of fear that had her bounding out of the bed.

Where was Mollie? Was she sick again?

'Max!' she called as she raced frantically through the house. She stopped briefly in her own room to haul on shorts and a T-shirt, wondering all the time what had happened. There was no one in Mollie's room, the lounge room was empty and so was the kitchen. She stopped for a moment, clutching the back of a kitchen chair, a little out of breath and on the brink of panic.

Calm down, she ordered herself. *You managed during a crisis last night and you'll manage again.* And as her breathing steadied, so did her thoughts. *Surely Max would have woken her if there had been an emergency?* She stood frowning as she considered where to look next. Then she heard sounds coming from the verandah.

Totally unexpected sounds—like a man and a baby laughing!

Curious, Gemma stepped through the doorway onto the verandah and saw them.

Max was squatting and Mollie stood beside him, her little feet firmly gripping the bare timber floor and one chubby hand on his knee to hold her balance. She was laughing and squealing with delight as the cutest little blue heeler puppy rolled and played in a pool of sunshine at her feet.

'For heaven's sake,' Gemma cried, hurrying towards them. 'Look at her! Who would have thought she would recover like this?'

Max scooped the gurgling Mollie in one hand and the puppy in the other as he jumped to his feet. 'Gemma.' His eyes held hers and the anxiety she saw in them made the breath catch in her throat. 'I looked in earlier and found Mollie wide awake, but you were still snoring.'

'Thanks for getting her. I slept like a log,' she lied. 'What about you?'

'I was fine,' he replied unhelpfully.

He didn't look as if his night had been 'fine', Gemma thought, noting signs of exhaustion and tension in the grim set of his face and the dark smudges beneath his eyes. 'I can't believe how well Mollie looks,' she said, dropping an impulsive kiss on the baby's cheek.

'The sister at the base told me it can be like that with babies. One minute they look like they're on their last legs and the next they're up and running as if nothing was ever the matter.' He chuckled as Mollie tried to clutch the puppy's ear. 'I wonder if her parents will let her have a puppy?'

'Knowing how crazy Dave was about dogs when he was a boy, I'm sure there's a very good chance.' Gemma scratched the puppy's forehead.

So this is how it's going to be, she thought. *We both pretend those kisses last night didn't happen.*

Some things never change.

'I guess Isobel and Dave will be here shortly after lunch,' she said in the most businesslike tone she could muster. 'I'd better get their room ready.' She turned to go.

'Steady on,' intervened Max. He let the puppy scamper away to join his brothers and sisters. 'You're not doing anything of the sort until you've had breakfast.'

'I guess I *am* rather hungry,' she admitted. 'Have you eaten?'

'No, not yet.' He raised a questioning eyebrow. 'We'll break with tradition this morning and eat together?'

'Good idea,' Gemma replied, almost enjoying the thought. But a memory of the day she'd arrived and their embarrassing discussion about women's breakfasts spoiled the short burst of pleasure.

Other women had eaten breakfast with Max. But what had happened beforehand? They certainly wouldn't have given him a blow-by-blow in-depth account of their inadequacies as a lover.

'Orange juice?' Max directed his question at Gemma as he helped Mollie into her high chair.

'I guess so,' she muttered. 'I'll get it.' She filled two glasses while Max fetched a packet of baby cereal from the pantry.

'Can you look after Mollie while I cook us something? What would you like? Do you fancy bacon and eggs?'

'Thank you. It's probably what I need.'

He must have heard the wintry edge in her tone, because he swung round and stared at her hard. 'Is something the matter?'

Oh, help me! Gemma thought, feeling suddenly much worse than she had last night. *Everything's the matter! I'm in love with you and I feel terrible instead of happy. And I've made you mad with me and I don't know what to do about it!*

With hasty, nervous movements, she began to spoon Mollie's cereal into a bowl. 'Of course there's nothing the matter. Everything's just hunky-dory.'

Max stood still in the middle of the kitchen and his brow creased momentarily as he scoured tense fingers back and forth through his hair. He looked as if he wanted to say something, but must have thought better of it and turned instead to the stove.

She stirred milk into Mollie's cereal and began to feed it to her while Max fiddled with a frying pan. In spite of her misery, Gemma tormented herself by watching his every move. She couldn't help admiring the easy roll of his wrists as he cracked eggs and slipped them into the sizzling pan. Couldn't help loving the way his thick, dark hair ended in a straight line just above his collar. And as for the way his backside neatly filled his jeans—that was nothing short of a work of art.

'Keep your mind on the job. You're getting cereal all over Mollie's face.' Max scowled when he caught her staring at him.

Gemma blushed as she dabbed away the blobs on Mollie's cheeks. 'I'm sorry,' she muttered. 'I got caught up in my thoughts.'

With an egg flip, he transferred the crispy bacon strips and sunny eggs from the pan to their plates, then set them on the table. As he sat opposite Gemma, he looked at her with a slight frown. 'Dare I ask what kind of thoughts you're having?'

Blushing again, she picked up her glass of orange juice. She had been thinking about the impossible—about making love with Max, of how he would look *out* of those jeans. Best to steer clear away from that subject. 'I was thinking it's kind of a relief that after we came out here more or less hating each other and fighting like we have since we were kids, that we've made a measure of progress. We—we've ended up—less antagonistic.'

Max placed a forkful of bacon back on his plate. 'I've *never* hated you, Gemma.'

The glass slipped in her hand and she quickly placed it back on the table before she spilled juice everywhere.

'But Max—'

'I know you always thought I did,' he continued. 'And in the end, I decided that perhaps it was best if you went on thinking that I didn't care about you.'

'But—but when we were young?'

'And you idolised Dave? Back then I was always jealous of Dave.' Max's gaze dropped to the plate of food in front of him and he toyed with his fork.

'You were *jealous*?' Gemma squeaked.

When he looked up again, she was startled by the intense emotion his eyes revealed. 'Even when you were a skinny little kid, Gem, your perky smile and bright eyes fascinated me. But my kid brother was the funny one—the one who made you laugh. You thought everything he did was so jolly admirable and adventurous.'

She reached a trembling hand to touch his arm where it rested on the table. 'But I was frightened of you, Max. You were always scowling at Dave and me.'

'That's because I was fairly young, too, and I didn't know how to handle my emotions.'

She let out a long, astonished breath and wondered if her poor heart could possibly bear the knowledge that Max hadn't hated her for all these years. 'All this time.'

But what good was knowing this now? Maybe she and Max weren't fighting any more, but an unbridgeable gulf of tension and doubt stretched between them.

'Anyhow,' he added gruffly, as if he regretted his admission, 'I've slaved over a hot stove, so we'd better eat and get on with preparing everything for our visitors.'

All morning, as together they tidied the house and made up a spare bed, getting ready for Isobel and Dave's return, Gemma felt as tense as tightly strained fencing wire. Max was polite and friendly, but the sexy teasing, the come-to-me-baby light in his eye that had thrilled her last night, had vanished.

When Isobel and Dave arrived, she was happy to stop thinking about herself and become absorbed in the excitement of the joyful parents reuniting with their daughter. She and Max grinned happily as they listened to their exclamations of surprise over how Mollie had grown in just two weeks and how she could stand all by herself.

But Gemma still found it incredibly difficult to drag her eyes away from Max. She was watching all the time for his expression to soften. But the Max of old, the reserved and frowning big brother was back.

At least he sat beside her on the lounge, while they explained as gently as they could about Mollie's croup. The parents accepted this news with remarkable calm. Gemma decided that, after dealing with armed rebels, croup probably seemed like a very minor drama.

Then Isobel and Dave told them the astonishing news that they'd heard radio coverage in Brisbane of the fiasco in the Goodbye Creek pub.

'I told you we'd attract media attention,' Gemma crowed triumphantly to Max. 'You watch. This is just the start of something big for Goodbye Creek.' But her excitement at the news was tarnished by his bored response.

'It's just a flash in the pan. Nothing will come of it.'

And of course they listened attentively to Dave as he expanded on his ordeal in Somalia. He was a good storyteller and the details of his capture and imprisonment were both alarming and fascinating, but with Max sitting some distance away, his fists firmly clenched on his knees, Gemma's thoughts kept straying. She kept thinking about the way he'd kissed her and held her last night—before everything had gone wrong.

When Dave finished, Isobel leaned forward in her chair and stared at them both shrewdly. 'I'm so grateful to you guys for everything you've done for Mollie,' she said. 'But I must confess, I'm also rather disappointed. I had high hopes that I would come out here and you would have some good news for us.'

'We've shown you how close Mollie is to walking,' Gemma replied quickly.

'Yes, but I'm not talking about Mollie. I'm talking about you two. You've been living together for almost two weeks and—and—' She shook her head and fixed them with an exasperated glare. 'You're still as wary of each other as opponents in a boxing ring.'

Gemma and Max exchanged self-conscious glances.

Dave jumped up and crossed the room to give Max a hearty slap on the shoulder. 'Cheer up, big bro. Isobel tries to matchmake wherever she goes. Gemma, don't worry, we'll take you back to the civilised coast with us and we'll leave this old grouch to his Brahman bulls and his bush.'

Max stood to return his brother's back slap. 'I can always rely on my family to understand me.'

Gemma's lips stretched into a very flat smile.

Straight after dinner, a jet-lagged Isobel and Dave took Mollie off to their room. The baby's cot had been moved in there, so the little family were alone together at last.

And, once again, Gemma and Max were alone in the kitchen. Max scowled at the pile of dirty dishes. 'My next investment will be an automatic dishwasher.'

'Great idea,' Gemma muttered. 'Although once we've all gone...' Her voice trailed away, and abruptly she turned to the sink, flicked on the tap and began rinsing dinner plates.

Max put the milk jug back in the fridge. 'It seems strange not having to worry about whether Mollie has settled for the night.'

She swivelled around to look at him. 'I know what you mean. I've become quite used to thinking like a mother.'

As he recrossed the room to return the salt and pepper shakers to their spot beside the stove, he commented, 'You've been absolutely fantastic with Mollie. The perfect little mother.'

His gentle words touched her. 'I really enjoyed looking after her. And I know you did, too, Max. You were so sweet with her.' She gathered up cutlery to be washed. 'You'll make a wonderful father.'

She hadn't really expected a response, but Max was silent for so long that eventually she glanced over her shoulder towards him. He was standing rock-still in the middle of the kitchen, his shoulders hunched with tension and his hands thrust firmly in the pockets of his jeans. He looked so wretched her heart jogged a crazy little war dance in her chest.

'Max, what's the matter?' she whispered.

'Gemma, I'm so sorry.'

'Sorry?' Snatching a kitchen towel, she hastily dried her hands.

He expelled his breath on a long sigh. 'I'm sorry I frightened you so badly all those years ago. You know—the night when you thought you were kissing Dave.'

An agonising lump wedged in Gemma's throat. She tried to talk, but nothing would come out.

'Ever since then, I've had a dreadful feeling that I really messed you up,' he went on, his mouth contorted by emotion. 'And now I know the truth, I can't forgive myself.'

Gemma shook her head and tried to get rid of the pain in her throat by swallowing. Behind her, she clutched the edge of the sink. 'Please,' she managed at last. 'Please, don't torment yourself. I'm the one who should apologise.'

'For Pete's sake, you were only a kid.'

'But you didn't frighten me.'

'Of course I did,' he stormed. 'I tricked you and scared you witless. You ran away. You wouldn't talk to me—couldn't bear to face me. You even got out of the country—and—now you tell me— For crying out loud, Gemma. I can't bear to think how I've hurt you.'

She raised a shaking hand to her mouth. The remorse in his voice shocked her. And his pain was her fault. She'd let him carry so much guilt—had never let him off the hook by admitting to her share of deception. 'You've got it all wrong!' On unsteady legs, she took a step towards him. Her eyes and throat stung. 'You didn't trick me or frighten me.'

'What's that?'

'You didn't trick me.'

He stared at her, his throat moving rapidly and his eyes disbelieving.

'I knew all along that I wasn't kissing Dave.' Gemma couldn't stand the pain she saw in his face. She stepped closer and took his hand. Touching him again made her feel stronger. 'Please believe me. I'm sorry I didn't tell you ages ago, but I've always been so embarrassed by the way I behaved that night.'

'But you said I've spoiled you for other men.'

'Oh, Max, that's not because I was traumatised. It's because I've never found any other man who can make me feel the way you did.' Bravely, she lifted his hand and pressed her lips to his palm. 'Your kisses were too—too wonderful, you see. You made me feel so full of *wanting* you.' She heard the sharp intake of his breath. 'I've never been able to dredge up that kind of wanting for anyone else.'

In his eyes, as he looked down at her, she saw a savage battle between hope and disbelief. Hardly knowing where she found her courage, Gemma stood on tiptoes and kissed his shadowy jaw. 'No one can kiss the way you do, Max. And all I want is for you to kiss me like that again.'

While her heart thumped crazily, she waited for his response.

'Struth,' he whispered at last. His hands reached for her hips and grasped them firmly. 'You mean there's nothing to keep us apart?'

'Nothing I can think of.'

She could sense the dreadful tension leaving him. 'And you'd like another kiss?' Already he was teasing her again. His mouth was curving into his beautiful, slow smile and his hands were moving possessively over her bottom.

Gemma's pulses throbbed. 'I could do with another of your kisses right now.'

'I'll see what I can manage.' He glanced around the kitchen with its dirty dishes. 'Let's find somewhere more romantic. Come outside,' he said softly.

She didn't know if she could bear to wait till they travelled the short distance, but without another word he swept her effortlessly into his arms and carried her out onto the verandah. Setting her down, he looked around them. 'Now where out here were we exactly on that night?'

And for Gemma it suddenly seemed as natural as saying 'hello' to lead him across the weathered timber floor to the railing in the shadows. With a little laugh, she pushed him against a wooden

BARBARA HANNAY

post. 'You were about here.' She stood close in front of him. 'And I think I was about—'

'You hurled yourself into my arms.'

'Like this?' She threw her arms around his neck and their eager mouths and bodies surged together. For Gemma, it was like coming home to be back in Max's arms, having his sexy lips reaching her mouth.

It was a kiss of pure seduction, starting slow and lazy and becoming bolder and more intimate until she felt fabulously dizzy and drowning.

Bursting with longing.

All she wanted was to give herself up to the wild fever his touch aroused. 'I want you so, so much,' she whispered.

'I love you, Gemma Brown.'

Oh!

For a stunned moment they stared at each other.

Gemma's heart pounded even harder than ever and her eyes welled with tears. She didn't want to cry. 'You—you do? You—*love—me?*' No, she mustn't cry. This was the happiest moment in her life. Or it would be if his understanding of love matched hers. 'What—what exactly do you mean when you talk of love, Max? Don't you also love Helena?'

'Helena?' His hands dropped to his hips and his head tipped to one side. Gemma took a cautious step away from him. In the dim light she could see that he was staring at her with an annoying, puzzled look in his eyes.

'You can't pretend you don't know what I mean.'

He shook his head. 'No, no. There's nothing between us. Please believe me.' He held out his arms to her in a gesture of innocence. 'When I first met Helena eighteen months ago, I guess something could possibly have developed, but it didn't. We've been exactly what I told you—good friends.'

'You seem so perfect together.'

He frowned. 'I don't see how you make that out. Helena's almost finished her two-year contract out here—doing her stint of country service. She can't wait to get back to the city in a few months' time. Life stuck out on an outback property wouldn't suit her at all. No, I've been a handy social escort for her and she's been a pleasant companion. But that's all it's been. Helena's an impressive woman and a competent doctor, but she's not the woman I need.'

He reached for her and hauled her towards him again, one hand cradling the nape of her neck. 'She's not you, Gem. It's you and I who are perfect together.'

Gemma wondered if her heart would actually explode. It seemed to swell so hugely in her chest. 'It seems too good to be true.'

'It's the absolute truth.'

She felt his hand under her chin, turning her face to look at him again. 'Gemma,' he said softly, with a strange little growl in his voice, 'you're the only woman I love and you're the only woman I want to share my life with.' He pulled her hard against him and she could feel his heart pounding away, just like hers.

He buried his face in her hair and his hands moved impatiently down her back and up again, as if he needed to know and touch every part of her at once. 'God, I need you, Gem. And I need you here. I need you to stay out here and love me and grow old with me. Is there any chance you could manage that?'

'Any chance?' How could so many wonderful, impossible dreams be handed to her in an instant? With a choked cry, Gemma slipped her hands round his waist and rested her head against his shoulder. 'There's a very, *very* good chance,' she whispered.

She pulled back slightly, so that she could look up into his face. 'Max, are you really asking me to—to—*marry* you?'

'Yes,' he told her with a shy smile. 'Please marry me, Gemma.'

'Oh, my goodness! Don't let me go. My legs have gone all shaky.'

He bent quickly and scooped her up in his arms again. 'Better?' he asked.

She grinned. 'Much better, thanks.'

His lips teased and tasted hers. 'So when can I expect an answer?'

'You know the answer, don't you?'

Crossing to the stairs, Max sat on the top step and settled Gemma on his lap. 'I know I claimed to be a mind-reader last night, but tonight I'd kind of like to hear you tell me what you're thinking. My guess might be wrong.'

'Actually,' she told him, relishing the feel of his tightly stretched denim beneath her, 'I happen to be madly in love with you.' She kissed him full on the mouth with a fresh burst of daring that both surprised and thrilled her. When she paused for breath, she added excitedly, 'I thought there was no chance you'd fall in love with me and I've been so sick at the thought of going back to Brisbane to live miserably ever after.'

Hardly believing how happy she felt, she dropped her head onto his shoulder again. It was a wonderful place to be. His smooth, tanned neck was temptingly close and she couldn't resist more flirtatious kisses and nibbles.

'So what's your answer?' he murmured huskily. 'Do you want to get married and stay here in the outback with me?'

'You bet I do, Max. I love this place. Try stopping me from living here.' With a laugh, she added, 'Think of all the breakfasts we can share from now on. Here in the homestead kitchen, or perhaps down by the creek, or out on mustering camps.'

He chuckled and she raised her lips to his. Groaning softly, Max took her mouth in a kiss so sexy she felt shivery and melting, totally electrified. Her mind threw up wild ideas, and, turning in his lap, she straddled him so they could be much, much closer.

Above them, the blue-black sky was spotted with stars, like the roof of a medieval cathedral. From the horse paddock nearby came the occasional soft clip-clop of hooves and, from further away, the soft call of a curlew. And floating all around them on the summer's night air wafted the sweet heady scent of the starry white jasmine that climbed latticework on either side of the steps.

Happiness zinged through Gemma and only one thought marred the moment and brought her stomach bunching into knots. 'Max?'

'Yes, sweetheart?' He nuzzled her neck.

'You're sure you don't mind?'

'Mind what?'

'That I'm so inexperienced.'

He relaxed his close hold on her, but kept his hands on her arms, rubbing them gently. 'Would this question be a sequel to that serious little discussion you started last night about modern social trends?'

'Yes.' Gemma looked straight into his eyes, trying to read his expression.

He kissed the tip of her nose. 'You're trying to tell me that I'll be your first lover?'

'Yes. Do you mind?

'Do I *mind?*' Locking his arms around her once more, he hugged her tight. 'Oh, Gemma, how could you ask such a question? Why, darling, I feel incredibly honoured to know that I'm going to be your first and only lover.' He kissed her forehead. 'Honestly, I'm a very privileged man.'

Deliriously happy, she trailed her lips over the underside of his jaw, and scattered more cheeky little kisses up and down his neck. 'I knew I was right to wait for you,' she murmured.

His lips caressed hers. 'We've both been waiting a long time to be together.' He nipped her soft lower lip between his teeth. 'Are you interested in making up for lost time?'

Gemma's smile widened as his lips moved slowly down her throat towards her breast. 'I'm very, very interested,' she whispered, and she opened her arms to her man—the one man in the world she wanted.

* * * * *

A Bride At Birralee

CHAPTER ONE

SOMEONE WAS COMING.

Callum Roper slouched against a veranda post and glared at the distant cloud of dust. In the outback, dust travelling at that speed meant one thing—a vehicle heading this way.

He wasn't in the mood for visitors.

Turning his back on the view, he lowered his long body into a deep canvas chair and snapped the top off a beer. He took a deep swig and scowled. Truth was, he wasn't in the mood for anything much these days! Even beer didn't taste the same.

'Why'd you have to do it, Scotty?'

He hadn't meant to ask the question out loud, but there it was, lingering like the dust on the hot, still air. *Why did you have to go and die? Damn you, Scotty.*

Taking another, deeper swig, he grimaced. How long did it last, this grief business? His younger brother had been dead for six weeks now and he still felt as raw and hurt as he had the day the helicopter crashed and he'd first glimpsed Scott's lifeless body in the cockpit.

Slumping lower in the canvas seat, he reached for the cattle dog at his side and rubbed the soft fur between its ears, willing himself to relax. But a picture of Scott's sun-streaked curls, laughing brown eyes and cheeky grin swam before him. It was the face of an irrepressible larrikin. And it had gone for ever.

Late afternoons like this were the worst. This was the time of day he and Scott used to sit here on the veranda, having a beer and a yarn. His brother had been such damn good company. Drinking alone without Scott's humorous recounts of their day wasn't any kind of fun.

He cast a bitter glance over his shoulder towards the encroaching vehicle. Entertaining visitors without Scott's easy banter would be hell!

Luckily, cars didn't foray into these parts very often. Birralee Station was beyond Cloncurry in far north-western Queensland, further outback than most people liked to venture.

But this particular cloud of dust was definitely edging closer down the rust-red track. He could hear the motor now and it sounded tinny, not the throaty roar of the off-road vehicles his neighbours used.

Surely no one with any sense would come all the way out here in a flimsy little city sedan? City visitors were even worse than well-meaning neighbours.

Scott had been the one for the city. He'd always been flying off to Sydney or Brisbane to seek out fun and female company. Callum was content to stick to the bush, restricting his socialising to picnic races and parties on surrounding properties. He'd never felt the urge to go chasing off to the city.

Almost never. His hand tightened around the beer can as a reluctant memory forced him to acknowledge that there had been one city woman he'd wanted to chase. A woman with crow black hair, a haunting, sexy voice and a gutsy, shoulders-back attitude. He'd wanted to chase her, catch her and brand her as his.

But his little brother had always had the happy knack of smiling at a girl in a certain way and rendering her smitten. Instantly. Accepting that the woman he'd desired had preferred Scott had been a bitter lesson.

Hell! What was the use of sitting here, thinking about all that again?

Callum jumped to his feet and frowned as he realised the car had stopped. He squinted at the stretch of bushland before him, searching for the tell-tale dust. Late afternoon sun lent a bronze glow to the paddocks of pale Mitchell grass, but there was no sign of movement. The cloudless sky, the trees and grass, even the cattle, were as still as a painting.

Crossing to the edge of the veranda, he stood listening. All he could hear now was the high, keening call of a black falcon as it circled above the cliff on the far side of the creek.

He frowned. By his calculations, the car had been close to the creek crossing. Perhaps the driver had stopped to check the water's depth before fording the shallow stream.

Leaning forward, he rested his elbows on the veranda railing and listened, watched and waited.

A good five minutes or more passed before the engine started up again. But when it did, it screamed and strained. Then there was silence again, before another useless burst from the motor.

'Silly sod's got himself bogged.' He listened for a few more minutes. There was more high-pitched whirring from the straining motor. More silence.

Shaking his head, he let out a heavy sigh. The last thing he felt like was playing hero to some uninvited city slicker, but he could hardly ignore the fact that someone seemed to be having car trouble so close to his homestead.

He had no choice. Cursing softly, he loped down the front steps and across the gravel drive to his ute.

Stella knew she was bogged. She was down to her axle in loose pebbles and sand in the middle of the outback—the middle of *nowhere*—and she was sick as a dog, more miserable than a lost puppy.

Another wave of nausea rose from her stomach to her mouth and she sat very still, willing her stomach to settle. It probably hadn't been very bright to stop in the middle of the creek, but she'd felt so ill she'd had no choice.

How hard was this going to get? She'd been in enough mess before she'd left home, but now she was stuck in this crummy little creek hundreds of kilometres from anywhere—and out of the mobile network. When she needed to phone Scott, she couldn't!

It was her own fault, of course. She should have tried ringing

him again before she'd left Sydney and told him she was coming.
Then he would have given her detailed directions. He might have
warned her about this creek crossing.

But if she'd rung him, he would have expected to know why
she wanted to see him. And she hadn't liked to explain about the
baby over the phone.

After their breakup, she *couldn't* have discussed her pregnancy
over the phone. There was just too much to talk about and it was
all too complicated. She wanted to work out the very best solution for their baby's future, and to do that she needed to discuss it
with him face to face.

And she hadn't wanted to waste precious money on air fares
when she might need it for the baby, so she'd spent five days—
nearly a week—driving all this way from Sydney.

Sighing heavily, she looked at her watch and then at the redden-
ing sky. It would be dark soon and, for the first time since she'd
left home, she felt genuinely frightened.

Fighting off the urge to panic, she forced herself to consider
her options. She couldn't spend the night sleeping in the car in the
middle of an outback creek; and trying to make camp under trees
up on the bank had no appeal. No, she'd rather gamble on how far
she was from the homestead and try to walk from here.

She reached into the back of her little car and groped for her
shoes, but before she could find them the sound of a motor came
throbbing towards her.

Her head shot up and she peered through the dust-streaked windscreen. Silhouetted against the sun, a utility truck crested the low
hill on the other side of the creek, then rattled effortlessly down
the dirt-and gravel-strewn slope.

'Thank you, God.' Smiling with relief, she dropped her shoe
and her spirits soared as she watched the ute rumble towards her
over the loose, water-washed rocks in the creek-bed. Perhaps it
was Scott driving. 'Please, let it be Scott.'

There was a male figure at the wheel and a blue heeler cattle
dog perched on the seat next to him.

The truck pulled to a halt beside her.

From her little low car, she looked up. The driver's face was shaded by the brim of his akubra hat, but she saw black stubble on a resolute jaw and dark hair on a strongly muscled forearm.

Not Scott. Oh, dear, no. Not Scott, but the one man she'd hoped to avoid. His brother, Callum.

Stella's breathing snagged and she lowered her gaze. *Callum!* This was a moment she'd dreaded, and she hadn't expected to have to deal with it right at the start.

She wet her lips and looked up at him with her chin at a defiant angle. 'Hi, Callum.'

He didn't answer.

'I—I'm afraid I'm stuck.'

The truck's door squeaked as he shoved it open. With an excessive lack of haste, his well-worn, brown leather riding boots lowered into the shallow creek. The boots were followed by an endless pair of blue jeans, a faded blue cotton shirt that stretched wide across powerful shoulders and, finally, a dark unsmiling face beneath a broad-brimmed hat.

It was a face she hadn't seen for twelve months. A face that still haunted her secret dreams. Dreams she never dared think about in the light of day.

For an agonisingly long moment, he didn't speak. He stood still as a mountain, his thumbs hooked through the loops of his jeans. 'What the hell are you doing here?'

What a beast! No greeting. No, How do you do, Stella? Long time, no see, or, Can I help? Not a trace of polite concern. Not even G'day.

For a heartbeat, she wondered if Callum Roper had forgotten her? That would be convenient but, short of his developing amnesia, she didn't think it was possible for him to have forgotten *that* party. Nevertheless, she deserved a warmer greeting than this!

At least when she found Scott and told him about getting bogged, *he* would be sympathetic.

She remained sitting in her car and held out her hand. It was about time this oaf was forced to remember his manners. 'How are you, Callum?'

Their eyes met. His expression was so fierce and hard that she knew, even before he spoke, that he hadn't forgotten her.

'Stella.' He nodded and grunted an incomprehensible greeting. After just a trace of hesitation, his big hand closed around hers.

It was the hard, callused hand of an outdoors man and she tried to ignore the goose-bumps that rushed up her arms in response to such simple contact. This was Scott's brother, her baby's uncle, and she really would have to learn to relax when he was around.

Easier said than done.

'You're asking for trouble if you stop in the middle of a creek,' he said.

Damn him. 'I didn't deliberately get myself bogged, you know. You should have a sign warning people about this creek.'

'If there was any sign, it would warn trespassers they'd be prosecuted,' Callum growled as he circled her car slowly, hoping his shock didn't show.

His heart was racing at a hectic gallop. The last thing he'd expected to find had been this particular woman stranded on his property. What the hell was *she* doing here?

Silly question. His stomach dropped like a leg-roped steer as he acknowledged there could only be one reason. She'd come to see Scott. Hell! She didn't know.

His brother hadn't shared details about his recent trips to the city, and Callum hadn't asked. He'd never even known for sure if Scott and Stella had still been an item, and she wasn't family, she wasn't a close friend, so he hadn't sent her word of the accident. At least that was the excuse he'd rationalised.

How the blue blazes could he tell her now?

He was uncomfortably aware of her cool grey eyes assessing him as he checked how far her wheels had sunk into the silty creek-bed. Only a class act like Stella Lassiter could look dignified in such a predicament.

Perhaps her dignity came from the way she kept her chin haughtily high as she sat quietly in her car. Or maybe it was an impression created by that broad, full mouth that made her look earthy rather than vulnerable. Maybe it was all that shiny hair, black as a witch's cat.

'How does it look? Am I salvageable?' she called. Her voice was another problem. Smooth and low, it had a syrupy cadence that kicked him at gut level and conjured a host of images he'd tried so hard to forget.

Hell, maybe she was a witch. In a matter of moments, some soft segment of his brain seemed to be slipping under her spell. *Just like last time!*

He forced his thoughts to practicalities. Her ridiculous little toy car was well and truly bogged, but it would be easy enough to haul her out.

Reaching into the back of his ute, he grabbed the D shackle and snatchem strap. 'Sit tight,' he ordered sharply and bent to shackle the long strap to a low bracket on the front of her car. 'I'll give you a tow.'

Leaping high into the truck again, he backed it around until it was positioned in front of hers and then, out of the ute once more, he looped the other end of the strap over the ball joint on his tow bar.

She opened her car door and leaned out to watch what he was doing. And Callum found himself staring at her feet as she sat in her car's open doorway with the skirt of her light cotton dress bunched over her knees and her bare feet propped on the doorway's rim.

Her feet were exquisitely shaped. Each neat toe was topped by perfectly applied, sky-blue nail polish. A fine silver chain threaded with blue glass beads was secured neatly around one dainty ankle.

Callum couldn't drag his eyes away. Her feet were as interesting and compelling as the rest of her.

Suddenly, she drew her legs into the car and pulled the door smartly shut. Had he been gaping? Perhaps he was more of a country hick than he realised. Through the window, she studied him and chewed her full bottom lip, showing a trace of vulnerability for the first time. 'I've come to see Scott. I hope he's home,' she said.

Callum swallowed. He knew she'd come looking for Scott and he should have been thinking about that instead of gaping at her mouth and her hair and her *feet!*

'Ah—' a painful constriction dammed his throat '—I'm—er— I'm afraid you're going to be disappointed. Scott's—' *Stuff this!*

He avoided looking at her as he blinked stinging eyes. 'Scott's not here.'

'What?' She stared at him, her eyes wide with disbelief and despair. 'Where is he?' Her strength seemed to leave her suddenly. She looked crumpled and crestfallen. 'I've—I've driven all the way from Sydney. I've got to see him.'

Callum shot a hopeless glance to the darkening sky. If it hadn't been so late in the day, he would have considered breaking the bad news and sending her packing! But there was less than half an hour of daylight left.

Forcing her to go back down the rough Kajabbi track in the dark wasn't an option. Chances were she'd get bogged again, or even worse she could hit a deep rut and turn this little death trap over.

'I'll tow you out of here and you'd better follow me up to the homestead,' he said.

'Thanks.' Her reply came in a whisper and she looked very pale, as if the stuffing had been knocked right out of her. 'But can I contact Scott from there?'

Callum cleared his throat. 'It'll be easier to explain about Scott when we get back to the house.'

Without waiting to see her reaction, he spun on his heel and climbed back into the ute, calling over his shoulder, 'Let your handbrake off and don't turn your engine on yet. Just leave it in neutral.'

He edged the truck forward and the creek-bed released her car easily. After towing her to the top of the small rise, he stopped while he unhitched the vehicles. 'The homestead's only a kilometre down the track. See you there.' Without looking her way again, he accelerated around a bend and headed for Birralee.

Scott wasn't here. It was more than she could bear. Stella fought to stay calm as she guided her little car over the last twists and turns of the bumpy track. She'd been keeping all her worries to herself for too long, but she couldn't hold on much longer.

She had never been one for confiding in her friends and the events of the past few months had snowballed into an unbearable, secret burden. First, when she'd realised that Scott hadn't been as committed to their relationship as she'd believed, there had been the unpleasantness of the breakup.

Then she'd discovered she was pregnant!

She'd almost lost the plot when she'd learned that, but after taking time to get used to the idea she'd tried to contact Scott. The message on his answering machine had said he would be out mustering the back blocks of Birralee for several weeks.

The final blow had fallen with a phone call from London and the job offer of her dreams! A British television network wanted to hire her skills as a meteorologist to head the research for a series of documentaries about global warming in Europe.

She couldn't believe the bad timing!

She'd studied so hard and had worked her socks off in the hope of scoring a contract like this, but the amount of travel involved and the primitive living conditions required on location meant it wasn't a job for a woman with a tiny baby.

If only she and Scott had been more careful! But there'd been too many laughs…too much country-boy charm…too many empty assurances that she really was the one and only woman for him…

Stella knew they were poor excuses. She was educated. She was a scientist! She knew better! But…for the first time in her life, she'd allowed herself to let go…

She'd let herself be just a little like her mother. And, just like her mother, her mistakes had caught her out.

She carried the consequences within her. The cluster of little cells, multiplying rapidly every day. Oh, God! She'd been carrying the secret burden of her pregnancy for four lonely months now and she couldn't keep it to herself any longer.

She had to speak to Scott.

The job offer had been too wonderful to resist and so she'd accepted it, but she couldn't fulfil her contract without Scott's help. *Scott, where are you? At the very least, I need to talk this through with someone.*

Ahead of her, Callum had pulled up in front of a typical outback homestead. She'd never visited one before, but she was familiar with the image—a low and sprawling timber house with a ripple-iron roof and deep verandas set in the middle of an expanse of lawn and shaded by ancient trees.

So this was Scott's home—Birralee. This was where the father of her baby had been born. He'd run on this grass as a little boy. He was at home in this wild, rough country with its rocky red cliffs, its haze of soft green bush and its vast wide plains, so flat you could see the curvature of the earth as you drove across them.

And of course this was Callum's home, too.

He stood waiting, his blue heeler squatting obediently beside him. His face remained fierce and unsmiling as she parked her car on the grass next to his truck. He'd taken his hat off and she saw the tangle of his dark, rough curls and the golden brown lights that might soften his eyes if he'd let them.

Callum had never looked very much like Scott. Where Scott was blond and boyish, full of sunshine and laughter, Callum was darker and older, more stormy and grim. OK…she had to admit he was still good-looking in his own hard way.

Who was she trying to kid? Callum was incredibly good-looking. Heaven knew, she'd been attracted to him from the very first moment she'd laid eyes on him. But he had a dangerous brand of good looks that fascinated yet unnerved her. There was a magnetic fierceness about Callum that pierced hidden depths in her and threatened her inner peace.

She'd recognised a perilous intensity in him on the night they'd met…

Get a grip! You'll be a complete mess if you think about that now!

Hopefully, she wouldn't have to spend too much time around him. She needed inner peace more than ever now. She needed cheering up.

She needed Scott.

Where was Scott? Why hadn't Callum told her straight away where he was? Her stomach churned and her smile was grim as she climbed out of her little car and stretched cramped limbs.

'Do you have much gear?' Callum asked.

'Just one bag and a bird cage.'

'A bird cage?' He didn't try to hide his surprise.

Her chin lifted. 'I had to bring my bird. My flatmate's absolutely hopeless about remembering to change Oscar's seed or water. Last time I left him with her, the poor darling nearly dehydrated.'

Carefully, she extracted the cage from the back of her car and eyed his cattle dog warily as she made introductions. 'This is Oscar.'

Callum scowled at the little blue budgerigar.

'What's your dog's name?'

Her question seemed to surprise him. 'Mac,' he muttered.

At the sound of his name, Mac's ears pricked and he sprang to his feet, tail wagging madly.

'Hi, Mac.' She shot Callum a cautious glance. 'He doesn't like to nip at small birds, does he?'

He cracked a brief smile. 'He's a true blue heeler. From when he was a pup he knew that his mission in life was to nip at the heels of cattle. I doubt he's ever paid any attention to birds.'

'That's a relief.'

Callum scruffed the top of the dog's head. 'Poor old fella's retired to home duties these days.'

Stella saw Callum's genuine affection for his dog and she felt a tiny bit better. Somehow it helped to know that the grim Callum Roper was as fond of his pet as she was of hers.

His smile faded as he nodded his head towards the house. 'You bring the bird cage. I'll grab your bag.'

'Thanks.' Reaching back into the car, she fished out her shoes and slipped her feet into them. Then, puzzled and curious, she followed the dog and his master up three wide wooden steps.

As Callum led her along the veranda, she couldn't help noticing that he made an art form of the loose-hipped, long-legged saunter of the outback cattleman.

With an easy dip of one broad shoulder, he pushed a door open. 'You'll have to stay here tonight, so you'd better have this room.' He stepped aside to let her enter, then placed her bag with surprising care on top of a carved sandalwood box at the foot of the bed.

She dragged her attention from him to the room. It was old-fashioned and simply furnished. There was no personal clutter and it was very clearly a guest room. The floorboards were left uncovered and the big double bed had brass ends and was covered by a patchwork quilt in various shades of green and white.

On the wall was a painting of a stormy sky and horses galloping down a steep mountainside with their manes and tails flying.

'I'm afraid I'm imposing on your hospitality.'

He didn't answer, but his gaze dropped to the bird cage she was still holding.

'I'll put this out on the veranda,' she suggested.

'You'd better bring it through to the kitchen. Mac won't touch it, but if you leave it outside the possums might knock it over during the night.'

'Really?'

A hint of mischief danced in his eyes. 'Or a carpet snake might fancy a midnight snack.'

'Oh, no!' Horrified, she clutched the cage to her. 'I'd be grateful if he could stay in the kitchen, thank you.'

Once again, she followed Callum's long strides. This time down a long hall with polished timber floorboards and rooms opening off its entire length.

Where was Scott? An uneasy tension coiled in her stomach. She hoped she wasn't going to be sick. The hardest part of her journey was still ahead of her.

When she found Scott, not only did she have to tell him he was going to be a father, she had to convince him that the plan she'd agonised over really was the best solution.

Best for him and the baby and for her.

It was a straightforward plan. She would resign from her current job, have the baby and then Scott would look after it while she went to London. Luckily the television project was so big that the company did their recruiting well in advance. She was due to give birth several weeks before her contract started and after twelve months she would come back and take over her responsibilities as a mother.

As she headed down the hall, she prayed that Scott would see the beautiful simplicity and fairness of what she was asking. If only she didn't feel so scared!

The rooms she glimpsed as she hurried after Callum were a little shabby, a little untidy, decidedly old-fashioned, but she had an impression of tasteful decor and comfort and an easy, unpretentious air that made them welcoming. Easy to live in.

Easy and charming like Scott had been. She could imagine him here. But could she imagine leaving his baby here at this house? Could she really leave a tiny baby way out here in the never-never while she spent a year overseas?

Everything depended on Scott's reaction.

And maybe Callum's.

They reached the kitchen at the back of the house. It was huge and cluttered and Stella fell in love with it at first sight.

The reaction was so unexpected. All her life, she'd been walking into other people's kitchens. There'd been a bewildering series of them during her childhood—dingy council flats, women's shelters and foster homes. Until she'd moved into the little flat she shared with Lucy, she'd never lived in one place for very long. Their kitchen was neat and trendy, but she'd never felt an immediate rapport with a room the way she did now.

She loved it. Loved the long wall of deep, timber-framed windows of clear glass with dark green diamond panes in the middle, pushed wide open to catch the breeze. Loved the spellbinding views of the twilight-softened bush as it dipped down to the creek and climbed on the other side to majestic red cliffs in the distance.

She loved the huge scrubbed pine table in the middle of the room, home to a wonderful jumble of odd bits and pieces—a flame-coloured pottery bowl overflowing with dried gum nuts, a pile of *Country Life* magazines, a horse's bridle and several bulging packets of photographs.

The collection of unmatched chairs gathered around the table enchanted her. With no effort at all, she could picture these chairs seating a party of happy, chatting friends or family. She could almost hear their bright, laughter-filled voices.

Standing in the kitchen's corner, was an old timber high chair with scratched red paint. Stella couldn't help staring at it, wondering...

'You can park the bird cage on that high chair if you like,' Callum said. 'We only use it when my sisters bring their tribes to visit.'

She did as he suggested. 'There you go, Oscar. You can have a lovely view of the gum trees and talk to all the other birds outside.'

Callum's mouth twitched. 'You don't think he might get ideas about escaping?'

She glanced again at the bush and couldn't help wondering if Oscar craved for freedom to explore that vast sky and all those trees, but then she shoved that disagreeable thought aside. 'I look after him too well,' she assured Callum primly.

He walked to the fridge. 'Would you like a beer?'

'No. No, thanks.'

'Scotch, sherry, wine? I'm afraid I can't manage any fancy cocktails.'

'I won't have any alcohol, thank you.'

He seemed surprised. 'Cup of tea?'

'Yes, in a minute. That would be nice, but first, please, you must tell me about Scott. How can I contact him?'

He stiffened and she felt a stab of panic. His face seemed momentarily grey and he turned quickly away from her and snatched a beer out of the fridge.

What's the matter? What's wrong? Her heart began to thud.

'You'd better sit down,' he said without looking at her. 'I'm afraid I've got bad news about Scott.'

CHAPTER TWO

CALLUM FIDDLED WITH his unopened beer. His guts crawled with dread as he imagined Stella's reaction to his news.

Scott's dead. The words were so hard to get out.

Telling his parents had been the worst, the very worst moment of his life. Scott had been the baby of the family—everybody's favourite. To tell his mother and father had meant inflicting unbearable pain.

If Stella was in love with his brother, she was sure to burst into noisy tears. What the hell would he do then?

'Callum,' she said, and her voice vibrated with tension, 'I need to know what's happened to Scott.'

He realised he was still holding the beer, rolling it back and forth between anxious hands. The last thing he needed on this night was another beer. Hastily, he shoved it back in the fridge and cleared his throat.

'There was a mustering accident a few weeks back. Scott was flying a helicopter.'

She looked pale. Too pale. And she sat stiffly, without speaking, staring at him. Waiting.

'I'm afraid Scotty was killed.' He couldn't keep the tremor from his voice.

At first he thought she hadn't heard him. She just sat there, not making a sound, not moving.

After some time, she whispered, 'No! *No!* He can't be dead.'

He braced himself for the tears, eyeing the box of tissues on the bench to his right.

But she didn't cry. She just kept sitting there looking stunned, while her face turned from pale to greenish.

'I'm sorry to have to give you such bad news,' he said, wishing she didn't look so ill and wishing he didn't sound so clumsy and obviously uncomfortable. Wishing she would say something. *Anything.*

Her hand wavered to her mouth and for a moment he thought she was going to be sick.

'Are you OK?'

'I—I—' She tried to stand and swayed groggily before moaning faintly and collapsing back into her chair, her head slumped sideways.

'Stella.' Crouching quickly at her side, he touched her shoulder and to his relief she moved slightly. Her dark hair hung in a silky curtain hiding her face and, with two fingers, he lifted it away. Her eyes were shut and her skin was cool and pale.

Hell! She'd cared about Scott *this* much?

A hard knot of pain dammed his throat as he scooped her in his arms and, edging sideways through the kitchen doorway, carried her back to her room.

'I'm all right,' she protested weakly.

He didn't answer. Her pale fragility alarmed him. In his arms, she felt too light, too slim. *Too soft and womanly.* He drew in a ragged breath as her satiny, sweet-smelling hair brushed his neck. One shoe fell off as he made his way down the hallway, and he saw again the delicate foot with its pretty blue toenails, the gypsy-like allure of her dainty ankle chain.

His chest tightened with a hundred suppressed emotions as he laid her on the bed and removed the other shoe.

'Thank you,' she whispered. Her grey eyes opened and they held his. A trembling, thrilling, silent exchange passed between them. She looked away. 'I felt a little faint,' she said and tried to sit up.

It only took the slightest pressure of his fingers on her shoulders to push her back onto the bed. 'You've had a shock. Take it easy there for a minute or two.'

Lifting a crocheted rug from the chair in the corner, he spread it over her.

Outside it was almost dark. He switched on the shaded bedside lamp, then retrieved her shoe from the hallway, and when he returned her eyes were closed again and she seemed to be calmer.

For too long, Callum stood beside the bed, taking his fill of her special style of beauty. Noticing the way her eyelids were crisscrossed by a fine tracery of delicate blue veins and how very black her long lashes were against her pale cheeks. Heaven help him, he'd spent too many nights imagining her like this—in bed. What a silly damn fool he was.

He crossed to the French doors that opened onto the veranda and stood quietly, leaning against the door jamb, watching the bush grow dark, watching this woman who'd been looking for his brother. Wondering if her fainting spell had been caused by more than the shock of his news and thinking that perhaps a little crying would have been easier to handle after all.

The bush beyond the house grew still and silent. All day the birds had filled the air with their noisy chatter and screeches, but now they'd stopped calling, responding to the approach of night as if obeying an unseen conductor. Very soon the cicadas would tune in.

After some time, Stella's eyes opened and she rolled onto her side.

'How are you feeling now?'

Her eyebrows lifted in surprise when she saw him standing in the doorway. Elbow crooked, she propped up her head. 'I'm OK. Truly. But I can't believe that Scott—' Her eyes glistened, but no tears fell. 'It must have been so awful. Can you tell me what happened?'

He nodded slowly. 'We were out mustering in the rough country on the far western boundaries of this property. We needed to use the helicopter to chase some stragglers out of a gully and Scott flew in close and somehow the tail rotor clipped a gum tree.'

He didn't add that it had been his fault Scott had been flying that day. He kept that guilty secret to himself, let it gnaw away at his insides like white ants in a tree stump.

Sighing, he glanced again at the darkening bush beyond the veranda. 'It all happened very quickly.'

'So you were with Scott at the time?'

'No.' His chest squeezed so tight that for a moment he couldn't breathe. 'Scott insisted on going solo and he was having the time of his life. I was on horseback down below.'

He closed his eyes. There was still no way to block out the memory. The terror of the chopper going down. The crazy, lurching fall. The horrifying, screeching sound of ripping metal. The hellish moment of finding Scott, blood-soaked and slumped in the pilot's seat, staring back at him with blank, sightless eyes.

Hell! Each day it seemed to become more vivid.

'Why didn't you contact me, Callum?'

The challenge in her voice piqued his pride, spurring sudden anger. 'I wasn't my brother's keeper. I didn't keep tabs on his women. How was I to know you were still in the picture? I thought he'd taken up with some girl in Brisbane.'

She swung her gaze away and bit down hard on her lip and Callum wished he'd been less brutal. 'I would have let you know, but I didn't...' *Didn't want to be reminded that you'd chosen Scott over me...* His Adam's apple felt the size of a rock melon. 'It's a damn shame you had to come all this way—without knowing.'

Closing her eyes, she smiled wryly as she gave a faint shake of her head. 'It's a damn shame all right.' Her smoky deep voice resonated with bitter self-mockery.

Again he asked, 'How are you feeling?'

'Like a dill-brain.'

'I was referring to your stomach. Has it settled? I'll make a cup of tea, or perhaps you can manage a bite to eat?'

She pushed herself into a sitting position. 'I suppose I should try to eat.'

'I'll get dinner, then. I'm afraid it's only leftover stew.'

'Anything will be fine, thanks. I'm not really hungry.'

Callum left the room and Stella lay there, watching his broad, straight back. She tried not to think. Tried not to worry. Not to panic!

She was alone now. Totally alone. There was no one to turn to. Her bright dreams were dead. There would be no trip to London. No father for her baby. She couldn't dream of asking Callum to help. Her last hope had died with Scott.

Oh, God! Poor Scott! She shouldn't be feeling sorry for herself. He hadn't deserved to die. He'd been too young, too healthy, too brimming with energy and love of life.

How could Scott be dead?

Her mother had died when she was fifteen and her death had never seemed real. This was even harder to believe.

And poor Callum. How terrible for him to see his brother die in such a terrible accident. And how hard to carry on alone out here without him!

She pressed a hand to her slightly rounded stomach. Her poor little baby, already fatherless before it drew breath. That was the worst of all.

Just like her mother, she was producing a child who would never know its father. Although, unlike her mother, Stella was quite clear about her baby's paternity.

Her mother had never been sure. 'It was one of the lecturers at uni.,' she'd admitted once, just once, in a mismanaged attempt to be close to Stella. 'One of the nutty professors—but I don't know which.'

By contrast, there was only one man who could be the father of Stella's baby's. The fact that he was dead was too much to take in. Her insides shook with fear. Fear for herself, for the baby. Especially for the baby.

Scott was dead.

Where did that leave her? She couldn't stand being alone any longer. All her childhood, she'd felt lonely—handed from one adult to another. Life had always been hard.

As an adult, she'd found it easiest to bury herself in study. When she'd discovered science, she'd found the laws of physics to be true and unchanging. They never let her down. Which was more than she could say for the people in her life.

And she'd really wanted the job in London! It would have allowed her to apply her scientific knowledge to a fascinating project. She'd been so excited. But the television network wouldn't want a woman with a tiny baby. She'd really needed Scott's help.

With a shaky sigh, she swung her legs over the edge of the bed and stood up. The dizziness seemed to have passed. So far so good.

She made her way back through the house to the kitchen, knowing the only thing that would hold her together now was habit. Old habits died hard and she'd learned as a child that it was best not to let others see how worried she was about all the mess in her life.

In the kitchen, Callum had everything ready. With rough movements, he placed a plate of food in front of her. 'My version of outback hospitality.'

The meal smelt surprisingly good. Rich beef and vegetables. 'Mmm. Good wholesome country fare.'

'Just like mother used to make?' he asked as he took his seat and pushed a knife and fork across the table towards her.

Stella rolled her eyes. 'Not my mother.'

He frowned and waited, as if he expected her to clarify that remark. When she didn't, he said stiffly, 'I don't want to pry, but I'm assuming this visit to see Scott was rather important?'

She felt her cheeks grow hot. 'Not really. I—I had a few days spare and I just thought I'd look him up.'

His eyes told her he didn't believe her and his mouth thinned into a very straight line. 'So you'll be leaving again in the morning?'

She hadn't been ready for his question. Her head shot up making her look more haughty than she intended. 'Sure. I'll be out of your hair as soon as the sun comes up.'

Standing abruptly, he crossed back to the stove and filled the teapot with boiling water from the kettle. Stella bit her lip. Callum had been hospitable and she'd been rude. 'Do you live here by yourself now?' she asked, trying to make amends.

'Yes.' He thumped the lid onto the pot.

'How do you manage such a big property on your own?'

'I manage. My father tried to persuade me that the property's too big for one man. He wanted to send someone out to help me.'

'But you refused help?'

'I don't want anyone else here.' The message was loud and very clear.

'So how do you do it all?'

Callum turned from the stove and shrugged. 'It's not that difficult if you're prepared to work hard. And there are plenty of blokes looking for mustering contracts. I can hire a team of fencers if I need to.'

'You mentioned your sisters before. Do they live in these parts?'

One of his eyebrows rose quizzically. 'Didn't my little brother tell you about the family?'

Stella concentrated on her food. She didn't want to admit to Callum that there'd been disappointments in her relationship with Scott. She forced a nonchalant smile. 'It was tit for tat. I didn't tell Scott about my family either. We liked it that way.'

It was partly the truth. After she'd let Scott make love to her, she'd expected they would become closer in every way, that he'd begin to share more of his life with her. But the minute he'd sensed she'd been getting serious, he'd become edgy and had backed away.

Callum brought the teapot and mugs to the table. 'My mob don't have any secrets. Both my sisters married North Queensland graziers. Catherine lives on a property near Julia Creek and Ellie is just outside Cloncurry. They both love the bush life. They're happy as possums up a gum tree.'

'Do they have children?'

'Three kids apiece.'

'Wow. That's quite a family. It must be crowded when they all visit.'

'It's great.' His eyes glowed and he actually smiled. And Stella wished he wouldn't. Callum Roper was far too attractive when his eyes lit up that way.

She glanced at Oscar in his cage in the corner. He was her family, the only living thing in the world that belonged to her. Apart from the baby. But the baby was invisible. Most of the time, she had trouble thinking of it as real.

Callum leaned back in his chair. 'And I suppose you know all about our old man?'

She frowned. 'Your father? Should I know about him?'

She was surprised when he almost laughed. 'He would like to think so, but then, all politicians have huge egos.'

'Politicians?' Stella almost dropped her fork. *Roper... Roper...* Was there a state politician named Roper? Suddenly she remembered. Not state government. Federal. 'Your dad is Senator Ian Roper?'

''Fraid so.'

'Oh, good grief!' In her head, she added a few swear words and the invisible cluster of cells in her body suddenly posed a whole new parcel of problems.

Just how much bad luck did a girl have to deal with? She was carrying the illegitimate grandchild of one of the country's most outspokenly conservative politicians!

Suddenly their efforts at conversation deteriorated. It seemed neither of them had much to say. Stella's curiosity about Scott's family vanished. She was back in panic mode again.

After they'd eaten, he asked, 'Are you feeling OK now?'

'Yes, much better, thank you. You're a great cook. Dinner was delicious.'

'Feel free to go straight to bed.'

'I'll help you clean up.'

His dark brows beetled in a deep frown. 'No, you won't.'

She had the distinct impression that he'd had enough of being sociable. He wanted her out of the room.

'You're sure I can't help?'

He nodded without speaking.

Standing slowly, she said, 'You'll be closing the kitchen windows, won't you?'

He frowned. 'I don't usually bother.'

'But—with Oscar in here—and the snakes and—everything.'

Callum almost grinned. 'Oh, yeah. The snakes. OK, I'll close the windows.'

CHAPTER THREE

STELLA WAS SICK the next morning.

As Callum came back from the holding yards, striding through the dewy bluegrass with Mac at his heels, he heard unmistakable sounds coming from the bathroom.

They stopped him dead in his tracks. She was supposed to be heading off this morning. Leaving him in peace. But how could he send her packing if she was sick?

He kicked at a loose stone and sent it rolling down the incline. Instantly alert, the blue heeler watched its descent then seemed to decide it wasn't worth chasing.

Callum watched it, too, as it bounced from rock to rock before disappearing into the scrub on the creek bank. This sickness of Stella's was rather unusual. The fainting last night and now this...

Perhaps she had a simple stomach bug, but she'd woofed down that tucker last night without any problems. He frowned. That was how his sisters had been when they'd been expecting. Fine one minute, then suddenly dizzy or racing to the bathroom.

Was she pregnant? No, surely not.

His head shot back. She damn well could be pregnant.

The more he thought about it, the more he was sure he'd hit on the truth. Of course she was pregnant. That was why she'd high-tailed it all the way from Sydney looking for Scott. That's why she'd been so upset.

Damn and blast you, little brother. What have you gone and done now?

If Stella was pregnant… If she was carrying Scott's child… If she was planning on heading back to the city…disappearing again as quickly as she'd appeared…taking Scott's baby with her…

He slapped his palm against the rough trunk of a bloodwood tree and stared blankly into the distance, while tumultuous thoughts raged. Thoughts of Scott, of his family, of his own guilt and grief, his parents' heartbreak.

Thoughts of Scott in Stella's bed.

Groaning, he kicked another loose stone. Distasteful as it was, he had little choice; he had to ask her. If Scott was leaving behind a son or daughter, he needed to know.

Fists clenched, he turned reluctantly and marched towards the house.

Stella was in the kitchen, hovering in front of the stove and squinting at the dials. She was wearing denim cut-offs and a simple white T-shirt and her feet were bare except for the silver ankle chain with its blue glass beads.

She turned and smiled at him warily. 'Good morning.'

He nodded. 'Morning. Did you sleep well?'

'Like a log, thank you. I didn't realise how tired I was.' She pointed to the stove. 'I thought I'd make a cup of tea, but I haven't quite worked out how to drive your stove.'

'It's fairly straightforward,' he muttered.

'Uh-uh.' She shook her head. 'An electric kettle is straightforward. A stove this size requires a licence to operate. I'm surprised you have something so complicated way out in the bush.'

'We needed it when all the family lived at home.' He reached past her to flick appropriate switches. 'My mother takes her cooking seriously.'

Stella gave a wry grin as she shrugged. 'I'm afraid I'm a victim of the microwave era. If it doesn't light up with little messages telling me what to do, I'm lost.'

She ran slim fingers through her shiny black hair. Her hands, like her feet, were elegantly shaped, although her fingernails weren't painted. The movements of her fingers in her hair made the silky strands shift and fall back into place. To Callum, the gesture seemed as natural and pretty as a jabiru stretching and folding its glossy wings.

'What would you like for breakfast?' he asked, unhappy to find himself still thinking about her hair, her hands, her feet.

She grimaced. 'I'm not sure. I thought I'd just try a cuppa to start with.'

'You're not hungry?' he challenged.

'Not really. Maybe some dry toast.' She looked away.

He took a deep breath. 'You were sick—just before.'

'It's nothing.'

'Nothing? Are you sure it's nothing, Stella?'

Her head swung back quickly and her grey eyes were defensive as she stared at him. 'Of course I'm sure.'

He knew she was lying.

'I can't let you head off on the long journey back to Sydney if you're not well. And if you can't manage more to eat than dry toast—'

She turned swiftly away from him again. He couldn't be sure but he thought she seemed to be trembling.

'Stella.'

She shook her head as if she wanted him to leave her alone. Then her chin lifted and he saw again the same haughty strength that he'd sensed in her yesterday. Or was it just stubbornness?

When he stepped towards her, she continued to keep her back to him, but he settled his hands firmly on her shoulders and forced her to turn around, too tense to take his time searching for delicate ways to pose his question. 'Stella, are you pregnant?'

'No!' she snapped and she tried to jerk her shoulders out of his grasp. 'Anyway, it—it's none of your business.'

He kept a tight grip on her shoulders. 'If you're carrying my brother's baby, I consider it my business.'

Her eyes blazed with sudden anger. 'Why? What would you want to do about it?'

'Are you telling me it's true?' His breathing felt suddenly constricted. 'You *are* pregnant?'

He let go and she jumped back quickly, like a trapped animal escaping.

'I'm telling you it's got nothing to do with you. I don't want you or your family trying to take over my life just—just because—'

'Just because you're having Scott's baby,' he finished for her. Out of the blue, he felt his eyes sting and his throat close over. Spinning on the heel of his riding boot, he marched away from her, clear across the room, kicking a chair out of his way as he went.

Bloody hell! He mustn't lose it and make a complete fool of himself in front of this woman, but the thought of Scott's seed blossoming inside her made him feel damn emotional.

Scotty Roper was gone for ever, but he'd left behind a part of himself. And, God help him, Callum couldn't block out the thought of his brother and Stella together—making that little baby—making *love*.

Whirling around again, he found that she was close behind him, standing with her hands clasped in front of her, as if she'd been thinking about touching him and hadn't dared, or hadn't wanted to.

'Are you quite certain it's Scott's baby?' he asked coldly.

The way she closed her eyes and compressed her lips told him she hated the question and hated him for asking. 'It's definitely his,' she said, matching his cold tone. 'And if you plan to stand there and make moral judgements about me, I'm going straight out that door and taking off for Cloncurry without even thanking you for your reluctant hospitality.'

'OK. OK.' He raised his hands in a halting action, then let out a long breath. Steam was pouring out of the kettle on the stove and he grabbed the opportunity to change the subject. 'I'll get you that cup of tea.'

In a weird way Stella felt better now Callum knew about the baby. It felt as if at least some of her burden was lifting from her shoulders.

Sharing the news with someone, *even Callum*, after keeping it to herself for so long brought instant relief. But she would have to make him promise not to tell the rest of his family—certainly not his father. Not the Senator!

He handed her a bright red mug and she took a seat at the table.

Snatching the chair he'd kicked aside, he turned it back to front and straddled it. Stella tried not to notice the very masculine stretch of his jeans over his strong, muscular thighs. He propped his elbows on the top rung of the chair's ladder back and held his mug in both hands.

She took a sip of tea. It was hot and sweet, just how she needed it. And her stomach seemed to accept it. 'Look,' she said, 'this is my problem, Callum. You don't have to worry about it.'

He eyed her thoughtfully. 'Did Scott know about the baby?'

She shook her head.

'And you came out here to tell him.'

'Yes.'

His brown-gold eyes continued to study her with the intensity of a hawk. 'What were you hoping? That he would marry you?'

Stella almost dropped her mug. 'No. Not marriage.' Did she imagine that slight relaxation of his shoulders?

'Do you need help? Money?'

'*No!*' She stared at him, shocked. 'And I'm not planning to get rid of it. Is that what you thought?'

He shrugged. 'I'm just trying to understand.'

She wanted to believe him. It was actually a comforting idea—having someone who wanted to understand.

Perhaps he was more sensitive than he appeared on the surface. Perhaps she could trust him. Her chin lifted. 'I know I'll be a hopeless mother, but the least I can do is give this little baby life.'

Draining his tea, he rocked the chair slowly forward and set his empty mug on the table. When he straightened once more, his gaze lifted slowly. 'What makes you think you'd be a hopeless mother?'

She felt her cheeks burn. *She couldn't tell him that.* No way! Honesty had its limits. It would mean confessing about Marlene, her own mother, the source of most of her hang ups. It would mean dredging up those sordid stories about the way Marlene had failed over and over in numerous attempts at motherhood.

It had been the ongoing pattern of Stella's childhood and it left her terrified at the thought of ever attempting to be a mother.

The pattern had always been the same. Marlene would plead

with the welfare people that she could take beautiful care of Stella and stay clean and sober. She would promise the earth.

And, because the government policy was to keep mothers and children together wherever possible, they would give in. For a few months, life would be grand. Stella would go home to her mother's new flat and they would eat meat with three kinds of vegetables and they'd go to the movies. They'd play music and dance in the lounge.

Marlene would wash her long black hair and she'd smell of lemon shampoo and talcum powder, and she would take Stella on her lap and read her stories about heroes. For some reason her mother had fancied tales about brave, fearless men.

At night, Marlene would tuck her into bed and tell her she loved her. And Stella would love her back fiercely, so fiercely she could feel her chest swell with the force of her emotion. Marlene was her mother, the very best mother in the world.

But then there would always be the black day when Stella came home from school and found Marlene incoherent and smelling of alcohol. Each day after that things would get worse...the house would turn into a pigsty...and there'd be a different man... She'd go hungry. Sometimes the man would be violent and she'd have to hide outside the house, crying and hungry, trying to sleep in the garage.

Eventually someone, usually a teacher, would report Stella's condition to the authorities. They would take her away again and Marlene would be broken-hearted. She would sob that she wanted to be a good mother...

Stella had wanted her to be a good mother, too. Had longed for it. She'd hated Marlene for failing yet again...

It wasn't the sort of story she could tell, certainly not to this earnest, solemn man, the son of Senator Ian Roper.

'Are you saying you don't want to be a mother?'

I'm terrified. I'm scared I don't know how to be a mother.

'I—I've worked very hard at my career.'

She saw his stony expression and she felt a distinct rush of resentment. It was impossible for anyone else to understand. She cast a frantic glance to the clock on the wall. 'Don't you have to go work or something?'

He rose to his feet slowly and she wished he hadn't. When he looked down at her from his considerable height, she felt smaller than ever.

'I'm waiting to hear from a ringer in Kajabbi,' he said. 'When he's free, we'll take the stock from the holding yards through to the road trains on the highway, but that probably won't happen till tomorrow or the day after.'

He walked to the sink and deposited their mugs into it. 'How about that dry toast?' he asked with a glimmer of a smile.

She had almost forgotten about breakfast. 'Thanks.'

As he dropped two slices of bread into the toaster he turned her way. 'You shouldn't leave this morning. You've barely had time to recover from the long drive up here. You should at least stay another night.'

He wasn't being friendly or warm. Just practical. And the long journey had been exhausting. She hated the thought of heading straight back.

'That would be sensible, I guess. Thanks.'

He brought her dry toast and spread his own with plenty of butter. It melted, warm and golden, into the toasted bread and Stella couldn't help looking at it rather longingly. Her morning sickness was fading and she was feeling hungry again.

'Sure you don't want some mango jam? My sister Ellie makes it.' He spread the bright-coloured fruit onto his toast and took a bite.

'It does look rather good,' she admitted and dipped her knife into the pot.

They munched for some time without talking. Then he said unexpectedly, 'You'd better tell me about this career and these big plans of yours.'

She sent him a hasty, troubled look, then just as quickly looked at her hands clenched in her lap.

'You never know,' he said carefully. 'I might be able to help.'

'How could you?'

'I don't have a damned clue. But if you tell me—'

She shook her head. 'There's no point. No one can help.'

But he wouldn't give up. 'What kind of work do you do? On the one brief occasion we met in the past, I don't think we talked about mundane things like jobs.'

They exchanged one lightning-quick glance, then both looked away. Stella fought to ignore the sudden memory of his strong body, hard against hers, his hot, hard mouth taking hers. 'I—I work with weather.'

'A weather girl? Like on TV?'

'Sort of. I'm not actually on TV, but I help to supply them with their information.'

He frowned. 'You're a meteorologist?'

'Yes.'

'And you couldn't do that if you had a baby?'

'Not—' She took a deep breath. *What the heck? Here goes...* '—not if I was on location in the Orkney Isles or Russia.'

There was no disguising his shock. 'Russia? What kind of job are you talking about?'

She told him about the documentary project scheduled to begin six weeks after her baby was due. 'I'd be based in London, but I'd be expected to travel, mostly studying coastlines. It's a job I've been working towards for ages and an offer like that is highly prized in my circle.'

Callum's lips pursed as he released a low whistle. 'I'll bet it is.'

'But, of course, a newborn baby doesn't fit in the picture.'

He was scowling again. 'I can see how this baby has completely wrecked your plans.' He didn't say anything more for at least a minute, just sat there as if he was carved from stone. At last he said, 'So you didn't want Scott to marry you and you didn't want his money. What was it you wanted from him?'

'It doesn't matter any more. It can't happen.'

'Tell me anyhow.'

Stella ran nervous fingers through her hair. Then she sighed loudly. 'I don't know how to say this without sounding crazy, but I was hoping Scott might be able to look after the baby for a while—so I could still go to London.'

Telling Callum had not been a good idea. He looked pale and distinctly unhappy. He sat staring at the table for several long, silent minutes. At last he spoke very quietly. 'You really are in a bind, aren't you?' And then he ran his big hand over his face, almost as if he was trying to hide his reaction.

Suddenly he jumped to his feet and mumbled that he'd better get on with some work. 'Help yourself to any books or magazines, rest up, watch TV. Eat what you like from the fridge or the pantry.' In the doorway, he turned back. 'I'll leave Mac behind for company.'

Then he hurried down the veranda as if he couldn't wait to get away.

Blackjack's hooves thundered beneath Callum, drumming the hard earth and pounding over the red plains of Birralee. Faster, harder, he pushed his mount, but nothing eased his raging, inner turmoil.

Eventually, he pulled to a shuddering halt on the crest of a headland that offered spectacular views down a red-walled gorge. It was the place he always came to when he needed to think.

Today his thoughts boiled. Why did it have to be Stella Lassiter who'd come to him with this problem? He didn't know what upset him more: the fact that the woman, who had roused him from apathy to passion in the briefest of encounters, now carried a part of Scott within her and might take it away to the far ends of the earth, or the knowledge that her relationship with Scott had become intimate.

Slumping in the saddle, he sat in a gut-clenched daze while his mind overflowed, teeming with memories of the night he'd met Stella...

He'd gone to Sydney with Scott to check out the prize-winning stock at the Royal Easter Show and, afterwards, Scott had taken him to a party. He'd seen Stella the instant he'd entered the room.

She'd been standing on her own at the far side of the crowd, watching the revellers with her chin at a haughty angle and an aloof expression on her face. Callum had been seized by an urge to stare.

She'd looked bold and bewitching. Her hair had been as dark and shiny as polished ebony and her sleeveless silk dress, the colour of rich claret, vibrant against the smooth ivory of her skin.

Her gaze had met his. She'd looked across at him and had smiled.

And the next moment had been like something out of a movie. He'd begun to walk towards her through the crowd. She'd watched him all the way. When he'd reached her, he'd been strangely out of breath, a little star-struck and suddenly shy, almost embarrassed by the spell that had seemed to have drawn him to her.

But then he'd looked into her clear grey eyes and had felt such a deep, immediate connection that he'd known that if he lived to be two hundred, he would never forget the moment.

Scott's laughing voice had sounded in his ear. 'Oh, so you've met Stella. Good.' He took her hand and placed it in Callum's. 'Stella, this is my big brother, Callum. Be nice to him. He's rough around the edges, but not quite as grim as he looks.'

Then Scott slapped Callum on the shoulder before disappearing off into the crowd to find a drink.

Callum asked Stella to dance and she hesitated at first. Her eyes followed Scott, watching as he reached the bar and started to chat up a pair of pretty girls. In hindsight, Callum realised he should have picked up on the obvious clue of her worried glance after Scott, but he'd been so determined to win her, he'd ignored anything that might get in his way.

When she warmly accepted his invitation to dance, he was as relieved as a nervous schoolboy.

The party's host had hired a band and the music was good. He enjoyed the physicality of dancing. Stella was a responsive partner and the electrifying spell that had drawn him to her continued to weave its sorcery.

Their smiling gazes linked and held as her slender curves brushed against him. He watched the growing warmth and awareness in her eyes as, time and again, their bodies met, tantalised, then swung apart.

When the music slowed, he couldn't wait another heartbeat to draw her closer, but when he did, the slow, sensual swaying of her slim hips beneath his hands and the sweet pressure of her breasts drove him to the limits of his control. He'd never been so highly sensitised, so exquisitely on edge, so jealous of the barriers of thin, teasing silk.

Dancing with Stella, gazing into her eyes, holding her in his arms, inhaling her…wasn't enough.

And the high colour in her cheeks, the wild smoky haze in her eyes and the catch in her breathing told him that she shared the same amazing need that was flaring in him.

He bent his lips to her ear. 'Let's get out of here.'

She nodded quickly and they fled from the brightly lit party rooms into the garden.

Moonlight sheened Stella's hair and silvered her pale skin as he tasted her at last. Her mouth was honey-sweet, yielding and passionate and he kissed her hard, taking everything with no more permission than the promise in her smile.

It was as if Stella was the first woman, the only woman he'd ever kissed, as if her mouth had been fashioned for his mouth and his alone, her breasts for his hands, her sweet femininity for his unforgiving hardness.

God knew what might have happened if the bright laughter of other party guests hadn't sounded close by. Entangled in each other's arms, they stood as quietly as their ragged breathing would allow, while laughing couples wandered past with a clinking of bottles.

When they were alone again, Callum drew her towards him once more, but he knew even before she stiffened and stepped away, that the magic had gone. For her the spell was broken.

'I shouldn't be here,' she moaned. 'We must go inside.'

'Stay,' he ordered, his voice thick and brusque with desire still rampant in his veins.

'I'm not a cattle dog, Callum,' she muttered before turning and walking quickly ahead of him back into the house.

Once inside, she asked for a drink. When he returned with wine, she drank half of it quickly, then placed the glass on a nearby table.

Her hands slid nervously down her thighs. 'Look, what happened out there—I apologise if it looks as if I've been leading you on, but—ah—' She pressed shaking fingers to her chest and shook her head. 'I shouldn't have let you kiss me.' She looked distressed.

He had to clear the tightness in his throat before he could answer. 'I'm not going to apologise for doing something I was sure we both wanted.'

'I'm not blaming you. I know I gave you all the signals. It's— it's just that I shouldn't have—'

His head was still reeling and he grabbed her hand roughly. Too roughly. Leaning close he muttered, 'You're fooling yourself, Stella. You were burning hot.'

'No. No, you don't understand.' She snatched her hand away and looked genuinely frightened. 'I'm sorry, Callum, but I should never have gone outside with you. I'm feeling so guilty.' She dragged in a heavy breath and her grey eyes were dark with confusion. 'You see, I—I already have a boyfriend.'

Just then Scott called to them from across the room. He beamed a cheery grin and waved. The giggling blonde at his side waved as well.

Stella's twisted, sad little smile as she waved back struck Callum like a savage blow. 'Not Scott?' he cried in disbelief. 'You're not trying to tell me my little brother is your boyfriend?'

Her chin lifted and she stared directly at him. For long, painful seconds she looked puzzled and helpless, but then she answered quite definitely, 'Yes, he is.'

He wanted to tell her she was making a huge mistake. There were a thousand reasons why she shouldn't be Scott's girl. Couldn't she see beyond his boyish charm? Didn't she know about his reputation with the ladies? And didn't she understand that she was destined to be with him, Callum?

'I'm very fond of Scott,' she said.

I'm very fond of Scott. Those words had pulled him up sharply as if he'd been snared by a ringer's lasso.

So in the end, the sum total of his relationship with Stella Lassiter had been a few measly hours and a frantic fumble. The brevity of the encounter made a mockery of the strong feelings that still lingered.

He knew he should have been grateful that she had been honest. She'd wanted Scott. Stubborn pride had stopped him from trying to change her mind, from trying to tell her how deeply and sincerely *he* would love her.

He'd left the city and he hadn't gone back.

With a squaring of his shoulders, he watched the flight of a black falcon, wheeling and cruising high above him. Enough of useless rehashing. What he was supposed to be thinking about, what he'd come out here to give deep thought to, was the fatherless baby. Scott's child.

He dug his heels into his horse's flanks and together they took off again at a steady gallop. He owed it to Scott to make sure this child didn't suffer by coming into the world without a father. Oh, yeah. Callum blinked at the sudden stinging in his eyes. He owed Scott big time.

At the far end of the paddock, there was a shallow dam and he led Blackjack there for a drink. Dismounting, he looped the reins over a post and, while the horse took water, he swallowed deep drafts from his water bottle and trickled some of the cool liquid over his hot and dusty face and neck. He rubbed roughly at his eyes.

His father had always joked that boys born in the outback had their tear ducts extracted at birth. They didn't wallow in sentimentality.

But hell! How could he hold back the flood of emotions that came when he remembered his part in Scott's accident? How could he hold back the *guilt?* If only he'd stopped Scott from flying that day. It had been a damn spider bite. One tiny arachnid had caused so much grief.

The morning of the accident, Callum had rolled out of his swag to find a painful welt on his wrist and a redback spider hiding in the depths of his sleeping bag. Although he'd tried to make light of it, he'd felt a little woozy and affected by the poison.

'You're not flying today,' Scott said when he saw Callum's condition. 'You have a spell on the ground with the horses.'

'I'll be fine,' Callum protested. He was a much more experienced pilot than Scott.

'No, mate. Don't try to tough this one out. We don't want you getting dizzy and dropping the chopper. It's a long way to fall.'

If only he'd argued harder! He should have called off the muster for that day. They'd both known that Scott hadn't been experienced enough for the risky flying required in a cattle muster.
But his little brother had always loved adventure, and since birth
he'd always found a way to get what he'd wanted. That day, he'd
wanted to fly.

Callum had been left with an unbearable burden of guilt.

His parents had never openly asked why he'd let Scott fly the
chopper, but he'd seen the silent questions in their eyes. They
knew that he could have prevented Scott's death and that knowledge ate at him day and night. He'd learned that the one person a
man couldn't forgive was himself.

With a heart-rending sigh, he mounted Blackjack again. He'd
made the wrong decision that day. Today it was time to make another decision and he knew now with certainty what it must be. If
he did nothing else worthwhile in this life, he had to do this. He
had to protect Scott's baby.

And if Stella Lassiter wouldn't agree to his plan, he would have
to find a way to make her.

CHAPTER FOUR

STELLA WANDERED ABOUT the homestead, unable to concentrate on reading even the lightest book. She kept thinking about Callum's reaction to her confession.

He probably thought she was incredibly selfish, wanting to chase off to London and ditch her responsibilities as a mother. If he hadn't rushed off in such a hurry, she would have explained that she'd already accepted the fact that London was out of the question now.

She drifted with uneasy curiosity from room to room in the Birralee homestead, trying out chairs, looking at family photos, listening to CDs, flicking through magazines...

She even forced herself to think about the letter she must write to the television network. *With deep regret... I am writing to inform...no longer in a position to accept your offer...*

She talked to Oscar and to Mac, but her budgerigar had never been trained to talk and the dog's conversational skills were even more restricted.

In the late afternoon, when she finally heard horse's hooves cantering up the track from the creek, she dashed to a window to look.

Astride a beautiful black stallion, Callum came flying up the slope towards the homestead. Behind him the sun blazed. Stella's breath caught. The man and beast seemed to be riding straight out of the sun like the gods of ancient legends. The sight stirred her. Disturbed her.

Later, when Callum had attended to the horse, he came into the house and she was relieved to see that he looked less like a god and distinctly more human—dusty, sweat-streaked and tired.

'You look like you've put in a hard day's work.'

'A hard day's thinking,' he corrected. Then his eyes narrowed and his intense gaze held hers. 'I'll take a shower and then I'll tell you about it.'

Her mouth dropped open. What on earth did this mean? 'Can't you give me a hint?' she asked his retreating back.

In the hall doorway he paused and looked back over his shoulder. 'I have a proposition to put to you.'

Then he was gone.

She paced the lounge, tense as a guilty schoolgirl summoned to the principal's office. A *proposition*? How could the man disappear for a day, return to drop a bomb like that, and then stroll calmly out of the room to take a shower as if he'd merely mentioned the sky was clouding over?

A proposition? What on earth did he mean? A dozen crazy thoughts chased through her head, but every time she tried to pin one down her mind screwed up with panic.

Pacing the carpet made her feel worse, so she threw herself back into the armchair where she'd spent much of the afternoon with a bowl of dry crackers and a can of lemonade beside her.

Hoping to look much calmer than she felt, she lounged casually in the huge, well cushioned chair with her legs curled beneath her while she flicked through the pages of an out-of-date women's magazine.

At last Callum's footsteps sounded in the hall and she fought the urge to uncurl her legs and to sit straight.

Stay cool. Don't let him think you're worried. After all, a proposition is just a grand word for a suggestion—for advice. You can deal with that. People have been handing out well-meant advice all your life.

When he entered the room, she kept her eyes on the magazine in her lap, flicked another page very slowly and then, just as slowly, allowed her gaze to slide his way.

Big mistake!

Freshly showered, with dark curls still damp, he stood in the middle of the antique oriental carpet and stared down at her. Suddenly her decision to slouch in a chair seemed like a very bad move.

From this position she was forced to look up...and up...to his great height and ridiculously wide shoulders...to his uncompromising jaw and no-nonsense mouth, his excessively brooding brows.

The golden lights in his brown eyes provided the only trace of warmth in his whole face. From this angle, everything else looked huge and grim.

And disturbingly handsome. His lean body, tiger eyes and born-to-be-wild hair carried a mix of danger and beauty that threatened her and yet thrilled her, too.

'Feeling better after the shower?' she asked, determined not to let her confusion show.

'I certainly feel cleaner.' He took a seat in the opposite chair and lounged back.

Stella watched the way he took his time settling his long rangy body into the chair. *He's trying as hard as I am to look calm and together.* The realisation helped to steady her. She picked up a cracker from the bowl beside her and munched it. 'Want one?'

He shook his head. 'We need to talk about your predicament.'

'My predicament?' she repeated slowly. 'I presume you mean my pregnancy?'

'Of course.'

Stay cool! With her legs still curled beneath her, she said, 'I told you not to worry about it, Callum. Good heavens, women have been dealing with this *predicament* since time began.'

'And too many times, they've ended up with the raw end of the deal.'

Bull's eye. That was a hitch she couldn't deny.

Her lips puffed as she let out a long, slow breath. OK, maybe Callum Roper was making a genuine effort to see things from her point of view, but that didn't mean his proposal would be user-friendly.

Reaching sideways, she lifted the bowl from the little table and rested it on her lap, taking her time to select another cracker. 'So what's your grand plan, Callum?'

'It's not so grand. Quite simple really... I'm proposing marriage.'

Her legs shot from under her. Crackers flew over the carpet and she completely forgot to stay cool. *Marriage?* Gripping the arms of her chair, she gaped at him. 'What on earth are you talking about?'

Ignoring the scattered crackers, he said solemnly, 'I see marriage as the best solution to your problem.'

Totally shocked, she struggled for breath. She needed several attempts at breathing before she could speak. 'Are you telling me you want to marry me off to someone?'

He gave the faintest of nods.

'How dare you?' She jumped to her feet. This wasn't something she could take sitting down. 'What right do you have to wreck my life?'

With a face as empty as a blank page, he said calmly, 'Let me finish and I'll explain everything.'

Hands on hips, she glared at him, her breath still shallow and uneven. 'OK,' she said at last. 'Who's the poor sucker you think I should trap into marriage?'

There was a beat of time before he said very simply, 'I am.'

Fresh shock waves sent her sinking back into the chair. Marry *him?* Impossible! A rush of heat engulfed her, bringing with it unwanted memories of that night a year ago when the flames of her desire had been so strong, so animal-like, they'd totally alarmed her.

Her breath came in desperate gasps. 'You're—you're crazy, aren't you?'

'Probably.'

'My God, Callum.' She gave a shaky little laugh. 'Don't joke like that. For half a minute I thought you were serious.'

He didn't move or speak. It was so maddening. He simply lounged lazily in his chair with one riding boot propped casually on the opposite knee. When it came to staying cool, he was winning hands down.

'I am being serious,' he said with an annoying lack of emotion. 'This is a perfectly sensible solution.'

'Sensible? What's sensible about it?' Jumping to her feet again, she flung her hands skywards to emphasise her distress. 'Callum, hello! This is the twenty-first century. Perhaps outback men haven't caught up, but most guys these days understand that women don't appreciate being forced to become a man's possession. That kind of thinking died out in—in the Dark Ages.'

How could he sit there looking so composed? So smug? He had to be crazy.

'No doubt you still think the earth is flat,' she cried.

She couldn't, wouldn't, hang around to listen to this nonsense! Before he could answer, she dashed out of the room and charged down the hallway, not sure where she was running, but needing space to think. To scream?

But the hall led to the front veranda and beyond that there was nothing but endless bush, red-soil plains and kangaroo grass. The outback! With a groan, she sagged against the veranda railing and stared at the darkening bush.

That was all there was out here. Bush, bush and more bush. She'd never realised till now what a luxury it was to have a little coffee shop around the corner from her Sydney flat. Just where did an outback girl go if she needed to have a quiet nervous breakdown?

There was a step behind her and she spun around to find Callum standing in the doorway.

'Are you OK?' he asked softly.

She almost spat another angry retort, but the expression in his eyes stopped her. The blank look was gone and instead she caught a glimpse of vulnerability. She released her own bewilderment in a sigh. 'I guess I'm OK. I can't think. I feel as if you've slugged my brain with a stun gun.'

Slowly he walked across the veranda and leaned against the railing. Too close for comfort. 'I apologise,' he said quietly. 'I guess I made a hash of that.'

His humility surprised her and it was hard to stay mad at him. 'I just don't understand where you're coming from.'

'I—I know marriage isn't the sort of thing you want to think about when you're still in love with my brother.'

She looked away, wondering what he would think if he knew that she'd slipped out of love with Scott with surprising ease once she'd finally accepted how little she'd really meant to him.

Callum cleared his throat. 'I'm not presuming that you'd be my wife in the usual sense. I'm not—I'm not trying to replace Scott. The kind of marriage I'm thinking of would be more of—of a business arrangement than a real marriage.'

Her startled gaze swung back to collide with his. 'What kind of business arrangement?' she whispered.

'Something purely practical so that you could stay here until after the baby's born and then go off to London just as you'd hoped.'

Still go to London? *Clump! Clump!* That was her heart taking off like an overexcited child.

A muscle in his jaw worked. 'Have you given serious thought to what it would be like to leave your baby behind?'

She pressed her fingers against her throbbing temples. Oh, Lord! Her feelings about motherhood were so confused. At times she thought how wonderful it would be to have a little baby of her own, but there were just as many times when she was quite sure that she would be as hopeless at mothering as Marlene had been.

'I have to think about what's best for the baby in the long term. This job could be pivotal to my career. It's something I've been working towards for so long and it will mean earning good money so that I can provide for the baby in the future.'

His expression was thoughtful, so pensive, almost sad, that she felt tears gather in her eyes. She looked away again as she asked in a choked voice, 'What would you plan to do with the baby— when I went away?'

'It would stay here with me. I'd have to get someone in to help of course, but that shouldn't be too hard. I'd make sure it was well looked after.'

'I see. But… Why would *you* want to do that, Callum? And why would you want to go to all the trouble of marrying me?'

An unreadable expression flickered in his eyes. Crossing his arms over his chest, he took his time answering, as if he wanted to get the words right in his head before he spoke. 'Marriage would make the baby legitimate. Part of the Roper clan. I'm afraid that's important to me.'

She nodded. Of course. The family name. 'I can imagine that

the son of Senator Ian Roper wouldn't want the embarrassment of an illegitimacy in the family.'

'I want this for Scott's sake. It would mean a part of him could go on living here.'

Then he blinked and turned away sharply, looking out into the darkening bush, and Stella felt that he was seeing things out there in the wide stretch of trees and earth and sky that she could never hope to see, feeling things she would never feel.

'And then when I come back—?'

He looked at her again. 'After London?'

'Yes.'

'You would be free to go.' His Adam's apple jerked in his throat. 'You can get on with your life.'

Free to go. Why did those words make her feel as if a door had been slammed in her face? 'What about the baby?'

'It would stay with me.'

'You mean you want to keep it here? To have it grow up here?'

For long, shattering seconds she waited for his answer.

'Yes,' he said at last. 'That would be part of the bargain.'

A cold, cruel emptiness swept through her. Oh, heavens. She clasped a trembling hand over her stomach. Could she bear to leave her baby behind *for ever?*

'You could see the child whenever you wanted to, of course, but this would be its home. Scott's child should have a chance to grow up in the outback. It's a good life. It builds healthy, independent youngsters.'

'I see.' She clutched at a veranda post for support as her legs turned to water.

She couldn't do it. There was no way she could leave her baby to grow up without her.

Don't be selfish, Stella. Think about what's best for the child. What have you got to offer as a single parent? And you don't have a clue how to be a good mother.

If she agreed to Callum's plan, her baby would grow up as part of the extended Roper family, with grandparents, uncles, aunts and cousins, belonging here on Birralee, loving the bush, just as its father had.

She struggled to keep her mind on practical details. 'So we'd say all the wedding vows about to have and to hold till death us do part, and then what? Would we get a divorce?'

Callum settled back against the railing, and stared at the scuffed toe of his riding boot as he answered. 'That's right. I know it sounds calculated, but I think our motives are justified.'

'You'd be doing it for Scott—for Scott's baby and I'd be doing it for—' Stella gulped. *To give my baby its only chance of a family—a proper family—and to save myself from making a hash of motherhood.* She couldn't admit to that. '—I'd be doing it for my career.'

He nodded grimly.

Surely things couldn't be that simple? There had to be a catch. 'I thought marriage was a rather messy business to undo.'

'I understand it isn't messy if there's never been any—' he swallowed '—any intimacy.'

'Oh?' She looked away and hoped he couldn't see how suddenly hot her cheeks were. 'But you plan for us to live together, as man and wife, until the baby is born?'

'More or less.' He cleared his throat. 'We can keep separate rooms.'

'Yeah, sure.'

He reached over and touched her cheek, just the lightest touch of his leathery finger against her skin, but she jumped. A tremor of pain twisted his mouth momentarily, but he kept his hand at her cheek as he said in a low raspy voice, 'You'd be quite safe, Stella. I won't make the same mistake I made in Sydney.'

'Of course,' she whispered breathlessly.

Then he withdrew his hand. 'My interest in you these days is simply as the mother of my brother's child.'

The remark made her ridiculously angry. 'You see me as an incubator?'

'Aren't you?'

The chauvinist pig! 'I refuse to answer that,' she huffed. 'But you can rest assured, Callum, if I do agree to this, I will *never* contemplate even trying to tempt you.'

'That's good,' he said rather loudly, accompanying his words with a slap of his hand on the timber railing.

'Yes, it's dandy,' she cried.

After another uncomfortable pause, he added, 'Look, this is rather a lot to get your head around. I've had all day to think about it. How about I rustle up some dinner and let you have a bit of space to think to yourself. We don't need to make a decision right now.'

'Sure.' She sniffed and, swinging away from him, she marched to the far end of the veranda where she stood glaring out into the dark lonely bush.

He began to walk back inside.

'Just a minute,' she called after him.

He was right. It *was* too much to get her head around and she didn't want to be left alone on the veranda with so many scary thoughts! 'I've still got too many questions.' Her hands flapped helplessly, echoing her confusion. 'I think I'm going to have to come and pester you. Talk it through.'

He shrugged. 'Whatever you like.'

As she accompanied him back to the kitchen, she clung to one thought: *What I must remember is that my baby would have a family. Not just for a year...but for ever.*

And in the kitchen, her eyes lingered on the mismatched chairs gathered around the big table and the high chair in the corner. Tonight they seemed more charming than ever. She pictured her little baby belonging in this room, a part of the big noisy Roper family, with aunts and uncles and six boisterous cousins.

How many lonely days had she spent as a child wistfully dreaming of a room like this filled with a big rowdy family? She had imagined them all—and in her head they had seemed so real.

Sweet, elderly grandparents who spoiled her; a pretty aunt who bought her brand new books for birthdays and perfume for Christmas; an annoying boy cousin who teased her; a cheery uncle who took time to listen to her dreams-and a father.

Oh, how good and kind her imaginary father had been!

Heavens! How could she bear to give her baby up? But how could she deny it a real chance to have all that?

Callum was rattling around in the pots and pans cupboard. 'Do you like spaghetti?' he called over his shoulder.

'Sure.'

'Good.' He pulled out a huge pot, filled it with water and set it on the stove.

'What can I do to help?'

'You can grate some parmesan cheese. I'm afraid all I'm going to do is heat up a bottle of sauce.'

She managed a smile. 'Now you're talking my kind of cooking.'

He disappeared into the pantry and came back with a packet of spaghetti and a large bottle of Italian-style tomato and garlic sauce.

Grateful for the distraction, Stella hunted down the cheese in the door of the refrigerator, found the grater and a small bowl in a cupboard next to the stove and sat down at the table.

'You know,' she said as she peeled plastic away from the triangle of cheese, 'if we went ahead with this scheme of yours, you'd be getting a pretty poor bargain. I can't cook and I don't know a thing about living in the outback.'

Suddenly the truth of her words hit home. She imagined meeting his family and felt a slam of panic. 'We couldn't do it,' she said quickly. 'It wouldn't work.'

'Why not?'

'Goodness, Callum. There are so many reasons. But number one is I don't fit in here. Look at me.'

'I'm looking. I see one head, two arms, two legs.' His mouth quirked unexpectedly. 'Unusual toenails.'

Suddenly self-conscious, she tucked her feet under the chair. To fill in time during the day, she'd repainted her toenails dark red and had stuck on tiny silver nail ornaments. 'That's what I mean. My toenails are an excellent example of what's wrong about me. My style is completely wrong. I'm a gypsy. I bet the women in your family have little pearl studs in their ears and wear classic country linen shirts with stretch moleskin jeans and are mad about horses...'

'Well...yes.'

'The only horse I've ever ridden was on a merry-go-round. And your mother and sisters are probably brilliant at cooking and sewing. You have a sister who makes jam for heaven's sake. I've never known anyone who didn't just buy it in a jar from the supermarket.'

As if to make up for her lack of skills, she thrust the cheese against the grater with fierce concentration.

'My father's a bit rigid in his ways, but the rest of my family are very easy going really,' Callum said. 'Besides, you won't have to see them very often.'

Not very often would still be too many times, she was sure. But as another dark thought hit, she groaned and the metal grater thumped loudly on the table top.

'What's the problem now?'

'There's an even bigger reason why your people would hate me.'

He stared at her. 'I would never have guessed you were so insecure.'

'Yeah, well, we won't go into that.' Now wasn't the time to confess she was a walking encyclopaedia of insecurities. She began to grate furiously again.

'Hey, we only need a little cheese to sprinkle on top,' he reminded her.

She stopped grating and stared in bewilderment at the ridiculous mountain of shaved parmesan. 'Callum, if we went ahead with this plan, your folks are going to think of me as the trollop who seduced your brother and then found a way to hoodwink you into marriage.'

Slowly, he turned away from the stove and stepped across to the table. His serious gaze held hers as his big hands gripped the back of a chair. 'For the time being,' he said, 'as far as my family are concerned, the baby is mine.'

Stella gasped. His words echoed and tumbled in her head. *The baby is mine.* For a shocking moment, she saw an image of herself and Callum—making love. Her chest seemed to squeeze all the breath from her lungs and an embarrassing coil of heat tightened her insides. *For Pete's sake, get a grip, girl. That's not going to happen.*

As soon as she could speak, she said, 'So you wouldn't tell your family about Scott and me?'

He shook his head. 'I don't think they're ready to deal with that kind of news.'

'You'd be prepared to let them think you and I had some kind of whirlwind romance-cum-shotgun-wedding?'

'Yes. That way we can protect both Scott's reputation and yours.'

'But don't you care what they think of you?'

He looked at the floor for a long, painful moment, was still looking at it as he answered her. 'This way is best. It won't hurt them as much.'

Stella stared at this big, dark, older brother of Scott's and wondered how she'd ever thought he lacked finer feelings. Here he was, calmly offering to sacrifice his reputation and his freedom and not one word of complaint.

'But you'll have to put up with me hanging around your house growing fat. I might drive you nuts.'

'Yeah, you might. I'll just have to cope, won't I?' He moved back to the stove and added sprinkles of dried basil and oregano to the deep red tomato sauce. Then his toffee-brown eyes found hers and he smiled. 'The daily change in toenail colour should keep me entertained.'

Stella knew she blushed. Arguing against his plan was getting harder all the time. She was beginning to feel as if she was in one of those crazy dreams where she'd try to run, but her legs would be made of air; she'd start her car, but the accelerator wouldn't depress; every time she'd try to stand up, she'd fall over.

With his back to her, he dropped long strands of yellow spaghetti into the boiling water. 'We have weather and global warming issues out here, too, you know,' he said without looking her way. 'I'd be the only cattleman in the district with a live-in weather forecaster. You could help me plan the best times to muster, when to bring in feed.'

She had to admit that she always jumped at a chance to apply her scientific knowledge to practical situations.

He must have sensed her interest because, without waiting for her to reply, he went on, 'Every way you look at it, my plan is the best solution.'

Then he turned to her, and the warmth fell out of his face and his mouth tightened with tension as he asked, 'So what do you say, Stella? Taking everything into consideration, will you marry me?'

CHAPTER FIVE

WILL YOU MARRY ME?

Callum stood stone still, his heart knocking against his ribs. Stella was looking as if she might weep. He couldn't blame her. How rotten could it be to be asked to marry a man under these circumstances?

She'd loved Scott. She was carrying his child. And now, she'd not only lost Scott, but was being asked to give up the child as well.

Was he asking too much?

Was it selfish of him to want to keep his family intact to protect the Roper name? And just how honest was he being with himself? All that high-sounding stuff he'd sprouted. *You'd be quite safe, Stella. I won't make the same mistake I made in Sydney.*

Could he be sure about that? Did he really expect to spend the next few months with this bewitching creature without giving in to all the hot and lusty urges that ravaged him? Was he man enough for the task he'd set himself?

Stella blinked.

Surely she wasn't going to disgrace herself by crying now?

She never cried, so she mustn't start now. She mustn't make this any harder for Callum. How much fun could it be to ask a woman he didn't love—hardly *knew*—to be his wife? She mustn't overload this scene with unnecessary emotion.

BARBARA HANNAY

She wasn't sure why she felt so choked up. It wasn't as if she'd spent half her girlhood mooning over dreams about her first proposal. Of course, if she had given it any thought, she might have imagined a rugged, dark and good-looking man like Callum in the picture.

That was beside the point!

The point was the job in London. And providing a family—a *real* family—for her baby.

But marrying Callum Roper? Living out here in the outback alone with him? It was such a scary thought. Scary because she didn't understand her see-sawing feelings for him. The pull of attraction…so thrilling and yet…so threatening.

His face had grown very dark as he waited for her answer. The intensity in his eyes forced her to look away.

'I think your offer of marriage is very generous,' she said quickly. 'But I can't accept.'

He sighed heavily.' You don't have to tell me why. I can guess. I know I'm not Scott.'

'No.'

'I'll never be like Scott.'

She was shocked by the heaviness in his voice. 'I don't expect you to be like him.'

He grunted something she couldn't make out.

Jumping to her feet, she began to circle the table. 'This marriage scheme can't be my only option!'

'Can you think of another solution?'

'I'm working on it.'

'Where else could you stay that's out of the way, where you can keep your pregnancy under wraps?'

'I—I'm sure I'd find another job for the next few months— something—somewhere.'

'And then when you leave, who would look after your baby? Scott's baby?'

She stopped pacing. 'I'd find someone.'

'You have family?'

'No.'

'None at all?'

'I'm afraid not. But—' Shaking her head, she stared at him helplessly. Oh, Lord. Once again she'd run full circle and was back at the same painful place. 'Your plan really is the best, isn't it?'

'No doubt about it.' His mouth thinned and he looked embarrassed. 'Look, I said it before, but I swear it. I won't make any— ah—marital demands.'

'Yes. Yes, I realise that.' Why did he have to make such a federal case of explaining that he'd lost interest in seducing her?

'And maybe in the future, after you've finished in England, we could come to some kind of fair deal about sharing access to the baby.'

'That—that would be good.'

'So?'

So she'd run out of objections.

When Callum's sisters had been married, their weddings had been at Birralee, with guests flying in from all over the country and caterers travelling the long journey from Mount Isa.

For Callum and Stella, things were different. As soon as Callum had moved the cattle to the road trains, they drove into Cloncurry to be married by an obliging, elderly minister who didn't ask too many questions.

Callum took the Range Rover, which at least provided air-conditioned comfort, but for much of the way, they rattled and bumped over a rough, red dirt track.

Beyond Kajabbi, they turned onto the main road, a thin strip of blue bitumen bordered by more red dirt which was, in turn, edged by grass the colour of pale champagne. Beyond the grass, wattle dotted the wide, terracotta plains in soft green and gold clumps, and above the whole brightly coloured land arched an enormous, very blue and cloudless sky.

Beside him, Stella sat without talking. She was dressed in a long white shirt over white wide-leg trousers. Every so often he glanced her way, but she seemed to be in a pensive mood and he could think of nothing really appropriate to say.

She didn't look as if she was in the mood for jokes, or small talk, or any kind of talk, for that matter.

She looked...lovely. Her clothes couldn't be simpler, but she'd
done something fancy with her hair. Bits of it were gathered on
top of her head and other bits hung in black silken strands around
her face. It should have looked messy, but Callum thought it made
her look especially glamorous.

He had donned a charcoal-grey suit, a brand new white shirt
and a silver and charcoal striped tie. The mirror told him he'd pass
muster as a bridegroom, but he preferred clothes with a lived-in
look and feel.

Today he felt citified, spruced up and starchy.

And nervous.

Stella's silence made him nervous.

He knew that one reason she avoided talking was because she
was still suffering from morning sickness and he drove as carefully as he could to avoid jolting her more than was necessary. But
he was the first to admit he knew very little about what women
wanted, and he worried that today she was having regrets about
her wedding—about how this day should have been.

No doubt she'd hoped for the whole traditional, romantic bit,
the full rhapsody. A proposal of undying love from a man on his
knees...a wedding gown and veil...church bells and a choir...
family and friends...

One thing was damn sure.

She would have preferred to be marrying his brother, the man
she'd loved. The father of her child.

But there was absolutely nothing he could do about that.

He didn't let his mind linger too long on his own reasons for proposing this marriage. That was a dead-end track. It always started
with telling himself that he genuinely liked the idea of having a
child to raise. He would have had one or two of his own by now
if he'd found the right woman.

But when his thinking reached that point, his mind stuck like
a needle in a broken record. The right woman. The right woman.
After that he couldn't get past the idea of Stella in his arms and
her sweet, passionate mouth surrendering to him...

When they reached Cloncurry, he didn't drive straight to the church. He pulled up outside a store managed by a hairdresser, who also doubled as the outback town's florist.

'Why are we stopping here?'

'I won't be a tick,' he reassured her.

Sandy, the shop's owner, grinned when she saw him. 'Wacky-do, Callum. Don't you scrub up a treat!'

A young girl, who was washing a customer's hair at a basin, stared his way and let out a low whistle. 'You look truly dude-some, man.'

'Were you able to get what I ordered?' he asked Sandy.

'I did my best. What do you think of these? They came in from Mount Isa only half an hour ago.'

She reached behind a partition and with an enormously bright smile, brought forth a pretty arrangement of white roses, carnations and baby's breath tied together with a broad white satin ribbon.

'They're terrific, Sandy,' he said and, as she handed them to him, he caught their heady, sweet fragrance. *This should help to make her feel a little more like a bride.* 'Thanks.'

Outside again, he leapt back into the driver's seat and handed the bouquet to Stella. For some ridiculous reason his hands were shaking and he could swear hers were, too, as she accepted it.

'Thank you,' she whispered. Her eyes glowed and she dipped her face towards the delicate blooms, breathing in their perfume. The movement sent fine strands of her hair falling forward, sweeping over her soft cheek. He'd never seen anything so captivating.

'Wouldn't seem like a wedding without flowers,' he said.

'No.'

He could sense her tension as he drove two streets further on to the little wooden church. Of course, he didn't blame her for feeling so edgy. He was as strung out as fencing wire.

There were no other cars parked outside when they pulled up, but that was what he expected. He and Stella had agreed that the wedding should be as quiet as possible. No family or friends. No fuss. Just get the papers signed and then get back to Birralee.

'But if you don't mind,' Stella had said, 'I'd like to wear white. I know it's supposed to be for virgins and all that, but—' she'd compressed her lips for a second or two, before flashing him a brave smile and saying '—this might be the only time I get married, so I'd like to look vaguely bridal.'

It had been then that Callum had decided to get the flowers and it had been since then that he'd found himself more and more worried about how desperately sad this day might be for her.

The day she should have married Scott.

As he turned off the ignition, he warned her, 'Being a bride means you have to let a fellow open the car door for you.'

'OK.'

He hurried to her side of the vehicle, opened the door and held out a hand to help her. She looked at him. Her face was pale above the white flowers but her grey eyes shone softly. 'Thank you.'

In one graceful movement, she left the car and was standing beside him in her simple loose white shirt and trousers, holding the flowers in both hands, close to her heart. 'Scott was the first man who ever opened a car door for me and you're the first man who's ever bought me flowers.'

Callum shrugged. 'You can't beat old-fashioned country boys.' Only just in time, he stopped himself from telling her that she was the first woman he'd ever bought flowers for. Buying flowers, making a fuss over a woman, wasn't his usual style.

Lifting her face to his, she kissed him suddenly. A quick, soft kiss, that lingered fragrant and warm just to one side of his mouth and sent him reeling into the church as dizzy as a drunken sailor.

The wedding wasn't quite the ordeal Stella had feared. She had planned to endure the ceremony bravely, getting through it by thinking of the excitement of going to London.

But she hadn't been prepared for the quaint appeal of the old wooden church with its sweet-faced, elderly minister, or the enthusiasm of his two middle-aged daughters, dressed in their best pastel frocks, who served enthusiastically as witnesses, wedding guests and choir.

One of the daughters cried, actually *cried*, when her father told Callum and Stella, 'I now pronounce you husband and wife.'

And when it seemed that her father had forgotten an important instruction, the other sister eagerly prompted Callum, 'You can kiss the bride.'

And Callum, apparently unwilling to disappoint them, took both Stella's hands in his and drew her close and then closer until his arms enfolded her.

'Let's keep up appearances,' he whispered against her ear.

She felt her face flame at the very thought of exchanging a kiss with him now, in front of witnesses. But before she could say anything, he had already started! His mouth was against hers, touching her politely, almost shyly, with only the subtlest of pressure.

Relieved to discover how easy he was making this for her, she kissed him back, returning the warm pressure. In contrast to the hard, muscled strength of his body, his lips felt surprisingly gentle and sensitive and...seductive.

But when she expected the kiss to end, his hands continued to hold her close. His warm breath mingled with hers and his lips brushed her mouth again, as if they were reluctant to leave her, and her blood hummed through her veins urging her to stay close to this sweetest of sensations.

And suddenly he was kissing her again and this time there was nothing, absolutely nothing chaste or proper about Callum's kiss. No longer was he simply going through the motions.

His mouth was demanding intimacy. She felt both shock and pleasure at his daring and her mind and body melted as the long lingering kiss drove everything else away.

She stopped thinking about the Reverend Shaw and his daughters, stopped reminding herself that this was a charade, even stopped thinking about the last time he'd kissed her. She focused completely on now and this kiss...

His powerful arms tugged her harder against him and he slipped his tongue boldly into her mouth, and he felt so right inside her, so necessary, that she felt herself dissolving into a helpless puddle of pleasure.

She heard one of the sisters sigh. 'Now, that's what I call a kiss.'

At last, too soon, Callum released her and she avoided touching a hand to her surprised lips or looking his way. It would be too embarrassing if he read in her eyes how incredibly affected she'd been. *Again.*

And she didn't want to see how he was feeling. He would be as aware as she was that this kiss hadn't been strictly in line with their plans.

To her dismay, she felt so overcome that she swayed on her feet.

'Are you all right?' Callum asked.

'Just a little dizzy.'

The Reverend Shaw and the Misses Shaw looked concerned.

Callum placed a steadying arm around her shoulders and she took a deep breath.

'Thanks, Callum,' she murmured. 'I'll be fine.'

'Take it easy,' he whispered, drawing her head onto his shoulder. 'Do you want to sit down?'

She shook her head and shortly afterwards the dizziness passed. They collected their marriage certificate and left, but the memory of that kiss lingered as they had a cup of tea in a Cloncurry café, made a quick round of the supermarket to stock up on stores, then drove back to Birralee.

It was so strange to come back to the homestead as husband and wife. Strange because nothing was different.

Callum disappeared almost as soon as he'd parked the Range Rover. Stella went into the kitchen, stacked the groceries away in the pantry and then changed from her white clothes into her everyday black jeans and dark red shirt.

She put her bridal bouquet into a crystal vase and set it on the antique sideboard in the lounge. It looked elegant and suitably old-fashioned, very at home amidst the mellow tones of rosewood and cedar furniture. But she felt more alien than ever—a complete outsider.

She'd been so keyed up about the wedding and now she felt as flat as the snake they'd seen run over by a road train on the highway. She was tired from her morning's ordeal, but not tired enough to sleep. Just weary enough to be moody. Depressed and lonely. Rattling around in this big empty house in the middle of nowhere with nothing to do but change Oscar's food and water and paint her toenails.

But she'd painted them yesterday—a pretty pearly silver. It had been the closest she could get to something bridal. Why had she bothered? She'd been a bride for five minutes.

And now she was simply a wife.

In name only.

Her hands wandered to her lips. Callum's kiss had been so different from the last time he'd kissed her. So sensitive at first, so sweet. So seductive. *But just as risky!*

Ye gods, all she could think about was wanting more. She was like a weak-willed moth drawn to his powerful flame. But just like the moth, she would be burned if she wasn't very careful. The kind of passion Callum could awake in her was too dangerous.

She needed to stay in complete control of her feelings...and her future.

After dinner, they sat on Birralee's front steps with Mac safely between them. Callum drank coffee and Stella sipped peppermint tea while they watched the full moon rise above the cliffs on the far side of the creek.

It started as a silvery glow lighting the sky above the cliff tops and silhouetting the rocky outcrops, making them jet black against an iridescent grey sky.

As they watched, Callum asked unexpectedly, 'So your middle name is Catalina?'

Stella shrugged. 'It's funny the things you find out when you get married, isn't it, Callum *Angus* Roper?'

He grinned. 'Angus is an old family name. It's been hanging around the Ropers for generations. What about Catalina? It sounds Spanish. Do you know where it comes from?'

'Ah...' Stella's mind raced. She didn't have a clue why her mother had selected her names. It hadn't been something she'd got around to discussing with Marlene. 'My mother found Catalina in a book and took a fancy to it.'

He accepted this invention with a slight nod. 'I suppose it's too early to start thinking about what you might call your baby.'

Startled, she stared at him. This afternoon she'd actually forced herself to look at websites dealing with pregnancy and childbirth and she'd ordered some books over the internet, but she hadn't given a moment's thought to baby names. It was easier to think about going away if she thought of the baby as an 'it', an embryonic entity—not a potential little boy or girl. Someone with a name.

She shook her head. 'I don't think I'll be pushing to call it Angus or Catalina.' And then, because she didn't want him to think she was hopelessly unmotherly, she said quickly, 'I think I'll call it Ruby if it's a girl.'

'Ruby,' he repeated slowly. 'Ruby Roper.'

'Look,' she said, jumping to her feet and needing to distract him from coming up with a string of names that were an improvement on Ruby. 'Here comes the moon.'

She pointed to the eyebrow of bright light glistening whitely above the cliff top. 'Watching the moon rise is very different from a sunrise, isn't it?'

'As different as night and day,' he said dryly.

But Stella ignored his sarcasm. She was determined to make a point—any point that had nothing to do with baby names. 'Even primitive people who didn't know anything about science could see for themselves how distinctly different the moon and the sun are. Look!'

In silence they watched the grandeur of the full moon rising like a dignified queen until its complete silver disc emerged above the cliff and sent shimmering light pooling over the bush.

'The moon is mysterious and magic,' she said, 'but the sun is bold and showy.'

'I guess so.'

'I'm sure that's why ancient people decided that the moon is female and the sun is male.'

'You're probably right,' he said, warming to the change of subject. 'And these days there's a new theory about women coming from Venus and men from Mars.'

Stella rolled her eyes. 'Now, I can't accept *that*. Men like to argue that there's a huge difference between the sexes, because it helps to keep women in their place.'

'So you don't think there are fundamental differences between males and females?'

'Well…no,' she hedged cautiously. This wasn't at all what she wanted to be discussing. 'If I'd listened to that kind of talk, I'd never have had the courage to study a male-dominated subject like physics.'

Suddenly he reached down, picked up her hand and placed it on top of his. In the moonlight, she saw how excessively white and slim her hand looked as it lay against the hugeness and darkness of his. The slim gold band he had placed on her fourth finger glowed. Ever so briefly, he touched the ring with one finger.

Stella's heart did a drum roll. Lord help her! How would she cope with this electric tension every time Callum touched her?

He flipped their hands over, palms up, showing the rough, callused pads of his fingers and the soft city-smoothness of hers.

She heard his low chuckle.

'You're right. There's absolutely no difference between a man and a woman whatsoever.'

Then he suddenly jerked his hand away from hers as if he'd realised just how much of a mistake it was for him to be touching her.

Stella felt instantly abandoned and miserable. She had been trying to forget that this was their wedding night, trying not to think of what would have happened if they'd been any other married couple. 'I'm incredibly tired,' she muttered and forced a loud yawn.

Stooping to pick up the empty mugs, she didn't look at him. 'I think I'll hit the hay.' And, feeling more miserable than ever, she hurried away so quickly she barely heard his 'Goodnight.'

Long after Stella had left, Callum sat on the steps with only Mac for company. At first he concentrated on the sounds of the bush at night. The whispering rush of a breeze as it rippled through the tree tops, the occasional low bellow from cattle down near the creek, the distant karoar, karoar, karoar of a lonely curlew.

Stella's deep, smoky, sexy voice.

He couldn't get enough of that voice.

Damn it! He was doing it again. Unless he kept his mind strictly under control he found himself thinking about her—thinking in ways that would lead him to trouble.

Sitting with his elbows propped on his knees, he gripped his head in his hands. This had to stop!

He was intensely aroused by everything about Stella: her sultry voice, her silky hair, the way she moved like a proud princess, the fact that she tasted of heaven when he kissed her.

'I was a prize idiot to kiss her like that,' he muttered to the dog at his side.

How had he ever thought he could have this woman living under his roof for months on end without falling under her spell?

The only, only thing that would keep him from breaking his own crazy rules would be remembering that she'd been Scott's woman. She was carrying Scott's child. And she would be leaving as soon as it was born.

CHAPTER SIX

Mornings on Birralee began with a screech of galahs. The pink and grey parrots, which looked ten times prettier than they sounded, took off from the trees along the creek at the crack of dawn. Shortly after that, Stella heard Callum moving about the house.

When she came into the kitchen, he was already tucking into bacon and eggs.

'How's the morning sickness?' he asked as she helped herself to a bowl of muesli and took a seat at the table.

'Seems to be calming down at last.' After a mouthful of food she added, 'I want to find ways of making myself useful around the place.'

His eyes widened over the rim of his big mug of tea. 'That spread-sheeting software you installed on my computer last week is exceptionally useful.'

'I like doing that sort of thing, but if I'm going to be here till the baby arrives, I should face up to some of the things I don't like.'

'You want to help me spey some cows?'

'Good grief, no.' She pulled a grimace of mock horror. 'I don't know if I could ever do that to a cow. Well, not unless she had counselling first.'

Callum laughed.

She grinned back at him. 'Perhaps I should develop a whole new career path for myself as a family planning consultant for cows.'

His smile faded. 'You're missing your work, aren't you?'

'I guess so,' she said as she reached for the milk jug. 'But I think what's bugging me most is that I don't feel I can contribute to anything here. At least I should be doing something about my deficiencies in the kitchen.'

'You're pretty good at washing-up.'

She shot him a give-it-a-miss scowl. 'You know I'm talking about cooking.'

Pushing his empty plate aside, he selected an orange from the fruit bowl and peeled its skin away from the flesh with long deft fingers. With a slow smile, he said, 'But, for a bright girl like you, cooking should be a breeze.'

'Well, it's not.'

His lazy smile lingered. 'I thought all women knew how to cook.'

'Shows you don't know much about women.'

'About city women,' he corrected.

'You know nothing about *this* city woman.' She sniffed and the friendly morning atmosphere was suddenly tense and strained. Closing her eyes, Stella took a deep breath. 'Sorry. It's a sore point. I'm afraid I know as much about cooking as I do about brain surgery or—or black magic.'

He chewed an orange segment thoughtfully. 'Perhaps you could look at cooking as a scientific experiment.'

'Oh, yeah?'

'Sure. Think about it. Cooking is simply a process whereby certain chemicals are combined. There are reactions and if you apply heat there are new reactions. If you vary the chemicals or vary the heat you get different results.'

She stared at him. 'For half a minute you almost convinced me.'

'But it's true!'

'Nice try, Callum, but I happen to know that cooking is a mysterious secret handed down from mothers to their daughters.' She pointed her spoon at him. 'Or occasionally their sons.'

He continued to eat his orange without offering a response.

'All my friends seem to have special secret family recipes. My flatmate, Lucy, could be tortured before she'd hand over her mother's recipe for cherry-ripe slice.'

'Doesn't your family have any cooking secrets?' he asked.

'No,' she answered sharply.

He looked at her for a long moment, as if waiting for her to say more, but she still wasn't ready to confess about her non-existent family. After a minute or two, he rose from the table and crossed to the old pine dresser that stood against the far wall.

Intrigued, Stella watched as he opened one of its drawers, extracted an old exercise book and brought it back to her.

'This is my grandmother's recipe book,' he said. 'It's rather old-fashioned, but she kept all her favourite recipes in here. And my mother's added to it as well. Why don't you take a look?'

'No one will mind?'

'Of course not.'

She stared at the tattered old book. In copperplate handwriting on the front cover was the name Eileen Roper and then, underneath it, Margaret Roper.

Eileen Roper... Margaret Roper...the wives of Roper men...

Stella Roper... Her spine tingled. OK, the other women were proper wives, but maybe, for just a little while, she could pretend she was really a part of this family...a link in the long chain of Roper women who had cooked in this lovely old kitchen.

Feeling like an intruder, she opened the bulging book. The very first recipe was for a rich fruit cake with a note in Eileen's handwriting saying, 'Keeps well and is excellent for the boys to take on a muster'.

Wow! Stella knew her friends would laugh if they could see how excited she was, but for her the idea of making a traditional home-made fruit cake seemed magical. The kind of thing *other* people did! She turned more yellowing pages. There were all kinds of recipes... 'Eileen's chicken and barley soup, good for patients with 'flu... Margaret's caramel rum pie, Angus's favourite... Ellie's beef strog...'

They weren't entered in any particular order and sometimes

there was different handwriting as if friends had also written their recipes into the book.

Stella was fascinated. 'Thanks, Callum. I wonder if I should try some of these?'

'Sure. Feel free.'

She flipped back to the first recipe at the front of his grand-mother's book. The fruit cake. What a buzz she'd get from making something like that. Perhaps Callum was right. Maybe it was purely a matter of science. If she followed Eileen's instructions to the letter, this scary collection of ingredients could emerge as a real cake.

She forced herself to think positively, imagining herself handing around slices of rich, fruity cake to members of Callum's family.

This is delicious, Stella. Did you make it yourself?

It tastes just like Mother's old recipe.

How could anyone be frightened of a fruit cake? All she had to do was throw fruit, butter, eggs and flour together. She ran her eye down the list of other ingredients Eileen had penned—lemon rind, golden syrup, marmalade, mixed spice, cinnamon and rum.

Already she could imagine this kitchen filling with the enticing smells of citrus and spice. 'I'm going to do this!'

'Do what?'

'Make a fruit cake.'

His eyebrows rose. 'I guess it doesn't hurt to aim high.'

She felt a stab of disappointment. 'You think I should start with something simpler?'

After only a moment's hesitation, he said, 'No. Not at all. You cook whatever takes your fancy.' He pointed to the set of keys hanging on the hook near the door. 'You'll need that big black key. It's the key to the storeroom. You should find everything you want there.'

'I'll have a beautiful big bowl of chopped raisins, cherries and dates soaking in rum for you to admire when you come home tonight, Callum. Prepare to be impressed.'

She smiled up at him, but wished she hadn't. There was a strangely ambiguous expression in his eyes, as if he didn't know whether to smile back or to scowl, and the very uncertainty in his look sent icy shivers skittering down her arms.

'I'll look forward to this evening,' he said quietly, and in one flowing movement he swept his hat from its peg and was out the door, leaving the fly-screen to swing shut behind him.

At noon the following day, Callum and two men from a neighbouring property were busy repairing the holding yard fences and they didn't hear the motor vehicle approach.

Callum was working with a chain-saw and it screamed and whirred shrilly. Sweat gathered beneath his hat and ran in rivulets down his back, making his cotton shirt cling to his skin. Sawdust coated his sweat-dampened arms.

A few metres away, Jim Walker, an aboriginal stockman, bent over a post-hole digger that shuddered and roared as loudly as Callum's chain-saw and, nearby, Jim's brother, Ernie, wielded an axe as he cut a mortise into a bloodwood post.

It was only when Callum caught a flash of white dancing at the edge of his vision that he looked up and was startled to see Stella.

Looking fresh and clean and heart-stoppingly pretty in a snowy white shirt and blue gypsy skirt, she was hovering some distance away, clutching a cane basket against her chest as if she was trying to keep its contents free of sawdust.

What on earth was she doing here?

He switched off the saw and waved and she called something back, but he couldn't hear her over the noise of the post-hole digger.

'Everything OK?' he yelled.

She nodded. She certainly didn't look as if she'd dashed down here in an emergency. But surely this wasn't a social visit? Wiping his grimy face with his sleeve, he set the chain-saw aside and hurried towards her.

A glance over his shoulder towards the other men assured him that their concentration was still firmly fixed on their work. They were tackling a big job and they needed to finish it today.

'Did you want something?' he asked when he reached her.

She looked embarrassed and made a little gesture with the basket. 'I—I brought you some lunch.'

'Lunch?' His jaw dropped so quickly it was a wonder it didn't hit the hard ground.

'Do you stop for lunch?' she asked.

'Well, yes, we do.'

'I wasn't sure. With all my sleeping in over the past weeks and everything, I've never noticed if you take lunch with you. I didn't know if you cut sandwiches, or what you do and—and—' she glanced towards Ernie and Jim '—I—I didn't know you had other men working with you.'

Suddenly the noise behind him stopped. Callum looked back to see the Walker brothers' big, white-teethed grins. 'These blokes have come over from Drayton Downs for the day to give me a hand with the fencing repairs.' He beckoned to them. 'Ernie, Jim, come and meet Stella.'

They continued to grin shyly as they ambled over and shook her hand. 'Pleased to meet you, Mrs Roper.'

'Mrs Roper?' Callum frowned at them. 'How did you blokes know I was married?'

They grinned some more and nodded. 'The boss was in Cloncurry yesterday. Word's spreadin' fast that you got yourself hitched, Callum.'

'Why didn't you say something before this?'

'We figured—maybe you was—' Jim shrugged '—maybe it was secret business.'

Stella fiddled with the blue and white tea towel that covered the contents of her basket.

'So what have you got there?' Callum asked her.

'Just—just a salad.'

He picked up a corner of the tea towel and saw two bowls lined with lettuce leaves and filled with dainty spoonfuls of tinned tuna and baby corn spears, cherry tomatoes and cubes of cheese. 'That—that looks great!' He hoped his enthusiasm didn't sound forced.

'I'm afraid I didn't bring enough for everyone.'

'No worries. There's plenty of tucker here for the boys.'

He shrugged in the direction of the Esky sitting in the shade of a gidgee bush. He'd packed it that morning with a loaf of bread, a generous hunk of corned beef, a jar of pickles and half a dozen cold boiled potatoes—enough for three hungry men.

Stella's chin lifted and her grey eyes flashed. Hell, she looked sexy when she went into haughty mode. If he wasn't so dirty, dusty and sweaty... If these two grinning blokes weren't gaping at them... If...

Dream on, mate. You're never going to do anything with this bewitching wife...except maybe eat her elegant lunch.

'You don't have to eat this, Callum. I just got carried away with being domesticated this morning.' There was a sudden gleam of triumph in her eyes as she added, 'The fruit cake's in the oven and it smells wonderful.'

'That's terrific.'

Her excitement about cooking was puzzling. Last night, she'd been bursting with pride as she'd asked him to admire the huge bowl of dried fruit she'd spent all afternoon chopping so she could soak it overnight in rum and sherry.

She was getting such a kick out of baking this cake. And yet, a few days earlier, she'd mentioned ever so casually that last summer she'd flown in a Hurricane Hunter jet while tracking a cyclone. They'd gone right into the eye of a storm. Now *that* was something to get excited about.

'The cake takes four hours to bake,' Stella said. 'So I thought I'd have plenty of time for a—' She looked around at the dry, dusty stock yards and pulled a rueful smile. 'I guess there's nowhere to have a picnic here.'

'We can manage a picnic,' he reassured her. 'Hop back in the ute and we'll go down to the creek.'

He did his best to ignore the chuckles of the two brothers as he followed Stella to the ute. Halfway across the yard, she turned back. 'I don't suppose we can avoid having people in the district know we're married.'

'Not much chance,' he agreed. 'Actually, I suppose I should have warned you. I rang my parents' place in Canberra, but there was no one home, so I left a message on their answering machine. But once they know, the whole world will know about us.'

She took a deep breath as if mentally preparing herself for the fateful day when she would have to face his family, then walked ahead of him again, keeping her head high and her shoulders very straight.

Callum found himself watching the silky sway of her hair and the gentle curve of her bottom beneath her soft cotton skirt and he hoped he'd get through this picnic of hers without making a fool of himself.

This wasn't a good idea.

Even before they reached the creek, Stella regretted her impulse to bring Callum a picnic lunch. The shock on his face when she'd arrived at the yards had been bad enough, but then she saw the poorly disguised smirks of the stockmen and Callum's polite but unenthusiastic reaction to the food she'd prepared and, suddenly, everything felt wrong.

She wanted to tell him she'd changed her mind. He should go back to Ernie and Jim. But he was starting up the ute, accelerating forward...and if she sent him back now, he'd lose face in front of the men.

By the time he parked the ute at the top of the creek bank, her stomach was tight with tension. When he led her to a soft grassy shelf on the lower bank, her mouth went dry.

'This is a good spot for a picnic,' he said, pointing to the shade cast by an enormous paperbark tree, but all she could see was a picture of the two of them sitting there...alone...and she knew a picnic was the most brainless idea she'd ever hatched.

The setting was faultless. Beside them, the cool clear creek bubbled charmingly over smooth water-washed stones. Blue dragonflies hovered and darted over the water, and a handsome kingfisher gave smooth presentations of precision diving. Yes, everything was perfect.

Not that Stella noticed once Callum crouched beside the creek and hauled off his shirt. She took one look at his wide, bronzed shoulders tapering down to a taut, lean waist and forgot how to breathe.

He began to wash away the sawdust and grime, evidence of his morning's work. Sloshing the water over his back, he let it run in a glistening cascade over his tanned skin and satiny muscles. Her palms grew hot with the thought of touching him, of learning the texture of that strong, smooth back, of feeling those muscles flex beneath her hands.

He stood and turned and she saw his broad, hairy chest and the teasing trail of dark hair disappearing into his jeans...

She shouldn't stare...

But what else, in heaven's name, could a girl do? Callum was truly breathtaking.

Unlike Scott, who'd worn his sex appeal like an advertisement, Callum moved with the natural, unaffected ease of a wild creature. He seemed to live in his body as if he were completely unaware of its charms. As he walked up the bank towards her, did he have any idea he was scrambling her brain?

Perhaps he did and took pity on her. With an easy shrug of his shoulders, he pulled the shirt back on, but when he reached her she was still completely tongue-tied. She handed him his lunch and neither of them seemed to have any idea what to say.

She kicked off her shoes and curled her feet beneath her, but her appetite had deserted her. Callum sat with his knees bent, staring at the creek and forking his lunch into his mouth so quickly she was sure he would get indigestion.

'You're repairing fences?' she asked. Dumb question, but they had to talk, had to find some way to relax and get over this silly awkwardness.

Still chewing, he grunted in agreement.

She tried another desperate tack. 'Have Jim and Ernie lived in this district long?'

He nodded and swallowed. 'All their lives. Their people are Kalkadoons.'

Kalkadoons! An exchange of information at last. 'The Kalkadoons were a very fierce aboriginal tribe in the old days, weren't they?'

He nodded.

'Ernie and Jim seem so shy and friendly.' She waited uneasily for Callum to comment, but he seemed to have forgotten that the art of conversation was a two-way process.

Embarrassed, she dumped her food back in the basket and

jumped to her feet. Sitting there on the velvety grass beside him was completely wrong. Dangerously wrong. She should never have suggested a picnic. They were too close, too alone, too awkward with each other...

Picnics were for courting couples.

Grabbing her skirt around her, she stepped down into the creek and dabbled her bare feet in the clear stream, hoping its coolness would reduce the heat racing through her.

'Stella, that isn't a good idea.'

The warning in his voice startled her. Clutching her skirt even higher, she hurried back towards the bank. 'Are there crocodiles here?'

'No!' A fleeting grin quirked his mouth, but next minute his face grew dark and he stared at her feet. 'You keep flaunting those naked feet in front of me and we'll both be sorry.' His voice held the hint of a growl.

Naked feet? She looked down and caught a glimpse of white toes, blue nail polish and her favourite ankle chain, then she lifted her eyes to Callum and seconds ticked by as she stood there with water swirling around her ankles, her gaze caught in his smouldering glare.

It was happening all over again. That spectacular rush of awareness that had drawn them together in Sydney. Hapless moths hurling themselves towards flames.

In one seamless movement he rose to his feet. 'I've finished my lunch. I should get back to work.'

'Of course.' She scrambled back out of the water and slipped her damp feet into her shoes. 'Let's go, then,' she said, knowing he was wise to leave. Now. They had no chance of a relaxing picnic.

Halfway up the bank, he turned and offered her his hand, muttering, 'This bit's pretty steep.'

Stella looked at his big brown hand and felt ridiculously self-conscious. And, when she placed her hand in his, electric shivers travelled under her skin.

He pulled her to the top of the bank so effortlessly that she stumbled against him and her breasts, tender from her pregnancy, collided with the solid musculature of his arm. An involuntary 'Ouch' escaped.

'What is it?' he whispered and he took half a step back, his eyes dark with emotion. And his gaze continued to hold hers as his hand skimmed the newly lush swell of her breast. He cupped its shape through the soft cotton of her shirt and she heard her heart-beats pounding in her ears as very slowly, very gently, his thumb glanced across the tip.

Oh, Callum. Oh, help! Melting, languorous yearning flowed through her and she blushed as she felt her nipples hardening and peaking.

'Are they tender?' he asked.

'Just a little,' she whispered.

For too long they stood together with his hand cupping her, heartbeats away from more touching. She could read the tortured questions in his eyes. Knew he was on the brink of breaking down every barrier he'd carefully erected. Understood that he was seeking painful answers in her eyes.

And all she knew was that she wanted him to caress her more boldly. To make the heat that was threading her veins blaze out of control.

But, with a sharp hiss of in-drawn breath, he dropped his hand to his side and stepped away. 'Best get back to work,' he said thickly.

Her breath rushed out in a noisy sigh. The danger was over. She knew she should be grateful that her inner weaknesses hadn't been exposed…but she wasn't grateful at all.

They turned and walked back to the ute.

Back in the kitchen, she knew she should never have left it. Dumping the basket on the table, she let out another long sigh. How had she ever thought the picnic could be a pleasant little domestic interlude?

It had been a disaster! She'd stopped Callum from getting on with an important job and she'd embarrassed him in front of the men. And she'd forced him into the kind of intimate situation that they'd been trying so hard to avoid!

Heavens! She'd wanted Callum to kiss her again. For a moment she'd thought she might die if he didn't. Thank goodness he was stronger than she was.

With a guilty grimace she looked around her at the hideous scene she'd abandoned when she'd left the kitchen for the holding yards. The table top was still littered with the remains of her morning's efforts. Flour, spilled milk and sticky egg shells...strips of buttered paper she'd used for lining the cake tin...scales for weighing sugar and flour...a sieve, a bowl lined with hardening cake mix...and a trail of floury footprints criss-crossing the floor.

No doubt virtuous outback wives cleaned their kitchens instead of frolicking in the creek. Even Oscar in his cage in the corner seemed to be looking at her with an accusing eye.

'OK. OK,' she growled at him. 'I'm a messy cook.' Feeling belligerent, she plonked her hands on her hips. 'But the important thing that you mustn't forget, Oscar, is that *I am now a cook!* This is a red-letter day!'

Bending low, she peeked through the glass window in the oven door and admired her cake. Its surface was transforming exactly as it should from a gooey mess to a nicely golden-brown cake top. And it smelt superb!

So what if she'd made a mess of the kitchen? And so what if the picnic idea had been pathetic? At least her cake was baking beautifully!

Dramatically, she hurled her hands into the air and shouted at the top of her lungs, *'Stella Roper can cook! Oh, boy, can she cook! Hey, look at the way this woman can cook!'*

Pausing for breath, she realised to her horror that there was a knocking sound coming from somewhere beyond the kitchen.

'Hello,' a woman's voice called. 'Is that you, Stella?'

She froze. *Not a visitor. Not now.* Not when the place looked like the set of a disaster movie.

The knocking started up again.

Oh, help! Casting a despairing glance around the kitchen she usually loved, she headed cautiously down the hall towards the front of the house.

Her stomach sank past her toes as she saw a middle-aged couple standing in the open front doorway and she recognised the well-televised, stern visage and impressive physique of the man. Tall and straight-backed, with the kind of thick, silver hair that always looked distinguished, Senator Ian Roper dominated the doorstep!

Oh, my God!

This sort of thing didn't happen. It just didn't. *Not to real people.* Parents-in-law couldn't just happen out of the blue, could they?

The woman beside him was smiling. She had youthfully brown and curly hair and her sleeveless black linen dress was simple but chic, a perfect foil for her long rope of chunky pearls.

Her smile was beaming as she stepped forward. 'You must be Stella,' she said, holding out her hand. 'I'm Margaret Roper, Callum's mother, and this is Ian.'

Stella stared stupidly at Callum's mother. 'How did you get here?' she asked. Oh, Lord. Where were her brains? 'I—I mean, hello. Hello, Mr and Mrs Roper. Senator Roper. What a—a pleasant surprise.' Cringe! First she'd been rude, now she was being overly sugary and polite.

Margaret Roper opened her arms. She kissed Stella's cheek and then, for a moment or two, she held her close. She smelt of something delicate and expensive, like a freshly delivered bouquet.

'I'm so sorry we didn't give you any warning,' she said, 'but we only accessed Callum's wonderful message this morning and, as Ian was already scheduled to fly to Mount Isa for a meeting, we couldn't resist coming out here to see you both the minute the meeting was over.'

Stella looked past them to the distant landing strip. A small plane was parked there and her memory stirred. She'd heard a plane flying overhead when she'd been coming back from the stock yards, but she hadn't given it a moment's thought. In the city planes flew overhead all the time. And they landed at airports.

What she'd completely forgotten was that, in the outback, planes, like everything else, behaved differently. They landed at people's front doors.

'How—how lovely to see you. Please come in. I'm afraid Callum's busy working on fences down at the yards.'

'Is he working on his own?' the Senator asked with a narrow-eyed glance that made Stella quite sure she was undergoing some kind of secret test.

'Oh, no. There are men from Drayton Downs helping him.'

'Ian,' Margaret Roper chided gently. 'Don't bombard the poor girl with questions the minute you arrive.' Her warm honey-brown eyes twinkled as she turned back to Stella. 'I'm just so excited about you and Callum. I always knew that my dear boy would find someone special. And this has been such a whirlwind affair. I think that's so romantic!'

'Yes,' Stella murmured weakly. 'Callum just—swept me off my feet. Ah—come and sit in the lounge. I'll make a pot of tea.'

Despite the fact that her legs felt like limp spaghetti, she managed to lead the Ropers into the lounge. It felt incredibly awkward to be showing them through the house they had lived in for umpteen years before Callum's father went into politics.

The Senator settled himself into the armchair by the window with the air of a king claiming his throne. With a frown, he surveyed the room slowly and thoroughly. No doubt he was making sure she hadn't helped herself to any of the antique silver.

Margaret didn't sit down. 'Why don't you let me help?' she suggested.

'Please don't bother,' Stella urged and she winced to hear the desperate note in her voice. 'I—I'm in the middle of—of things—in the kitchen.'

'You've been baking,' Margaret said, sniffing the air and smiling.

'Smells good,' added the Senator.

'Yes,' Stella agreed. 'It's not quite ready yet.'

'Don't worry. We're not hungry,' Margaret assured her. 'But some tea would be divine. And Stella...' Margaret hesitated slightly '...we were hoping it wouldn't be too much of an imposition if we stayed tonight. There's a rodeo in Mount Isa and all the hotels are booked.'

Help! They couldn't stay. There was nowhere for them to sleep. She was in the guest room. Callum was in the main bedroom. There were only single beds in the other rooms! Stella felt as if her head might explode.

'Of course you can stay. That would be—lovely. I'll make that tea.' Stella fled.

She reached the kitchen at a flat run, her heart thumping wildly. *Don't panic! Think!*

Think priorities. What's more important? Hiding this disgraceful mess in the kitchen or hiding the fact that Callum and I aren't a blissfully happily-ever-after married couple?

A quick recollection of the dreamy, sentimental look on Margaret's face and she knew there was only one answer.

But that meant she had to ferret her gear out of the guest bedroom and into Callum's room. Her heart did a fair imitation of a ballerina's pirouette. It also meant that tonight she and Callum would have to share his room. *His bed.*

Best not to think about that now. That kind of thinking could fry a girl's brain.

Her hands shook as she filled the kettle, but she forced her thoughts into order. In her work, whenever she'd had to track and report a natural disaster like a cyclone, there'd been procedures to follow. Now she developed a quick mental list of procedures for this disaster.

One, make cups of tea. Two, empty her things out of the guest room and into a suitcase. Three, new sheets on the Ropers' bed. Four, clean kitchen. Between steps one and four, run to the lounge for snippets of meaningful conversation with the in-laws. Five—

Forget it. She would never make it to five.

Sundown. The last post was in place. Using a crowbar and a long-handled shovel, Callum tamped the earth hard around it while Ernie and Jim slipped the final rail home.

A good day's work.

'Are you coming up to the house for a beer?' Callum asked.

Ernie shook his head. 'Thanks, mate, but I think we better push off home.'

Callum considered trying to change their minds, but he knew the thought of Stella waiting up at the homestead was making the men coy. And, as he waved them off, he realised that the thought of Stella waiting at home was making him feel a few things, too.

Hot, hard and brainless would have to head the list. These days, just being around her was an ordeal. Looking at her and talking to her was sweet torture. He'd nearly gone mad at her blessed picnic. All he could think about had been hauling her close and pushing her down into that soft grass, taking her mouth, kissing her sense-less…making her want him.

Him. Not Scott.

Over and over, like a video recorder stuck on replay, he kept seeing the way it could happen: her hair, black and shiny against the velvet green grass; her eyes changing from cool grey to stormy smoke as he lowered himself over her; her lips, wide and sexy, part-ing to smile at him; her body, warm, becoming hot and tense with longing; her voice—her sultry, tough-girl voice urging him closer.

Damn! He didn't have enough brains to give himself a head-ache. He was such a fool!

Cursing, he tossed the crowbar and shovel into the back of the truck. *Damn you, Scott. Damn you for deserting your woman.*

What had Stella been playing at by coming down to the yard for a picnic?

As he stepped onto Birralee's back veranda, he heard voices and his first reaction was relief. Company. For once he was grateful. Visitors would be the distraction he needed. They would provide a buffer between himself and Stella.

But as his hand reached for the fly-screen door, ready to push it open, he froze. That was his mother's voice! *'Struth!* His par-ents were here with Stella! How on earth was she coping? How would *he* cope?

His parents had always looked on him as their steady, earnest son, the one who, even as a little tyke, had been eager to please them. If they discovered the truth behind this marriage, they would be devastated. His heart plummeted as he entered the kitchen.

But, if he'd had all day to think about this moment, he never would have come up with the scenario he found.

His mother, wearing an apron, was up to her elbows in washing-up water. Stella, looking pale and tired, was drying a huge mixing bowl, and on the table in front of her was a range of sparkling clean cooking utensils. His father, sitting at the far end of the table with newspapers spread in front of him, was calmly peeling prawns.

Talk about surreal!

Everybody spoke at once. His mother began to explain that, as her hands were wet, she couldn't hug him. Stella was offering excuses he couldn't follow about tea and changing sheets.

Eventually the hubbub died and his father looked at him with a steely eye. 'You turned out to be a sly old dog, son.'

Callum nodded and swallowed a constriction in his throat. 'I take it you got my message about the—about our—good news.'

'Darling, we're delighted,' Margaret said warmly and he saw that her face was glowing.

Stuff this! It should have been such a happy moment, but Callum felt a lead weight settle in his chest. It actually hurt to see his mother looking so happy. She hadn't looked like that since before Scott died and she was going to be so disappointed when she eventually learned the truth about him and Stella.

'You know you've done Margaret out of the biggest wedding in the district,' his father said.

Callum tried to smile. 'Sorry, Mum. It was just one of those things that happen out of the blue.'

'Love at first sight?' Margaret asked, her brown eyes shining with excitement and pleasure.

More like lust at first sight. Callum squashed that thought.

'It certainly took Stella and me by surprise,' he said. As he spoke, he looked at Stella and forced a smile and the answering wistful expression in her eyes made his heart spin.

He wanted to tell her he was sorry. Sorry he wasn't Scott. Sorry he hadn't prepared her for this. Sorry for the thousand probing questions his father was sure to ask.

But luckily, right now, the Senator had less threatening things on his mind. He gestured to the pile of prawns in front of him. 'Can't shake your hand, son. I've got seafood all over me. Bought these prawns in Mount Isa. Freshly caught and flown in from the gulf. Thought they might be good for tonight.'

'Excellent,' Callum managed. 'Saves cooking dinner.'

'We didn't want to arrive empty-handed,' Margaret added.

Callum's eyes returned to Stella. To his amazement, she put down the bowl she'd been drying and hurried towards him, flashing a tight smile. 'Darling, how was your day?' She raised her face to his for a kiss.

Blood pounded through his body.

Settle, boy. Don't overreact. This is simply a demonstration for the parents of how the little wife greets her husband at the end of the working day.

He kissed her cheek. 'Hi, sweetheart. I'm afraid I can't kiss you properly. I'm covered in dirt and dust.'

Fortunately, his parents laughed.

And with heightened colour in her cheeks and downcast eyes, Stella removed herself back to the far side of the kitchen.

He looked again at the collection of cooking gear. 'How did the cake turn out?'

'Don't ask!' three voices snapped in chorus. And any hint of pink drained from Stella's cheeks.

'No, Stella! Not the cake. What happened?'

She didn't answer at first, but her chin lifted in that familiar, haughty way she adopted when things got tough and her eyes flashed him a warning. *Don't you dare make a joke about this!* 'It burned.'

'That's—that's really bad luck.' He cleared his throat. 'I'm sorry...but...if you'll excuse me, I'll go and have a shower. Make myself presentable.'

He hurried to his bedroom to collect clean clothes. Two steps into the room he saw Stella's suitcase poking out from under his bed and he came to a heart-thudding halt.

Her hairbrush and mirror were on his dresser. Stepping closer, he saw the little silver chain with its blue glass beads lying on the cut-glass tray that held his cuff-links.

His pulses leapt as he stepped into the adjoining bathroom and found her multicoloured toothbrush in the rack beside his.

He realised immediately what she had done and why, but his wave of admiration for her quick-thinking was rapidly swamped by a more pressing thought. If he and Stella had to follow through with this charade, he was facing the most difficult and potentially dangerous night of his life.

In bed with Stella.

CHAPTER SEVEN

CALLUM CLOSED HIS bedroom door and leaned his back against it as he released a long sigh of relief. As far as he could tell, he and Stella had made it through the first part of the evening without any major mishaps.

But how to deal with the long night ahead? If he wasn't excruciatingly careful, this was where things could get really tricky.

Right now, Stella was standing in the middle of his bedroom with her arms crossed over her chest as if she half expected him to pounce on her.

'You were terrific tonight,' he told her. 'Anyone would think you'd had years of practice at being married.'

She gave a dismissive little laugh. 'I got an A for drama in high school.'

Easing himself away from the door, he tried not to think about his own performance this evening. Whenever she'd touched him, or when she'd called him 'darling', he'd tried to keep his breathing steady, but each touch, each look, each word, had made him want her more than ever.

'What happened when your father took you away for a man-to-man talk?' she asked.

'I thought he made a pretty good fist of coming to terms with his shock,' Callum admitted. 'His comments were all positive apart from chewing over the fact that we rushed into marriage without telling them.'

'Your mother told me they've been hoping you would settle down and—and start a family.'

'Yeah.' Callum sent her a wry grin. He'd heard that message from his mother many times. 'Well, I'm halfway there.'

She was rubbing her left hand nervously up and down her right arm.

'I should have warned you that Mum would want to invite my sisters and their families to come over here tomorrow. But that's my family, I'm afraid. Any sniff of a chance for a celebration—'

Stella shrugged. 'She assures me that Ellie and Catherine are bringing enough food to feed an army, so at least I won't have to panic about a catering crisis.'

'That reminds me, I'm sorry about the cake.' She looked so suddenly miserable, he wanted to offer some comfort—a hug or even a pat on the shoulder—but any kind of touching was not a good idea tonight. He shoved his hands in his pockets. 'I know how much it meant to you.'

She blinked and gave a little shrug. 'I'm over it.'

'Nothing could be salvaged?'

'Your mother was very good. She helped me cut off the burnt top and sides. There's a bit in the middle that's not too bad.' Her lip curled in a twisted smile. 'It was going so well until they arrived.'

Exhaling a loud sigh, he looked around the room that had suddenly grown too small—way too small if it was to accommodate the two of them for a whole night. 'How on earth did you get all your gear out of the guest room and into here?'

'It was a dicey exercise.' She rolled her eyes. 'It's part of the reason I burned the cake. But what we've got to worry about now is—'

'How we spend the night,' Callum finished for her and he wondered what he could do about the way his body primed itself for action at the merest thought of having Stella share his bed.

'I'll get changed in the bathroom,' she offered.

'Sure. Good idea.'

With nervous haste, she pulled purple silk pyjamas from her suitcase and hurried through to the adjoining room.

Callum hunted through his drawer, searching for something that would serve as pyjamas. He usually slept bare, but tonight a strait-jacket or a suit of chain mail would come in handy. He settled for a pair of solid black cotton boxer shorts and changed into them quickly. Then he turned down the old fashioned, cotton waffle bedspread.

And Stella walked back into the room.

The purple silk of her pyjama top clung to her breasts and the short bottoms revealed far too much of the shapely length of her legs. Bright colour flared along her cheekbones. She looked as breathless and edgy as he felt.

He made a desperate decision. 'You take the bed. I'll be fine over there in the armchair.'

'You're sure?'

'Absolutely.' Snatching a spare pillow and a light throw from the top of the wardrobe, he hastily switched off the wall light and settled himself in the chair. 'This is great,' he lied.

Stella climbed onto his queen-size bed and sat to one side. In the light cast by the bedside lamp, she looked distinctly ill at ease. Sexy, desirable…but uneasy.

Across the room, they watched each other and the air seemed to throb with their tension.

'How are you going to sleep there?' she asked. 'Your legs are far too long.'

'Don't tempt me out of this chair, Stella.' He grimaced as he heard the unmistakable growl of desire in his voice.

She must have heard it, too, because she suddenly reached for the sheet and drew it over her legs.

Closing his eyes, Callum prayed for sanity. 'Why don't you tell me about Scott's visits to Sydney?' he suggested.

'I beg your pardon?'

'Scott never talked much about his trips away.' He needed to have his little brother where he belonged—as a fixed, immovable wedge—between them.

Perhaps she understood because, after a moment or two's hesitation, her shoulders seemed to relax against the pillows. 'What exactly do you want to know?'

'Whatever you're prepared to tell me. Of course, I only want a censored version.'

She raised both hands and ran them through her hair, lifting it and then letting it slip silkily back into place. It was a habit that seemed to help her relax and, no matter how many times she did it, Callum never tired of watching.

'Actually, I'm glad you've asked,' she said. 'I've been wanting to explain about that because I don't want you to get the wrong idea about me. Scott and I were—were just good friends for ages.' She pleated the sheeting with her fingers. 'I'd never met anyone like him. He was so much fun.'

Callum nodded. 'Scotty was fun all right.'

'One Saturday night, we went to a really exclusive Sydney Harbour restaurant and he pretended to be a prisoner just released from jail. He told the poor waiter I was his parole officer.'

'That'd be Scott.' Callum couldn't hold back his chuckle. 'He loved pulling pranks like that. I remember having dinner with him in a restaurant in Cairns once and he pretended to be a German tourist. He kept up the accent all evening.'

'I can imagine. He missed his calling as an actor. On our date he kept up this whole spiel about how much Sydney had changed in the five years he'd been "inside". He rattled on about how the items on the menu had become so cosmopolitan. I found myself playing along with him. We certainly fooled the restaurant staff.'

After a stretch of silence, she added softly. 'It's just terrible that he died.'

And wasn't that the truth.

She did the thing with her hair again and Callum's hands balled into fists. *Don't think about running your fingers there!*

He sighed. 'Scott liked to get away. I think he tended to think of living way out here as being in a kind of jail. Most of the time he didn't mind it, but every so often he just had to break out.'

Stella's expression was thoughtful as she lowered herself forward until she lay stomach-down on the mattress and propped her head on her hand. Over the end of the bed, she looked at him with searching directness. 'I would have thought living in the city was more like being in jail. Out here there's so much freedom. Nobody breathing down your neck. How do you feel about living here?'

'There's no other place I'd rather be.'

'That's what I guessed,' she said softly. 'I think I'd feel that way too. If I really belonged here.' She traced the geometric pattern of the folded bedspread with one finger. 'But I've never really belonged anywhere.'

Their gazes reconnected and held. What was she saying? Callum didn't dare think. She couldn't possibly mean she wanted to go on living here with him. His heart almost stopped at the thought of having her here in his life, his wife for ever, the mother of his children...

But no, that definitely wasn't what she was saying.

'Where do your family live?' he asked.

She groaned and dropped her head so that her hair fell and covered her face. 'Please, let's not talk about that.'

After a puzzled pause, he shrugged. 'If you insist.' Every time the subject of her family came up she behaved the same way. He knew her anxiety about cooking was somehow tied up with this family of hers. He suspected that her agreeing to leave her baby behind was connected to that, too.

'One of these days I'll tell you about my mother,' she said.

'OK,' he said softly, hoping she couldn't tell how exceptionally pleased he was by this very small sign of trust.

'But tonight's not the time.'

'Perhaps we should try to sleep.'

'I suppose so.'

She sounded doubtful and he was secretly relieved. Truth was, he could go on listening to her husky, honeyed voice all night. It wound around him like wood smoke from a warming camp fire.

'Unless you want to tell me some more about Scott,' he said, wondering just when he'd become partial to self-inflicted pain.

She seemed to consider this suggestion, then shrugged her shoulders. 'Well—there was one wet Sunday I'll never forget. My flatmate went to watch her boyfriend play football in the rain and Scott and I stayed in my apartment and had pizzas delivered and listened to music and—'

Made love. His stomach crawled. 'It's OK. You don't have to tell me every intimate detail.'

Stella ignored him. 'And I painted Scott's toenails.'

Her words hit him like a grenade going off in his face. *'You what?'*

She smiled shyly. 'I know it sounds wacky. A big tough bush bloke letting me paint his toenails just for fun.'

Hell! He struggled to breathe. Never had he been so painfully aware of the vast difference between himself and his young brother.

Callum knew there was absolutely no way he could get involved in toenail painting with a woman. And it wasn't that he was hung up about gender roles. It was the sheer intimacy of the act.

Sure, sex was intimate...but sex was intense and fuelled by passion. It wasn't the same as being so totally at ease with a woman as to be able to do something as off-the-wall and unexpectedly personal as having one's toenails painted! Just for fun!

I'm so tied up in knots I couldn't even enjoy her simple picnic.

In his mind's eye, he could see Scott and Stella together. He could hear the private laughter, the jokes; he could sense the touching, the shared companionship. Suddenly he felt desperately lonely and hopelessly inadequate as a stand-in for his brother.

'What colour?' he managed to ask at last.

'Colour?'

'The nail polish.'

'I'm not sure if I remember. It was a shade of red. I think it was ruby.'

His voice shook slightly as he asked, 'Is that why you want to call your baby Ruby?'

Stella looked surprised, as if the link had never occurred to her. 'I don't think so. I just think Ruby's a cute name.'

They lapsed into an awkward silence.

'Callum, there's something else I should explain about Scott.'

He braced himself mentally for bad news. 'Explain away.'

'It's just that Scott and I split up—before I knew I was pregnant.'

He stared at her, unable to speak.

'It was pretty awful. You see I finally realised that I'd been clinging to a relationship that just wasn't going to work. I'd been hoping that Scott would settle down… He was fun, but he didn't want to get serious…'

What a joke! How ironical could life get? Callum's fists clenched. Here he was, bursting to get serious with Stella and she was still breaking her heart over Scott, who'd been terminally allergic to getting serious with a woman. 'I'm sorry if my little brother hurt you, Stella.'

She didn't answer.

The chiming clock in the lounge struck midnight and from beyond the homestead came the soft call of a mopoke.

'I guess we'd better get some sleep,' she said.

'Yeah.' He tried to settle his long body into the cramped chair. 'Goodnight.'

"Night, Callum.'

After a minute or two, she switched off the lamp and he could hear her movements as she made herself comfortable in the bed.

Then silence. No sound but the wind in the trees. No light except for faint bars of creamy moonshine seeping through the slats in the blinds. He closed his eyes and tried to ignore the pain in his heart and the disturbing pressure in his loins. Just as well he was cramped up in this chair. A little discomfort might straighten out his useless, X rated thoughts.

There was more silence till the lounge clock chimed a quarter past the hour.

Then, through the darkness, came Stella's voice, low and excited. 'Callum, come here.'

He jolted upright, peering through the pale light cast by the moon. She'd kicked the sheet away and was lying on her side, holding her hand against her lower abdomen. He stared, but didn't move.

'Are you all right?'

'Yes, but come here. Quickly.'

'Stella, I—'

'It might stop soon.'

'What is it?'

'The baby. At least I think it's the baby. There's this tiny little flutter-kick thing happening down here.'

'Are you sure you want me to—?'

'Yes, hurry.'

Crossing the floor quickly, he sat on the side of the bed. Stella grabbed his hand and, slipping it under the waistband of her pyjama bottoms, pressed it firmly against her lower stomach.

Sweat broke out all over him! So close to the most womanly part of her! He was trembling as his palm pressed against her soft… smooth…warm…luscious…skin. Heaven help him! She felt so sensual…so good.

'You have to push me in a bit because it's still quite little, but can you feel that?'

Drawing on will-power he didn't know he had, he ignored how incredibly sexy this moment was and concentrated on the tiny movement bumping against his palm. He held his breath and the movement came again. And again. Like the soft bump of a duckling's bill tapping the inside of an egg. 'Yes,' he whispered huskily. 'I can. I can feel it.'

She looked up at him and her face was so close he could feel her soft breath against his cheek and he could see the warm, vulnerable sense of wonder in her eyes.

'It's Ruby,' she whispered.

He wanted to kiss her. Oh, God! He wanted to kiss her from head to toe. 'It's going to be a perfect little baby,' he whispered back and still he wanted to kiss her. Yes, he would start by kissing her pretty toes and then he'd move slowly up her long silky legs. Or perhaps he would start at her mouth and then move down. Either way, he would explore every sweet and secret part of her. This was Stella and she was so lovely, so gutsy, so maddeningly sexy. So near!

And she was looking at him with eyes swimming with emotion. Her soft lips were parted in sensual invitation. *They were married.* Married and alone in bed together. There was absolutely no reason on earth that they couldn't kiss.

He'd never desired any other woman the way he wanted Stella. He edged closer.

Come to your senses, man! Hell! Wake up! Think about Scott! She chose Scott, not you! Besides, you made her a promise that this wouldn't happen!

Seconds from making the worst mistake possible, he withdrew his hand from her warmth and softness and slid from the bed to stand beside her, hands safely on his hips.

'That was an enlightening experience,' he said and winced as he heard how sarcastic and rude that sounded.

She looked understandably hurt. 'I wanted to share a special moment with you.'

'I know,' he said more gently. 'I—er—' How could he explain to her what he couldn't explain to himself? His thoughts were plunging and scattering like tumbleweed in a storm.

He was trying so hard not to say something really stupid. He wanted, he needed, to make love to her. Right now! But he also wanted to love and protect her in the future as much as he wanted to love and protect her baby, but if he said that, she'd pack up and run. She didn't want his love. All she wanted from him was a roof over her baby's head.

She pulled the sheet back over her. 'Look,' she said huffily when she was safely covered up, 'I told you all that stuff about Scott because I thought that getting everything out in the open would be good for both of us.'

He nodded.

'So we can put this pretend marriage into its proper perspective.'

'Which perspective would that be?'

'Well—Scott and I weren't careful enough. We made a silly, immature mistake but, thanks to this arrangement, you and I can go part way to correcting it. This marriage is a practical and adult solution,' she said solemnly.

'Oh, yeah. I'm—glad you see it that way.'

'But if we're going to keep on being practical and adult, you can't spend the night in that chair. It's ridiculous.'

Callum coughed. 'Stella, give me a break. If I got into bed with you it would be very—very adult, but I'm not sure it's practical.'

Passionate, deep thrusting sex could hardly be described as practical. Unless there was a baby to be made...

And that had already been accomplished by his brother.

Stella lay stiffly with her arms folded across her chest as if for protection. 'There's plenty of room here. You take that side of the bed, I'll stick to my half, and we should both get some sleep.'

Sleep? Sure...as if I won't notice the minuscule space separating your luscious, semi-naked body from mine.

'We both know nothing's going to happen,' she said tightly.

'Of course!' he replied, too quickly and way too loudly!

CHAPTER EIGHT

STELLA LAY BESIDE Callum, stiff as a mummified corpse, staring at the ceiling. Wide awake. There was no way she could relax and drop off to sleep.

She was too aware of Callum in her bed. Oh, man! The picnic had been difficult enough, but now! He looked ultra-divine wearing nothing but skimpy boxer shorts. And he was just here, in easy reach!

For the sake of her sanity, she had to drag her mind away from those dangerous thoughts. She pressed her hand against the warm little mound of her growing baby and couldn't help smiling into the dark as it responded with yet another little thump. Tiny Ruby. Somehow she was sure it was a girl. What a cute little mover her baby was.

But still, she hadn't been prepared for the way those little movements made her feel. Most of the time she only allowed herself to think of her pregnancy as a kind of inconvenient illness, but tonight it really hit her that this was a proper little person she carried inside her.

And suddenly she could visualise it clearly. At first it would be tiny and cute and helpless like a baby doll, but in a few short years her baby would be a laughing, impish child. A skinny and long-limbed outback tomboy with sun-streaked curls and a freckled nose.

Her throat tightened painfully as she thought about Ruby grow-ing up with Callum and the rest of the Ropers.

Without her.

Ruby would have Callum to watch over her and love her and teach her to ride. Stella could picture them charging off on horse-back together across Birralee's vast plains. Tough and free and open-hearted like the country they loved.

And where would she be?

Alone in a city somewhere?

Alone as she'd been for most of her life?

Her mother had thrown away her only doll in one of her drunken rages. And now she was going to give this baby away.

She bunched the sheet into a ball and shoved it into her mouth to stop herself from moaning aloud. How aching and empty she felt.

How could she bear the thought of other arms holding her little one? Other ears hearing her laughter, her first word...seeing her first steps...comforting her...knowing the warmth of her chubby arms.

But it was *her* baby! How could she have ever thought it was right to give it away? How could she let Callum's family become the most important people in her child's world?

If only...

She turned her head to look at the dark silhouette of Callum's shoulder as he lay on his side with his back to her. Each day that passed, she felt more and more drawn to him in every way. If only he had married her for a more romantic reason than his sense of duty to Scott!

If only they could be like a normal married couple—lovers who raised their baby in their own little close-knit family. But that wasn't what he'd planned at all. Callum married her for one rea-son—to give the baby legitimacy and to raise it at Birralee. Sure, he was attracted to her physically. But he'd made it clear that his prime interest was Scott's baby. Not her.

With a groaning sigh she rolled over in the other direction and stared at the far wall. Tomorrow his sisters and their husbands and children would arrive. So much family. So many questions.

Help!

* * *

By noon the next day, Birralee's huge kitchen looked and sounded like something out of one of Stella's fantasies.

Every chair around the table was occupied and the table was laden with food. Excited talk and laughter filled the room and drifted out through the windows that were opened wide to catch the breeze.

As she'd expected, Callum's sisters were attractive and capable. Their husbands were predictably tall, sun-tanned and good-looking, and their children healthy and glowing. To her relief, everyone was amazingly friendly. They hugged Stella and welcomed her into their fold without a moment's hesitation.

It was actually frightening to see how easily they accepted her and how naturally they assumed she was wonderful—as if Callum would only choose the most suitable, very best woman to be his wife.

His younger sister Ellie kissed Stella and stood holding her by the arms and looking deeply into her eyes. Her own eyes were the same warm toffee as Callum's and they glowed as she said, 'Oh, yes, Stella, you're so perfect for Callum. I can feel it in my bones.'

Stella thanked heavens for her years of practice at hiding her innermost thoughts and feelings. Those times helped her now as she returned Ellie's frank gaze. She hoped her smile was friendly and assured, even though her mind was whispering, *I'm a fake. I'm a fake. I'm a big fat fake.*

How bitterly disappointed this family would be when she left Callum! Stella clung to the faint hope that, eventually, the baby she left behind would make up for her sins.

Her self-esteem wasn't helped by the discovery that Ellie and Catherine were as gifted in the kitchen as she suspected and they'd brought a mountain of gourmet delights—home-made sausages wrapped in bread for the children and cold roast beef with a special pepper crust for the adults.

And the accompaniments were just as impressive—white radish and wild rocket salad and spicy coriander rice. There was even dessert—crunchy biscotti and a soft meringue roll oozing raspberry-flavoured mascarpone.

Stella had never seen a meal quite like it outside a restaurant and, all the time she ate, she kept recalling her blackened cake and Margaret Roper's initial shock when she'd discovered the state of the kitchen yesterday.

Thankfully, that was behind her. Today Oscar's cage had been moved to a hook just outside the back door and she'd scoured the kitchen until once again it was the epitome of country charm.

Ellie's daughter, Penny, occupied the high chair and she beamed at everyone like a baby princess on her throne, looking impossibly cute as she solemnly speared pieces of cold sausage and halved cherry tomatoes with her fork.

Every so often Ellie would lean over and help her baby. She would kiss Penny's round cheek and the little girl would dimple with delight. At one point they rubbed noses and laughed into each other's faces and the perfect, open love that passed between the two of them made Stella's eyes sting.

That could be me. Ruby and I could be like that. She struggled to block out memories of Marlene sobbing, 'I want to be a good mother but I don't know how.'

Maybe I don't know how either, Mother. You never showed me the way.

Oh, Lord! This kind of thinking would send her into a mess! Closing her eyes, she took a deep breath and willed her nerves to settle. If only she'd had a chance to talk to Callum about a plan of attack for handling this meal.

He was sitting beside her and, at that moment, he squeezed her hand and the skin on her arms prickled warmly. Leaning close, he whispered, 'How are you holding out?'

She turned slightly to meet his gaze and he traced a pattern on her palm with his thumb. His touch and the understanding in his eyes made her as warm and melting as a birthday candle. Goodness, he was good at this! No wonder his family believed he really loved her.

Margaret was sitting opposite them, watching them fondly. She reached across the table and patted Callum's free hand. Her eyes shone and her mouth wobbled a little, but she smiled bravely as she said, 'Callum, darling, how clever of you to discover Stella. You've found such a wonderful way to help us get over—over Scotty.'

Stella's face flamed and a weird choking cry forced its way from her throat.

Callum quickly drew her head against his shoulder, dropping warm kisses on her forehead as he did so and she was grateful that her hair fell forward, creating a shielding curtain that hid her face.

'Stella knew Scotty, too,' she heard him explain to his mother, and, feeling dreadful, she kept her flushed face pressed into the warm hollow of his shoulder. 'That's how—how we met.'

'What did you say Stella's maiden name was, Callum?' came the Senator's voice, booming from the far end of the table.

Her head shot up and her dismay was replaced by a new fear. Was this the moment when everything came completely unstuck? How many questions would she have to answer about her family?

'My name was Lassiter,' she told her father-in-law and she realised that every adult at the table was listening and watching her carefully.

'Lassiter,' he repeated with a thoughtful frown. 'So does that mean you're related to the Lassiters who own Janderoo station over near Pentland? Don and Freda Lassiter? They come from a big family.'

'No,' Stella answered hastily. 'I don't think so. My people have always been city folk.'

'Callum's not one for the city, so how did you two meet?' This came from Catherine. Her eyes were very dark and piercing like her father's and Stella suddenly felt like a squirming bug impaled by an entomologist's scalpel. All she could think of was the truth—that she had met Callum once at a party and then had told him she'd preferred his brother.

To her relief, Callum answered his sister for her. 'Scott introduced us. Then Stella came up here on holiday and I kind of moved in on her.' He turned to her again and sent her a beautiful, tummy-flipping smile.

'Smartest move you ever made, brother,' cheered Ellie.

'Yeah.' He flung an arm around Stella's shoulders.

'Sweetheart!' There was a broken note in Margaret's voice. 'It's so lovely to know that Scott played a part in your happiness with Stella. Somehow it feels so right.'

Help! Stella focused downcast eyes on the lacy pattern of the tablecloth in front of her. Deceiving this fine, grieving woman was terrible. Putting Callum in a position where he had to deceive his own mother was unforgivable!

A momentary respite was provided by the children, who had eaten their fill and were becoming bored. As they gained permission to leave the table and to run on the veranda or explore the garden outside, the adults settled down to coffee. A platter of cheese and fruit was handed around.

But before Stella could relax, Catherine's husband, Rob, fired another question her way.

'What kind of work did you do in the city, Stella?'

For a moment her mind froze, scared that the truth might be her undoing, that somehow everything about the London job would come out. But to her intense relief, when she mentioned her background in meteorology, the conversation actually steered into safer waters. Soon everyone was discussing the outback cattleman's favourite topic—the weather.

Stella understood the fragile, dependent relationship people on the land shared with the elements and she soon became totally absorbed in discussions about tropical cyclones, bush fires, severe thunderstorms, floods and droughts.

In fact, she found herself the centre of attention as she outlined some of the ways meteorological research could support the cattle industry to plan the best uses for their land and water resources.

There were murmurs of agreement. Senator Roper was watching her with a narrowed-eyed, speculative gaze, but she tried not to let it unnerve her.

Ellie grinned broadly. 'This gal of yours is much more than a pretty face, Callum.'

She saw a flash of agreement in the eyes of the others at the table, but she held her hands out to indicate the remains of the spread in front of them. 'But I can't cook.'

And there was a ripple of indulgent laughter.

Eventually, the meal drew to a close and Stella could feel the knots in her stomach beginning to loosen a little.

'Now, let's attack the dishes,' Ellie suggested.

'Please don't,' Stella cried. 'I didn't prepare one crumb of the food, so I want you to leave the clearing and the washing-up to me.'

'We can't leave you with all this,' interjected a horrified Catherine. 'We always pitch in.'

'That's how families do things in the bush,' added Ellie with a grin.

Families? For a moment, Stella almost faltered. Perhaps she was breaking some ancient family law? But then she shook her head and insisted, 'Honestly, thanks for the offer, but I'd like to look after this.' After all, a girl had to have some pride. She felt bad enough eating all their food.

There were more protests but, eventually, they gave in. While Stella remained alone in the kitchen, they wandered outside to round up their children, search for discarded shoes or socks and to talk about hitting the road if they wanted to be home before dark.

Stella was busily stacking plates on the draining board when she heard heavy footsteps behind her. She turned and her heart tripped several beats when she saw Senator Roper standing quite close.

'I wondered if I could have a quick word, Stella?'

Oh, crumbs! 'Of course.'

Without smiling, he gestured towards any empty chair at the half-cleared table. 'Please, take a seat.'

She gulped. 'Thank you.' Then she sat with her damp palms clasped in her lap.

At first she was afraid he was going to remain standing but, to her relief, he drew out a chair and sat facing her. His face remained as serious as a heart attack. 'My son seems to have lost his head over you,' he said.

She was so surprised and alarmed, she couldn't think of one sensible word to offer in response.

'My wife is a romantic,' Senator Roper continued. 'She's over the moon about this marriage. But I know my son. I know it's totally out of character for Callum to behave this way—on a whim. And I have to admit that I was extremely surprised that he rushed so quickly into marriage with a woman who was prepared to tell him so little of her background.'

Stella's chin lifted. She guessed that her background would have been of vital importance to this man. Well, that was too bad! She wasn't about to enlighten him.

Her cheeks were hot, but she hoped she didn't look anywhere near as frightened as she felt. 'Your son didn't require details of my pedigree before he asked me to be his wife.'

Her father-in-law's eyes widened.

'Are you telling me you're unhappy with his choice?' she challenged.

He shook his head, but there was no softening in his expression. 'If my son really loves you, that is enough.'

But it obviously wasn't enough. The Senator's eyes narrowed as he went on. 'But I must warn you, Stella, that Callum is a man whose feelings run deep. He still mourns the loss of his brother profoundly.'

'Yes, I do realise that.'

'His emotions are probably more vulnerable now than they have been at any other time.'

'I understand.'

He watched her carefully through an uncomfortable minute of silence. What could she say? If he had been hoping to make her feel small and guilty, he'd succeeded.

He rose and offered her his hand. 'All I'm asking is that you take care of him for us, Stella.'

There was still no smile and she fancied she could hear what he *wasn't* saying: *If you hurt the only son I have left, I'll never forgive you.*

She wasn't sure if her legs would support her as she tried to stand. She could only force one reluctant smile. 'I promise you, I want the best for Callum, too,' she told him.

They shook hands and with a curt little nod of his head he turned and left the room as quickly as he'd entered.

Stella sagged against the sink, feeling ill. She knew that Callum had made an enormous sacrifice of his own pride and dignity by marrying her, but the worst was yet to come—after the baby was born, when she left him to face his family.

Oh, Lord! She should never have agreed to this marriage. Callum had been so insistent that it was the best decision, and at the time it had seemed like the right solution for the baby, but now she just felt terribly selfish—as if she was merely using Callum to suit her own ends!

Turning to the dishes in the sink, she attempted to finish the task of stacking plates, but her hands were shaking so much she feared she might break them.

Then there were more footsteps heading her way and she turned to see Ellie hurrying into the room.

'We'll be heading off soon,' she said.

Stella nodded. 'Thank you so much for coming.' She spoke quickly, feeling totally out of her depth as she struggled to shrug aside the aftershocks of her conversation with the Senator and to adopt the calm warmth required of a hostess. 'The food was superb. I don't know how you did it at such short notice.'

'Oh, all sorts of things can be managed at short notice,' Ellie replied with a knowing sparkle in her eyes. 'Even weddings.'

'Well, yes. I guess so.'

Ellie's hand rested on Stella's arm. 'I know your secret,' she said softly.

'You do?' Stella's nervous stomach bunched into even tighter knots. What secret could Ellie know? That the marriage was a sham? That Stella was going to walk out on Callum in a few months' time? That she would be leaving him holding a baby that wasn't even his?

Oh, Lord! Ellie couldn't know about Scott, could she? Could he have told his sister about his visits to Sydney? Her heart fluttered in her chest like Oscar flapping in his cage.

'You're pregnant, aren't you?' Ellie said.

Stella's hand flew to her stomach. 'How—how did you know?'

The other woman's mouth twisted in a wry smile. 'I've been there three times. I know the signs. You didn't touch the alcohol or the coffee. You avoided any of the smoked and soft cheeses— just ate the crackers on their own. You've got a glow.'

'A *glow*?'

Ellie laughed. 'It's nothing toxic. Not a glow-in-the-dark kind of glow—just a nice bloom in your cheeks. I always think we women look our best when we're pregnant.'

Stella didn't know what to say. She really liked Ellie. From the moment they'd met she'd felt a genuine kinship, but she doubted the friendliness would last if Callum's sister knew the whole truth.

'When are you due?' Ellie asked.

Stella hesitated. Admitting to dates could incriminate her—but then so would avoiding the question. Her baby was due in October, but she added a couple of weeks to her dates and left her answer vague. 'Before Christmas.'

Ellie frowned. 'Callum might need to do a final muster before the wet season sets in. Could be dicey. Have you booked into Mount Isa hospital or are you going in to the coast?'

'We haven't really talked about that yet.'

They could hear Ellie's husband, Andrew, calling to her. 'Coming,' she called back. To Stella she said, 'Better get all the hospital stuff sorted out straight away. It can catch up with you sooner than you think.'

'OK. I will. Thanks.' Stella followed her out of the kitchen. In the doorway, she said, 'Ellie, I haven't wanted to broadcast news about the baby just yet.'

'I don't blame you. Dad's a bit of a dinosaur. Let him get used to one bit of startling news at a time.' She slipped an arm around Stella's shoulder and gave it a squeeze. 'I'm just so wrapped about you and Callum. Anyone can see how into each other you two are.'

Gulp! Stella managed an awkward smile and nodded and then they joined everyone on the front veranda and soon she was absorbed in the general fuss and clamour of farewells. The two young families piled into their four-wheel drive vehicles and Callum's parents headed off for the light plane which Senator Roper would fly back to Mount Isa.

Stella and Callum were left standing alone at the top of Birralee's steps. She felt exhausted, confused and guilty.

'Thank God that's over,' Callum said, staring grimly at the diminishing speck of his parents' aircraft.

They were alone again. All around them stretched the wide, silent plains and the even wider, more silent skies of the outback. Alone—surrounded by an ancient land—trees, rocks and sky—and not another human within eighty kilometres.

Maybe Callum was thinking about this, too. In profile, his face was hard and stony and, when he looked at her, the warmth that had filled his eyes at lunch-time was replaced by a cold, bleak regret. She guessed at once that he was feeling very badly about so much deception.

'Thank you for covering for me,' she said.

His sigh was long, loud and bitter. 'I know this marriage was my idea, but I didn't enjoy pulling the wool over my parents' eyes.'

Before she could respond, he strode away as if he couldn't bear to talk about it. With leaden steps, and an even heavier heart, she went back into the house to do her penance at the mountain of dirty dishes in the kitchen.

A fortnight later, a letter arrived from Callum's father. Stella left it on the sideboard with the other mail, and when Callum came home in the evening she watched as he stood, with his back to her, slit the envelope and scanned the hand-written page. She saw his deep frown and a tremor of fear skittered through her.

When he'd finished, he folded the letter slowly and then examined other pages of printed matter that had come with it. Finally, he thrust everything back in the envelope and stood tapping it against his thigh as he stared at the floor.

She had to ask. 'Is something the matter?'

He sighed. 'You may as well read it.' Unsmiling, he handed her the envelope.

'Are you sure you want me to?'

He nodded, but he looked so unhappy her hands shook as she pulled the fine sheet of letter paper away from the others and read.

Dear Callum,

Because of the speed with which you married (which in my view fell just short of elopement), your mother and I haven't had a chance to give you a wedding present.

As you know, Birralee has been in the family for almost one hundred years and it would have been going to you and Scott eventually. I made handsome settlements on the girls when they were married. And so, son, Callum Angus Roper is now the official owner of the family's business. Birralee Pastoral Company is yours. It's all signed and sealed.

Look after the place and it will take care of you. And just make sure that you and Stella get on with the job of raising a family so you can hand it on when the time comes.

Love,

Dad

Stella read the letter through twice. She felt terrible. Callum's family were placing so much weight on this marriage. 'You weren't expecting anything like this?' she asked.

He shrugged. 'I doubt it would have happened if Scott hadn't died. Knowing my old man, it probably wouldn't have happened if I hadn't married.'

'You don't sound very happy.'

'I don't know. I can see Mum's hand in all this and I—' He clamped his lips together as if he had to hold back what he really wanted to say.

'You wish you could have told her the truth.'

He gave another shrug.

She hated to see him looking so unhappy. Especially when it was her fault. 'Why don't you let me tell your parents what we're doing?'

He couldn't have looked more shocked if she'd announced that she wanted to discuss their situation on talkback radio.

'Not now,' he snapped. 'They couldn't handle it. It'll be different when there's a grandchild. That will help to make up for—' His fists clenched, and for a long tortuous moment he stared at her.

'—For their disappointment when they realise you didn't marry for love?' Stella supplied.

His eyes seemed to burn into her and she sensed that he was struggling with a vicious inner demon. Then his lip curled. 'My mother's always been a hopeless romantic. She loves weddings. But she loves babies, too. She'll be tickled pink about your baby.'

Her baby. *The Roper family's baby.* A cold shiver crept through her and settled around her heart as she pictured her baby surrounded by Scott's family.

Now that she'd met them, she could fill in details. She could see their faces, voices and mannerisms. Her baby would love them and she'd be a sunshiny, happy soul just like Ellie's Penny.

Except…except…among those people who hugged and loved her baby…its mother would be missing.

Oh, hell! Her whole body was trembling. She had to shake that thought aside. It wouldn't do to give in to self-pity at this stage of the project, when it was Callum who deserved her concern.

For her, the future held adventure and hope—the TV documentary and who knew what else? But Callum had little choice about his future. Between them, she, Scott and his parents had put restrictions on his life, until they'd reduced it to something as predictable and unvarying as the ebb and flow of the tides. Callum would work Birralee and raise her child.

She watched him now as he stood stiffly in the middle of the room. 'I've never asked what you had planned for your future before—before I came along and made a mess of your life.'

He looked away. 'No use talking about what might have been.'

'When I'm gone, maybe you'll—get married again. I mean, properly married.' Nervously, she ran her hands through her hair.

'Maybe.' For another scorching minute, his burning gaze returned to her. He stared at her hands as she fiddled with her hair and she found herself dropping them behind her back.

'Your family will forgive you, Callum,' she said gently, searching for ways to soothe his obvious pain. 'They *love* you.'

A muscle pulsed in his cheek, but he didn't answer.

Stella rushed on, trying to find words to make him feel better, to make them both feel better. 'When they realise why you married me—that you did it out of love for Scott and his baby—they won't be angry with you.'

Again, he said nothing. In tormented silence, she watched as he put the letter in his pocket and walked out of the room.

CHAPTER NINE

FOR CALLUM, THE day-to-day business of living with Stella got harder and harder. On the surface things were fine. She became much more confident with cooking and meal times became something to look forward to.

She also became totally involved in researching the management methods of some of the really big cattle companies, and they talked for hours about his growing vision for Birralee now that it was in his sole care.

At times he got the feeling that she really loved the challenge of the outback, but then he worried that she was trying so hard at cooking and learning about station life to help her forget about Scott and to ward off her unhappiness.

And, each day, it became more and more difficult to hide his feelings for her. His efforts to avoid touching her bordered on the ridiculous. It was more than a straight physical thing. His mother had recognised that. She knew he was deeply in love with Stella and she'd told him how happy she was that he'd found the right woman at last.

But when Stella left him, his family would know that his heart was broken and the burden of this impending disappointment made his own situation worse.

What a mess! What a crazy, hopeless mess!

Time was marching on. Stella's figure was changing. In Callum's eyes, she grew more womanly, more beautiful each day as her shape expanded, but luckily she seemed unaware of his fascination.

Books on pregnancy and new clothes arrived for her and she modelled up and down the veranda. Dropping her gaze to her round tummy, she gave it a little pat. 'At least I'm starting to look pregnant and not just as if I've eaten too much.'

He wanted to tell her she looked gorgeous. Softer, sweeter—more womanly and desirable than ever. But what could be more stupid than messing up their careful plans with talk that sounded like seduction?

At times it was a relief to get away. He threw himself into new strategies for the management of Birralee, and one of his first decisions to help streamline production was to contract a top cattle vet to spey the female cattle he had ready for the live export market.

He hired Joe Ford whose new speying technique was basically painless and much faster than any method Callum was familiar with. The task was accomplished in a day. As they drove back to the homestead in the evening, Stella came flying down the back steps.

'Oh, thank heavens you're still here,' she said to Joe as he clambered out of the truck.

'What's the problem?' Callum's heart picked up pace when he saw her wild-eyed, worried look.

'It's Oscar.'

He frowned. 'Oscar?'

'Yes. He's looking terribly sick.'

Embarrassed, Callum explained to the vet. 'Oscar's a pet budgerigar.'

Joe cleared his throat. 'I—I see.'

Wringing her hands together, Stella pleaded, 'Can you come and take a look at him, please? I'm afraid he's dreadfully sick.'

'Stella, Joe's a cattle vet. He's not a budgerigar doctor. I don't think—'

Whirling back to face Callum, her eyes flashed sparks. 'A vet's a vet and Oscar needs a vet. Surely vets are like doctors.' She shot a sharp glance in Joe's direction. 'Don't you take some kind of oath to protect all animal life?'

Joe gave a helpless shrug. 'I'll take a quick look.'

'Thank you.' Hurrying ahead, she led the way to the kitchen and very soon all three of them were staring at the bird as it huddled on the bottom of the cage looking thoroughly miserable.

'He certainly looks pretty crook,' Callum admitted.

'You can do something, can't you?' Stella asked Joe. Her grey eyes were pleading and her face was far too pale.

Joe looked quite shamefaced as he shook his head. 'I'm sorry, but I don't think I can.'

She stared at him, appalled. 'But you have to. You're a vet. If you can fix a great big bull, surely you can fix a tiny little bird!'

'That's the trouble,' Joe said, shuffling his feet uncomfortably. 'I specialise in large animals. Large-animal vets are quite separate from small—'

Stella didn't wait to hear more. 'In Sydney when Oscar was sick, I took him to an excellent female vet and she weighed him in a little basket so she could tell how bad he was. Surely we can find some way to weigh him? I remember she told me that a healthy bird weighs about forty grams, but a sick one might only be thirty.'

Callum did his manful best to keep a straight face and wondered what Joe was making of this.

'She gave him antibiotics in a little plastic syringe and he was completely better in three days.'

'I'm sorry, but I don't carry antibiotics for budgerigars. Anything I have would kill him.'

She groaned melodramatically. 'I can't believe this! Honestly, who in their right minds would choose to live in the outback? Are you telling me there's absolutely nothing you can do for him?'

'If you keep him quiet and clean, he might recover.'

She ran a distracted hand through her hair and blinked her eyes.

'Stella,' Callum said. 'The trees out here are full of budgerigars. There are thousands of them—'

'*What are you saying?*' she yelled. 'I hope you're not suggesting that there's plenty more where Oscar came from.'

'I guess—I—'

'You have absolutely no idea what he means to me.'

She dashed out of the room leaving the two men to exchange embarrassed grimaces.

After Joe had flown off, Callum went to look for her and found her in the study, examining the spines of the books lined along the shelves. A pile of discarded books lay on the floor beside her.

'Don't you have anything about animal health?' she muttered between tensely gritted teeth.

'I really don't think we have anything that covers budgerigars.'

She let out an exasperated sigh and stood with her eyes downcast, her arms folded over the mound of her tummy and her chin jutting at a belligerent angle. Her foot tapped impatiently.

'I'm sorry, Stella. I shouldn't have said that about the other birds. I know how much Oscar means to you. You went to all the trouble of bringing him up here from Sydney and I've seen how carefully you look after him.'

'How would you feel if it was Mac?' she demanded.

'I'd be pretty cut up,' he admitted and tactfully refrained from adding any clichés about a man's best friend.

He searched for ways to distract her from worrying about the bird but, no matter how hard he tried, he couldn't find the right words to cheer her. She stayed upset for the rest of the evening. Dinner was a very tense and tight-lipped affair.

Next morning, when Callum came into the kitchen, he saw immediately that Oscar hadn't improved. The bird was still huddled on the floor of the cage.

He heard Stella's footsteps coming down the hall. 'How is he?' she asked, white-lipped.

'Not much better, I'm afraid.'

'Oh, Callum, what are we going to do?' She stood beside the cage staring at the poor little creature, her restless fingers trailing helplessly up and down the bars of his cage.

Callum squeezed her shoulders gently. 'There's still a chance that he might pull through.'

She lifted her face, her mouth turned square and her eyes squinted and he knew she was making a huge effort to hold back tears. He couldn't resist drawing her closer and she sank into him, warm and unresisting, needing his support, which he gave gladly.

The bulge of her baby pressed against him and he felt an instant rush of overwhelming tenderness for her. For her, for her baby... even for the pathetic little bird she cared so much about.

She clung to him, burrowing her face into his shoulder. He gave in to the impulse to thread his fingers through her shiny black hair. It was as silky and soft as he knew it would be and slipped through his fingers like glossy satin ribbons.

He touched her cheek and her skin was as soft as wattle blossoms. He knew the rest of her was soft, too. Soft and warm and sweet and womanly and sexy as hell and...

She lifted her head and looked into his eyes and he could see the full force of her emotions. And he knew it was totally inappropriate, but all he could think of was taking her back to his room right then, and kissing her, losing himself in her.

'Poor Oscar,' he heard her say and he came zinging back to reality. 'I know I'm being pathetic about him,' she said, 'but he's the only pet I've ever owned. He's the only family I have. I don't know if I'll be able to bear it if he dies.'

He dropped his hands to his sides and tried to concentrate on her words. Tried not to think about sex.

'Maybe he's elderly. Maybe it's his time,' he suggested helplessly.

Shaking her head, she walked away from him and slumped into a chair at the kitchen table.

'Perhaps you should give in and have a little cry,' he suggested.

She shook her head. 'I can't. I mustn't.'

Puzzled, he pulled out another chair and sat opposite her. 'Hey, you're a woman. You're allowed to cry.'

Her chin lifted and she glared at him. 'That's sexist rubbish.'

Of course. This was Stella the feminist scientist—not one of his sisters. 'OK, I'll try again. You're very upset. Crying is supposed to help release your emotions.'

'But I can't cry,' she whispered.

They were looking straight into each other's eyes again and he saw a vulnerability in her that completely contradicted the harshness of her claim. 'Stella,' he said, 'what do you mean? Don't you ever cry?'

'No.'

'Not ever?'

She drew in a deep, shuddering breath. 'I can't possibly cry for a sick bird when I—I didn't even cry when my mother died.'

Fine hairs rose on the back of his neck as he recognised the significance of this moment. This was the taboo subject. Her mother.

Cautiously, he asked, 'When did your mother die?'

She stiffened.

'Were you very young?'

'I—I was fifteen.'

Only fifteen. 'And, at fifteen, you had already learned to hold back your tears?'

She didn't answer and he could picture the teenage Stella with her chin up, her shoulders back and her eyes glinting fiercely.

'You promised to tell me about your family sometime,' he reminded her gently.

She shook her head wearily. 'You might hate me if I do.'

'Hate you?' He was truly shocked.

'Your family are so perfect.' She patted her stomach and her voice was edged with bitterness as she said, 'Ruby will be inheriting thoroughbred genes from your side.'

'But Stella, what about your contribution? Your baby will have a mother who's a very clever scientist.'

'And a grandmother who was an alcoholic and a prostitute!'

She flung the words at him harshly, so harshly he almost flinched. But he knew that was what she expected. This was what she'd been trying to hide from him for so long.

Determined to show no sign of shock, he asked, 'So…did you live with your mother?'

'Now and again. In between a string of foster homes. She could never keep me for very long.'

'But she tried?'

'Oh, yes. She tried. Over and over.' She pressed her lips together and took a deep breath through her nose. 'I guess the maternal instincts were there, but the grog got in the way.'

'Well, you might have inherited her instincts. There's every chance you'll be a fantastic mother.'

She shook her head. 'I doubt it. Anyway, now you know why it's best that I leave my baby with you.'

This was another shock. 'You mean your real reason for going away is because you have no faith in yourself as a mother? It's not just the job in London?'

Stella covered her face with her hands. 'There are a thousand reasons why I'm going.'

He was tempted to suggest that running away never solved problems, but he suspected that it wouldn't be wise to start lecturing her right now when she'd waited so long to take him into her confidence. 'What about your father?'

Her lip curled. 'The news gets better and better. I know absolutely zilch about my father. Not even his name.' She looked impossibly tense as if she was waiting for his reaction to fall on her like a heavy blow. 'On my birth certificate it says, "Father Unknown".'

'That's tough.'

'Aren't you glad you know all this?'

What he knew was that he wanted to hold her again.

Her eyes narrowed. 'What would Senator Roper think of this news?'

'What he thinks is irrelevant.'

'Won't he be horrified that his grandchild has such a black pedigree?'

'Stella, in the outback we judge people by how they live day to day. When you're dealing with an unforgiving land, what counts is what a man does now. Today. The past no longer matters. Right now I'm looking at you and I'm seeing a very clever woman, who's achieved a great deal on her own, without any family support. That takes guts.'

She smiled wanly, reached over and patted his hand. 'Thanks.' After a pause, she added, 'I want Scott's baby to experience your kind of family. Not mine. Yours is such a jolly perfect family— stable, salt of the earth and all that.'

'I can't imagine how hard it must be to have no idea who your father is.'

Her face crumpled and for a moment he thought that this time she would let a tear or two fall. But no. She took another deep breath and fixed him with a steady gaze. 'That's why you must tell Ruby all about Scott. I want her to know everything about her father. What a great guy he was.'

'Yeah.' His throat felt rough and choked. 'You—you can count on that.'

'The only thing my mother ever told me about my father was that he was a university professor. I was born when she was quite young—before she went downhill so to speak.'

'Well, there you go!' Callum exclaimed. 'A professor. At least you know where all those brains come from.'

'When I was at university, I used to look at all the professors and try to guess if my father was one of them. I would think that I could be sitting in his lectures—right under his nose—and he would never know about me. There was one professor of physics I really liked. He was incredibly clever and kind and he cracked jokes that were actually funny.' Her mouth tilted. 'I used to pretend he was my father.'

'You never know. I suppose there's a small chance that he might have been. You could probably try to find out if you wanted to.'

She shook her head. 'I wouldn't want to lay that kind of shock at his feet. Anyhow, I could never imagine him getting together with Marlene.'

'Was that your mother's name?'

'Yeah.'

'Did she look like you?'

Stella shrugged. 'A bit.' Then she gave a self-deprecating little laugh. 'A lot.'

Callum had no problems imaging a kind, clever guy wanting to get together with a woman who looked like Stella.

'I don't like to think about either of my parents very often.'

So is that why you're running away? Do you want your baby to grow up without the baggage of either of her parents? The questions hovered in his mind, but this wasn't the right moment to ask them. Not when she was feeling so low.

Suddenly her head jerked up and she stared past him, her eyes wide and a blast of joy lit her features. 'Callum, look at Oscar!'

He turned to see the little bird hopping across the floor of the cage to peck at his tray of seed.

'He's eating!' she cried.

'Blow me down.'

She jumped up and hurried over to the cage. 'Do you think he's better?'

'It's got to be a good sign,' Callum said, coming to join her. And as he stood watching the hope and happiness linger in Stella's eyes, he wished to hell he could find a way to make her look at him that way.

CHAPTER TEN

STELLA THOUGHT SHE knew about weather, but experiencing steamy northern temperatures was quite different from recording them on a chart. As the weeks passed and her stomach grew rounder, the days grew hotter. She longed for the cool southerly winds that brought relief to hot days in Sydney, but she knew she hoped in vain.

It was even too hot for Callum to work. He'd spent several afternoons stretched on the sofa, reading through a pile of cattle industry journals with his shirt unbuttoned and wearing denim shorts rather than his usual jeans.

Oscar had recovered, thank God, but he'd given her such a terrible fright that she fussed over him more than ever. Today she'd placed a pedestal fan near his cage in the kitchen and now she was trying to find a comfortable spot for herself on the lounge carpet directly under the ceiling fan. She was dressed in a skimpy pink T-shirt-style smock and she knew she looked a mess.

Given the size of her tummy, she was quite certain she looked more like a giant strawberry than a human being. And because it was too hot to have her hair down, she'd scrunched it into a knot on top of her head, but fine bits of it kept escaping.

She was having another go at reading a book about childbirth. When the book had first arrived, she'd skimmed through it and hadn't liked what she'd found. Everything about giving birth had sounded way too gruesome and she'd filed the book away and had tried to put the whole subject out of her mind.

But now she was eight months' pregnant and the issue was becoming harder to ignore. Callum's mother and sisters had been asking her if she was preparing for natural childbirth. And on her regular trips to Mount Isa, the midwife at the hospital kept mentioning the benefits of breathing techniques, birthing positions and relaxation exercises.

Relaxation? They had to be joking.

She had just read an entire chapter of relaxation exercises and had tried them out and none of them seemed to work. Flipping back to the beginning, she puffed out her lips with a resigned sigh and decided she had better give it one more try.

Imagine you're floating on a huge fluffy cloud. You're sinking into it. Let it support you totally. Your whole body is relaxing. First your feet and legs let go, then your hips, your torso, your chest. Breathe in regularly and slowly.

A fly buzzed past her nose and settled on her foot. She tried to ignore it, but eventually she had to shake it away.

'Damn,' she muttered. And that was the end of her relaxation. She'd have to start on the fluffy cloud all over again.

Callum lowered his journal and looked at her. His gaze rested on her feet and she saw his frown.

'You don't paint your toenails any more.'

'No, I've given up.'

'Any particular reason?'

'A very simple one, Callum. I can't.'

His frown deepened. 'Why not? Have you run out of paint?'

She rolled her eyes. Men could be so dense. 'Haven't you noticed? There's an enormous bump where my waist used to be, which means I can't reach my toes. Half the time I can't even see them.'

He dropped the magazine and sat up, swinging his long legs over the edge of the sofa. His unbuttoned shirt fell open, offering her a tempting view of his very masculine chest with its nice shadowing of dark hair.

He smiled. 'We'll have to do something about this. Stella without toenail polish is like—like the Mona Lisa without her smile, the Statue of Liberty without her lamp—'

'It's not that big a deal.'

His eyes widened and it was hard to tell if he was making fun of her or deadly serious. 'I mean it, Stella. We can't have you going around with your toenails bare. Not that there's anything wrong with your nails, but they should be coloured. They're an important part of who you are.'

'You really think so?'

'Too right.'

She wanted to give him a hug, but that would be silly since she and Callum were avoiding that kind of closeness. But how had he guessed that her painted toenails were important to her, like a badge of courage? How did he know that she'd hated not being able to reach them any more?

Ever since she'd been little when one of her foster mothers had told her that her face was plain but she had pretty feet, she'd been pathetically vain about her feet.

Now an unexpected glow warmed her insides. Callum understood. He cared.

'Would you like me to paint them for you?' he asked.

She hid her pleased surprise behind a mocking chuckle. 'I'd like to see you try.'

His eyebrows rose. 'You don't think I could do it?'

'I can't imagine it.'

He stood up and towered above her and his smile broadened to a grin. 'I'm not going to let a slight like that go unchallenged, young lady. Prepare to have your toenails painted by an expert.'

Oh, heavens, he was serious. Suddenly she pictured his big brown hands holding her feet. 'I was joking,' she cried. 'I don't need them painted.'

'Yes, you do. Now, don't get up. Tell me where you keep all the toenail stuff.'

'Um…' Stella gulped. This was silly. She and Callum didn't do this kind of thing. It was too—too intimate.

'If you don't tell me, I'll just hunt around in your bathroom till I find what I need,' he said.

Secretly thrilled, she gave in. 'There's a blue and silver striped bag in the cupboard on the left.'

'I'll be right back.'

He was gone before she could voice a protest, and back before she'd thought up an excuse. By the time he was kneeling on the carpet beside her, with his shirt still undone and all that naked chest exposed, her brain was going into meltdown. Heavens! She needed to think of a smart retort that would send him away again.

She and Callum avoided situations like this. It was as if they'd tacitly agreed that anything remotely touchy-feely was no-go territory. For Stella's part, she still feared the powerful attraction she felt for him. She feared losing control and she suspected that, if Callum tempted her, there was every chance her control would scatter to the winds.

For weeks now, an uncomfortable chemistry had been mounting between them. If they were sensible—if they kept their distance—it stayed at an only-just-bearable low simmer.

So far they'd been sensible.

So what on earth did Callum think he was doing? How could he spoil it all now by playing with her feet? Maybe he thought her feet were a safe extremity but, as far as Stella was concerned, having Callum touch any part of her body posed a problem.

He unzipped the pack and pulled out several bottles of nail polish. 'What colour would you like? Blue?'

'Pale pink would be safer. If you muck it up, it won't be so noticeable.'

'If I muck it up!' He managed to look affronted. 'I'd appreciate a little more faith, woman. If I can paint a machinery shed, I can paint a toenail.' He selected a bottle of Baby Blush. 'This one do?'

She nodded.

'Are you comfortable?'

Before she could answer, he dragged an armchair closer and piled a mountain of cushions between her back and the chair.

'That's great. Thanks.'

'OK. Let's see.' He settled comfortably in front of her and held her foot between his legs and she tried not to look at his chest, or the latent power in his bare thighs, or—*gulp*—the very masculine shape that strained against the centre seam of his denim shorts.

'Now, what do I have to do?' he asked. 'Do I need to sand your nails back? Is there an undercoat that goes on first?'

'Just a coat of colour will be fine,' she said breathlessly.

Carefully, he shook the little pot of polish, then slowly unscrewed the lid and extracted the tiny brush.

Stella smiled as she watched the intense concentration on his face as he wiped excess polish from the brush and began to apply paint to the nail of her big toe with the serious attention of a heart surgeon. He looked so dreadfully conscientious, she wanted to giggle.

'Callum, you can lighten up on this. It's not as if anyone else is going to see my feet. *I* only glimpse them occasionally these days.'

He didn't answer, didn't even acknowledge that he'd heard her, as he drew a final stripe of colour neatly over the nail. Bending his head, he blew gently on her toe and Stella felt so suddenly hot, she knew she must be blushing. He looked at the next toe and frowned.

'There's a toe separator in the bag,' she told him.

'A toe separator,' he murmured, but he didn't seem too interested in hunting for it. Instead of rummaging through her bag, he put the brush back into the pot, re-screwed the cap, blew on her nail once again and then ran his finger down the little valley between her big toe and the next.

What was he doing?

His eyes were downcast, concentrating on her foot, so she couldn't see his expression. And perhaps it was just as well he wasn't looking at her face. He might see how hot and bothered she was feeling. 'That toe will be dry. You can keep on going.'

He acted as if he hadn't heard her and began to trace his fingers with teasing slowness between the rest of her toes.

'Callum,' she whispered.

'Just separating them.' He looked up. Their gazes locked and her insides went into free fall when she saw the languid burning in his eyes.

'You're supposed to be painting my nails, not giving me a foot massage.'

'Patience,' he murmured. But instead of returning to the task, he trailed his hand down the sole of her foot. Her heart began to clatter as he cupped her heel in the palm of one hand while he rubbed gentle circles around the tip of each toe. 'Don't you like this?'

Oh, help! This shouldn't be happening. Not with Callum. He shouldn't be touching her like this. It felt so incredible. Each touch seemed to reach deep inside her. Too deep. Too much. 'I hate it,' she whispered.

'Liar.' He lowered his mouth and kissed the inner curve of her arch.

Flaming rivers rippled under her skin and spread like a runaway fire from her toes, up her legs and along the insides of her thighs until they pooled low and urgent inside her. *She mustn't moan.* 'What—what do you think you're doing?'

His smile was both shy and wild and it definitely spelled danger. 'I don't know. What do you think I'm doing?'

Trying to seduce me? With total success! 'Maybe you have heatstroke?'

'Can't be heatstroke. Feels too good.' He was kissing her toes. No, not just kissing them—he was running his tongue over their sensitive tips. And it felt—

Stella was coming undone. Slowly, quickly, she wasn't sure. The lazy afternoon seemed to be spinning away as her sense of time and place melted into *now* and *this.*

He lowered one foot and took up the other and his smile lost any trace of shyness as he held her foot against his thigh.

'Callum, we shouldn't be—' she cried, but even as she said it she was pushing her foot boldly forward, sliding it out of his hand until she touched him. She couldn't help herself. She had to touch him. Through his shorts. *Right there!*

He stilled. 'Stella, what do you think you're doing?'

'I don't know,' she whispered, feeling too hot, too gone to think. All she wanted was to feel. To feel Callum at last.

She ran daring toes over the tough cotton of his shorts, and the fever inside her roared as she felt his response surge hard beneath her foot. She heard her own gasps—heard his groan.

And next minute, he was pulling her down beside him on the carpet. Cushions scattered and his mouth turned savage and hungry.

It was terrifying yet wonderful! They'd waited too long for this. Far too long. Too many days, weeks, months of not touching. Now, every good intention exploded and scattered all around them.

Callum kissed her mouth and she adored the feel and the taste of him, loved the deep thrust of his tongue, so male and wonderfully intimate. So good. So right.

She ran excited fingers through the hair on his chest and shivered with pleasure as he kissed her neck. When his mouth found her breasts through the thin cotton of her dress, she couldn't hold back soft moans as she arched and yearned for more. Oh, yes! Yes!

He whispered her name and it had never sounded so lovely, so sexy.

She could tell he was being careful not to hurt her baby, but their bodies strained for the closest possible contact.

'We mustn't,' she protested weakly.

'I know. I know.'

'But I want you,' she cried. And she did. There had never been a time when she'd felt such wanting. She had never felt like this with Scott. Never. Now she accepted the truth that she'd always wanted this man.

'Oh, God, Stella.'

They were on fire. It was far too late to pull back.

But surely they couldn't take the last plunging leap into complete intimacy?

'Just let me touch you, Stella.'

'Oh, yes, Callum!'

Yes! She was losing control. The overwhelming urgency in her demanded release. No more protests. No more words. Too late to fear this. All she wanted was to surrender.

His impatient mouth covered hers again and, pushing her clothing aside, his hand grew more daring.

His caresses became more loving, each touch an intimate gift. And then she was lost, disintegrating in a wild, glorious star burst.

Lifting damp strands of hair away from her cheek, Callum tucked them behind her ear and watched as she opened her beautiful eyes. Eyes that shimmered with such strong emotion that his heart leapt like a high-vaulting stallion.

He almost said something crazy. A dead give-away like, *I think I love you.* But memories of that first time in Sydney—that other time when their strong attraction had flared out of control—kept him quiet. He had scared her off then.

Now, despite the self-conscious shyness in her eyes, she was smiling up at him. 'If that's how you paint toenails—you must be amazing—in—in bed.'

He smiled. 'With you I'd win medals.'

She blushed and he watched as her smile turned wistful and dreamy. Suddenly she looked very young and vulnerable and guilt sent his heart plummeting. Hell! She'd been trusting him to keep his promise that there would be no intimacy in their marriage. 'But we can't find out, Stella, can we?'

Her smile vanished. 'No, of course not.'

Their glances slid away and he sat very still beside her on the carpet with his hands locked around his bent knees. His guilty thoughts seemed to hover unspoken in the steamy room and the only sound was Mac's panting as he lay sprawled in the hallway leading out to the veranda.

Stella was the first to move. She propped herself up on one elbow and studied Callum with a typically level Stella-style gaze. 'You broke your promise.'

He nodded and grimaced. 'I did. I'm sorry.' What else could he say? If he tried to explain his actions, he would end up telling her how he really felt about her and that could scare her off completely.

When she made no response, he cleared his throat. 'About those toenails.'

'What about them?'

'I—I still want to paint them. I've become used to seeing all those different colours trotting around the place.'

Awkwardly, she pushed herself higher until she was sitting cross-legged on the carpet. 'Callum, is this your way of saying let's not talk about what just happened?'

His airways seemed to contract. 'No. We can talk about it.'

'Do you think it was a mistake?'

'Well, I guess it was, but it was my mistake, not yours.'

She dropped her gaze. 'It doesn't change anything, does it?'

'How do you mean?'

The colour in her cheeks deepened. 'What I mean is—it was just sparks, wasn't it? Just chemistry? Nothing deep and meaningful.'

Fear flickered in her eyes and a stab of regret speared his heart. What a dent to the ego this girl was. It was just as he'd feared. The last thing Stella Lassiter wanted was a deep and meaningful relationship with Scott Roper's brother.

He shook his head slowly. 'Don't worry, Stella. I'm sure what just happened was simply the result of a healthy man and a woman spending too much time alone together in the bush.'

Nervously, she chewed at her lip and pulled at a loose thread in the carpet. 'We'd really stuff things up if we take this any further.'

He tried for a grin, but it faltered. 'Of course.'

'You made it very clear about this marriage and legalities—'

'Yeah. From a legal point of view, things would be more complicated if we consummate the marriage.'

She pulled harder on the thread until it began to unravel. 'I hope you don't think I'd try to get my hands on a share of Birralee.'

Callum stared at her. 'That sounded like a round about way of saying you want to have sex with me.'

Her face turned bright red and she almost choked on her shocked gasp. 'No! Heavens, no! Of course, I didn't mean—'

'OK, OK!' He jumped in quickly before she expanded her protest into a five-minute speech. 'Look, I'm not worried that you're going to start demanding a share of this property. I'm just trying to make things easier for everyone concerned when you—when you come back from London.'

The thread in her hand snapped.

His heart stilled. 'You still want to go away, don't you?'

'I—think so,' she whispered.

A small boulder seemed to wedge itself in his throat. 'You're not sure?'

She sighed and gave her middle a pat. 'These days I can't seem to think beyond this little one's arrival.'

'That's—that's understandable.'

He laid his hand beside hers on her stomach. It was so very round and tight and burgeoning with life. He felt the baby move. The kick was surprisingly strong. He could feel the outline of the little foot and he could picture the baby curled safely inside Stella's womb, ready and eager to escape into the world. He was gripped by a sudden urge to see it, to hold it in his arms. 'It won't be long now,' he said gently.

There was a sudden flash of panic in her eyes. Her whole body seemed to sag and her attention darted to the book she'd been reading. 'Don't remind me,' she whispered.

'Are you scared?'

'Too right.'

He picked the book up. 'What about all this reading you've been doing? Hasn't it been any help?'

She shrugged.

'I'm sure you'll be OK, Stell. You're young and healthy and I've promised to make sure you fly into Mount Isa in plenty of time.'

'I know. But—oh, Callum. There's more to having a baby than arriving at the hospital in time. I don't know if I can bear the thought of all that pain. I think I'm going to be queen of the wimps.'

'You'll be OK. You're tough.'

She compressed her lips and closed her eyes as if she was holding back tears. 'It's all bluff. Deep down I'm a quivering coward.'

He saw the unmistakable tension in her and remembered her fears about motherhood. He'd seen plenty of animals in labour and had a fair idea how fear could make the process so much more difficult.

Suddenly he was afraid for her. Given her circumstances, there was a good chance she would fight against giving birth rather than working with it. That could mean she would have a very hard time.

He looked at the book in his hands. 'How about I read up on

all this childbirth stuff, too? Maybe I could help somehow—be
your coach.'

The wash of relief in her face was amazing. Her smile couldn't
have been warmer if he'd offered to buy her the moon and the stars.
'Would you really do that?'

His heart quaked at the thought of seeing her suffer, but he'd
leap tall buildings in a single bound if it made her look at him that
way. 'Yeah. I'll be there if you want me to.'

'Oh, Callum,' she cried and she threw herself forward, wrapping her arms around him. 'That would be so wonderful. I know
I could manage if you were there.'

It was hard to believe this was Stella. Stella the tough girl. The
feminist scientist. She was looking at him with eyes that were
glowing with trust and she was literally begging him to be her
knight in shining armour.

And he couldn't resist cupping her face in his hands and dipping his mouth to hers. He had to taste again the sweet, moist
lushness of her parted lips. 'I'll be there,' he murmured. 'We'll be
a great team.'

'Promise?'

'I promise.'

'What if you're away on a muster or something when I go into
labour?'

He kissed the tip of her nose, and stroked her soft lower lip with
his thumb. 'We've each got a satellite phone. I'll keep mine with
me all the time and, come hell or high water, I'll be there with you,
Stella. I promise.'

Stella knew Callum was a man of his word, but she was truly
surprised by how seriously he approached the preparation for her
labour. After two weeks with him as her personal childbirth coach,
she was beginning to feel like an athlete training for a big race.

He read every book she'd bought and each evening he made her
practise the relaxation exercises and the various breathing techniques over and over until he was satisfied that she was totally familiar with them.

But the best part was how good she felt just knowing that he was going to be there in the delivery room with her, checking her breathing, helping her to relax, cheering her on to the finish line.

The electric tension still zapped between them, but now that they'd discussed it they could deal with it more easily. At least that was what Stella tried to tell herself. But, in reality, she was finding it harder than ever to ignore the way she felt about Callum.

The way she felt about leaving him! The paperwork from the British television network had been forwarded from Sydney confirming what she'd known all along: she was expected to arrive in London in eight weeks' time.

Eight weeks! It was as if she'd been running merrily along through an obstacle course, pretending that because she couldn't see the hurdles they weren't there. Now she'd run smack bang into the big one.

'What's that?' Callum asked when he saw the official-looking yellow envelope.

'Oh, just some forms I have to fill out.'

Vertical creases ran between his brows. 'So this is it, the final commitment?'

'Yes.' Suddenly she could hardly breathe.

Callum stood stock still before her and she saw his hands clench tightly against his sides. He looked so unexpectedly white and *sick*, Stella's heart boomed like a bass drum.

And in a flash she knew exactly how she felt about going. If he told her not to sign the papers, she would stay here. All he had to do was say that he needed her.

She could keep her baby and she could keep him. Was it selfish to want them both? Her heart twisted so sharply it was hard to think straight. Surely if she stayed here she could make herself useful. With a background in environmental studies there were many ways she could adapt her knowledge to assist a cattleman.

Oh, Lord, should I tell him that?

Her mouth opened, the words quivering on her lips, but suddenly Callum gave a shake as if he were ridding himself of an unwanted thought. 'You'd better get everything signed, sealed and delivered straight away,' he said. 'In case you have to dash off to hospital. You'd never forgive yourself if you forgot to post important stuff like that.'

She felt the blast of disappointment like a slap in the face. He sounded so matter-of-fact. Perhaps she'd imagined that fleeting moment when he looked ill at the thought of her leaving?

'I suppose I should send them straight back.' She couldn't hold back a sigh.

'You wouldn't want to mess things up at this stage.'

'No.'

Strange how truly dreadful she felt. Lately she'd found it more and more difficult to dredge up excitement about the job overseas. Other dreams kept nudging it aside. Dreams of the little human being who was sharing her body. A little pink and white baby. Someone who called her Mummy.

When she tried to picture herself as part of a fascinating team of scientists and television people working their way around European coastlines, she kept seeing the red earth and blue skies of the outback. And the recognition of colleagues didn't seem nearly as important now as the smiling approval of honey-brown eyes.

But of course, Callum was right.

She couldn't give up on London now and she had no right to hold him to this marriage. It would be unfair after he'd given up so much for her to suddenly change her mind and plead with him to let her stay. If he'd wanted her to stay, he would have admitted it weeks ago, after they'd been so intimate.

After dinner, she filled in the forms, signed them and slipped them into a clean envelope ready for the mail truck in the morning.

Callum saw the envelope sitting ready, but made no further comment. Instead he told her, 'There's a section of fence down near the Paroo gorge. I'm rather unhappy about it. Some of the cattle have already found their way through it and if they get right down into that really wild country, I'll have hell's own job getting them out again.'

'So you want to go out there tomorrow?'

'I should muster those strays back through the fence. But it's further away from base than I like to go these days.'

Stella tried to squash a little spurt of panic. 'Go, Callum. The baby isn't due for another two weeks and apparently first babies are nearly always late.'

His eyes were dark with concern. 'You're sure you'll be OK?'

'Of course. I can always get you on the satellite phone if I have to, but I haven't felt the faintest twinge.'

'I'll be as quick as I can.'

He left in the four-wheel drive straight after breakfast, taking Nugget and Cleo, two of the station's working dogs and his stallion, Blackjack, in a trailer. Mac stayed behind at the homestead.

'To keep you company,' Callum told Stella. 'Don't mention the word muster in his hearing or he'll twig that we've gone without him and he'll spend the whole morning whining.'

When he reached the section of broken fence, he parked the vehicle and continued on horseback, crossing a wide and sandy river-bed. Gums grew in the river-bed and in a narrow strip along each bank. On the far side he reached the rough scrub where the cattle were most likely to have strayed.

There was a good chance the herd had been joined by some cleanskins—wild cattle that had never seen a branding iron, a drench gun or an ear tag. Some might never have seen a human.

Mustering on his own wasn't wise, but with Stella's time drawing so close he didn't want to delay things by waiting till one of his neighbours was free to lend a hand.

He held the reins lightly in one hand, while with the other he tugged at his akubra, pulling it low over his eyes as protection from the savage brilliance of the sun.

In the past, he'd always found that he could think more clearly when he was riding, but this morning, as he trailed through the scrub, he didn't want to think, didn't want to remember how he'd felt last night when he'd seen the large official envelope addressed to Stella. Didn't want to think about how he felt about her, how bone-deep lonely he would be when she was gone.

He kept his eyes peeled looking for colour, for the movement that would betray the presence of the herd but, in spite of his concentration, thoughts of Stella elbowed their way back into his head.

He'd always maintained that a man in the bush developed a gut instinct for recognising a certain rightness about some things and as he rode this morning, taking his fill of the landscape he loved, the more he thought, the more he became absolutely, no-doubt-about-it dead certain that he knew what was right for him—and for Stella, the baby, Mac, even Oscar, damn it.

They should all be together at Birralee. For ever.

He'd been crazy to try to pretend things should be any other way.

No matter how hard he tried to shake the conviction, it wouldn't budge. Hell, it was the truth and he had to tell Stella. It was time to wear his heart on his sleeve. To be honest and up front.

She could go to London if she had to, but then she had to come back to him. *Soon as the time's up, I'll get her. Even if I have to track her down in some Norwegian fjord, I'm going to get her and bring her back.*

With that decision made, his heart felt lighter. Just as soon as he'd found these flaming cattle, he'd tell her.

Topping a slight rise, he saw the herd scattered below. He and the dogs moved in quickly. Nugget, the speedier animal, expertly covered the far wing of the herd while Cleo took the other flank and Callum, yelling fiercely and cracking his whip, came at them from behind.

Years of experience had taught him how to read cattle and he was ready for the cantankerous scrub bull when it charged. With an angry roar and a loud crack of his stock whip, he turned it from its frenzied dash towards the heavy timber to his right and soon it was back in with the herd, not happy, but more subdued.

Confident that the dogs could handle the mob, he made a quick check of the gullies to the left. There were stragglers there, too. Digging in his heels, he pushed Blackjack down the rocky shale, anxious to get the job over, urging him further down the steep gully, closer to the rogue beasts.

Neither he nor Blackjack saw the melon hole. Without warning, he felt the horse lose balance beneath him. He fought to stay in the saddle, but next moment his valiant, sturdy stallion was pitching forward and Callum was thrown.

CHAPTER ELEVEN

IT WAS A bad fall. As Callum hit the ground, his right foot caught in the stirrup and he felt the sharp-shooting agony of his ankle being wrenched apart. Damn it to hell! He'd broken bones.

Rocky shale dug into his back and he gritted his teeth as he lay there, fighting back pain while he waited for the world to stop spinning and his vision to clear.

Eventually he could turn his head. Squinting against the cruel sun that blazed directly overhead, he made out the dark shape of Blackjack standing nearby. The startled animal was shaking. But at least he hadn't bolted and he didn't look hurt. That was a relief.

Callum knew what he had to do. There was no time to examine his injury. He had to move very quickly, before the ankle went cold and shock set in. Swallowing a groan, he edged himself up the slope. Just a little closer and with a clumsy lurch, he was able to reach for the dangling reins.

It was only sheer strength of will that got him to his feet. Just for a moment he had to take his weight on his busted leg while he clung to the saddle and yelled curses as he raised his good foot into the stirrups.

Waves of dizziness claimed him as he slumped forward over the saddle. Then, grimacing with the effort, he unbuttoned his shirt pocket and extracted his phone. He hated the thought of ringing Stella and telling her what had happened, but it had to be done.

But as soon as he depressed the buttons, he realised the phone was dead. He checked the batteries, tried again. Still no luck. Must have damaged it during the fall.

He swore, knowing there was nothing for it but to get himself home.

A flick from the reins sent Blackjack heading back up the slope in the direction of the vehicle. On the ridge ahead of him, he could see the stragglers at the end of the mob. The dogs were still working them, leading them back to the fence, but there was no way he could mend the broken panel today, so the cattle would soon be back. A morning's effort wasted.

Molten blasts of pain were shooting through his ankle by the time the horse came to a halt next to the truck. It was hard to keep thinking and moving with so much discomfort, but somehow he managed to dismount.

But getting Blackjack back into the trailer was beyond him. Breathing hard, he leaned against the side of the truck, loosened the girth straps and let the saddle drop to the ground, then he slapped his hand against the stallion's rump and sent him to find his own way home.

By crikey, his leg was bad. Cursing bad. Callum let fly with another loud volley of swearing as he levered himself up into the truck. Once he was behind the steering wheel, he had to sit there for several minutes, taking big breaths, trying to beat the pain. Eventually, he whistled the dogs and they leapt into the ute's tray back.

OK. He wiped the sweat from his face with his shirt sleeve. Driving with his left foot on the accelerator was going to be tricky, but he had to do it. Had to get home as soon as he could.

A couple of times on the long trip back, shadowy darkness threatened to consume him and he thought he might lose consciousness. His energy seemed to be draining away and he wasn't sure how he kept the truck going, how he kept the steering wheel steady, how he kept his eyes open...

It seemed like twenty years before he reached Birralee, and by then he knew he couldn't move. All he could do was sit with his hand on the horn, waiting for Stella.

* * *

The long, drawn out blast of the truck's horn terrified Stella. Mac began barking immediately, terrifying her even more as she rushed to the window. It was Callum's truck. What on earth? What was wrong?

As quickly as her rotund shape would allow, she raced after Mac, through the house, across the veranda, down the steps and over the sloping paddock to the truck.

'Callum, what is it? Oh, my God, what's happened?'

He was slumped over the steering wheel and she saw dried blood on his forehead. *Was he dead?* Her heart seemed to crash against the wall of her chest and she thought it might burst through as she wrenched the driver's door open. 'Callum!' she screamed.

Oh, God, no! Callum! He couldn't be dead. Not like Scott. No, No!

'Callum!'

He lifted his head and his face was deathly white as he peered at her. 'Came off my horse.'

'Oh, heavens—' A sob disrupted the already ragged rhythm of her breathing and she gulped as she tried to draw in a breath. 'Where—where are you hurt?'

'Busted my leg.'

'What about your head?'

'Think it's OK.' He looked at her groggily. 'Stell, I want to talk to you.'

'What about?'

''bout us.'

'Bad timing,' she whispered. 'Don't try to talk now. Let's think about how we can get you out of there. Can you lean on me?'

'Don't even think about it—too heavy for you.'

'You need a doctor.'

''Fraid so.'

'Right.' She was calming down, forcing herself to think straight. She could do this. She wasn't about to cave in. She could be tough. Hadn't she already planned for medical emergencies like this? Just last week she'd programmed the number for the Flying Doctor into the phone and she'd written Birralee's latitude and longitude onto a wall chart in the office so she could give the doctor their precise location. 'Stay there, Callum. I'll be right back.'

'Not going anywhere.'

Again she was flying over the grass, but now, instead of feeling sheer terror, she felt purposeful. Frightened but *almost* composed. One press of the correct button and her call was connected straight to the flying doctor base. The news was good. There was a plane in their vicinity and it could be with them soon.

Next she found a blanket to keep Callum warm, and once she had that tucked around him she fled back to the kitchen to make him a Thermos of tea. Back down the steps and across the paddock.

As she lifted the strong, sweet brew to his lips, he muttered, 'You'll wear yourself out, Stell. I'm OK, don't fuss over me.'

'I like fussing over you.' He looked awful—his skin was pasty and caked with dust, sweat and dried blood. His eyes were bleary and bloodshot, his lips as colourless as rain.

'I want to talk to you.'

'Not now, Callum. Shut up and drink.'

'Since when did you get so bossy?'

'Since you showed signs of suffering from shock. At least the doctor's on his way.'

'He'll probably want to take me into Mount Isa.'

'Then, I'm coming, too. You can talk to me when we're safely on the plane.'

He groaned. 'Sorry about this. I've really stuffed up!'

'Of course you haven't. Now, listen, my hospital bag's already packed, but I'm going back to the house to pack a few things for you. And I'll ring the neighbours on Drayton Downs.'

'Good idea.'

'I'll ask them to take the dogs and Oscar over to their place.'

He nodded and grimaced, and his face leached whiter than ever.

'Oh, Callum, you poor darling.' She kissed his cold cheek. 'I feel bad about leaving you even to make another phone call.'

She couldn't be sure what deep emotion she saw in his dark gaze, then he closed his eyes. 'I'll be fine.'

By the time she had Callum's bag packed and had contacted the neighbours, the flying doctor's plane was already landing. He and the nurse hurried over the paddock. They were calm, friendly and competent, although they looked a little startled when they saw Stella's advanced state of pregnancy.

'I'm not the patient,' she told them as she led them behind the homestead to Callum in the truck. 'At least, not yet.'

In no time they had Callum out of the vehicle and were examining his ankle.

'We'll need X-rays,' the doctor told her. He gave Callum an injection for the pain. 'OK, mate. Let's immobilise this leg then we can get you back to town and patched up.'

Stella was glad she'd been prepared for her own trip to hospital. Everything was happening so quickly. In no time, they were carrying Callum on a stretcher to the small plane while she followed with the bags.

The take-off was smooth and soon Birralee homestead looked like a tiny matchbox way below them. The nurse was happy for Stella to sit beside Callum, holding his hand. Not that he noticed. He was so heavily sedated he wasn't aware of her presence.

'Don't you dare die,' she whispered, squeezing his hand tight. She felt frozen inside. The doctor had muttered something about the possibility of internal injuries. Callum couldn't die. He mustn't. He was too special, too kind, too loving...

Touching shaking fingers to the rough curls tumbling over his forehead, she felt a painful uncoiling of emotion. She gazed at the features she'd come to know so well and felt agony... It was as if a powerful emotion was being dragged to the surface from way deep inside her...from a place she'd kept locked up tightly since childhood.

The force of it was shaking her.

Oh, heavens! She'd tried to resist this! But she'd always known from the first night they'd met, that Callum had the power to make her feel this kind of out-of-control flooding of emotion.

As a little girl, she'd felt like this about her mother, Marlene, and she'd been hurt, time and again.

But Callum? She'd tried to resist his kisses, his kindness. Had he won? Lying there, completely unconscious, had he reached in and touched that place deep inside her where body meets soul?

'Callum,' she whispered, ignoring the nurse sitting quietly to one side. 'You mustn't die. Not you, too.' She bit back a sob. She mustn't cry. She mustn't. 'I think I might be in love with you. Really in love. I think Ruby and I might need you. Oh, Callum, I need to talk to you about it.'

Suddenly she remembered that he'd wanted to tell her something. Perhaps she should have listened, but at the time she'd been too frightened to stop for a chat.

Now, she was more frightened than ever.

Margaret Roper was understandably upset to get a phone call from the hospital.

'Right now Callum's in the theatre having his ankle set,' Stella told her. 'There are no internal injuries, thank heavens, and the doctors are confident that he will heal without complications.'

'Poor Callum!' Margaret sighed. 'And how unfortunate for you, dear, with the baby due so soon. This is the last thing you need.'

'Don't worry about me. I'm fine,' Stella assured her. It was almost the truth. For the past half-hour, she'd been getting cramp-like twinges in her lower abdomen and they were scaring the hell out of her, but there was absolutely no point in alarming her mother-in-law when she was thousands of kilometres away in Canberra.

'Where will you stay tonight, Stella?'

'I've found a motel right near the hospital.'

'Good. Now, don't you wear yourself out with running back and forth after Callum. Would you like me to fly up? Maybe there's some way I could help.'

A sharper twinge took Stella by surprise.

'Are you all right, dear?'

'Yes.' She took a deep breath. 'Thanks for the offer, Margaret, but I'm sure we'll be just fine. But I'd better go now. I'll get an early night and ring you in the morning with an update.'

'We'd certainly appreciate that. Take care, dear.'

Stella replaced the receiver and gave a little moan as she sagged against the wall of the telephone booth. Ouch! The cramps were moving out of twinge range and into something definite and scary.

Just as the books had predicted, they were gaining momentum. Like an advancing menace. And every pain was taking her down a path that would ultimately lead her away from Callum for ever. Away from Callum and her baby.

As the pain eased, she straightened and stepped out into the hospital corridor. She wondered if Margaret Roper would still call her dear after she'd run out on Callum.

Fat chance.

Callum was angry. He'd been kept sedated for most of the night and it was the early hours of the morning before he woke properly.

'Where's Stella?' he bellowed to the first unfortunate nurse who ventured near his hospital bed.

She frowned. 'I beg your pardon?'

'Where's the woman who came with me? Mrs Roper. My—my wife.' He'd used that word so rarely it still felt both strange and wonderful.

'The pregnant woman?'

'That's the one.'

'I think someone said she's over in the maternity wing.'

His throat contracted. 'What's she doing there?'

She favoured him with a smug smile. 'Having a baby I should think.'

'She can't be!' he shouted. 'It's not due for another twelve days.'

'Shh, Mr Roper. You'll wake the other patients and you shouldn't get yourself all het up. You've had a bad fracture. Last night you had surgery on your ankle and your lower leg has been set in a plaster cast. You need to take it easy.'

'It's only a busted leg and I've been taking it *too* flaming easy! You've kept me doped to the eyebrows for hours. Now I want to know about Stella.'

She let out a resigned sigh. 'Would you like me to check on her condition?'

'Of course.' After a moment he remembered to add, 'Please.'

As the nurse hurried away, his brain churned. Surely Stella wasn't in labour? He'd promised to be there. Oh, hell! She would be terrified.

* * *

Swinging her legs over the edge of the bed, Stella reached for her handbag on the bedside table.

'What are you doing?' asked the startled midwife.

'I've changed my mind,' she said. 'I've decided I don't want to have a baby today.'

'But my dear, you can't—'

Stella clenched her lips and did her best to ignore the new pain that threatened. 'Just watch me.' She tried to wriggle her hips forward so she could slide her ungainly body off the high bed, but the pain was beating her, building up too fast, too sharp, too strong! 'Oh-h-h!'

'Come on, dear. You're not going anywhere. You must try to relax.'

'I can't relax,' she wailed. 'I've never heard of—oh—oh!' She panted and groaned under another mountain of pain. 'There's no way anyone could relax through that,' she grunted when at last it was over. 'I'll come back tomorrow and try again then. Maybe I'll be feeling more ready for all this by tomorrow.'

'I'm sorry, Stella. You're having this baby today.'

'I can't!' she cried.

The midwife was looking determined. But Stella could be determined, too. 'I can't have this baby without Callum,' she said. 'He promised to be with me.'

'Callum? Is that your husband?'

'Yes. He was admitted yesterday with a broken ankle.'

The woman looked as if she was about to ask another question, but the phone on her desk began to ring. 'Just try to breathe through the pain,' she said then hurried away to answer it.

'Mr Roper, I've been talking to a midwife. Mrs Roper has been in the labour ward since midnight.'

'Midnight?' He looked at his watch. That was five hours ago! 'You've got to get me to her.'

'You can't possibly go in your condition.'

'You don't understand. She can't have this baby without me.'

The nurse smiled sweetly. 'Maybe she couldn't start it without you, but I can assure you that she can and she is having this baby on her own.'

'The hell she is. I insist you get me over there.'

The nurse laughed as if he'd cracked the joke of the century. 'Look, I've ordered a nice cup of tea and a snack for you. You must be starving. Why don't you settle back and try to relax? By the time you've eaten, you could be a daddy.'

'Forget the food,' he barked. 'I won't be eating it. I have to be there with her. I promised.'

The nurse's patience was wearing thin. She forgot to smile as she said, 'But that was before you had an accident.'

'Bull dust! Being a patient is a state of mind. I'm cured. Now, if you won't help me, I'll find my own way to the labour ward.'

She placed a nervous hand on his arm. 'Don't be foolish. It's very sweet of you to want to be with your wife, but you have to think about your own condition, too. The surgeon left strict instructions, there's to be no weight on your leg. I don't have permission to move you just yet.'

'Then get permission.'

Her eyebrows rose and her voice sharpened. 'Rudeness is not going to help your wife. I can tell you one thing, Mr Roper,' she said as she hurried towards the door, 'until the surgeon does his rounds, you won't be going anywhere.'

We'll bloody see about that!

The breathing patterns and relaxation had seemed so easy when Stella had been sitting with Callum on the carpet in Birralee's lounge, but they were a darned sight harder now. Why, oh, why had her baby decided to come today when Callum couldn't help her?

She hadn't known such strong pain existed. Why hadn't anybody told her how bad this would be? Or that it went on and on and on. When the books talked about contractions building stronger and getting closer, they hadn't explained *how* strong or how close.

She was so tired of breathing and panting her way through each one. As for relaxing the rest of her body—that always came as an afterthought. So much for floating on fluffy clouds! What a joke! She'd never felt so *un*-relaxed, so uncomfortable in her life.

She was exhausted. And tense!

She needed a break.

And she didn't want her baby to be born now. It was imperative to sort things out with Callum first. Oh, help! She drew in a deep, starting breath and began another cycle of breathing as more fiery pain consumed her.

'How much longer?' she groaned as the contraction faded at last.

'There, there,' came a voice that was meant to be soothing. 'You're doing just fine.'

'Maybe I need some drugs or something.'

The midwife examined her again. She beamed. 'You're almost fully dilated, Stella. Hang in there, sweetie. It really shouldn't be too much longer now.'

Her baby would be coming soon? Without Callum? The slam of panic almost flattened her. 'But I—I can't have a baby yet,' she moaned.

'Of course you can, dear.'

Another pain started. Lower, harder, hotter, fiercer. She felt warm liquid flow between her legs and spread on the sheet.

'There you go,' the midwife announced cheerily, 'your waters have broken. Things will really start to happen now.'

Oh, Lord! Stella knew that she shouldn't be so tense, but couldn't help it. She wanted Callum.

A sudden collision outside distracted her momentarily.

'Good heavens!' cried the midwife, but already Stella had stopped caring what was happening anywhere else. Right now, her body was the centre of the world.

With another loud bang, the double doors of the delivery room swung open. Through a haze of pain, Stella saw the midwife jumping out of the way as a wheelchair spun into the room and almost crashed into the bed. The chair's occupant was wearing a hospital gown and his leg was encased in plaster.

It couldn't be.

It was. It was Callum!

He was levering himself out of the chair.

The midwife was protesting. 'What do you think you're doing? How did you get in here?'

'Hijacked a wheelchair,' he muttered. 'I had to be here. This is my wife.'

'But you can't. You're supposed to be in—'

'Don't you start telling me what I can't do!'

There was silence and Stella could sense a battle of wills waging beside her.

Then suddenly she didn't care as another contraction gripped her. When it was over, she felt Callum's hands smoothing damp strands of hair away from her forehead and he pressed his lips to her cheek. 'Sorry I'm late, sweetheart,' he whispered. 'You're doing just great.'

'Can you stay?'

'You bet.' He ran a gentle hand down her arm. 'But, hey, you went ahead and started having this baby without me.'

'I didn't want to,' she whispered. 'I've been trying to stop it.'

'Don't do that, Stell. We need this baby out.'

'Do we?'

His warm eyes looked at her so tenderly, she wanted to weep. 'Sure we do.'

'How's your leg?'

'Fine.'

'You know you're crazy for coming in this condition.'

'Yeah.'

'But it's so good to see you.' She rubbed her cheek against his arm, but then another pain arrived. She'd been brave for hours and hours and hours. She couldn't turn into queen of the wimps now. Somehow, she had to be strong for a little longer.

'The sister says you're in transition.' Callum was stroking her back softly. 'Breathe fast and shallow like we practised. Pant like Mac on a hot day.'

She was feeling very dizzy and ill. Worse than ever. Oh, dear. She didn't want him to see her like this. She'd planned to be so courageous. She tried to tell him she was sorry, but a strange, noisy grunt broke from her lips. And a completely new sensation crashed down on her. The bottom half of her body seemed to be straining away from the rest of her.

'Aha!' she heard the midwife cry. 'I think your baby is coming. You can start pushing now, Stella!'

She clutched Callum's hand. The midwife was doing things to the end of her bed. Callum's free arm slipped under her shoulders, supporting her, his voice close to her ear. 'Good girl. At least I got here just in time for the best part. It won't be long now.'

'Excellent. The head's crowning already,' the midwife called.

Every cell in Stella's body was urging her to go with this incredible force. There was nothing she could do but push. In the slight lulls between contractions she sank against Callum, exhausted and dreamy, sure that she had no more strength, but then the urge to push was there again, and she had no choice but to cooperate.

It was so much better now with Callum there. He didn't let her give in to fear. 'You're doing so well, kiddo,' he kept telling her. 'I can't wait to see your beautiful baby!'

The strain was becoming unbearable, but somehow, with Callum and the midwife urging her on, Stella kept pushing until at last she felt something warm and wobbly between her legs.

'I can see the baby's head,' Callum told her.

There was no time to be scared.

'Keep pushing, Stella,' the midwife was calling, 'I'm going to guide the shoulders out now.' To Callum, she said, 'If you help Stella up, she can see her baby being born.'

Did she want to see the baby? For a split second the old panic returned, but it was too late. Callum's arms were slipping lower down her back, helping her to lift away from the mattress, supporting her.

She looked down. And saw damp, dark, blood-smeared hair, a little red face with eyes tight shut, a little squashy nose and a tiny, tiny ruby-red mouth.

'Another push,' called the midwife.

'Deep breath,' reminded Callum, 'and then push! Go, Stella, that's the way. You little beauty! Here she comes. Oh, darling!'

'It's a girl!' cried the midwife.

Stella looked down again and saw her.

Saw a little red and perfect baby girl, her skin still shiny and wet.

She heard Callum's quiet exclamation. 'She's perfect!'

Trembling all over, she watched in awe as her baby experienced her first seconds of life: watched her tiny red hands uncurl, saw her fine, delicate fingers stretch and hit at the air, saw her dark wet hair plastered to her head in little curls. Before the midwife could start suctioning her, she heard her baby let out a gentle, inquisitive cry.

'It's Ruby!' Stella whispered.

Callum kissed her forehead. 'She's just beautiful, sweetheart.' His voice sounded as choked as she felt and it was so good to have his strong arm around her shoulders, still supporting her.

Stella saw the baby's little eyes open and blink then stare silently at the strange new world around her. 'She's gorgeous.' She couldn't believe this moment was really happening. This live, squirming baby was the wriggling bump she'd been carrying around for all those months. These were the little feet that had kicked against her ribs and had kept her awake at night.

This was her daughter. She was the mother of the cutest, most amazingly compact little girl. 'Hello, Ruby. I had no idea you'd be so sweet.'

Next minute the little face screwed up tight and the baby's lower lip trembled as she broke into a loud and lusty yell.

'Hey there, Ruby. No need to cry.' With the tip of her little finger, Stella reached to touch one tiny waving hand and she gasped with surprise as the baby's fingers instinctively closed tightly around her.

Ruby was drawing her very first breaths and yet her tiny hand was clinging to Stella, as if she already knew she was her mother, as if she needed her.

As if she knew her mother might leave her. *Would leave her!*

Stella couldn't believe the sudden swoop and rush of her emotions. Joy for this moment. Fear for the future. She looked up to Callum and saw his eyes swimming with bright tears.

It was too much! A painful swelling burst in her throat, her eyes stung and her heart raced. She heard a strangled moan breaking through her lips as she tried not to cry.

But the force was too strong.

She burst into tears.

Callum's fingers stroked the nape of her neck, then drew

her head against him. She was crying for herself, for Ruby, for Callum…for Scott who would never see his baby…for her own mother. Oh, goodness, yes. She was crying for Marlene. She couldn't help thinking of her mother at this moment. Had Marlene felt this awe-filled wonder when she'd been born?

Stella felt as if she was crying for every mother and daughter who'd shared this precious moment of meeting for the very first time.

She clung to Callum and heard his heart pounding, as his arms enfolded her and he rocked her against his chest. She heard his soothing murmurs and felt him stroke her hair aside. His lips pressed against her forehead; she felt the warm wetness of his tears and couldn't hold back her loud heart-shattering sobs.

'You're a champion, Stell.'

'Oh, Callum,' she spluttered through her tears. 'I had no idea she'd be so beautiful.'

'Have you noticed?' he whispered. 'She has the cutest little toenails.'

She tried to smile but burst into more noisy sobs.

'This is a miracle,' she heard him tell the midwife.

'It always is,' came the reply.

'I mean, the fact that she's crying.'

'Oh?' The midwife sounded surprised, but then her manner turned matter-of-fact as she said to Stella, 'Let's put the babe to your breast, while I deal with the placenta.'

Stella's hospital gown was briskly pulled aside and, as Ruby was lifted up to her chest, she felt the skin-to-skin touch of her soft little body. She held her baby in her arms and the tiny mouth nuzzled her. And she fell helplessly, completely in love.

CHAPTER TWELVE

'Ruby's twenty-four hours old, Callum. Do you think she's grown?'

He returned her broad smile. 'She's grown more beautiful,' he said and he meant it. The way he felt about Ruby was incredible. Ruby Roper. Scott's daughter. His daughter now. The sense of connection he felt to this tiny scrap of humanity was beyond anything he'd anticipated—almost mystical. Seeing her being born had been such a life-changing experience.

And Stella was looking so happy. Surrounded by dozens of flowers, she was wearing a glamorous, pale pink nightdress, a gift from his mother. He'd never seen her wearing anything so obviously feminine and she looked amazingly pretty and so proud as she gazed at the sleeping infant in the cot beside her. 'You love her, don't you?' he said.

'I'm crazy about her.'

He reached for her hand. 'I know I've said it before, but I'm so proud of you and I really am very grateful for the way you rescued me the other day.'

'I didn't do much.'

'You were fantastic the way you took charge and knew exactly who to ring and how. Anyone would think you'd lived in the bush all your life.'

She looked pleased. 'When Ruby's old enough, you'll have to teach her how to press that button on the telephone.'

Then her eyes suddenly lost their sparkle and Callum's heart sank to the bottom of his plaster cast. The wash of misery that clouded her face was all the evidence he needed. She was still planning to head off in a few weeks.

'Stella,' he said.

And at the same moment she said, 'Callum,' with her eyes downcast as she nervously smoothed the sheet over her legs. 'There's something I've been wanting to tell you.'

A giant fist squeezed his heart. Could he bear to hear what she had to say? 'I have something to tell you, too.'

'What is it?'

Fear held his tongue. 'Ladies first.'

'OK.' Closing her eyes, she spoke very quickly, 'I'm-not-going-to-London.'

It took a moment or two for her words to sink in and then he could hardly speak above the pounding of his heartbeats. 'Really?'

'I rang them and it's OK.'

'I see.' He shot a glance towards the tiny form in the crib. 'Now you've seen Ruby, you can't bear to leave her?'

'I made up my mind before I saw her—the day before she was born.'

His heart and lungs were doing crazy things. 'Uh-huh.'

'I had an attack of sanity in the plane when we were flying in here. I realised it would be irresponsible of me to head off to an important scientific position when I was so newly postnatal. I wouldn't be in the right frame of mind and I would let the team down.'

He nodded.

'As soon as I got you settled here in the hospital, I rang London and explained that I couldn't go. They were a bit put out, but they weren't overly worried. There are so many people queuing up for that job.'

'But—but how do you feel? It was such a big dream for you.'

She shrugged and smiled sadly. 'It's strange what can happen to dreams. They can fade away until you can hardly see them any more.'

'I see.' He wondered why he didn't feel better. Stella wasn't going away. Why wasn't he ecstatic? Perhaps it had something to do with the fact that she wasn't looking very thrilled as she shared this news. What was missing from all this?

'So do you agree that I did the right thing?' she asked.

He picked up her hand. It felt cold. 'If it's really what you want.'

'I'll go back to Sydney instead,' she said.

'Sydney?' *Sydney?* A terrible mix of emotions clawed at the back of his throat. 'Why—why Sydney?'

'My flatmate hasn't taken anyone else in, so I can go back there and there's a good chance I can get a job back in the office.'

Dropping her hand, he used the end of the bed for support to swing into an upright position and clumped away from her clear across the room. There was something mightily out of whack here. Stella was giving up her big dream—her fantastic job in the UK for—for her old job in *Sydney?*

'But what—what about—?' *What about Ruby? What about us?* He wanted to shout.

What about the way I feel about you? The way you wept in my arms when Ruby was born? How can you just sail off to Sydney after we shared all that?

She looked as if she was holding her eyes extra wide to keep from crying. 'What are you asking me?' she asked. 'What about—?'

'What about Ruby?'

Silvery tears sprang into her eyes. She sniffed and dabbed at them with the backs of her hands. For what seemed an age, she didn't answer and Callum almost forgot to breathe.

'I love Ruby so much,' she whispered, then her voice grew stronger as she continued, 'but when I accepted your proposal, I agreed that Ruby belongs on Birralee with you. You've kept your promises, Callum, so it would be rather selfish of me to start making new demands just because I'm not going to the northern hemisphere any more. I don't want to ruin Ruby's chance of a good family life. Or yours.'

'So you think you'll make our lives bright and beautiful by leaving us here and dashing off to Sydney?'

She didn't answer, but her chin lifted to that haughty angle that was so familiar to Callum and suddenly he *knew* she was trying to cover up how she really felt. He couldn't help grinning. 'Well, that actually makes things easier for me.'

'How?'

'If you race away from here and I have to come after you, the air fare to Sydney is a lot cheaper than a ticket to London.'

She looked puzzled. 'Come after me?'

'That's what I was going to tell you. If you insist on running away, I'm going to insist on coming after you and explaining a few important home truths. Of course, you could save us both a lot of effort if you let me explain them now.'

'What sort of home truths?

He hobbled back to the bed again. 'Let's start with the fact that you love me.'

Her mouth gaped. 'What makes you think that?'

'I have an intuition about these things.'

'Oh, yeah?' She sniffed again, reached for a tissue and blew her nose. 'Don't you remember? We had a business arrangement. You wanted to protect Scott's baby. You—you said our intimacy was a mistake. Falling in love was never part of your plan.'

'Maybe not, Stell, but it's happened anyhow, hasn't it?'

She stared at him, shaking her head with disbelief, but he could see hope shining through her tears.

Emboldened by that faint sign, he sat on the bed again, picked up her hand and placed it against the hammering in his chest. 'You see, you love me and Ruby. And we love you back. You've no idea how much we love you, Stell.'

More tears glistened, grew fat and spilled down her cheeks. 'Callum, you know about my background. I'm so afraid I have no idea what love really is.'

'But you've already admitted you love Ruby.'

'Yes,' she said. 'But a mother's love is spontaneous. It's uncon-ditional. What makes you so sure I love you?'

He raised his free hand and traced the path of a tear with his thumb and then he bent close and gave her a sweet, slow kiss and she kissed him back just as sweetly, just as slowly. He smiled into her eyes. 'I've grown up surrounded by lots of happily married people, so I'm an expert. Believe me, I can tell you love me by the way you—' he paused and grinned '—by the way you look at me.'

'How do I look at you?'

'Like you can't wait to jump my bones. Like you can't wait to finish what we started the first time I painted your toenails.'

She blushed and rolled her eyes. 'That's not love. That's straight lust.'

'Well, let me put it another way. You force yourself to get up at the crack of dawn just so you can have breakfast with me. You've never been on a cattle station before, but you want to find out every darn thing there is to know about running my property.'

'Yes, but I'm a control freak.'

'And you like the idea of living with me and having me in your bed for the next forty, fifty maybe sixty years.'

She sucked in a surprised breath.

'You do, don't you?' he urged.

'What if I do? Aren't you still talking about lust?'

'No, Stell. That kind of staying power involves the other L word. The one you're so afraid of.'

She smiled shyly. 'I guess it might.'

'No doubt about it. Together for ever—just like we promised Reverend Shaw when we were married—that's how I see us.'

'Oh, Callum.'

He pressed his lips to her hand. 'I have this vision for Birralee that includes you and me as partners in every sense of the word… and Ruby and maybe two or three other little Rubies…'

Gathering her close, he kissed her again, showing her his love the best way he knew how. 'So if that's my version of love, how does it sound to you?'

He held his breath as he watched her face and saw her doubt give way to bright, shining joy.

'It sounds like the dream that shoved London out of my head,' she whispered. 'And it sounds as if I'm going to be absolutely, totally, up to my eyebrows in love for the rest of my life.'

Blissful seconds passed as their eyes lingered and they absorbed each other's happiness and felt at long last a beautiful peace entering their hearts.

Stella couldn't resist scattering a shower of happy little kisses
all over Callum's face, his neck and finally she settled for his wonderful mouth.

'Callum, I don't think you have any idea how drop-dead gorgeous you are.'

Sudden shyness tilted his smile.

'I've been wanting to tell you things like that for so long.'

His hands caressed her shoulders through the soft fabric of her
nightie. 'If anyone's drop-dead gorgeous it's you, sweetheart.'

Stella laughed softly as she tightened her arms around his neck
and nipped his lower lip softly between her teeth. 'I should warn
you, I'm very susceptible to flattery.'

His answering laugh was playful, rippling with happiness. 'And
I've been meaning to tell you what a sexy mouth you have. And
your hair. I love your silky hair. As for your—'

'Toenails?'

'Them, too,' Callum said. 'Sexiest toenails in the whole damn
world.'

And of course, they had to kiss again.

'Just as well you have a private room,' came a voice from the
doorway.

Stella looked over Callum's shoulder to see a smiling nurse
standing there. 'Mrs Roper, your parents-in-law are in reception
and they wish to know if you're receiving visitors.'

'Oh,' she cried. Her eyes sought Callum's and he nodded. 'Yes,
of course.'

As the nurse left, Stella took a deep happy breath and sank back
against the pillows. 'They'll love Ruby, won't they?'

He grinned and leaned forward to kiss the tip of her nose.
'They'll adore her. They'll want to spoil her rotten.'

Stella's face grew serious. 'Callum, I'd like to tell them the
truth—that she's Scott's baby.' The idea hit her suddenly and she
knew instantly that it was important to her long-term happiness to
get everything out in the open with Callum's family.

He frowned. 'I don't know if they're ready for it.'

She reached for his hand, linked her fingers with his and
squeezed. 'It'll be OK when they understand how much we love

each other and how much we both love Ruby... I think we should trust them to cope, Callum. They're Ropers. They're the same as you—intelligent, compassionate and tough.'

Footsteps were approaching down the corridor. Callum's hand tightened around hers. 'You're braver than I am about this, but I suspect you're right.'

Margaret and the Senator hesitated when they reached the doorway, but the minute they saw Callum and Stella together, their faces broke into joyful smiles.

'Hello! Do come in,' Stella cried keeping Callum's hand firmly clasped in hers. 'It's so good you got here safely. Come and see our darling little girl.'

They hurried forward eagerly. 'Stella, dear, you look so well.'

'Congratulations!'

'Oh, look at her! Isn't she the sweetest little duck!'

Stella and Callum had to separate and submit to hugs and kisses. Ruby slept through all the noise while she was admired extravagantly. Margaret wept happy tears. Senator Roper kept thumping Callum on the back. Everyone grinned broadly.

After the first excitement settled down, the Senator stood beside the crib and stared at Ruby. 'Who does Ruby look like—Stella or Callum?'

Stella's heartbeats raced as she watched him study her daughter's little cap of fuzzy light brown hair, the hint of a dimple in her chin and her turned up nose.

Her hand sought Callum's again. 'I think she looks like her father,' she said softly and she felt Callum's grip tighten like a vice around her fingers.

'Do you?' Margaret frowned. 'I can't really see much resemblance to Callum.'

'No,' Stella said. She had to do this. She *had* to do it. She couldn't go on living a lie for another minute. 'But don't you think she looks a little like Scott?'

'*Scott?*' came Margaret's astonished cry.

Then there was total silence. The room seemed to swim as Stella watched their shocked faces. Callum's hand was gripping hers so tightly her fingers felt numb.

She dared to look at him and his face was so stony it might have been carved from granite. But his eyes shimmered with tears and were riveted on her. Lifting a trembling hand, she touched his cheek.

Then she looked at his mother's pale face, at his father's dark glare and she took a deep breath. 'Ruby is Scott's daughter.'

As soon as the words were out, Stella felt sure that her strength and courage would desert her. She felt dizzy as stunned exclamations and gasps of shocked amazement circled around her. Tears threatened. These days she was getting very good at crying.

'What I want you to know,' she said as steadily as she could, 'is that Callum has been very gallant.' She did her best to swallow the pain that was filling her throat. 'As soon as he knew that I was expecting Scott's baby, he offered me his hand in marriage, so that—so that Ruby could be a legitimate member of your family.'

'I see,' whispered Margaret. She shot worried glances to her husband, to Callum and back to Stella.

There was a horrible, painful, awkward silence and Stella wished she could crawl into a hole and stay hidden for a decade or two.

Then Callum cleared his throat. 'Actually Stella's account of what happened isn't quite accurate,' he said. 'Sure, I wanted to keep Scott's baby in the family, but marrying her wasn't a matter of gallantry at all.' He raised the hand he'd been crushing so fiercely and pressed it to his lips as he sent her a smouldering smile. 'I wanted to make Stella mine from the first minute I saw her. One smile from her and I became twice the man I was before.'

A little cry escaped Stella.

'I happen to love her very much,' Callum told his parents. 'And it seems that, by some miracle, she loves me.'

'I certainly do.' Stella looked straight at the Senator knowing she'd never felt so sure of anything or as happy as she did at this moment.

'Marrying Stella is the best, the very best thing I've ever done,' Callum continued. 'You can be sure that Ruby will grow up on Birralee surrounded by love.'

'Oh!' cried Margaret, tears streaming down her face as she rushed forward to hug them again.

At that moment a lusty little cry erupted from the crib. Everyone looked at everyone else.

Callum's father was closest to the crib and, after a moment's hesitation, he leaned forward and lifted the baby gingerly. They watched as he stood there, holding tiny Ruby awkwardly while he stared down into her little face.

Stella steeled herself for the Senator's reaction to her bombshell. It seemed they were all waiting for him to say something.

He cleared his throat. 'I'm overjoyed to be welcoming this very precious little girl into our family.' His Adam's apple worked hard in his throat and his eyes gleamed as he dropped a gentle kiss on Ruby's forehead, then smiled at Stella. 'Thank you, Stella, for bringing Scott's daughter to us.'

'Yes,' cried Margaret, and she gripped Stella's hand. 'Thank you so much, you dear girl. Thank you for Ruby.' Her other hand shook as she reached with it to grasp Callum's, so that the three of them were linked. 'And thank you for making Callum so happy.'

Stella smiled at them all through her tears. Thank you, she wanted to say. Thank you for becoming my family. But she'd said as much as she could manage for now. The rest could come later.

For now she couldn't believe she was so lucky.

There were more happy tears as Ruby was passed to Margaret for a grandmotherly cuddle and then to Stella. Callum was on his feet and he and his father were shaking hands, then clasping each other.

Ruby's cries grew stronger and Callum and his parents went outside so that Stella could feed her baby in peace. She was tucking her back into the crib when she heard the clump, clump of Callum's crutches. He looked very pleased as he came into the room.

'You were right, my clever girl, it was good to get everything out in the open,' he said. 'Those parents of mine are over the moon.'

'About everything?'

'About absolutely everything.' With another clump, clump he crossed the room and took her in his arms. 'Oh, Stella, you've no idea how happy I am, too. I'm so very much in love with you.'

'I love you more,' she said and she smiled into his eyes. Wrapped in happiness, she clung to him, marvelling at her good fortune.

'You told your parents that you wanted me from the first moment you saw me,' she whispered.

'It's true. I did. I fell head over heels in love with you at that party in Sydney and I've been helplessly in love with you ever since.'

'Same here.'

He pulled away slightly to study her. 'You're joking.'

'No, Callum. I wouldn't joke about that. The minute you walked into that room it was as if someone had let off sky-rockets inside me.'

'But you rejected me.'

'Because I was frightened,' she admitted, wondering how she could have ever been so foolish. 'I didn't know how to deal with the strong feelings you roused in me.'

'You're not frightened any more, are you?'

'Only a little.'

'Oh, Stell,' he whispered hoarsely, 'don't be frightened.' With one finger beneath her chin, he tipped her face so that he could look directly into her glistening eyes. 'My darling, I'm the one who should be terrified. Don't you know the power you have over me? You hold my heart in your hands.'

This time they were both trembling as they kissed. And Stella knew they were both thinking of the long nights yet to come and the bedroom they would share when they went home with Ruby to Birralee.

* * * * *